THE ESSENTIAL
PHANTOM OF
THE OPERA

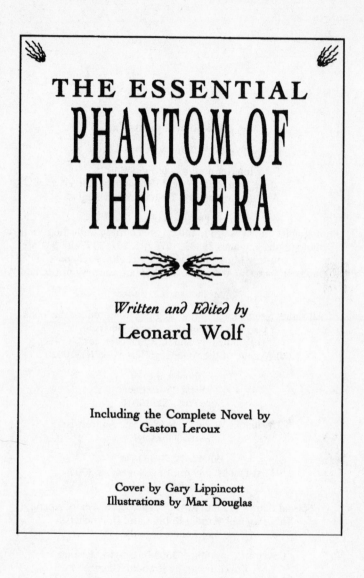

THE ESSENTIAL
PHANTOM OF
THE OPERA

Written and Edited by
Leonard Wolf

Including the Complete Novel by
Gaston Leroux

Cover by Gary Lippincott
Illustrations by Max Douglas

ibooks

new york
www.ibooks.net

DISTRIBUTED BY SIMON & SCHUSTER, INC.

A Publication of ibooks, inc.

Copyright © 1996 by Leonard Wolf

Interior design copyright © 1996
by Byron Preiss Visual Publications, Inc.
Artwork copyright © 1996 by Max Douglas

PHOTO CREDITS:
Photographs on pages 9, 13, and 20 are courtesy Collection Viollet.
Photographs on pages 25, 83, 127, 201, 287, 317, and 341 are
courtesy Museum of Modern Art Film Archive.
Photographs on pages 57, 155, 227, and 256 are courtesy of Leonard Wolf.

An ibooks, inc. Book

Distributed by Simon & Schuster, Inc.
1230 Avenue of the Americas, New York, NY 10020

ibooks, inc.
24 West 25th Street
New York, NY 10010

The ibooks World Wide Web Site Address is:
www.ibooks.net

ISBN 0-7434-9836-4
First ibooks, inc. printing November 2004
10 9 8 7 6 5 4 3 2

Special thanks to Keith R.A. DeCandido, Rosemary Ahern,
Kari, Paschall, Arnold Dolin, Carol D. Pinchefsky,
and Robert Legault.

Cover art copyright © 2004 by Sergio Martinez
Cover design by Brandon Diaz;
copyright © 2004 by ibooks, inc.

Printed in the U.S.A.

Acknowledgments

⋙⋘

A great many people have helped me in the completion of this book. I cannot thank them all, but I would be remiss if I did not express my thanks first to the librarians at New York University, Columbia University and The New York Public Library.

Then I want to thank Jean Luc Maeso of the *Opéra Comique*, Marie Josaë Kerouas of the *Musée de l'Opéra*, and particularly Francis Lacassin, who is the editor of in the indispensible French Bouquins edition of Gaston Leroux's work and whose kindness and courtesy helped ease my task. I want to thank, too, Elizabeth Atkins, for her help with research and translation, and Catherine Fletcher for her work on the history of Garnier's *Opéra*.

Mary Corliss of the Film Stills Department of the Museum of Modern Art and David Del Valle have once again been helpful in the location of stills.

Nancy C. Hanger and Keith R.A. DeCandido, my editors at Byron Preiss, will know how grateful I am for their help.

Introduction

>>€€<

"You want the secret of my success; my recipe? I'm happy to give it to you. I have always brought the same care to making an adventure novel, a serialized novel, that others would bring to the making of a poem. My ambition was to raise the level of this much maligned genre." Gaston Leroux

If we consider briefly the twentieth century's most popular film monsters: Dracula, the Frankenstein creature, the wolfman, King Kong, Jekyll and Hyde, and the Phantom of the Opera, we are struck by how much sympathy each of them demands—and gets—from the same audiences that look forward to being frightened by them. Even Dracula, who, after all, is a creature of Satan, can be seen as someone doomed, compelled to do evil until the good guy Christians drive a stake through his heart, after which a look of peace spreads over his face and he crumbles to dust. The others are each pathetic in their own way: the Frankenstein creature is a model of the absolute orphan, abandoned by Victor, his mother-father creator, and because of his size and ugliness, doomed to a loveless existence; King Kong, Universal Pictures' gargantuan ape, is another sufferer. Hopelessly in the throes of an interspecies Beauty-and-the-Beast affair which can never be consummated, he achieves nobility by dying to save Ann Darrow,

1

who is by no means worthy of him. As he crashes to his death, we are told, "It was beauty that slew the beast" and, if we have normal instincts, we shed a tear. The werewolf, too, entices our compassion because he does not choose his brutality. He is reluctant before his transformation and remorseful after he has committed his crimes.

As we go down our list of monsters we will notice that by the time we get to Jekyll and Hyde, and especially when we get to the Phantom of the Opera, that our monsters begin more and more to resemble ordinary mankind. They are mortal, and they are people. When we first meet Dr. Jekyll, there is nothing about him that would suggest monstrosity. Indeed, that was Robert Louis Stevenson's point: that within the ordinarily decent Jekyll there lies coiled, waiting, the sensuous and murderous Hyde, flesh of his flesh and bone of his bone,

As we turn our attention to the Phantom of the Opera, our understanding of the word "monster" turns suddenly vague because Erik, hero of Gaston Leroux's fiction, is a superbly gifted human being whose physical repulsiveness drives him to crime as it exiles him from the human condition. As with Mary Shelley's Frankenstein creature, the fault lies not with him but with his maker. In Erik's case, that maker is unambiguously God Himself, whose inattention allowed a man as ugly as Erik to be born.

From a literary point of view, Gaston Leroux's novel, published in France in 1910, is, like Bram Stoker's *Dracula,* a strange sort of masterpiece. Its genre is not surprising. Like Stoker's novel, it is governed by the conventions of gothic fiction, where the story is organized around the perils of a young, beautiful, and sensitive heroine who, with malign sexual intent, is pursued from one cold, dark, dank, and macabre place to another by a tall, dark stranger who is infinitely more interesting than the good-looking and (often) wealthy or titled young hero who rescues her.

As in Stoker's fiction, there are no profoundly or subtly imagined characters. Indeed, the *Phantom*'s protagonists are hardly more than stick figures: Erik is ugly and lonely; the twenty-year-old Viscount Raoul de Chagny, who loves Christine, is young, ardent, brave, and profoundly foolish; Christine, as the heroine of a gothic novel, is beautiful, sensitive, and in sexual peril. Count Philippe, Raoul's much older brother, is a man about town, given to backstage visits to dancers at the opera with one of whom, La Sorelli, he has the kind of friendship that is supposed to raise the eyebrows of admiring or envious or disapproving other men. He, too, has virtues. He loves his brother and would die for him, but as we will see,

2

he is not much more effectual than his good intentions and he comes to a pretty bad end. As for La Sorelli, she is another sort of cliché. She "is an imposing, beautiful dancer whose face is at once grave and voluptuous and whose figure is as supple as a willow branch." But, adds Leroux, "Speaking of brains, it was a known fact that she had hardly any . . ." Though she is present in the early chapters of the fiction, she disappears from the novel without comment. The same can be said of the singer, Carlotta, who serves Leroux as the protagonist of the painfully comic "croaking" scene in Chapter 8 after which she, too, drifts out of view. The Persian is Leroux's *deus ex machina.* Clearly, once he was stuck with the incompetent Raoul as his book's romantic lead, had to invent the Persian so that the plot could be moved forward with some semblance of intelligence.

All the other people in the novel serve either as comic backdrop figures, such as Armand Moncharmin and Firmin Richard, the opera's managers, and Madame Giry, the box attendant who is the Phantom's ally. They are momentary passersby who briefly demand our attention, like the "rats," the children of the ballet corps; the trapdoor closers, the scene-shifters, and the rat-catcher. Finally, there is Madame Valerius who, being too good to be true, is the perfect fairy godmother to Christine's Cinderella. All sweetness and no light.

Leroux's achievement is that with such frail threads he wove his comparatively simple story of the pursuit of a beautiful woman by a horridly ugly man into a tapestry of myth that frequently feels both complex and moving. It is all done with smoke and mirrors, no doubt, but what we finally have is a compelling and important work of fiction. How he achieved that is worth some additional comment.

Let us consider first Leroux's decision to put a mask on Erik. Masks everywhere create the same sort of mystery that is implicit in walls and doorways which, because we meet them as impassive and implacable facades, taunt our curiosity by raising the question of what lies behind them. But with masks, that curiosity has a special poignancy, since they, unlike walls and doors, have the form of the human face even as they conceal it. In Erik's case, we learn what has been concealed. Once his mask is removed, what we see compels both horror and compassion. If we knew nothing else about Erik except what that ruined face looked like, we would recognize him as an exile from the human condition. Indeed, his ugliness is so great and so central to our understanding of his behavior that by the time the Persian asks at the end of the novel, "Why did God make a man

3

so ugly?'' the question, banal and sophomoric in any other context, resounds with the sort of profundity we find in the Book of Job or in the phrase at the end of Melville's "Bartleby the Scrivener," "Ah Bartleby! Ah humanity!"

More important even than providing Erik with a mask, there is Leroux's decision to set his story mostly within the walls of Charles Garnier's opera house. It is an ambience that allows Leroux's simple tale to carry the burden of any number of rich meanings, most of them related to loves lost or betrayed: within the pages of *The Phantom of the Opera* there resonate the stories and the music of *Faust, Le Roi de Lahore, La Juive, Don Giovanni, Otello,* and *Romeo and Juliette.*

Given the structure of the opera house, with its various levels, Erik and Christine can also be seen as Cupid and Psyche, as Beauty and the Beast, as Pluto and Persephone. Even Raoul searching for Christine can be glimpsed as an Orpheus figure descending into Hades hunting for his lost Eurydice.

Leroux's stratagem, then, pays off, because what we have in *The Phantom of the Opera* is a truly fabulous fiction. A novel in which so many fables are at work that we experience it as a multidimensional allegory. If his characters do not become real people, they become something perhaps even grander: recognizable elements in an allegory of pain, compassion, and redemption to which we find ourselves entirely responsive.

The ambience of the opera serves Leroux in another way. It becomes the overriding metaphor for the creative process itself. It is in the opera house that the full transformational power of a work of art can be seen to take place. There, grease paint and music, set designers, composers, carpenters, tenors, seamstresses, children in tutus, horse trainers, seat attendants, painters, electricians, violin and tuba players, divas and prima donnas are at work taking the dusty, gritty, dangerous, and disappointing world we know and turning it into one in which we catch glimpses of high romance as well as high tragedy.

There is another aspect of Leroux's achievement which requires comment, and that is his mastery of the macabre. In *Phantom,* we get it in the conception of Erik's ugliness, in the account of the rosy hours of Mazendaran and in the episode of the torture chamber. But there are other of Leroux's fictions in which the macabre overshadows everything else. In his collection of short stories, *Aventures Incroyables (Incredible Adventures,* collected in 1977), for instance, we have the story *"La Femme au Collier de Velours"* ("The Woman With the Velvet Collar"), whose protagonist is a woman who has survived a beheading and who wears a ribbon to hide the guillotine's scar. In that same collection there is *"Le Diner des Bustes"* ("The Dinner of the Busts"), the story of the annual meeting of a group of armless and legless men who survived a shipwreck by eating each other's arms and legs.

But to get at the triumphantly macabre in Leroux, one must say something about *La Reine du Sabbat* (*The Queen of the Sabbath,* 1911). Even the barest of plot summaries will give us a sense of just how far Leroux is willing to test his reader's capacity for a willing suspension of disbelief. There, we learn that the emperor of the Austro-Hungarian empire has beautiful twin blond granddaughters, one of whom is at the same time the elected queen of the gypsies who are part of a vast plot to overthrow the empire. The queen is, moreover, protected by two men, one of whom is so beanpole thin that he can climb up and down chimneys with ease, while the other is a man with three arms who, when he is in a hurry, simply turns himself into a cartwheel and rolls along. The story involves a clockmaker who is also a vengeful nobleman; a version of the Mayerling saga most bloodily retold; a woman circus horseback rider who sews her rapists' eyelids shut; as well as other scenes so ghastly that one prefers not to describe them.

And yet, it is all of it readable, beyond belief, because for Leroux the macabre is a form of energy that propels his narratives. And the source of that energy is unquestionably what he understands about our dream life.

He was candid about that. When asked where he got his strange ideas from, he replied,

"Ah well, I'll tell you: It's not by listening to the song of the nightingale . . . It's by sleeping.

"Yes . . . I go to sleep with a still embryonic idea in my head and then, tap, tap, I am awakened . . . What? What? I don't know, the thing is found, the problem is solved. The point is, the mystery. There is nothing left to do but write it." (Jean Claude Lamy, ed., in the introduction to *Histoires Epouvantables*. Paris; Nouvelles Editions Baudiniere, 1977, p. 23.)

It is as if his waking intelligence had immediate access to and could control the logical-illogic of dreams. As if, like Hieronymous Bosch, or like Shakespeare in *Macbeth,* he could, with no trouble at all, plumb the unconscious, that chasm in the mind where all fantasies—exquisite, lurid, violent, inane, or insane—are in constant motion, and where there is no question

5

of right or wrong. There, everything is vibrant, and it is precisely the vitality of the awful that Leroux re-creates for us. Sometimes, at his best, as in *Phantom,* what he reveals about the awful acquires larger meanings, and he achieves the "honest literature" at which he aimed.

A cursory glance at a portrait of Edgar Allan Poe is enough to reassure us that he has the features appropriate for a writer of horror fiction. With his slim build, his dark, somber, haunted, inward-gazing eyes, Poe's appearance satisfies our sense of how a man should look who broods over the ghastly way things are.

But it is far otherwise with the Frenchman Gaston Leroux, who, in addition to *The Phantom of the Opera,* wrote more than a score of other novels of mystery, madness, or horror. Even as a young man, Leroux was a portly figure who tipped the scale at two hundred and fifty pounds and who usually carried that weight with good-humored pride. Henri Jeanson writes,

"One needed to see him moving along the boulevards, his cane in his hand, wearing his swaggering hat, his belly three paces out before him . . . his eyes sparkling with pleasure behind his eyeglass lenses. . . . Arrived before the Napolitain [cafe], he went by it quickly lest he succumb to temptation and, at the Place de l'Opéra, he turned brusquely, retracing his steps, and settling into a table at the Napolitain. . . . He was sensible and sentimental. A glimpse of the sky over the Faubourg Montmartre would start a tear from his eye, and the rhythm of Paris in motion, the flow of its traffic, the smiles of its women, would entirely discombobulate him." (Jean-Claude Lamy, ed., *Europe,* June–July 1981, p. 111)

He was the very model of a Parisian boulevardier, a gourmand who, it almost goes without saying, kept a sharp eye out for beautiful women. Portly and genial, his usual greeting was, "Ah, old fellow, how good it is to be alive." He was a man with a teasing intelligence who, in 1925, when he was fifty-seven years old, would say,

"Very well, then . . . I was born in Paris on the sixth of May, 1868. That's the mathematical truth, I dare say . . . but the real human truth is that I am fifty years old. . . . And I have decided to be fifty years old for as long as possible, until my death, which I hope will come as late as possible.''

The house in which he was born is on the Rue Faubourg Saint Martin, Number 66. He came into the world a month before his parents would legitimize his birth by getting married in Rouen on the thirteenth of June. His father, Dominique Alfred Leroux, who was originally from Mayenne, was a public works contractor. His mother, of Norman extraction, was Marie Bidault, the daughter of a Fécamp bailiff. Eventually, there would be four children in the household: Gaston, the eldest, then Joseph and Henri, and finally a sister named Héléne.

At the age of twelve, Gaston was sent away to a primary boarding school in Eu, where among his other schoolmates he counted Philippe of Orleans, son of the pretender to the crown of France. His years at the school made a deep impression on him. In his novel *The Perfume of the Woman in Black,* there is a poignant description of the school's stone-walled courtyard and its chapel. There, the novel's protagonist, Rouletabille, describes the excitement he felt when, as a child at the school, he was sent for to meet his mother in the parlor beside the chapel when she came on one of her rare visits. Rouletabille says,

"I lived only in the hope of seeing her . . . I clung to her memory and that of her perfume until her next visit. Having never distinctly seen her dear face, I was intoxicated to the point of giddiness when she hugged me and it was not so much the image of her that I retained as her odor. On the days that followed her visit, I would escape from time to time . . . to the parlor when it was empty as it is now, and I would religiously breathe the air that she had breathed. I nourished myself on the atmosphere through which she had briefly passed, and I left [the parlor] with an uplifted heart." (*Le Parfum de la Dame en Noir* [*The Perfume of the Woman in Black*], Francis Lacassin, ed., p. 209.)

When he was done with his schooling at Eu, Leroux was sent to Caen to prepare himself for a law career. He received his degree, *avec mention bien* (with honors) when he was eighteen years old.

Late in the course of his adolescence, Leroux's mother died. Leroux was twenty when the death of his father suddenly turned him into the head of the family. Jean Claude Lamy tells us that Leroux wrote the words, "I don't want to be the oldest member of the family," on a fogged window-pane (*Histoires Epouvantables,* p. 24).

From Caen, Leroux went on to Paris where, to please his grandfather, he took up studies to prepare himself to become a lawyer, but his distaste for the law was expressed early on, and for a long time he was a desultory student who rarely went to class. He was irritated by the law's solemnity and the way the system allowed people to pry into the personal lives of young lawyers, transforming them into children who accepted their scold-ings meekly. The ritual of exams received his particular scorn.

"I've never seen a hoax like those exams. Four were examined at a time. And you were selected alphabetically. If your name was Durand you were certain to be examined; if you happened to be named Tartempion you would more than likely have to come back another time."

Still, after cramming for eight days, he took the exams and passed them and received his license to practice, but he never became anything more than a *stagiare,* a probationer. His years as a lawyer, combined with his personal charm, served him well later in the journalism career toward which he was drifting. In 1892, having met Robert Charvay, an editor at a gossip newspaper called *L'Echo de Paris,* Leroux contributed poems and squibs to that journal. Then, because of his legal training, he was asked to become the law correspondent for the newspaper *Paris.*

His big break came when he was assigned to cover the trial of Auguste Vaillant, an anarchist who on December 9, 1893, had exploded a bomb in the Chamber of Deputies. Leroux's reportage for *Paris* was noticed by Bunau-Varilla, editor of the prestigious *Le Matin.* Bunau-Varilla offered Le-roux a regular position as a reporter.

Leroux would continue to work at *Le Matin* for nearly thirteen years, during the course of which he would prove to be an ace reporter, turning in accounts of the trials of the famous anarchists of his day, Émile Henry and Santo Caserio. In 1899, Leroux was at Alfred Dreyfus' second trial at Rennes. He wrote of the verdict, "This moment . . . will be a date in the history of justice and future schoolchildren will be no more able to ignore it than they would the date of the battle of Actium or that of the crowning of Charlemagne" (Gilles Costaz, *Europe,* June–July 1981, p. 46).

Indefatigable, intensely curious, and scrupulously observant, Leroux

8

Cover to *Le Parfum de la Dame en Noir* (*The Perfume of the Woman in Black*)

pulled off one famous journalistic coup after another. One such coup was a series of interviews with the Swedish South Pole explorer Nordenskjöld and his men, who were returning home after spending two years on the ice. Leroux joined their boat at St. Helena. Since Nordenskjöld was wary of reporters, Leroux did not bother to identify himself as one and managed to draw details of their harrowing experiences from Nordenskjöld and his men. When the ship stopped at Funchal, Leroux cabled nine long articles to his paper with details of the adventures of the expedition. The articles were so rich in detail that when Nordenskjöld submitted his memoirs to the publishers Flammarion, they made it a condition that they would only publish if Leroux promised not to collect his reportage into a book.

He pulled off a similar coup when, by boarding their ship in Suez, he interviewed the so-called "heroes of Chemulpo," Russian survivors of the Japanese fleet's shelling at Inchon. On another occasion he left his colleagues gasping when he filed a story in which he asserted that Kaiser Wilhelm of Germany was planning to have a private meeting with Czar Nicholas of Russia. Both countries officially denied that such a meeting would take place, and Le Matin so informed Leroux. He however insisted that he was right. In the event, the emperors did in fact meet on board a gunship in the Baltic.

How had Leroux gotten wind of the meeting when no other journalist had a clue? By talking with the czar's chef, who had been informed of the meeting so that he could cater the affair.

In his years as a journalist, Leroux lived an exciting if often frenzied life as he traveled from one hot spot to another. He covered the Russo-Japanese war in 1904 for Le Matin. In October 1905, he went to Baku and Balakhany, where thousands of Armenians had been massacred by the Tartars. In December of that year, the 1905 Revolution exploded. There were mutinies of soldiers, arbitrary arrests, strikes, and Leroux covered them all.

Busy journalist that he was, some time during these years, Leroux managed to acquire a wife, Marie Lefranc, from whom he was soon separated, but who refused to give him a divorce.

In 1902, when he was thirty-four years old, he met the one true love of his life. By then he had acquired the two-fold reputation of a gambler and a womanizer who "liked to take chances at a roulette table or a poker game the way he liked to try his luck with a pretty woman, being sure that with her, too, he was putting all his trumps in play" (Lamy, p. 30).

In the lobby of a Swiss hotel, Leroux's interest was attracted by a young woman, Jeanne Cayatte, who was reading an article by him in Le

Matin. The portly Leroux's brown eyes widened under his thick eyebrows and he mounted his attack. Obtruding himself on Ms. Cayatte's attention, he observed that he had little respect for journalists, and even less for the journalist, Gaston Leroux, whose work she was reading.

"And what sort of work do you do?" asked Ms. Cayatte.

"I," replied Leroux, "am a cattle dealer."

"Yes, one can tell," sniffed the lady. That was the beginning of an enthusiastic courtship which, since Marie Lefranc continued to refuse Leroux a divorce, ended for him and Jeanne Cayatte in that irregular relationship that in France has the name *concubinage*. Three years later, in St. Petersburg, to which she had accompanied Leroux, Jeanne Cayatte bore a son, Miki.

It was not until 1917, when Marie Lefranc died, that Jeanne Cayatte and Leroux were finally able to marry. Theirs was a stable and evidently satisfactory marriage because, writes Lamy,

"Though she was very beautiful, [Jeanne Cayatte] was not very temperamental, and the love she bore Gaston was of a character essentially maternal. . . . [Leroux], to gain her pardon, took her to jewelers where together they could choose the gift that would heal the rupture and write *finis* to his last passing fancy." (Lamy, p. 30.)

In 1907, Leroux's career as a journalist came to an abrupt end. He had just returned from Italy, where he had been sent by *Le Matin* to cover an eruption of Vesuvius. There, fleeing the lava, he had spent three days in a shack playing poker. When he returned to France, he settled down to savor some vacation time when, one night, he was wakened from sleep by a messenger from his newspaper bringing him an order from Bunau-Varilla, his editor-in-chief, to go posthaste to Toulon, where the gunship *Liberté* had been damaged by an explosion. Leroux, perhaps exasperated because he had been wakened from sleep or, because he had been thinking of changing his mode of life, shouted down, "Shit! Go tell Bunau-Varilla, shit!"

That dramatic gesture put paid to a brilliant journalistic career, but confronted by a loss of income, Leroux made the long-deferred decision to devote himself to writing popular fiction. He had already had a taste of what that might be like. Before the famous *"merde"* message to Bunau-Varilla, Leroux in 1903 had published a novel, *The Double Life of Théophraste Longuet,* which appeared in installments in the pages of *Le Matin*. It was avidly read far beyond its literary deserts, because within its pages, readers

11

were told, were hidden the clues to the whereabouts of a treasure in the form of silver medals supposed to have been buried by a famous gangster named Louis Dominique Cartouche (1693–1721). "Cartouche's Treasure" consisted of seven plaques. Six were worth 3,000 francs each, while one, the grand prize, was worth 7,000 francs.

Now, in 1907, he took up the fiction writer's burden once more. From then on and until the day of his death he would write indefatigably, prodigiously, publishing some thirty-three novels, a dozen short stories, and half a dozen screenplays.

Here, in an introduction to *The Phantom of the Opera,* I have chosen to comment only on those of his novels in which, as in *Phantom,* Leroux's predilection for the theme of the human face and what lies behind it are the theme.

That fascination with the meaning of faces is to be found even in that early puzzle-novel, *The Double Life of Théophraste Longuet.* There, Théophraste Longuet, an honest and pliable manufacturer of rubber stamps, is possessed by the transmigrated soul of a seventeenth-century Parisian gang leader named Cartouche, and from time to time he is transformed into a man with a temperament so ferocious that, without a qualm, he snips off an offending neighbor's ears.

The Double Life is severely marred by the unhappy fusion of several quite different stories: the first, and the one with the most interest, deals with personality swings poor Théophraste goes through as he switches from being Longuet to Cartouche and back again. The second, a comic counterpoint to the main story, is about how Longuet's wife Marceline and his best friend, Adolphe, cuckold him. The third theme, dragged in by the heels, describes how Longuet and the police inspector, Mifroid, who is pursuing him, literally fall into the catacombs that lie beneath the streets of Paris, where they discover a lost civilization of people from the seventeenth century. The story of their sojourn among these erotically complaisant people, all of whom have pig snouts instead of noses, is no doubt meant to be Swiftian satire. It comes off instead as a callow misjudgment on Leroux's part. The best that can be said of this early Leroux fiction is that, like almost every story he ever told, it is constantly inventive, frequently macabre, more than occasionally comic, and, at surprising intervals, quite lyric.

For the French, the most important of Leroux's fictions are the seven novels that feature the young detective Rouletabille and the five Chéri Bibi novels.

Cover to *Le Mystère de la Chambre Jaune* (*The Mystery of the Yellow Room*)

The best of the Rouletabille novels, and the most appropriate to the present discussion, are *Le Mystere de la Chambre Jaune* (*The Mystery of the Yellow Room,* 1907) and *Le Parfum de la Dame en Noire* (*The Perfume of the Woman in Black,* 1908). *The Mystery* introduced the French reading public to Joseph Josephin Rouletabille, the eighteen-year-old journalist–detective whose intellectual acumen is one of the great wonders of the world.

The Mystery is a locked-room detective fiction in the tradition of Poe in "The Murders in the Rue Morgue" and Conan Doyle's "The Adventure of the Speckled Band." In Poe's story, the murder is committed by an ape that gets into the locked room by coming down the chimney, while in the Conan Doyle story, the victim is killed by a snake that has been lowered through a hole drilled in the ceiling. Leroux felt that he ". . . had to go beyond Poe in 'The Murders in the Rue Morgue,' much farther than Conan Doyle in 'The Adventure of the Speckled Band'; it was necessary to have a murder committed in a hermetically sealed room that stayed as tightly closed as a strongbox, while at the same time the assassin gets away. By what means?" (Francis Lacassin, p. 994).

The young Rouletabille (his name means "roll your ball," or "roll your marble") is a master of logic. Armed with what he calls "*le bon bout de la raison* (the good end of reason)", he undertakes to see his problem steadily and to see it whole. Rouetabille is made to say,

"Reason has two ends, the good and the bad, There's only one on which you can depend with confidence, that's the good end. One recognizes it because it will not shatter, no matter what you may do or say. . . . I do not ask for exterior clues to teach me the truth. I ask simply that they do not contradict the truth indicated to me by 'the good end of reason.' (*Le Mystère de la Chambre Jaune,* pp. 395–396.)

In *The Mystery,* Leroux meets his own challenge to tell the story of a crime committed in a truly impenetrable room that has a single barred window and a heavy door locked from the inside. The victim in the room is Mathilde Stangerson, daughter of the American Professor Stangerson. Professor Stangerson and his assistant are in the professor's laboratory when they hear the sound of a shot coming from Mathilde's room. When her door is broken open, they find Mathilde, who has been hurt by an intruder.

That is how *The Mystery* begins. When the young newspaper reporter Joseph Josephin Rouletabille is called in to investigate the crime, he finds

14

himself is working alongside Police Inspector Larsan, Paris' most brilliant detective. We learn, too, that Mademoiselle Stangerson is presently engaged to marry young Darzac. As the novel progresses, the culprit attacks again, but each time he makes his getaway, baffling the police and, after hundreds of pages, the reader. Finally, Rouletabille, armed with the "good end of reason," exposes the criminal. Of course the culprit is the least likely person in the story to be suspected. Without giving away his identity, there is no harm in saying that he is in fact a world-renowned criminal who has been long sought by the police. He is, moreover, a master of disguise who, gifted with superb mimetic skills, can assume whatever face he pleases.

Le Parfum de la Dame en Noir (*The Perfume of the Woman in Black*), though it can be read as a separate novel, is actually a sequel to *The Mystery*. The central cast of characters remains the same, and indeed, in certain respects the plot is duplicated. Again, the villain is intent on harming Mademoiselle Stangerson, but this time the novel takes on a psychological density that is missing in *The Mystery,* because Rouletabille's own identity becomes a factor in the fictional equation as, in the course of combating the master criminal, Rouletabille finds himself removing layer upon layer of the mystery surrounding his own parentage.

In these first two Rouletabille novels, there is no trace of the macabre sensibility I have spoken about above, which would later characterize much of Leroux's fiction. There is crime, and there is a criminal, and the detective, Rouletabille, has an intellectual problem to solve. Except for choosing to be good or evil, none of the characters are in any way bizarre.

Things are quite otherwise in the first of the Chéri Bibi novels, *Le Cage Flotant* (*The Floating Cage*). There, like Erik, Chéri Bibi, the criminal hero of the novel, commits his crimes only after society has mistreated him. Though he is not quite as horrid as Erik, Chéri Bibi's face is a craggy map of power and dismay. Leroux writes,

"The large, square head; the large mouth with its thickened lower lip; a short, powerful nose; imposing, large ears; small, round, extremely piercing eyes intensely on guard under the arch of his tufted eyebrows; his hair, cut close, showed the outline of his skull revealing the kinds of bumps that [the phrenologists] Gall and Lavater would say showed a man of feeling, of courage [and yet one capable] of violence; the sort of man who could be either a vagabond defending his girlfriend to the death or a general who loves his mother. (*Le Cage Flotant,* Lafont edition, p. 55.)

15

The description goes on at some length, but it comes at last to this: ". . . At the same time, he was hideous."

While Chéri Bibi is a master criminal, he is not at heart a villain. As his devoted friend, La Ficelle, puts it, "He was a brave man, good natured. But it was people who made him wicked. People, and worse: unhappiness; and worse, fate! *Fatalitas!* as he always said . . ." (pp. 160–161).

The plastic surgery episode in which Chéri Bibi is transformed by the rogue surgeon, Kanak, into the semblable of his hated enemy, the Marquis Maxime du Touchais, is hardly less appalling than those in H. G. Wells' *The Island of Dr. Moreau*. There, however, it is animals that are being tormented into human shape. Here, it is the features of the Marquis du Touchais that are being grafted piece by piece onto Chéri Bibi's face. Leroux, taking his cue from the Greek tragic authors, intensifies the horror by keeping it out of sight—but not out of hearing. Chéri Bibi's weak cry of protest (and pity for his victim) as each phase of the operation is about to happen will ring in a reader's ears for a very long time. "Not the hands!" Chéri Bibi groans at one point. "No! No! Not the hands! . . . Leave him his hands, leave him his hands"(p. 147).

The physical awfulness, however, is as nothing compared with the psychological disaster that follows the surgery. Cheri Bibi, who above all men hated the Marquis du Touchais, whom he believed to be the initiator of the disasters that had befallen him, has had himself surgically re-created in the marquis' image, and now must assume his life, which includes being the husband of Cecily, Cheri Bibi's first and only love. But there, *fatalitas* plays a dreadful hand. Cecily had always detested Maxime du Touchais, and when Cheri Bibi, wearing the face of the dead Maxime du Touchais, comes home to Cecily in the guise of her husband, he finds that Cecily's loathing for Maxim remains undiminished. *Fatalitas!*

In the opening chapters of *Balaoo,* a murder is committed at an inn in St. Martin-des-Bois. The chief clue to the identity of the killer is the footprints he has left *on the ceiling*. We learn later that the killer is the mostly gentle Balaoo, a young "man" whose external features are apparently human, but who is in fact the sort of creature who in an earlier day would have been called "the missing link" between man and ape. Born in the Batavian jungle, he is brought back to France by his master, a scientist named Coriolis. Coriolis performs surgery on Balaoo's vocal chords so that Balaoo, able to speak, can pass as human. For the most part, he carries off the charade so well that he actually qualifies as a lawyer. The tragedy for Balaoo is that his master's daughter, Christine, whom he loves, knows what

16

he is and that he has prehensile feet over which, through much of the story, he wears slippers. Though there can be no question of love between them, Baloo's yearning for Christine, like Erik's for his Christine, drives both his violent and his compassionate behavior.

The two linked novels *La Machine à Assassiner* (*The Assassination Machine*) and *Le Poupée Sanglante* (*The Bloody Puppet*) are two of Leroux's most bizarre fictions. Here we have a bouillabaisse of themes: a vampire nobleman; a Frankenstein-like scientist who makes a humanoid; straightforward detective fiction; and an Indian murder cult. The protagonist of both novels is, once more, a harmless ugly man, Benedict Masson, a bookbinder who is passionately in love with Christine, a woman who cannot possibly return his love. Then, like Chéri Bibi, he is suddenly rendered handsome, but in a fashion that makes it impossible for his good looks to be of any use. His brain is surgically implanted inside the skull of a handsome humanoid that can neither love nor make love.

Before closing this introduction to *The Phantom of the Opera,* Leroux's best known work in America, I think the reader might find charming this excerpt from his son's description of his father's work habits. He writes that when beginning a novel Leroux worked only in the mornings, between five and eight. As the work neared its end, his father's focus became intense.

"But what calm was demanded then! The household sank into a stupefying silence. No more piano, no more songs or cascading laughter, no more visits . . . Hush. The housework was done on tiptoe. . . .

" 'It'll be [finished] tomorrow,' he would announce one evening. . . .

"We knew what that meant. The next morning, everybody, from the moment they got up, was on the qui-vive: my mother, my sister, I and all the servants, still fairly numerous in those days, and who, in our house, given their long service, were considered family.

"The more the minutes passed by, the more we were on tenterhooks. My father, revolver lying on his bureau, was finishing the epilogue. When he wrote the word 'end' he squeezed off a shot in the direction of the balcony window. It was the signal so long awaited. From then on bells rang, drums and trumpets were unleashed, as well as iron pot covers, pots, hammers, and any other utensil capable of making noise . . . until we were breathless, and in Indian file, a howling mob we would run through the garden and the house, from the pantry to the drawing room." (Jules Gaston

Leroux, in the introduction to Jean Claude Lamy's edition of *Histoires Epouvantables,* pp. 50–52.)

Violence, good humor, creativity, self-display. In short, Gaston Leroux.

Leroux's hope that death would delay coming for him as long as possible was disappointed. On April 27, 1927, Gaston Leroux, whose enthusiastic curiosity about life had driven him as a reporter from one hot spot in Europe to another, and who, as a fiction writer was capable of imagining the most extreme human behavior, died suddenly of uremic poisoning.

Surely, with his sense of irony, he would have smiled at the train of events his death set into motion. Since his demise was totally unanticipated, neither he nor his family had taken the precaution of finding a burial site for him. His family knew, however, that he had often expressed his desire to be buried in the cemetery of the chateau at Nice. The trouble was that by the time of his death, there were no more sites available. But fame has its uses. The local press set up a sufficient clamor so that, somehow, a burial plot overlooking Nice and the sea was discovered, and there Gaston Leroux, who in life was an aficionado of cemetery silence, was buried. He was fifty-eight years old.

DEDICATION

"To
my good old brother Jo"[1]

---

[1] Joseph Leroux, ten years younger than Gaston, is described by Jean-Claude Lamy as being as much like Gaston as if he were his twin. Lamy writes, "Stout [like Gaston] and wearing the same kind of beard and spectacles, Joseph loved the bohemian life, which, as soon as he arrived in Paris, led him to Montmartre. . . . He became a singer and was on the stage in various theatres. He was, for a while a director of the Grand Guignol and was the spirit behind a literary and artistic periodical, " 'L'Echo de Montmartre.' Gaston Leroux, who was extremely fond of his brother, gave his name to Rouletabille, [the fictitious journalist-detective he invented], but this mark of esteem did little to make [Joseph] more famous. A dilettante who was careless of what tomorrow might bring, he lived the sort of life that comes to a quick end: stricken by diabetes, he died in his brother's arms at the age of thirty-nine . . ." (Jean-Claude Lamy, *Histoires Epouvantables*. Paris: Nouvelles Editions Baudiniere, 1977, p. 47.)

Gaston Leroux

Preface

IN WHICH THE AUTHOR OF THIS SINGULAR WORK TELLS THE READER
HOW IT WAS THAT HE BECAME PERSUADED THAT THE PHANTOM OF THE
OPERA REALLY EXISTED

The Phantom of the Opera existed. He was not, as was believed for a long time, a creature imagined by artists; a superstition of directors; a droll creation of the excitable minds of young women in the corps de ballet, their mothers, or the box attendants, the cloak room employees or the doorkeeper.

Yes, he existed, in flesh and blood, despite the fact that, he appeared to everyone to be a veritable phantom—that is to say, a ghost.

I was struck very early on in my researches in the archives[1] of the National Academy of Music[2] by the surprising links between the phenomena attributed to the Phantom and a more mysterious, more fantastic tragedy,

---

[1] "archives"
    There is a research library in the Paris Opera which contains a splendid archive of works relating to every conceivable aspect of the opera's history. Visitors get to peek at it on conducted tours, while accredited scholars have access to it for their work.

[2] "National Academy of Music"
    A synonym for the Paris Opera building. The National Academy of Music was the original name for what is now called the Paris Opera (*Académie Nationale de Musique*). The Royal Academy of Music (*Académie Royale de Musique*) was founded in 1669, in Paris. It was established to nurture operas based on French texts. It was known also as the Imperial Academy and the National Academy of Music and Dance.

and I was led to the notion that perhaps the tragedy could reasonably be explained by the phenomena.

The events take place not much more than thirty years ago,[3] and it would not be at all difficult to find even today among dance circles very respectable old-timers whose word no one could doubt, who would remember, as if it had happened just yesterday, the mysterious and tragic conditions which accompanied the disappearance of Christine Daaé,[4] the disappearance of the Viscount de Chagny and the death of his older brother, the Count Philippe, whose body was found at the edge of the Rue Scribe[5] side of the lake that lies beneath the Opera. But to this day, none of those witnesses has thought to link that frightful adventure to the more or less legendary Phantom of the Opera.

The truth was slow to penetrate my mind because I was troubled by a search that collided at every instant with events which, at first sight, one would have judged unearthly; and more than once, I was ready to abandon the pursuit of a vain image that was exhausting me. Finally, I had the proof that my premonitions had not deceived me, and all my efforts were rewarded on the day that I became certain that the Phantom of the Opera had been more than a shadow.

On that day, I had passed long hours reading the *Memoirs of a Director,*[6] the lightweight work of the too-skeptical M. Moncharmin, who in the course of his tenure at the Opera understood nothing about the shadowy conduct of the Phantom, and who sneered extravagantly even at the moment when he was the first victim of the strange financial operation that took place inside the "magic envelope."

In despair, I was about to leave the library when I met the charming administrator of our National Academy, who was gossiping on a landing with a stylishly dressed, lively old fellow to whom he cheerfully introduced me. The administrator knew about my researches and knew also how impatiently and fruitlessly I had been trying to find the whereabouts of M.

---

[3] "thirty years ago"

Since *The Phantom of the Opera* was published in 1910, we have some authority to set the real time in which the story is set as 1880 or thereabouts. For reasons that will be indicated later, we have fixed on 1881 as the likely year.

[4] "Christine Daaé"

There are two nineteenth-century figures with the name Daae listed in the *Nordisk Familjebok*. One is Ludvig Daae, a Norwegian political notable, and the other is Ludvig Ludvigsen Daae, a Norwegian historian. Christine, however, was born in Sweden.

[5] "Rue Scribe"

Named for the librettist Augustin-Eugène Scribe, who worked with the composers Halévy, Verdi, and Meyerbeer (see Chapter II, Note 12; Chapter V, Note 6; Chapter VIII, Note 2).

[6] "*Memoirs of a Director*"

This is a wholly imaginary work.

Faure,[7] the Examining Magistrate of the famous Affair Chagny. It was not known what had become of him, or whether he was alive or dead. This old fellow was M. Faure himself. And now, having returned after spending fifteen years in Canada, his first move had been to ask the secretary of the Opera for a complimentary seat.

We spent a good part of the evening together and he told me as much as was known to that point about the entire Chagny affair. Lacking other proofs, he had been forced to believe in the viscount's madness and in the accidental death of his older brother. But he remained persuaded that there had been a terrible struggle between the two over Christine Daaé. He was unable to tell me what had become of Christine, or of the viscount. It goes without saying that when I spoke to him of the Phantom, he only laughed. He, too, had been informed of the unique phenomena that seemed to attest to the existence of an exceptional being who had chosen to live in the most mysterious corners of the Opera; he knew the story of the "envelope," but in his view none of that would have required the attention of a magistrate charged with examining the Chagny affair; and it was enough that he had devoted a little time to listening to the deposition of a witness who had presented himself and who claimed that he had met the Phantom. This person—this witness—was no other than the man whom all of Paris called "the Persian" and who was well known to opera-goers. The judge believed him to be touched in the head.

You may suppose that I was tremendously interested in the story about the Persian. If there was still time, I wanted to find this valuable original witness. My luck held good and I was able to find his little apartment in the Rue de Rivoli,[8] which he had never left, and where, five months after I visited him, he died.

At first, I was doubtful, but when the Persian, speaking with the candor of a child, had told me all that he personally knew about the Phantom, and particularly when he had turned over to me the proofs of the Phantom's existence (especially Christine Daaé's strange correspondence, which cast a

---

7   "M. Faure"

    An examining magistrate who is charged with investigating crimes.

    Leroux, who spent more than ten years as a legal or judicial reporter, held the legal profession in very low esteem. We will see that the unfortunate M. Faure will turn out to be a not particularly quick-witted fellow.

8   "Rue de Rivoli"

    Traversing the First and Fourth Arrondissement, the Rue Rivoli begins at 45 Rue François Miron and 1 Rue de Sévigné, and ends at Place de la Concorde and 2 Rue St. Florentin. The street was constructed from 1800–1835 and, in its early years, the kinds of establishments that were permitted to exist there were extremely restricted: artisans and workmen who employed hammers, or who used furnaces in their work. Placards or signs were forbidden to be affixed to the facades of buildings.

    The street was given its name to commemorate Napoleon's victory at Rivoli, January 14–15, 1797.

dazzling light over the Phantom's frightful destiny), it was no longer possible for me to be skeptical. No! No! The Phantom was not a myth.

I have been told that perhaps this correspondence was not authentic, and that it might have been fabricated out of whole cloth by someone whose imagination had been nourished by seductive tales, but I have fortunately been able to find examples of Christine Daaé's handwriting elsewhere than in the packet of letters, and have been able therefore to make a comparative study of the handwriting; a study which has entirely erased my doubts.

I have also been able to find substantiation as regards the Persian and, as a result, I have come to see him as an honorable man, incapable of inventing a plot that would have misled justice.

Moreover, my opinion is shared by some highly placed people, friends of the family, who have been more or less closely involved in the Chagny affair, and to whom I showed my documents and with whom I discussed my conclusions. From them I received the most generous encouragement, and in that regard, I will take the liberty of reproducing a few lines which have been addressed to me by General D. . . .

Monsieur,
I cannot urge you too strongly to publish the results of your research. I remember perfectly well that some weeks before the disappearance of the great singer Christine Daaé and the tragedy which plunged the entire Faubourg St. Germain[9] into mourning, there was considerable talk about the "Phantom" in the dancers' lounge, and I do believe that the talk continued until after this event, which was on everyone's minds; but if it is possible, as I think it may be after having heard you, that this tragedy can be explained by the Phantom, then please, sir, speak to us of him again. As mysterious as he may appear at first, he will still be easier to explain than this dark tale in which ill-intentioned people see two brothers who loved each other quarreling to the death.
I remain, etc.

Finally, with my documents in hand, I examined once again the Phantom's vast domain, that formidable building in which he had constructed his empire, and there all that my eyes and mind perceived admirably confirmed the Persian's documents. Then there followed a marvelous discovery that definitively crowned my work.

It may be recalled that not long ago, while digging in the basement of

---

[9] "Faubourg St. Germain"
A fashionable quarter of Paris.

From *The Phantom of the Opera* (1925)

the Opera in order to bury phonograph recordings[10] of the singers' voices, the workmen's picks unearthed a cadaver. I was soon able to prove that this was the body of the Phantom of the Opera! I had the administrator touch this evidence with his own two hands, and now it matters little to me whether the newspapers say that it was a victim of the Commune.[11]

---

[10] "recordings"

In 1907 such a time capsule was buried a few paces from the large underground lake that was made to be a reservoir from which water could be pumped at the slightest alarm. A plaque was affixed to the wall that said, "The gift of Alfred Clark, 28 June, 1907. On this date, vacuum-sealed, twenty four records were buried and which, according to the wishes of the donor, were not to be unearthed until a hundred years had passed."

There, doomed to a century of silence, were the voices of Patti, Melba, Tetrazzini, Caruso, Tamagno, Frantz, Chaliapin. On June 12, 1912, thirty-two more records were buried in two additional urns. This time a record player, a speaker, as well as a box of needles were also buried. A complete listing of the fifty-six pieces was sealed in a copper cylinder along with instructions on how to use the machine. This time instrumentalists were included: Paderewski, and the violinist Kreisler. (Duault, p. 68)

[11] "Commune"

The revolutionary government briefly installed in Paris from March 18, 1871, to the 28th of May by insurrectionary forces after the Revolution of March 18, 1871. It held power only briefly and was overthrown on May 27 of that same year.

The revolt, before it was over, was singularly bloody. Estimates of casualties range from 17,000 dead to 36,000, and there were 38,000 arrests.

The revolt had its origins in the mass dismay over the armistice that was signed by a royalist-leaning government with the victorious Germans after the Franco-Prussian War. Though the revolt spread to the provinces, it was quickly suppressed there.

The poor wretches who were massacred during the time of the Commune in the cellars of the Opera are not buried on that side. Later, I will specify where their skeletons can be found, far from this immense crypt where all sorts of provisions[12] had been stored during the seige. I came upon the trail of the skeletons while searching for the remains of the Phantom of the Opera, which I never would have found if it had not been for the unlikely burial of the recordings.

But we will come back to this cadaver and the question of what to do about it. Now I must conclude this very necessary preface by thanking the all too modest minor players in this drama such as police chief Mifroid (who was called to the preliminary hearings after the disappearance of Christine Daaé); as well as the former secretary Monsieur Remy; the former administrator M. Mercier; the former choral director, Mr. Gabriel; and especially the Baroness Castelo-Barbezac, who was once known as "little Meg" (and does not blush to admit it), the most charming star of our admirable ballet company, the eldest daughter of the honorable Madame Giry, deceased—the former attendant of the Phantom's box—all of them were most helpful to me, and thanks to them the reader and I will be able to relive these moments of horror and pure love in close detail.*[13]

---

* I would be an ingrate if, on the very threshold of this frightful and true story, I did not also thank the present management of the opera[14] which so kindly lent its cooperation to my researches, and in particular, M. Messager, as well as that sympathetic administrator, M. Gabion, and the amiable architect who was so devoted to the conservation of the building, and who did not hesitate to lend me the works of Charles Garnier, though he was practically certain that I would not return them. Finally, it remains for me to recognize publicly the generosity of my friend and former collaborator, M. J. L. Croze, who permitted me to browse through his admirable theatrical library and to borrow rare editions of books he valued highly.

[12] "provisions"

During the siege of Paris by the Germans in 1870, during the Franco-Prussian War, the cellars of the Opera were requisitioned and turned into a vast military warehouse. For about six months, some 4500 tons of food were stored in them. That included 17 tons of wheat, 624 of flour, 280 tons of biscuit, 224 of rice, as well as quantities of salt, sugar, and coffee; salt or pickled pork, beef, and fish. There were seven tons of cheese. But, since these were French supplies, we need not be startled to learn that there were 1,154,786 liters of wine and 511,138 liters of brandy. (Jacques Moatti, L'Opéra de Paris, unpaged; and Alain Duault, L'Opéra de Paris, p. 37.)

[13] "in close detail"

Leroux's preface is a masterly premonitory overview of the entire plot line of The Phantom. Most of the main characters are introduced, as well as a central theme: the relationship between illusion and reality.

[14] "present management of the opera"

Since our narrator claims to have Gailhard as an informant, it may be useful to know that Gailhard was a comanager of the opera with Ritt after December 1, 1884 until December 31, 1891. In 1893, he was again comanager, this time with Bertrand. From 1899 to 1900, he was the sole manager when he became comanager once more, this time with Capoul. From 1905 to 1908, he again managed the opera by himself. As well as being, at intervals, a director of the opera, Pedro Gailhard had a considerable career as a bass singer. What is of interest to us is that, among other roles, he played Mephistopheles in Gounod's Faust, in 1871.

Chapter I

❧ ❧

IS IT THE PHANTOM?

It happened on that evening when Messieurs Debienne and Poligny,[1] who were retiring as directors of the Opera, put on their last gala performance. Suddenly the dressing room of La Sorelli, one of the principal dance personages, was unexpectedly invaded by half a dozen of the girls from the corps de ballet, who came up from the stage after having "danced" *Polyeucte*.[2] They rushed in tumultuously, laughing excessively and not quite naturally while others uttered cries of terror.

La Sorelli, who wanted to be alone to rehearse the speech she would shortly need to recite in the foyer[3] before Messieurs Debienne and Poligny,

---

[1] "Debienne and Poligny"

In the period that interests us (1875–1915) there were seven directors of the opera. Between 1907 and 1914, the director was André Messager and his codirector was Leimistin Broussan. Messager, like one of the new directors, Firmin Richard, was also an accomplished composer of symphonies, ballets, and one famous opera, and was deeply involved in the musical life of France. He won a gold medal from the Society of Composers in 1875 for a symphony. He composed a cantata, "Don Juan and Haidée," based on Byron's "Don Juan," and was the winner of a Ville de Paris second prize for another cantata, "Prometheus Unbound."

[2] "Polyeucte"

Based on a play by Corneille, this Gounod opera, with a libretto by Jules Barbier and Michel Carré, was first performed at the Paris Opera on October 7, 1878. Though its music has been admired, the opera, with its deeply Christian theme, has rarely been performed. Mlle. Krauss (see Chapter 2, Note 8, p. 40) played the role of Pauline.

[3] "foyer"

looked disapprovingly at the scatter-brained crowd surging in behind her. She turned toward them and asked the reason for so much excitement. It was little Jammes—the girl with the snub nose dear to Grevin, and forget-me-not eyes, rosy cheeks, and lily-white throat—her voice choked and trembling, who answered in three words, "It's the Phantom."

And she locked the door. La Sorelli's dressing room had an official and commonplace elegance. A cheval glass, a couch, a dressing table, and closets made up the necessary furniture. There were various engravings on the walls, mementos of her mother who had had a fine career in the old opera on the Rue le Pelletier.[4] There were portraits of Vestris, de Gardel, of Dupont and Bigottini.[5] This dressing room seemed like a palace to the gamines of the corps de ballet, who were lodged in common rooms where, until they heard the sound of the warning bell, they passed the time singing, quarreling, and slapping the hairdressers and costumers, and buying each other little glasses of cassis or beer or even rum.

The French word here is *foyer*, which has a large number of meanings, including fireplace, home, club, or lobby. If the farewell ceremony is to take place in a small room, the word "lounge" would apply. But, in Chapter III, page 53, it becomes clear that the farewell ceremony took place in the *Foyer de la Danse*.

The *Foyer de la Danse* of the Paris Opera was enhanced with paintings by Gustave Boulanger and sculptures by Felix Chabaud. One entire wall of the Foyer was covered with three great mirrors. It was lighted by a bronze chandelier that contained 104 lamps.

[4] "Rue Le Pelletier"

The opera house in the Rue le Pelletier was in the former Hotel de Choiseul, and was meant to be a temporary replacement for the Theatre des Arts. It remained in use until 1873, when it was destroyed by a fire in the course of which one fireman died. For a while, the fire imperiled the Garnier Opera which was not yet fully completed.

The decision to build the new opera had its genesis in an assassination attempt. The Rue le Pelletier, on days when traffic was heavy, was susceptible to what we now call gridlock. It was a street on which a traffic accident could produce tragic consequences. Indeed, such an accident happened on January 14, 1858. As the cortege of the emperor and the empress was approaching number 19, Rue le Pelletier, which faced the theater, a bomb exploded, but without harming the royal coach. Still, the narrow escape speeded the decision to erect a new imperial academy of music. (J. G. Prud'homme, *L'Opéra 1669–1925*. Paris: Librarie Delagrave, 1925, p. 42.)

[5] "Portraits of Vestris, Gardel, Dupont, Bigottini"

Gaëtan Vestris (1729–1808), a dancer at the Paris Opera. Born in Florence. Or Leroux may have Gaëtan's equally renowned dancer son, Auguste (1760–1842), in mind. It was said of Gaëtan that no one had ever danced a *pas de deux* with as much feeling and elegance as he did. He was distinguished also for his talent as a mime.

There were two Gardels. The first was Claude Maximilien Léopold Philippe Joseph (1741–1787), who was a dancer, choreographer, and later ballet master at the opera. The second was his brother, Pierre Gabriel, who, like Claude, was a dancer, choreographer, and ballet master at the opera.

Dupont is perhaps Pierre Dupont (1821–1870), French poet and songwriter. Or, possibly, Auguste Dupont (1827–1890), the Belgian pianist and composer. Another candidate would be Pierre Auguste Dupont (1796–1874), who sang "exquisitely" at the Paris Opera.

Emilie Bigottini, a French dancer (1785–1858). She began her career at the opera in 1801 in the role of Psyche. Famed for her skills as a pantomimist, her most triumphant role was that of Nina in *Nina, or Mad for Love*, a ballet based on a work by Marselier and d'Alayrac, created by her brother-in-law, the choreographer Milon Bigottini.

La Sorelli was very superstitious. Hearing little Jammes speak of the phantom, she shivered and said, "Little fool." And, since she had been the first to believe in ghosts generally and in the Phantom of the Opera in particular, she wanted to be informed at once. "You've seen him?" she asked.

"As clearly as I see you," wailed little Jammes who, no longer steady on her feet, let herself fall into a chair.

At once, little dark-eyed Giry, with the jet-black hair and swarthy complexion—that poor little skin stretched over those poor little bones—added, "If it is the Phantom, he's awfully ugly."

"Oh, yes," said the dancers in unison.

They all spoke at once. The Phantom had appeared to them as a gentleman in evening dress who had stood suddenly before them in the corridor, without anyone knowing where he had come from. His appearance had been so sudden one might have thought he had stepped out of the wall.

"Nonsense!" said one of them, who had kept more or less calm. "You see the Phantom everywhere."

And it is true that, for several months, there had been talk of nothing else but the Phantom in evening dress, who walked about like a shadow from top to bottom in the building, and who never spoke a word to anyone, and to whom nobody dared to speak, and who, in any case, disappeared as soon as he had been seen, but where or how he disappeared no one could say. As befitted a real phantom, he made no noise when he walked. At first they had laughed or sneered at a phantom dressed like a man of fashion, or like a pallbearer, but among the corps de ballet, the legend of the Phantom had very soon taken on colossal proportions. All of them, more or less, claimed to have met this supernatural being and to have been the victim of his malice. And those among them who laughed the loudest were not necessarily those who were most reassured. Though he did not let himself be seen, the Phantom made his presence or his movements known by comic or disastrous events for which, according to nearly universal superstition, he was responsible. If anyone had had an accident, or if a friend had played a trick on one of the young women in the corps de ballet, or if a powder puff had disappeared—whatever it was, it was the Phantom's fault. The Phantom of the Opera!

And, in fact, who had seen him? There are so many men in dress suits to be met at the opera who are not the Phantom. But he had a characteristic that most men in dress suits did not have: his suit was worn by a skeleton.

At least, that's what the young dancers said.

And, naturally enough, his head was a death's head.

Could any of that be taken seriously? The truth is that the notion of the skeleton had its birth in a description of the Phantom made by Joseph Buquet, the chief stagehand who had actually seen him. He had bumped into him—one could not really say "nose to nose" because the phantom had no nose—he had bumped into a mysterious person on the little staircase which descends near the ramp directly to the "cellars." Though the Phantom had fled, Buquet had had time to see him for a single second, and he had retained an unforgettable memory of what he saw.

And this is what Joseph Buquet said about the Phantom to anyone who would listen: "He's terribly thin and his dress suit floats over a skeletal framework. His eyes are set so deeply that it's hard to see their pupils. In fact, one sees only two large black holes, as in the skulls of the dead. His skin is stretched over his bones like that of a drum. It's not white at all, but an ugly yellow; there's so little of his nose that, seen in profile, it's invisible, and the *absence* of that nose is something horrible to *see*. And all he has in the way of hair is three or four long brown hanks hanging down in front and behind his ears."

Joseph Buquet had pursued the strange apparition, but in vain. It had disappeared as if by magic, and he had been unable to find any trace of it.

This chief stagehand was a serious man, orderly, slow to imagine things, and temperate. What he said was heard with amazement and interest, and it was not long before there were other people found who told stories of their encounter with a man in a dress suit and a death's-head skull.

Sensible people who got wind of that story said at first that Joseph Buquet had been the victim of a practical joke played on him by one of his subordinates. And then, there was a series of incidents, one after the other, so curious and so inexplicable that even those inclined to be malicious found themselves disturbed.

Certainly a fireman, a fire lieutenant, is a brave man. Someone who fears nothing. And especially someone who has no fear of fire!

Well then, this fireman, this lieutenant in question,* went down into the cellar to make an inspection and, it would appear, ventured a bit further than usual. Suddenly, his eyes starting from their sockets, he reappeared on stage, pale, terrified, and trembling, and almost fainted in the arms of little Jammes' noble mother. And why? Because he had seen a disembodied

* I have this absolutely authentic story from M. Pedro Gailhard, the former manager of the opera.

head of fire coming toward him at eye level. Let me say it again: a lieutenant, a fireman who has no fear of fire!

Papin was the name of this fire lieutenant. The corps de ballet was dismayed. First of all, this fiery head had no resemblance at all to the description of the Phantom that Joseph Buquet had given. The fireman was questioned closely, and the chief stagehand was interrogated once again, and as a result, the girls were sure that the Phantom had more than one head, which he changed at will. Naturally, they imagined that they were in great danger. If a fireman, a lieutenant, had no hesitation about fainting, then solo dancers and members of the chorus could excuse the terror that set them scuttling away on all their little paws when they passed by some dark hole in an ill-lighted corridor.

On the morning after the incident with the fire lieutenant, La Sorelli—surrounded by her dancers and followed even by the hordes of children in leotards—put a horseshoe[6] on the table in the concierge's vestibule, which anyone who was not a member of the audience had to touch before starting up the staircase. This was her way of warding off the evil that seemed to threaten the place. Anyone who failed to touch the horseshoe was in danger of becoming prey to the occult power that, from the cellars to the rafters, had taken possession of the building.

This horseshoe, which, alas, like the rest of this story I did not invent, can still be seen[7] on the vestibule table in front of the concierge's booth if one enters through the administration courtyard.

We have then a quick insight into the state of mind of the corps de ballet on this evening as we follow them to La Sorelli's dressing room. "It's the Phantom," little Jammes had cried, thereby increasing the dancers' anxiety.

An agonized stillness reigned in the room. One heard nothing but the sound of rapid breathing. Finally, Jammes, terribly frightened, huddled into the farthest corner of the wall and murmured one word: "Listen."

Indeed, it seemed apparent to them all that a rustling could be heard

---

[6] "horseshoe"

For the superstitious, the horseshoe has a double power. First, it is made of iron, a metal that was believed to repel witches and other uncanny creatures. Then the curved shape of the horseshoe links it to the luck-bringing lore that is attached to the crescent moon. It was believed that the devil could not enter a home that had a horseshoe over the door. It is usually placed with the "horns" pointing upward, otherwise the luck it should bring will run out. (Maria Leach, ed., *Funk & Wagnalls Dictionary of Folklore, Mythology and Legend*. New York: Funk & Wagnalls, 1950.)

[7] "can still be seen"

Not in the present-day opera building.

behind the door. Not the sound of a footstep. One would have thought it was the sound of something sliding across a panel in the wall. Then, nothing more. La Sorelli tried to appear less fearful than her companions. She walked to the door and asked, in a strained voice, "Who's there?"

But no one replied.

Then, feeling all eyes scrutinizing her smallest gestures, she forced herself to be brave and said loudly, "Is there anyone behind the door?"

"Yes, yes. Of course there's someone behind the door," cried that dry little prune,[8] Meg Giry, who heroically restrained La Sorelli by clinging to her tutu. "Don't open it. My God, don't open it."

But La Sorelli, armed with the dagger that she always had with her, dared to turn the key and opened the door while the dancers shrank back into the dressing room and Meg Giry sighed, "Mama. Mama."

La Sorelli looked courageously into the hallway, but it was empty. A butterfly of flame in its glass prison cast a bizarre red glow over the passing shadows, but did not dissipate them. The dancer shut the door quickly and, heaving a great sigh, said, "No. There's no one there."

"Just the same, we saw him clearly," Jammes said again as, with fearful steps, she resumed her place beside La Sorelli. "He has to be prowling about somewhere. I'm not going back to dress. We ought to go together, at once, to the meeting room for the 'speech' and then come up again together."

At that, the child piously touched the coral ring[9] she wore to ward off bad luck. And La Sorelli, using the rosy tip of her right thumb, secretly drew a St. Andrew's cross[10] on the wooden ring she wore on the third finger of her left hand.

A celebrated journalist has written that:

La Sorelli is an imposing, beautiful dancer whose face is at once grave and voluptuous and whose figure is as supple as a willow branch. It is commonly said of her that "she is a beautiful creature." Her hair, blond and pure as

---

[8] "that dry little prune"

This slightly contemptuous reference to Meg Giry is at odds with the fulsome gratitude to her that the imagined narrator expresses in the preface (see page 26).

[9] "coral ring"

In many parts of the world, coral was believed to provide powerful protection against bad luck. The *Funk & Wagnalls Dictionary of Folklore, Mythology and Legend* says, ". . . a list of its properties reads like a catalogue of the ills suffered by mankind from the mind, the body and the elements" (p. 250).

[10] "St. Andrew's cross"

A cross in the shape of a letter "X" because St. Andrew, one of the Twelve Apostles, was supposed to have been crucified on such a cross (c.60 A.D.). St. Andrew, the patron saint of Scotland, is often represented as a white-haired old man holding the Gospel book and leaning on such a cross.

gold, crowns a forehead beneath which her emerald eyes are set. Her head is balanced gently as an egret's on her long, proud and elegant neck. When she dances, her hips make a certain indescribable movement that sets her whole body trembling with an ineffable languor. When she raises her arms and leans forward to begin a pirouette, accenting thereby the outline of her bosom, and causing the hips of this delicious woman to sway, she appears to be in a tableau so lascivious that it could drive a man to blow his brains out.

Speaking of brains, it was a known fact that she had hardly any. But no one ever reproached her for that.

Again she said to the little dancers, "Pull yourselves together, girls. As for the Phantom . . . maybe no one has ever seen him."

"Yes, yes. We've seen him. We saw him just a little while ago," replied the youngsters. "He had a death's head and a suit like the one he wore on the night that he appeared to Joseph Buquet!"

"And Gabriel saw him, too," said Jammes. "Not longer ago than yesterday afternoon . . . in broad daylight."

"Gabriel the choirmaster."

"Of course. What, you don't know that?"

"And he was wearing his evening clothes in broad daylight."

"Who? Gabriel?

"No. The Phantom."

"Of course he was wearing evening clothes," insisted Jammes. "Gabriel told me so himself. That's how he recognized him. And here's how it happened. Gabriel was in the stage manager's office. All of a sudden the door opened and in came the Persian. You know, the Persian who has the evil eye."

"Oh, yes," the little dancers responded in unison. No sooner had the image of the Persian been evoked then they made the hand gesture against the evil eye[11]: putting out their forefinger and little finger while they kept their middle fingers closed.

---

[11] "evil eye . . . gesture against the evil eye"
There are several kinds of gestures against the evil eye
  1. The *mano fica* is made by doubling together all the fingers and inserting the thumb between the forefinger and the middle finger. It is both a guard against the evil eye and an expression of indifference (I don't care a fig). It has, too, the implications of sexual insult, since in Europe, the fig is perceived as representing the female genitals.
  2. The *mano cornuta* is made by extending the forefinger and the ring finger, while keeping the thumb and the other fingers folded. Since the extended fingers imply horns, the *mano cornuta* is notorious as a sign indicating that the man pointed at with it is a cuckold.

"You know how superstitious Gabriel is, just the same he's always polite, and when he sees the Persian he contents himself with putting his hands in his pocket and touching his keys.[12] Well, as soon as the door opened for the Persian, Gabriel leaped from the armchair in which he was sitting all the way over to the closet so that he could touch the iron lock. In making the leap, he tore a whole piece of his vest on a nail. In his hurry to get out, he banged his head on a clothes peg and gave himself a huge bump. When he backed abruptly away, he scratched his arm on a standing screen next to the piano. He wanted to lean against the piano, but his movement was so awkward that, unfortunately, the cover fell and crushed his fingers. He bounded out of the office like a madman and ran down the stairs so clumsily that he tumbled down the entire first flight on his back. Mama and I were passing by just then. We hurried to help him to his feet. He was badly bruised and his face was so bloody he frightened us. Then, all of a sudden, he smiled at us and exclaimed, 'Thank God for letting me off so lightly.'

"Well then, we questioned him and he told us the whole frightening story. he had been scared by what he had seen behind the Persian: the Phantom. The Phantom with his death's head, just as Joseph Buquet described him."

An alarmed murmur greeted this story at the end of which Jammes was breathless from having told it in such haste—as if she was being pursued by the Phantom. There followed another silence, which was interrupted by little Giry speaking in a small voice even as Sorelli, in sheer funk, polished her nails.

"Joseph Buquet would do better to keep still," Meg Giry said.

"Why should he keep still?" she was asked.

"It's my mother's opinion," replied Meg in a low voice looking around as if she was afraid that she might be overheard by other ears than those of the girls who were there.

"And why is that your mother's opinion?"

"Hush. Mama says the Phantom doesn't like to be bothered."

---

3. The *mano pantea* is made by extending the index and middle fingers, while holding the ring and little fingers close to the palm with the thumb. (See Leonard Wolf, *The Essential Dracula*. New York: Plume, 1993, pp. 10–11.)

[12] "touching his keys"

In many parts of the world, keys are considered to be powerful amulets. In Greek mythology, Athena, Janus, and Hecate are key bearers: Athena carries the keys to Athens; Janus, who faces in two directions carries keys in both hands; Hecate carries the keys to the universe. In Mediterranean cultures, keys are believed to ward off the evil eye. In France it was believed that a werewolf struck in the face by keys would return to his human shape. (Maria Leach, ed. *Funk & Wagnalls Dictionary of Folklore, Mythology and Legend.* New York: Funk & Wagnalls, 1950.)

34

"And why does your mother say that?"

"Because . . . because . . . nothing."

This knowing reticence provoked the curiosity of the girls, who gathered around little Giry and begged her to explain herself. There they were, elbow to elbow, bent forward in a position that was part fear and part prayer. They communicated their fear to each other, shivering with pleasure.

"I swore not to say anything," said Meg in a whisper.

But they would not let her alone and promised so persuasively to keep her secret that Meg, who was burning with the impulse to tell what she knew, began, her eyes fixed on the door.

"All right, then. It's because of the box. . . ."

"What box?"

"The Phantom's private box."

"The Phantom has a box?"

At the idea that the Phantom would have a box, the dancers could not contain their fearful joy. Uttering tiny cries, they said, "Oh, God, tell, tell."

"Not so loud," Meg commanded. "It's the first box, number five. You know, it's the box nearest the left-hand side of the stage."

"Impossible."

"It is, too. My mother is the box attendant. But you swear not to say anything."

"Of course, go on."

"Well then, it's the Phantom's box. No one has been there for more than a month. Except the Phantom. And the administration has been ordered never to rent it again."

"And the Phantom goes there?"

"Well, yes."

"So someone goes in there?"

"The Phantom goes in, but there is no one."

The little dancers looked at each other. If the Phantom came to the box, one ought to see him, since he wore evening clothes and had a death's head. That's what they explained to Meg, but she replied, "Precisely. No one sees the Phantom. And he has no evening clothes and no death's head. All that they've said about his death's head and his head of fire—that's all nonsense. He has nothing at all. One can only hear him when he's in his box. Mama has never seen him, but she's heard him. And she really knows, since she's the one who gives him his program."

La Sorelli thought it her duty to interrupt. "Little one, you're making fun of us."

Little Giry burst into tears. "I'd have done better to keep still. If Mama ever knew . . . But it's certain that Joseph Buquet is wrong to worry about things that are none of his business. That's going to get him into trouble. Mama said it just yesterday."

Just then heavy and hurried footsteps were heard in the corridor and a breathless voice called, "Cécile! Cécile! Are you there?"

"That's my mother's voice," said Jammes. "What's wrong?"

And she opened the door. A respectable lady built like a Pomeranian grenadier surged into the dressing room and, groaning, let herself sink into an armchair. Her eyes rolled frantically, shedding a somber light over her brick-red features.

"Oh, dreadful. Dreadful."

"What, what?"

"Ah, Joseph Buquet."

"What about Joseph Buquet?"

"He's dead."

The dressing room filled with exclamations, with astonished protestations and terrified demands for an explanation.

"Yes, they just found him hanged in the third basement. But the worst of it is," the poor woman continued, panting, *the worst of it is that the stagehands who found the body claim to have heard a sound like the death song.*"

"It's the Phantom," exclaimed little Giry, as if she could not help herself, but then took the words back right away, pressing her fists against her mouth. "No, no. I didn't say anything. I didn't say anything."

Terrified, her friends repeated softly, "It's the Phantom, for sure."

La Sorelli was pale. "I'll never be able to make my speech," she said.

As she emptied a little glass of liquor that was on the table, Jammes' mother gave her opinion: "It must be the Phantom behind it."

The truth is that no one has ever really known how Joseph Buquet died. The hastily improvised inquest gave no details beyond calling the death a *natural suicide*.

In his *Memoirs of a Director,* M. Moncharmin, who was one of the two directors to succeed Messrs. Debienne and Poligny, reports the hanging incident as follows,

A disturbing incident marred the little celebration that Messrs. Debienne and Poligny gave to mark their departure from the Opera. I was in the administrative office when suddenly I saw the administrator, Mercier, come in. He was terribly disturbed as he informed me that they had just discovered the body of a stagehand hanging in the third subbasement of the stage between a flat and a piece of scenery from *The King of Lahore*.[13] I said, "Let's cut him down."

In the time it took to run down the stairs and set the ladder the rope that had hanged the man was gone.

And that's the event that M. Moncharmin found natural: A man is hanged from a rope; they go to cut him down and find the rope is gone. Oh, M. Moncharmin found a simple explanation: Listen! *The ballet was in progress. The lead dancers and the chorus took precautions against the evil eye.*[14]

Period. End of discussion. No more to be said.

You are to suppose that the corps de ballet comes down the ladder then cuts up the hanged man's rope and divides it among themselves in less time than it takes to write. It's ridiculous. When, on the other hand, I think of the exact place where the body was found—in the third subcellar under the stage—I imagine that someone might have had an interest in seeing the rope disappear after it had done its work, and we will see later whether I am wrong to have imagined such a thing.

The dreadful news spread quickly throughout the Opera, where Joseph Buquet was much loved. The boxes emptied out. And the little dancers, gathered around La Sorelli like fearful sheep around their shepherd, made their way to the lounge through corridors and poorly lit stairways as fast as their pink-stockinged legs could carry them.

---

[13] *"The King of Lahore"*

The name of an opera by Jules Massenet. Its libreo was written by Louis Gallet. The work was first performed at the Paris Opera on April 17, 1877, and was revived again in April 1879. Since it was performed sixty times in the three years after it was staged, we can situate the time of the action of *The Phantom* as either at the end of the seventies or early in the eighties of the nineteenth century.

The King of Lahore (Le Roi de Lahore) is set in eleventh-century India in Lahore, the capital of the Punjab. The opera's convoluted plot involves a love triangle that includes King Alim, his prime minister, Scindia, and the priestess Sita. At one point, King Alim dies, but he is restored to life by the god Indra. At the story's tragic climax, Sita, who is Alim's beloved, stabs herself, and Alim, who is fated to die when she does, meets his doom.

[14] *"The ballet . . . evil eye."*

Gaston Leroux's idiosyncratic use of italics has excited considerable critical comment. They usually serve the narrative in the way that film music serves movie plots—that is, they point to feelings or signal coming shifts in the action.

The italics frequently have considerable lyric resonance. So much so that the poet Jean Rogeul has made a poetic collage of italicized lines selected from a wide range of Leroux's fictions.

Chapter II

THE NEW MARGUERITE

On the first landing, Mlle. Sorelli bumped into the Count de Chagny, who was on his way up the stairs. The count, who was usually so calm, seemed very excited.

"I was on my way to your house," said the count, greeting the young woman in a very gallant manner. "Ah! Sorelli, what a beautiful evening. And Christine Daaé: what a triumph."

"Impossible," protested Meg Giry. "Not six months ago, she was singing like a crow. But let us get by, *my dear count,*" said the youngster with an impish curtsy. "We're on our way to find out about a poor man who was found hanged."

At that moment, a preoccupied administrator, hearing these words, stopped abruptly. "What, mademoiselles, you already know?" he said more or less rudely. "Don't talk about it, and above all don't let Messieurs Debienne and Poligny know about it. It would cause them too much grief on their last day." Everyone went to the dancers' lounge, which was already full.

The Count de Chagny was right: there had been no evening like this one before. Those who were privileged to be there still speak warmly of it to their children and to their grandchildren. Gounod,[1] Reyer,[2] Saint-

Saëns,[3] Massenet,[4] Guiraud,[5] Delibes,[6] each in their turn mounted the podium and conducted their works. Among the other performers there were Faure[7] and Mlle. Krauss.[8] It was on that night that Christine Daaé, whose mysterious destiny I wish to describe in this work, revealed herself to a stupefied and intoxicated Paris.

---

[1] "Gounod"

Charles François Gounod (1818–1893). Gounod, son of a painter father and a mother who was a pianist, is best known as the composer of the music for the opera *Faust*. Early in his life, he thought of becoming a priest, but eventually chose music as his life's work. His first opera, *Sapho*, was performed at the Paris Opera in 1851. As we have seen (Chapter I, Note 2) he also composed the music for *Polyeucte*. *Faust*, considered the most famous opera in the repertory, appeared at the Theatre Lyrique in 1859. Since then, it has been performed thousands of times.

[2] "Reyer"

Ernest Reyer (1823–1909) was a composer and music critic. His Nibelungen opera *Sigurd* was performed in Brussels and in Lyon in 1884. It reached the Paris Opera in 1885.

The *Sigurd* story is taken from the Scandinavian *Edda*. There is some resemblance in the plot of *Sigurd* to that of *The Phantom*, especially in the early part of the story. Both involve a mythic journey in which the hero is required to rescue an imprisoned heroine. Sigurd, the Scandinavian hero, rescues Brunhild from a palace in Iceland which is enclosed by walls of flame. To reach her, he must pass through a forest and a desolate plain. He overcomes all obstacles and reaches Brunhild, whom he wakes from her sleep.

Christine, we remember, is a Scandinavian, but in her case, there is no resourceful hero. His place is taken by the Persian, who has no higher motive than his intrinsic humanity.

[3] "Saint-Saëns"

Charles Camille Saint-Saëns (1835–1921). A composer whose musical career began at the age of six when he was given the orchestral score of Mozart's *Don Giovanni*. Saint-Saëns was a friend of, and influenced by, Franz Liszt. He was a composer of operas, symphonies, and piano concertos. His operas were frequently performed at the Paris Opera. His most famous opera, *Samson et Dalila*, was first produced at Weimar in 1877. Fifteen years later, it reached the Paris Opera on November 23, 1892.

Saint-Saëns' "Danse Macabre" or "Dance of Death" (1874), a symphonic poem, was inspired both by a poem by Henri Cazalis and the woodcuts of Franz Holbein. What is of interest to readers of *The Phantom* is that the work contains a scene in which Death plays the violin and dances in a graveyard at midnight (see Chapter VI).

[4] "Massenet"

Jules Massenet, 1841–1912, a French composer with some twenty-five operas to his credit, puts in an appearance here playing his "Marche Hongroise" ("Scenes Hongroises") (1871).

Note that a stage flat and a set piece from a production of Massenet's Opera *Le Roi de Lahore* play an important role in the plot of *The Phantom*.

[5] "Guiraud"

Ernest Guiraud (1837–1892) wrote and staged his first opera *Le Roi David* (1852) in his native New Orleans, when he was fifteen years old. I have been unable to find a piece called "Carnaval" on any list of his works. Other of his orchestral works include: "Artevald" (1882), "Caprice" (1884) and "La Chasse Fantastique" (1887).

[6] "Delibes"

Clément Philibert Leo Delibes (1836–1891), who was famous as a composer of music for ballets, is most remembered for the music he composed for the ballet *Coppelia*.

[7] "Faure"

Jean Baptiste Faure (1830–1914) was a baritone who was also gifted with a comic genius. Before coming to the opera, he sang at the Opera Comique. His first great success came with his role in Auber's *Manon Lescaut*. He came to the opera in 1861 and for the next sixteen years was an increasingly successful singer there. He had roles in *Don Carlos, Hamlet, Faust, La Coupe du Roi de Thulé*, and *Jeanne d'Arc*.

[8] "Krauss"

Gabrielle Krauss (1842–1906) was a celebrated soprano who commanded an annual salary of 64,000

Gounod had performed *La Marche Funebre d'une Marionette;*[9] Reyer, his beautiful overture to *Sigurd;* Saint Saëns, *La Danse Macabre* and a *Reverie Orientale;*[10] Massenet, un unpublished *Marche Hongroise;* Guiraud, his *Carnaval;* Delibes, his *La Valse Lente de Sylvia* and the pizzicatti of *Coppelia.* Mlles. Krauss and Denise Bloch[11] had sung: the first sang the bolero from the *Vépres Sicilliennes;*[12] the second, the brindisi[13] of *Lucréce Borgia.*[14]

But the triumph of the evening belonged to Christine Daaé, who first sang several passages from *Romeo and Juliette.*[15] It was the first time the young artist sang this work of Gounod's. It had not yet been performed at the Opera; and the Opera Comique[16] had only recently put it on its program many years after it had first been staged at the Theatre Lyric by Mme. Carvalho.[17] Ah, one must pity those who did not hear Christine Daaé in the role of Juliette, who knew nothing at all of her naïve grace, who did not thrill to the melody of her seraphic voice, who did not feel their souls

francs a year. Playing Rachel in *La Juive,* she made her debut at the Paris Opera in the first performance given in the Garnier building, January 5, 1875.

[9] *"La Marche Funèbre d'une Marionette"*

Listed as *Convoi Funèbre d'une Marionette.* One of Gounod's compositions for the piano.

[10] *"Reverie Orientale"*

I do not find a *Reverie Orientale* in a list of Saint-Saëns' compositions. On the night imagined here by Leroux, Saint-Saëns might have played a medley of pieces taken from his "Egyptian Concerto—The Fifth Concerto in F" (1896), "Orient et Occident," a march (1869), and "Melodies Persanes," songs (1870).

[11] "Denise Bloch"

No Denise Bloch is listed among the women who sang at the Paris Opera. There is a Rosine Bloch, who began singing at the opera on November 13, 1864, in a brilliant debut in the role of Fidès in *The Prophet.* Her singing career at the opera ended in 1880.

[12] *"Vépres Sicilliennes"*

The *Sicilian Vespers* is an opera by Giuseppe Verdi, with a libretto by Eugène Scribe and Charles Duveyrier. Commissioned by the Paris Opera, it was first performed in Paris in 1855.

[13] "brindisi"

Brindisi is the Italian word for a toast, as in *fare un brindisi,* to make a toast in honor of someone.

[14] *"Lucréce Borgia"*

An opera by Gaetano Donizetti with a libretto by Felice Romani. It was first performed in Milan in 1833.

[15] *"Romeo and Juliette"*

Another of Gounod's operas with a libretto by Jules Barbier and Michel Carré., It was performed first at the Theatre Lyrique in 1867. The *International Dictionary of Opera* says that there are more than eighty operas based on Shakespeare's *Romeo and Juliet.* Gounod's is a much simplified version of Shakespeare's play.

Romeo and Juliette was not performed at the Paris Opera until November 28, 1888, a fact that helps to establish a date for the action of *The Phantom* before that year.

[16] "Opera Comique"

After the eighteenth century, *opéra comique* became the term used to describe musical productions that had spoken dialogue, whether they were comic or not. The name applies also to the Opera Comique theater in Paris.

[17] "Mme. Carvalho"

Marie Miolan Carvalho (1827–1895), a member of a famous French family of musicians, was a gifted soprano who had a long and successful career as an opera singer. She sang in Halévy's *La Juive* in 1849. The year of the opening performance of *Romeo and Juliette* at the Theatre Lyrique was 1867.

fly, together with hers, over the tomb of the lovers of Verona. *"Seigneur! Seigneur! Seigneur! Pardonnez-nous!"*[18]

Well, all of that was as nothing beside the superhuman melodic loveliness which was heard during the prison scene[19] and the final trio[20] of *Faust*,[21] which Christine sang as understudy for Carlotta, who was indisposed. No one had ever seen or heard anything like it.

It was a "New Marguerite" that Daaé revealed. A Marguerite of a splendor and brilliance unsuspected until then.[22]

The entire audience, profoundly moved, burst into overwhelming applause as a sobbing Christine fell into the arms of her friends. Apparently unconscious, she had to be carried to her dressing room. The great critic P. de St.–V. recorded indelibly that unforgettable and marvelous moment in an account which he justly entitled "The New Marguerite." Like the great artist that he was, he understood that this beautiful and gentle child had brought to the stage of the opera something more than her art—it was her heart that she had brought. None of the Opera's aficionados could fail to know that Christine's heart had remained as pure as that of a fifteen-year-old and P. de St.–V. declared that "to understand what had just happened to Daaé one *would need to imagine that she had fallen in love for the first time.* It may be indiscreet of me to say, but only love is capable of accomplishing such a miracle, such a stunning transformation. Two years ago, we heard Christine Daaé at her tryouts at the conservatory,[23] at which

---

[18] *"Seigneur! Seigneur! Seigneur! Pardonnez-nous!* [Lord! Lord! Lord! Pardon us!]"
The opera ends with these words, after which the stage directions read, "They die."

[19] "the prison scene"
Act V, scene 1, Gounod's *Faust*.
Marguerite, imprisoned for killing her child by Faust, is asleep. Faust comes in, remorseful. Faust calls to her; she wakes but, her mind disordered, imagines herself in the garden in which Faust first made love to her. When Faust urges her to flee from the prison, she is unable to understand him. (Opera libretto, Gounod's *Faust*.)

[20] "the final trio"
Act V, scene 2, Gounod's *Faust*.
Mephistopheles, Faust, and Marguerite are on stage. Mephisto urges Faust to persuade Marguerite to fly with them, but she prays to Heaven instead. As the curtain falls, we know that Faust is damned and that Marguerite's soul has been wafted up to Heaven.

[21] "*Faust*"
Gounod's *Faust* (1859), based on Goethe's play (1808), has been called the most popular opera of all time. It will be seen that the story of Christine, who sings the roles of Juliette and Marguerite, has been influenced to some degree by *Romeo and Juliette* and *Faust*.

[22] "Marguerite"
The young woman whom Faust seduces in Goethe's *Faust*.

[23] "Conservatory"
The Conservatory of Music and Declamation in Paris was founded in 1789. In 1795 the name was changed simply to the Conservatory of Music. Supported by the government, the conservatory provided its students with a wide range of instruction: instrumental music, composition, voice lessons, recitation, and dance.

time she raised our hopes charmingly. *What, then, is the source of today's sublime performance? If it does not come down from heaven on the wings of love, I would have to suppose that it rises from hell* and that Christine, like the master singer Ofterdingen, had made a pact with the devil. Anyone who has not heard Christine sing the final trio from *Faust* does not know *Faust*: that exaltation of voice, that sacred intoxication of the pure soul could not be surpassed."

Just the same, some of the subscribers complained. How could one have hidden such a treasure for so long? Until now, Christine had simply been an appropriate Siebel[24] next to Carlotta's somewhat too splendidly sensuous Marguerite. And it had required the inexplicable and incomprehensible absence of Carlotta to give la Daaé her chance to show what she was capable of in a part of the program usually reserved for Carlotta. Moreover, why, deprived of Carlotta, did Messieurs Debienne and Poligny approach Daaé? Did they know about her hidden genius? And if they knew, why had they concealed it? And why had she herself hidden it? Strangely enough, it was not known whether, at the moment, she had a teacher. She had said many times that henceforward she would work alone. It was all inexplicable.

Count de Chagny, standing in his box, had witnessed the delirium and added to it his enthusiastic bravos.

Count de Chagny (Philippe-Georges-Marie) was at that time precisely forty-one years old. He was a great nobleman and a handsome man. He was a little taller than the average, with agreeable features, despite a somewhat forbidding forehead and a slightly cold look in his eyes.[25] He manifested a certain polite refinement toward women and a disdain toward men who were not always willing to forgive him his worldly success. He had an excellent heart and a clear conscience. On the death of the old Count Philibert, he had become the head of one of the oldest and most illustrious families in France, whose patent of nobility went all the way back to the time of Louis le Hutin.[26] The Chagny fortune was a large one, and when

---

[24] "Siebel"

A young man who, in Goethe's *Faust*, is Faust and Mephistopheles' drinking companion. In Gounod's opera, he is a youth who is smitten by Marguerite and who defends her honor.

[25] "forbidding forehead . . . slightly cold look"

We will not get to know the older de Chagny very well, but the brief sketch we have of him here is not of a particularly attractive man: An unmarried man of forty-one with the approved sexually exploiting vices of a man of his class. Leroux wants us to see him as dutiful, honorable, condescending and, except for doting on his younger brother, cold.

[26] "Louis le Hutin"

It is a long genealogy indeed. Louis X, king of France (1289–1316), was also known as "Louis le Hutin." *Hutin* is an archaic word for stubborn, opinionated, or quarrelsome. Louis died after drinking chilled wine on a hot day just after a strenuous tennis match.

the old count, who was a widower, died, Philippe undertook the considerable task of managing the large patrimony. His two sisters and his brother Raoul would not hear of dividing the estate, and it remained intact under Philippe's control, as if the right of primogeniture still existed. When the two sisters married—on the same day—they took their share back, not as if they were entitled to it, but rather as a dowry, for which they expressed their gratitude.

The Countess de Chagny—née Moerogis de la Martyniere—had died giving birth to Raoul, who was born twenty years after his older brother. At the time the old count died, Raoul was twelve years old. Philippe took an active part in the child's education. He was admirably supported in this task first by his sisters and then by an old aunt, a sailor's widow who lived in Brest,[27] and who gave the boy a taste for the maritime life. The young man signed on to the training ship *Borda*,[28] achieving high scores, and he completed the requisite tour of the world without incident. Thanks to his powerful connections, he was chosen to participate in the official expedition of the *Requin*,[29] whose mission was to search the polar ice for the survivors of the *d'Artois*,[30] of which there had been no news for three years. While he waited for his assignment, he was enjoying a long vacation which would last at least six months.[31] The matrons of the Faubourg St. Germain, seeing the handsome youngster, who seemed so fragile to them, pitied him already for the rough work that awaited him.

The young sailor's shyness—I would almost be tempted to say, his innocence—was remarkable. He seemed to have just emerged from the pampering hands of the women who raised him—his sisters and the old aunt. From that purely feminine education he retained a candid manner

---

[27] "Brest"

A port city in Brittany with a long history as a military port. During World War II, Brest was occupied by the Germans (1940) and was, for a while, a principal submarine repair station for them until 1944, when the town was liberated by invading American troops.

[28] "Borda"

There was a naval training ship named *Borda*, whose home base was Brest. The ship was named after Charles Borda (1733–1799), a mathematician and naval officer who played a significant role in the establishment of the metric system in Europe.

[29] "Requin"

The French word *requin* means shark.

[30] "d'Artois"

A French county. Also, the name of a noble family descended from Robert I, brother of St. Louis.

Leroux, as a reporter, was the European journalist who had the first interview with Nordenskjöld, the Norwegian explorer who, with his men, was marooned on Antartic ice for nearly two years from the *d'Artois* and was presumed to be lost. (See the Introduction, p. 10)

[31] "six months"

This would appear to be a very unhurried rescue mission if one of its young mariners has a six-month leave before setting off.

and a charm which nothing until now had been able to tarnish. He was now twenty-one years old,[32] but looked eighteen. He had a small blond mustache, beautiful blue eyes and the complexion of a young woman.

Philippe spoiled Raoul. For one thing, he was very proud of him, and was delighted at the prospect that his younger brother would have a career in the navy in which one of their ancestors, the famous Chagny de la Roche, had attained the rank of admiral. He took advantage of Raoul's leave of absence to show him Paris, whose luxurious pleasures and artistic delights his younger brother had hardly known until then.

The count believed that, at Raoul's age, it was not too good to be too good. The count was a man with impeccable manners, an equable temperament, as thoughtful in his work as in his pleasures, and incapable of setting a bad example for his brother. He took Raoul with him wherever he went. He even introduced him to the dancers' lounge at the Opera.[33] I know that it was said that the count was "on intimate terms" with la Sorelli. Well, what of it? Was it a crime for such a bachelor gentlemen with plenty of time on his hands—especially after his sisters had married—to spend an hour or so after dinner in the company of a dancer who, though she was not what one would call terribly witty, had, nevertheless, the prettiest eyes in the world? And then, there are places to which a true Parisian of the count's rank must show himself. In that era, such a place was the dancers' lounge at the Opera.

Still, it may be that Philippe would not have taken his brother backstage at the National Academy of Music if Raoul had not asked it of him first with a gentle persistence that the count would later have reason to remember.

Philippe, having applauded Daaé that evening, turned toward Raoul and was horrified to see how pale he was.

"Don't you see," said Raoul, "that the woman is about to faint?"

And, in fact, Christine onstage was being held up by the other actors.

"It's you who are about to faint," said the count, leaning toward Raoul. "What's the matter?"

---

[32] "twenty-one"
Later, in an oversight, Leroux will say that Raoul is twenty years old (see page 131).

[33] "dancers' lounge"
It was usually an extension of the stage in which the dancers congregated just before or after appearing on stage. It was often equipped with mirrors and warm-up bars for the use of the dancers. It was a place for last-minute straightening of seams, and for quick glances in the mirror just after hearing the prompter's bell. It could serve, too, as a rehearsal space.

A long tradition that ended only in 1935 permitted opera subscribers to go backstage at the opera during intermissions and, writes Duault, "one could see, at each intermission, handsome men in white gloves and evening dress converging in the Foyer de la Danse bearing goodies to their protégées, inquiring about their caprices and planning their after-the-performance projects." (Duault, p. 65)

But Raoul was already standing. "Let's go," he said, his voice trembling.

"Where do you want to go?" asked the count, astonished by his brother's emotional state.

"Let's go see. This is the first time she's ever sung like that."

The count looked at his brother and a slight smile of amusement played at the corners of his lips.

"Well . . ." Then he added quickly, "Let's go. Let's go." He seemed enchanted.

It was not long before they were at the crowded subscribers' entrance. While they waited to get through to the stage, Raoul, in an unconscious gesture, removed his gloves, and the kindly Philippe was too sensitive to tease him for his impatience, but the gesture was instructive. He knew now why Raoul was distracted when he talked with him and why his brother seemed to take such pleasure in turning every conversation to the subject of the Opera.

They pushed through to the stage. A throng of men in evening dress was hurrying toward the dressing rooms, or to the dancers' lounge. There were the mingled cries of stagehands and foremen, the extras departing from the last scene, the walk-ons, a backdrop being lowered from the flies, a platform being nailed down with heavy blows from a hammer—the usual hubbub of the theater; the eternal theater, the noise of which sounds so threatening that you fear for the fate of your top hat, or an attack from behind—the normal elements of an intermission, which never fail to trouble a novice like the young man with the small blond mustache, blue eyes, and the complexion of a young woman, who moved as quickly as the jumble permitted across the stage on which Christine Daaé had triumphed and under which Joseph Buquet had just died.

There had never been more confusion than on this evening, but Raoul had never been less timid.[34] He pushed every obstacle to one side with a solid shoulder and was oblivious to what was being said around him by the frightened stagehands. He was uniquely focused on his desire to see the woman whose magical voice had ravished his heart. Yes. He knew well that his poor young heart no longer belonged to him. He had tried to defend it since the day that Christine, whom he had known as a child, came back into his life. In her presence, he had felt a very tender emotion

---

[34] "less timid"

   We will see that Raoul, though he will be courageous, is almost never dynamic. This moment, when he is hurrying to Christine's side, is the only time in the story when he acts aggressively.

which, on reflection, he had wished to drive away, because, consonant with his respect for himself and for his convictions, he had sworn that he would never love a woman who could not be his wife and, naturally enough, he could not—even for a second—consider marrying a singer.[35] Yet now, that very sweet emotion had been followed by an atrocious sensation. Sensation? Or feeling. It encompassed the physical and the moral. He had a pain in his chest as if someone had opened it and taken out his heart. It felt horribly hollow. He felt a dreadful emptiness that could never be filled except by the heart of the other! These are the manifestations of a particular psychology which, it would appear, can only be understood by those who have fallen in love, or as they say, "who have been struck by Cupid's arrow."

Count Philippe, still smiling, was having trouble following his brother.

At the back of the stage beyond the double door which opens onto the steps that lead to the dressing rooms and those which lead to the boxes on the left side of the first floor, Raoul was brought to a halt in front of a little troop of children who, having just come from their attic, crowded the passageway through which he meant to go. He did not respond to any of the quips sent his way by their little painted lips; finally he was able to pass and descend into a shadowy hallway still vibrating with the shouts of enthusiastic admirers. One name reverberated throughout: Daaé, Daaé. Behind Raoul, the count said to himself, "The rascal knows the way," and he wondered why. He himself had never taken Raoul to see Christine. One had to suppose that Raoul had gone there alone, while the count, as usual, stayed chatting with La Sorelli, who often kept him with her until the moment she had to go onstage. Sometimes it was her tyrannical foible to ask him to hold the little gaiters which preserved the luster of her satin and the cleanliness of her skin-colored tights. She had an excuse for all this: she had lost her mother.[36]

The count, putting off for a few minutes the visit he was supposed to make to La Sorelli, followed the corridor which led to Daaé's dressing room and ascertained that this hallway had never been frequented as much as on this evening, when the entire theater had been overwhelmed by the success of the singer and the fact that she had fainted. The lovely youngster

---

[35] "consider marrying a singer"

Though Leroux strikes the note of class-consciousness here, we will see that the difference in rank between the two young people plays only a small part in their story.

[36] "lost her mother"

La Sorelli's self-indulgence is presented here with a certain irony. Christine, too, has lost her mother. In fact, every major character in this work is parentless: Raoul, his brother Philippe, Christine Daaé, and above all, Erik, the Phantom.

had not yet regained consciousness. Just then, the theater doctor, who had been sent for, arrived, and pushed his way through the people. He was followed by Raoul, who trod close on his heels.

Thus it happened that the doctor and the lovestruck young man found themselves beside Christine at the same moment, and she received the care of the first even as she opened her eyes in the arms of the second. The count, along with many others, stayed in the suffocating air of the doorway.

Audaciously, Raoul asked the doctor, "Don't you think those gentlemen should clear the room? One can hardly breathe in here."

"You're entirely right," the doctor agreed, and sent everyone else away except Raoul and the maid. The maid stared at Raoul, her eyes wide with amazement. She had never seen him before. Just the same, she did not dare to question him.

And the doctor thought that if the young man behaved in this fashion, then evidently he had the right to do so.

That's why the viscount stayed in the dressing room, gazing at Christine as she came to life, while the two directors, Messrs. Debienne and Poligny, who had come to express their admiration for her, were pushed back into the corridor among the men in evening clothes. The Count de Chagny, thrust out into the hallway like the others, burst out laughing.

"Ah, the rascal. The rascal." And he added, under his breath, "Beware of these lads with their innocent, girlish airs."

He was radiant. "But of course, he's a Chagny!" He started toward Sorelli's dressing room. But, as we know, the count met her, accompanied by her frightened little flock, on their way to the lounge.

In her dressing room, Christine Daaé heaved a great sigh, which was answered by a groan. Turning her head, she saw Raoul and trembled. She looked toward the doctor and smiled, then at her maid, then at Raoul once more.

"Monsieur!" she said in a voice that was no more than a whisper. "Who are you?"

"Mademoiselle," replied the young man, who got down on one knee and ardently kissed the diva's hand. "Mademoiselle, *I'm the little boy who went into the sea to retrieve your scarf.*"

Christine looked again at the doctor and the maid, and all three of them began to laugh. Blushing, Raoul got to his feet.

"Mademoiselle, since it pleases you not to remember me, I'd like to say something to you in private—something very important."

"When I feel better. Do you mind . . . ?" Her voice trembled. "You're very kind."

"But, you really must go," added the doctor with his most pleasant smile, "so that I may look after the young lady."

"I'm not sick," Christine said suddenly, with a vitality as strange as it was unexpected. She got up, passing a hand across her eyes. "Thank you, doctor. I need to be alone. Go, all of you, I beg you. Leave me. I'm very nervous this evening."

The doctor wanted to offer various objections, but given the young woman's condition, it seemed to him that a better remedy was not to oppose her. He went into the corridor with the distraught Raoul. The doctor said, "I don't recognize her this evening. She's ordinarily so gentle." And he left him.

Raoul was left alone.

That part of the theater was now deserted. They were about to proceed with the farewell ceremony in the dancers' lounge. Raoul, thinking that Christine might be going there, waited silently. He hid himself in a convenient shadow made by a corner of the door. He continued to feel an atrocious pain where his heart had been. And that's what he wanted to talk to Christine about, without delay. Suddenly the dressing room opened and he saw the maid carrying packages and leaving by herself. He stopped her in the hallway and asked for news of her mistress. Laughing, she replied that Christine was doing very well, but that she ought not to be disturbed because she wanted to be alone. Then she left.

An idea crossed Raoul's inflamed mind: Christine, no doubt, wanted to be alone for *him*. Had he not told her that he wanted to talk privately to her, and was that not the reason she had sent everyone else away? Barely breathing, he approached the dressing room and pressed his ear against the door in order to hear whatever response might be made when he knocked. But his hand fell when he heard *a man's voice* in the dressing room saying, in a singularly commanding fashion, "Christine, you must love me."

And Christine's trembling voice, so sad that one guessed it was accompanied by tears, replied, "How can you say that to me? To me, who sings only for you."

Raoul was in such pain that he had to lean against a panel. His heart, which he thought he had lost forever, was now back in his chest and beating wildly. The whole hallway resounded, and Raoul felt his ears deafened by the sound. Surely, if his heart continued to beat so loudly, it would be heard; the door would be opened and he would be chased ignominiously away. What a position for a Chagny. Eavesdropping behind a door! With all his might, he tried to quiet his beating heart. But a beating heart is not a dog's muzzle, and even when you seize an intolerably barking dog's muzzle with both hands, it can still be heard growling.

The man's voice resumed. "You must be very tired."

"Oh, tonight I gave you my soul—and I'm dead."

"You have a beautiful soul," said the man in his deep voice, "and I thank you for it. There isn't an emperor in the world who has received a similar gift. *This evening, the angels wept.*"

After these words, "*This evening, the angels wept,*" the viscount heard nothing more.

Meanwhile, he stayed where he was, but since he feared being discovered, he hid himself in a shadowy corner intending to wait there until the man should leave the dressing room.

He had, in the same moment, encountered both love and hate. He knew that he loved. He wanted to know whom it was he hated. Much to his surprise, the door opened and Christine Daaé, wrapped in furs and her face veiled in lace, came out of the room, alone. She shut the door, but Raoul noticed that she did not lock it. She went by. He did not even watch her going, because his eyes were fastened on the door, which did not open again. Since the hallway was once again empty, he went across to the dressing room. He opened the door, then closed it behind him at once. He found himself in the most complete darkness. The gaslights had been turned off.

"Someone is in here!" Raoul said, his voice trembling. "Why are you hiding?"

As he spoke, he leaned his back against the closed door. Night and silence. Raoul could hear nothing but his own breathing. Evidently he did not realize how amazingly indiscreet his conduct had been.

"You won't leave without my permission," the young man cried. "If you don't answer, you're a coward. But I'll expose you."

He lit a match. The flame illuminated the dressing room. There was nobody in it. Raoul, having taken care to lock the door, lit lamps. He went into the bathroom, opened the closets, searched, felt the walls with his moist hands. Nothing.

"Oh," he said aloud, "am I going mad?"

He stayed thus for ten minutes, listening to the hissing of the gas in the calm silence of the abandoned dressing room. Though he was in love, it did not even occur to him to steal a ribbon, scented with the perfume of the one he loved. He left the dressing room, no longer knowing what he was doing or where he was going. At some point in his incoherent wandering he felt a chill breeze on his face. He found himself at the bottom of a narrow stairway. Behind him there descended a procession of workers bent over a homemade stretcher covered by a white cloth.

"Which way is the exit, please?" he asked one of the workers.

"It's right there, in front of you," was the response. "The door is open, but let us pass by."

Mechanically, he asked, indicating the stretcher, "What's that?"

The worker replied, "That's Joseph Buquet, who was found in the third subcellar hanging between a flat and the backdrop for the *Roi de Lahore*."

He stepped to one side, nodded, and went out.

Chapter III

⇒»€

IN WHICH, FOR THE FIRST TIME, MESSRS. DEBIENNE AND POLIGNY SE-
CRETLY TELL THE NEW DIRECTORS OF THE OPERA, MESSRS. ARMAND
MONCHARMIN AND FIRMIN RICHARD, THE TRUE AND MYSTERIOUS REASON
FOR THEIR DEPARTURE FROM THE NATIONAL ACADEMY OF MUSIC.

Meanwhile, the farewell ceremony was taking place.

I have said that this magnificent celebration marking their departure
from the Opera had been given by Messrs. Debienne and Poligny because
they wanted, as we say nowadays, to go out with a bang.

They had been helped in this idealized, if somewhat sad, project by
everyone who was anyone in Parisian society and the arts.

They had all planned to meet in the dancers' lounge, where Sorelli
was waiting for the departing directors, a glass of champagne in her hand
and a small speech ready at the tip of her tongue.

Behind her, her fellow dancers, young and old, crowded about her,
some of them gossiping in whispers about the events of the day, while
others exchanged knowing winks with their friends, a crowd of whom were
already gathered around the buffet which had been placed on the sloping
floor between Boulanger's[1] *Danse Guerrière* and *Danse Champêtre*.[2]

Some of the dancers had already put on their street clothes; most of
them still wore their tutus, but all of them thought it their duty to assume

53

a grave manner. Only little Jammes, at the happy, insouciant age of fifteen, seemed to have forgotten the Phantom and the death of Joseph Buquet. She was so continually prattling, babbling, skipping about, and clowning with her friends, that, when Messrs. Debienne and Poligny appeared on the steps of the dancers' foyer, she was severely called to order by an irritated Sorelli.

It was clear to everyone that the retiring directors had a cheerful air which, in the provinces, might have appeared strange to everyone, but here, in Paris, was considered in good taste. Any true Parisian has learned to hide his grief under a mask of joy, or his innermost delight with a look of melancholy or indifference. If you know that one of your friends is in pain, don't try to console him; he'll tell you he's all right. But if some happy event should befall him, be careful not to congratulate him; he will suppose his good fortune to be so natural that he'll be astonished to hear you speak of it. In Paris one is always at a masked ball, so Messrs. Debienne and Poligny, sophisticated as they were, would not have dreamed of showing their real feelings in the dancers' lounge. And they were already smiling forced smiles at Sorelli, who was beginning to recite her speech when foolish little Jammes cut short the directors' smiles with an exclamation so abrupt that the fear and anguish hidden in their faces was suddenly clear to everyone.

"The Phantom of the Opera."

Jammes uttered this phrase in a tone of unspeakable terror. Her finger pointed to a face in the crowd of men in evening dress,[3] a face with a death's-head look, so pale, so grim, and so ugly, with its profoundly cavernous eye sockets, that it created an immediate sensation. "The Phantom of the Opera. The Phantom of the Opera."

There was laughter and jostling, and there were those who wished to offer the Phantom a drink, but he had disappeared. He had slipped into the crowd and was sought for in vain while two elderly gentlemen were trying to calm little Jammes even as little Giry uttered piercing cries.

Sorelli was furious; she had not been able to finish her speech. Messrs. Debienne and Poligny had hugged her and thanked her, and then made their escape as quickly as the Phantom himself. No one was surprised by

---

[1] "Boulanger"

Gustave-Rodolphe Boulanger was a French painter (1824–1888) who decorated the walls of the opera's foyer.

[2] "*Danse Guerrière* and *Danse Champêtre* [Warrior dance and rustic dance]"

There are actually four types of dance depicted by Boulanger on the panels in the *foyer de la danse*: Bacchic, Amorous, Warrior, and Rustic.

[3] "a face in the crowd"

This is the first glimpse a reader gets of the Phantom.

this, because they knew that the directors had to go through the same ceremony on the floor above in the singers' lounge, and that, finally, their close friends would be received one last time in the large vestibule of the directors' office where a real supper awaited them.

And it is there that we find them now with the new directors, Messrs. Armand Moncharmin and Firmin Richard. Neither set of directors knew the other very well, but the protestations of friendship flowed and were responded to by a thousand compliments, to such a degree that the faces of the guests, who had anticipated a dreary evening, lighted up at once. The supper was almost jolly, and since there were plenty of opportunities for toasts, the official representing the government showed himself to be so skillful at mixing the glories of the past with the successes of the future that a warm cordiality soon reigned among the guests.

The transfer of powers had taken place the day before in the most simple fashion. Because there was a great desire for agreement, remaining matters had been resolved between the incoming and the outgoing administration under the supervision of a government commissioner. As a result, no one could be surprised on this memorable occasion that the faces of the four directors were radiant.

Messrs. Debienne and Poligny had already turned over to Messrs. Armand Moncharmin and Firmin Richard the two tiny master keys that opened all of the thousands of doors of the National Academy of Music.[4] These keys, objects of general curiosity, were being nimbly passed from hand to hand when several of the people in the crowd had their attention drawn at the table's end to a strange, pale, fantastic hollow-eyed face that had already appeared in the dancers' lounge, where it had been greeted by little Jammes' cry, "The Phantom of the Opera."

He was there, like any normal guest, except that he was neither eating nor drinking.[5]

Those who had begun by smiling at him ended by turning away their heads because the sight of him roused such dark thoughts. No one repeated the jokes that had been made in the lounge. Nobody cried, "Look, it's the Phantom of the Opera."

---

4   "keys"
    This is one of Leroux's oversimplifications. There were 2,531 doors that were opened variously with 7,593 keys, some 5,052 of which were used in the administrative parts of the building.
5   "He was there . . ."
    The fictive narrator, having asserted that the Phantom *was* there, dances away from the direct statement and takes refuge in the speculative, "because the thing is entirely possible". Then, having raised the possibility that the Phantom was *not* there, he reverses himself again and has him reappear in the vestibule, where he announces the death of Joseph Buquet.

He had not said a word, and those who sat beside him were not themselves able to say at what precise moment he had taken his seat there, but each of them thought that if the dead sometimes returned to sit at the tables of the living, they could not show features more macabre. The friends of Firmin Richard and Armand Moncharmin thought this emaciated guest was a friend of Messrs. Debienne and Poligny, while their friends thought that this cadaverous being was a guest of Messrs. Richard and Moncharmin. As a result, nobody risked asking for an explanation, or made an unpleasant remark or tasteless joke that might have irritated the visitor from beyond the grave. Some of the guests who were familiar with the legend of the Phantom and who knew the description given of him by the chief stagehand—they did not know Joseph Buquet was dead—thought privately that the man at the end of the table could have passed for a living embodiment of the imagined being created, according to them, by the superstition of the Opera staff; and yet, according to the legend, the Phantom had no nose, and this person had one. But Monsieur Moncharmin asserts in his *Memoirs* that the guest's nose was transparent. "His nose," he said, "was long, thin, and transparent"—and I would add that it could have been a false nose. Monsieur Moncharmin may have taken what was glistening for what was transparent. Everyone knows that science is capable of making admirable false noses for those who, by nature or because of an operation, have been deprived of them.

Is it in fact true that the Phantom came to sit at the directors' banquet without having been invited? And can we be sure that this face was that of the Phantom of the Opera himself? Who dares to say? If I speak of the matter here, it is not that I want to make the reader believe, even for one second, or even tempt him to believe, that the Phantom was capable of such superb audacity, but only because the thing is entirely possible.

And here, it would seem, is a sufficient reason to think so. Monsieur Armand Moncharmin—still quoting from his *Memoirs*—says, verbatim, Chapter XII:

When I think of that first evening, I am not able to separate the secret confided to us in their office by Messrs. Debienne and Poligny from the presence at our supper of the *ghostly* personage whom none of us knew.

Here is precisely what happened. Messrs. Debienne and Poligny, seated at the middle of the table, had not yet noticed the man with the death's-

The modern chandelier of the Opéra Garnier

head, when suddenly he began to speak. "The *rats* are right," he said. "The death of poor Buquet is perhaps not as one might think."

Startled, Debienne and Poligny cried, "Buquet is dead?"

"Yes," the man—or the shadow of a man—replied calmly. "He was found this evening hanging in the third subcellar between a flat and a backdrop for the *Roi de Lahore*."

The two directors, or, better, the ex-directors, stood at once and stared strangely at him. They were unreasonably agitated, that is to say, more than they had reason to be by the announcement that the chief stagehand had been found hanged. The two directors looked at each other. They had turned paler than the tablecloth. Finally Debienne gestured to Messrs. Richard and Moncharmin; Poligny uttered some words of excuse to his guests, and the four directors made their way to the administrative office.

I turn now to Monsieur Moncharmin's account.

In his memoirs, he says that "Messrs. Debienne and Poligny seemed to be more and more agitated, and it appeared to us that they had something to tell us that was extremely embarrassing to them. First, they asked us if we knew the person who sat at the end of the table who told them about the death of Joseph Buquet, and when we replied in the negative, they seemed to be even more disturbed. They took the pass keys from us and examined them for a moment, shook their heads, and advised us to have new locks secretly made for the rooms, closets, or for any of the things we might want to keep especially secure. They were so droll as they spoke that we started to laugh and asked them if there were thieves at the Opera. They replied that there was something worse, and that it was the Phantom. Again, we laughed, persuaded that they were indulging in some kind of joke that was meant to crown the evening's festivities. Then, at their request, we assumed a more serious mien, meaning to please them by participating in their joke.

"They told us that they would never have spoken to us about the Phantom if they had not received a formal command from the Phantom himself to ask us to treat him well and to give him anything for which he might ask. However, happy to be leaving a place over which there hung such a tyrannical shadow, they had delayed until the last moment giving us an account of such strange events, for which, certainly, our skeptical minds were in no way prepared. However, the news of Joseph Buquet's death was a brutal reminder that each time they had failed to obey any of the Phantom's requests, some fantastic or grim event had quickly brought them back to a realization of their dependence. In the course of this unexpected account, confided to us in a tone of the gravest and most absolute secrecy, I was watching Richard. Richard, as a student, had had the reputation of being a practical joker; that is, he was skilled in the thousand and one ways available to people who wished to poke fun at each other. And the concierges on the Boulevard Saint-Michel knew all about him. Without missing a mouthful, he seemed to be enjoying the dish now set before him, even though its seasoning, because of the death of Joseph Buquet, was a bit macabre. He nodded his head sadly, and as the tale was being unfolded to him, his features darkened, like that of a man who bitterly regretted taking over the Opera now that he had learned there was a Phantom in it.

"For my part, I could do no better than to slavishly copy his grim look. Finally, however, we could no longer restrain ourselves and burst out laughing at Messrs. Debienne and Poligny, who, seeing us pass from a very dark mood to an insolent hilarity, behaved as if they thought we had gone mad.

"When the joke seemed to be lasting a bit too long, Richard, half jokingly, half in jest, asked, 'But what is it that this Phantom wants?'

"Monsieur Poligny went to his office and came back with a copy of the Opera's instruction book.[6] The book begins with the words, 'The management of the Opera will give to the performances of the National Academy of Music the splendor that is appropriate to the premier lyric stage in France.' And it ends with Article 98 in the following terms:

This privilege may be revoked
1. If the director contravenes the rules stipulated in the Book of Instructions.

"The rules then follow.

"This copy," said Monsieur Moncharmin, "was in black ink and was exactly like the one we own, except that we saw that at the end of a paragraph in the book shown to us by M. Poligny there was an addition in red ink—in a bizarre and tormented handwriting, as if the words had been traced with the tips of matchsticks dipped in ink—the handwriting of a child who was still making only vertical strokes and who had not yet learned to connect his letters. That added paragraph which so strangely extended Article 98, said, verbatim:

5. *If the director delays for more than fifteen days the monthly sum that he owes the Phantom of the Opera—that sum, fixed, until further notice at 20,000 francs—240,000 francs per year.*

"Monsieur Poligny pointed, with a hesitant finger at this final clause, which we had certainly not expected.

" 'That's all? *He* wants nothing more?' asked Richard, perfectly self-possessed.

---

[6] "instruction book"

The French name for this document is *Cahier des Charges*. Signed both by the Minister of Fine Arts and the incoming new director(s) of the opera, the *Cahier* specifies minutely what the rights and duties of the director(s) are vis-à-vis the state.

For example, in the *Cahier des Charges* negotiated for, Pedro Gailhard (see note p. 30) and Eugene Ritt, who became codirectors of the opera in 1885, one learns that they were entitled to 25,000 francs each as salary plus 16,000 francs toward the upkeep of their carriages. (Duault, p. 92.)

" 'Yes,' replied Poligny. He leafed through the instruction book and read:

'Art. 63.—Box number one in tier number one will be reserved for all performances for the head of state. On Monday loge number 20 on the ground floor on Wednesdays and Fridays loge number 30 are at the Minister's disposal.

The second loge, number 27, will be reserved daily for the use of the prefects of the Seine and of the police.'

"Monsieur Poligny showed us that here, once again, at the end of that article, there was appended a line in red ink: '*At all performances, box five of the first tier will be put at the disposition of the Phantom of the Opera.*'

"At this last sally, there was nothing for us to do but to get up and shake the hands of our predecessors warmly and congratulate them for having imagined such a charming joke which proved that the ancient French sense of humor was still alive and well. Richard thought it necessary to add that now he understood why Messrs. Debienne and Poligny had retired from the management of the National Academy of Music: there was no way to conduct business with such a demanding Phantom.

"Unamused, Monsieur Poligny said, 'Clearly, one doesn't pick two hundred and forty thousand francs out of the air. And have you considered what it costs us, since we cannot rent loge number five in the first tier because it is reserved for the Phantom at every performance? And that doesn't include the sums we have had to disburse to the subscribers. It's dreadful. Really, we can't work just to support phantoms. We prefer to leave.'

" 'Yes,' Monsieur Debienne repeated, 'we prefer to leave. Let's go.' He got to his feet.

"Richard said, 'But it seems to me you're on very good terms with him. If I had such a troublesome phantom, I wouldn't hesitate to have him arrested.'

" 'But where? How?' they cried simultaneously. 'We've never seen him.'

" 'Not even when he's in his box?'

" '*We've never seen him in his box.*'

" 'Well then, rent it.'

" 'Rent the Phantom's box! Just try it, gentlemen.'

"At which the four of us left the managers' office. Neither Richard nor I had ever laughed so hard.''

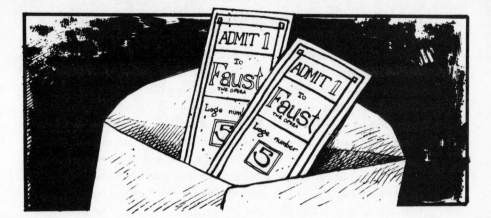

Chapter IV

BOX NUMBER FIVE

Armand Moncharmin has written such voluminous memoirs concerning that long period of his comanagement that one has a right to wonder if he had the time to devote himself to the Opera beyond giving an account of what transpired. Monsieur Moncharmin could not read a note of music, but he could use the familiar "tu" form of address when he spoke to the Minister of Public Instruction and of the arts; he had done a bit of society journalism and enjoyed a reasonably large fortune.[1] In short, he was a charming fellow who did not lack intelligence since, having undertaken to run the Opera, he had been wise enough to look for a competent manager and had gone directly to Firmin Richard.

Firmin Richard was a distinguished musician and a gallant gentleman. Here is the portrait of him that appeared in the *Revue des Theatres* at the time of his appointment:

M. Firmin Richard is about fifty years old, tall, stocky without being over-weight. Imposing in bearing, distinguished, ruddy-featured, his full head of hair is neatly cut with bangs over his forehead. He has a beard to match.

---

[1] "fortune"

Leroux encapsulates quite neatly what was required of candidates for the position of opera director.

There is a tinge of sadness in his features which tempers his frank, candid look and charming smile.

M. Firmin Richard is a very distinguished composer, skilled in harmony and counterpoint.[2] Grandeur is the principal element of his compositions. He has published chamber music that is much appreciated by connoisseurs— music for the piano, sonatas, and fugitive pieces full of originality as well as a collection of melodies. Finally, his *La Morte d'Hercule,* performed at one of the concerts of the Conservatory, breathes an epic air which reminds one of Gluck,[3] one of M. Firmin Richard's venerated masters. Still, if he adores Gluck,[4] he has no less admiration for Piccinni;[5] M. Richard appreciates music of every sort. Full of admiration for Piccinni, he honors Meyerbeer[6] and delights in Cimaros,[7] and nobody appreciates better the inimitable genius of Weber.[8] As for Wagner,[9] M. Richard is not far from claiming that he, M. Richard, is the first, if not the only one in France, who has truly understood him.

---

[2] "harmony and counterpoint"
In music, the intertwining of melodies with each other or melodies with chords to achieve richness of texture. *Webster's Third New International Dictionary* says that in music, counterpoint is achieved when "one or more melodies [are] added as accompaniment to a primary melody."

[3] "Gluck"
Christoph Willibald Gluck (1714–1787), an Austrian composer. He wrote the music for more than a score of operas, including *Artaserse* (1741), *La Nozze d'Ercole e d'Ebe* (1747) and *Orfeo ed Euridice* (1762). One notes that Leroux's Firmin Richard, influenced no doubt by Gluck's *Marriage of Hercules and Ebe,* has written a concert piece titled *The Death of Hercules.*
It is notable, too, that Gluck composed the music for two operas on the theme of Orpheus and Eurydice—whose legend considerably influenced Leroux's treatment of the Christine–Raoul story.

[4] "if he adores Gluck"
This is a tongue-in-cheek line, since the two composers, Gluck and Piccinni, were at the center of a long-standing professional feud. (See Note 5, below.)

[5] "Piccinni"
Niccolò Piccinni (1728–1800), the Italian-born composer, moved to Paris in 1776, enticed there by Marie Antoinette, who took singing lessons from him. Before his death, he had composed more than 130 operas.
Piccini's success in France was consistently opposed by Gluck's partisans. The director of the Paris Opera was not averse to pitting the two composers against each other. He asked them both to write an opera on the theme of Iphigenia in Tauris. Gluck won the competition.

[6] "Meyerbeer"
Giacomo Meyerbeer (born Jakob Liebmann Beer) (1791–1864). Meyerbeer, a dominant force in the development of nineteenth-century French opera, was the son of a Jewish banker in Berlin. *L'Africaine,* performed in Paris in 1865, is the most famous of his operas.

[7] "Cimarosa"
Domenico Cimarosa (1749–1801) was an Italian composer. For a time, he served as Kappelmeister to King Leopold II, following the departure from the post of Mozart's rival, Salieri. It was at Leopold's court in 1793 that Cimarosa composed *Il Matrimonio Segreto (The Secret Marriage),* his best-known operatic work.

[8] "Weber"
Carl Maria von Weber (1786–1826) was a German composer of intensely sensual music. He was, as well, an accomplished pianist, symphonic conductor, and novelist. His most famous operas are *Der Freischutz* (1820) and *Euryanthe* (1823). In addition to his ten operas, he composed symphonies, masses, lieder, ballads, and cantatas.

I stop quoting here at the point at which it seems clear to me that if M. Firmin Richard loved practically all music and all musicians, it then ought to be the duty of all musicians to love M. Firmin Richard. Let us say, as we conclude this brief portrait of M. Richard, that because of his difficult temperament, he was what one might call an authoritarian.

The comanagers spent their first days at the Opera pleased at being masters of such a vast and magnificent enterprise. They had certainly forgotten the curious and bizarre story about the Phantom when there occurred an incident which proved that—if there was a joke—it was not over yet.

M. Firmin Richard arrived at his office one morning at eleven o'clock. His secretary, M. Rémy, showed him half a dozen letters that he had not unsealed because they were marked "personal." One of the letters caught M. Firmin's attention at once, not only because the envelope was addressed in red ink, but also because it seemed to him he had seen that handwriting somewhere before. He was not puzzled for long: it was the red handwriting that had so strangely ended the book of rules. He recognized the childlike up and down strokes. He unsealed it and read:

Dear Director,

I ask your pardon for troubling you at such a serious time when you are busy deciding the fate of your best performers at the Opera in which you will be renewing important contracts and concluding new ones; and all of that with a clarity of vision, and a theatrical understanding, a knowledge of the public and its tastes, and an authority that I, with my long experience, find astonishing. I am aware of what you have done for Carlotta, la Sorelli and little Jammes, and for several others whose admirable qualities (talent or genius) you have discerned. You know very well who I mean as I write these words; evidently it is not for Carlotta, who sings like a banshee, and who ought never to have left the Ambassadors or Cafe Jaquin; nor for Sorelli, who owes her success to her shape; nor for little Jammes, who dances like a calf in a meadow. Nor is it for Christine Daaé, whose genius is inescapable, but whom you have sedulously kept from any important role.

Of course, you are free to run your business any way that you see fit. Just the

---

[9] "Wagner"

Wilhelm Richard Wagner (1813–1883) wrote his first opera, *Die Feen* (*The Fairies*), when he was twenty years old. Beethoven and Weber were early influences on his work. At the time of his death, he had created at least half a dozen imperishable operas: *Tannhäuser* (1843–45); *Lohengrin* (1846–48); *Der Ring des Nibelungen* (1853–74); *Tristan und Isolde* (1857–59); *Die Meistersinger von Nürnberg* (1862–67) and *Parsifal* (1877–82).

On the day of his death in Venice, he was at work on a treatise to be called "On the Feminine in Human Nature." He had finished page two of the essay when he was stricken by a heart attack. The last two words he wrote were *"Liebe-tragik"* (*love tragedy*).

same, I'd like to take advantage of the fact that you have not yet dismissed Christine Daaé to hear her in the role of Siebel tonight, since the role of Marguerite, ever since her triumph of the other day, has been kept from her. And I beg you not to dispose of my box for today, nor for any subsequent days.

I will not end this letter without conveying to you how disagreeably surprised I was recently when, arriving at the Opera, I learned from the reservations desk that, by your orders, my box had been rented.

I have not protested sooner first because I am an enemy of scandal, and then because I thought that your predecessors, M. Debienne and Poligny, who have always been charming to me, had neglected, before their departure, to tell you about my little idiosyncrasies.

But I have just received M. Debienne and Poligny's answer to my request for an explanation, and their response proves that you are aware of my book of rules, and that, therefore, you are mocking me outrageously. If you want us to live in peace, it is better not to begin by taking away my box!

Having made these small observations, please consider me, my dear director, your very humble and obedient servant.

Signed: Ph. of the Opera

This letter was accompanied by a clipping from the "personals" column of *La Revue Théatrale*, where it said, "*Ph. of the O.: R. and M. have no excuse. We warned them, and we left them with a copy of your book of instructions. Greetings.*"

M. Firmin Richard had barely finished reading when the door of his office opened and M. Armand Moncharmin was standing before him, a letter in his hand precisely like the one his colleague had received. They looked at each other and burst out laughing.

"The joke's still on," said M. Richard. "But it's not funny."

"What does this mean? Do they think that, just because they have been the directors of the Opera, we're going to let them have a free box forever?"

Neither of these two men had any doubt that the letters were the result of a practical joke devised by their predecessors. "I'm not in the mood to be the butt of this joke much longer," declared Firmin Richard.

"It's harmless," said Armand Moncharmin.

"Well, anyway, what is it they want? A box for this evening?"

M. Firmin Richard ordered his secretary to send tickets for Loge Number 5, if it had not already been rented, to Messrs. Debienne and Poligny.

It had not been. The tickets were sent at once. M. Debienne lived at the corner of Rue Scribe and the Boulevard des Capucines;[10] Poligny on the Rue Aubert.[11] The two letters from the Phantom of the Opera had been posted on the Boulevard des Capucines. It was Moncharmin who noticed it on examining the envelopes. "You see," said Richard.

They shrugged their shoulders and regretted that people of such advanced years should still be amusing themselves with such childish tricks.

"Just the same, they could have been polite," Moncharmin pointed out. "Did you see how they treated us as regards Carlotta, Sorelli, and little Jammes?"

"Well, my friend, those fellows are sick with jealousy! When I think they went to the trouble of paying for an ad in *La Revue Théatrale*! Have they nothing better to do?"

"By the way," Moncharmin continued, "they seem to be very interested in Christine Daaé."

"You know as well as I do that she is reputed to be virtuous."

"Often enough, one may borrow a reputation," said Moncharmin. "I have a reputation for knowing music, and I can't tell the difference between the F-clef and the G-clef."

"You never had that reputation," declared Richard. "You don't need to worry."

At this, Firmin Richard gave orders that the performers be sent in. They had been waiting in the corridor for two hours for the managers' door to open—the door behind which waited fame and fortune—or dismissal.

The whole day was spent in discussions, negotiations, the signing and the breaking of contracts—also, I beg you to believe that that evening, the evening of January 25, our two directors, fatigued by tempers, intrigues, recommendations, threats, protestations of love or of hate, went to bed early without even the curiosity to cast a glance in the direction of Loge Number 5 to see whether Messrs. Debienne and Poligny found the performance to their taste. Since the departure of the previous directors, the Opera had not been idle, but M. Richard had had various repair work done without interrupting any of the performances.

---

[10] "Capucines"

    The Boulevard des Capucines, named for a Capucine monastery, traverses the IInd and IXth Arrondissements in Paris. Number 1, Boulevard des Capucines, was the site of the Cafe Napolitain, a haunt of journalists, writers, and artists during La Belle Epoque (1885–1915), the period in which Gaston Leroux flourished. In 1874, the first Impressionist exhibit opened at Number 35.

[11] "Rue Aubert"

    The Rue Aubert, in the IXth Arrondissement, begins at Number 5, Place de l'Opéra, and ends at Number 53, Boulevard Haussmann. Originally named the Rue Rouen, it was renamed in honor of the composer Daniel-François-Esprit Aubert (1784–1871) in 1864.

The following morning, Messrs. Richard and Moncharmin found among other things in their mail a thank-you note from the Phantom, as follows,

My dear director,
Thank you. A charming evening. An exquisite Daaé. Fix the choruses. Carlotta, a magnificent and banal instrument. Will write soon regarding 240,000 francs—to be exact, 233,424 and 70 centimes. Messrs. Debienne and Poligny having given me 6575 francs and 30 centimes representing the first ten days of this year's pension—their responsibilities ending on the evening of the tenth.
Your humble servant,
Ph. of the O.

They also received a letter from Messrs. Debienne and Poligny:

Messieurs,
We thank you for your kind attention, but you will easily understand that the prospect of hearing Faust *once more, however delightful that would be to the former directors of the Opera, ought not to keep us from remembering that we have no right whatsoever to occupy loge number five in the first tier which belongs exclusively to the person of whom we spoke at the time that we read, together with you, and for the last time the final paragraph 63 of the Instruction Book.*
We remain etc.

"Ah, these people are beginning to annoy me," Firmin Richard said angrily as he snatched up the letter from Messrs. Debienne and Poligny.

That evening, Loge Number 5 in the first tier was rented.

The next day, when Messrs. Richard and Moncharmin arrived at their office, they found an inspector's report relating to events that had transpired the evening before in Loge Number 5 of the first tier. Here is the essential paragraph of that brief report:

Twice this evening, at the beginning and at the middle of the second act [the inspector had written the report on the previous evening], I was forced to call the police to expel the occupants of Loge Number 5 of the first tier. These people, who had arrived at the beginning of the second act, caused a veritable scandal by their laughter and their absurd comments. The noise of people hushing them could be heard from all sides and people were beginning to protest throughout the theater when a box attendant came to get me. I entered the box and made such comments as were necessary. The occupants seemed to have entirely lost their wits and made stupid replies. I warned them that if they continued their behavior I would have to expel them from the box. I had no sooner left when I once again heard their laughter and renewed protests from the house. I returned with a policeman, who made them leave. Still hilarious, they said they would only go if they got their money back.[12] Finally, they calmed down and I let them go back into the box. They were no sooner in it when their laughter began again. This time, I had them expelled once and for all.

"Send for the inspector," cried Richard to his secretary, who had been the first to read the report and who had already made comments on it in blue pencil. The secretary, M. Rémy, was an elegant, distinguished-looking twenty-four-year-old, with a thin mustache. He was fashionably dressed— in those days it was the thing to wear a frock coat during the day. Intelligent and timid in the presence of the director, who paid him his salary of 2400 francs a year, he monitored the newspapers, replied to letters, distributed the complimentary tickets and box seats, arranged meetings, talked with people in the waiting room, visited sick performers and found understudies for them, and corresponded with department heads; but above all his task was to weed out visitors. He could be fired at a moment's notice, because his job was not recognized by the management. The secretary, who had already sent for the inspector, ordered him into the office.

The inspector came in a bit nervously.

---

[12] "their money back"

Since they were sitting in a box, their refund would be fifteen francs per person. The range of opera ticket prices was as follows:

Apron (forestage) and facing loges: 17 francs

Balcony seats and boxes facing stage and first level loges on the side: 15 francs

Orchestra, second loges facing and baignoire [boxes] on the side: 14 francs

Second level, side: 10 francs

Third level, facing stage: 8 francs

The pit: 7 francs

Apron (forestage), level three: 5 francs;

Stalls in the amphitheater, fourth level, facing stage: 2.50 and 3 francs

(Karl Baedeker, *Baedeker's Guide to Paris.* London: Dulau & Co., 1907.)

A curious fact: Freud paid four francs for his "stall" seat in the orchestra in 1885 at the Theatre Porte-Saint-Martin.

We get a sense of the money values of the period when we read what it cost to eat in a dining car on the train: "Dinner at 6 francs; lunch at 4 francs. (By way of comparison, the cost of a horse-drawn conveyance in Paris was 2 francs per hour; a bottle of Margaux or sauterne cost 4 francs; the daily median salary of an industrial workingman was 5 francs peer day.)" (Jean-Francois Six, *1886 Naissance du XXe Siècle en France,* p. 16.)

"Tell us what happened," said Richard brusquely.

The inspector stammered at first and referred to his report.

"Well," said Moncharmin, "*why* were those people laughing?"

"M. Director, they must have dined unusually well and seemed better prepared for horseplay than to hear fine music. They had no sooner entered their box when they came out again and called for the box attendant, who asked them what was wrong. They said, 'Look into the box. There's nobody there, right?'

" 'No, nobody,' she replied.

" 'Well,' they insisted, 'when we went in, we heard a voice saying *someone was there.*' "

M. Moncharmin could not help smiling as he looked at M. Richard, but Richard was not smiling at all. He was much too familiar with the kind of practical joke that he discerned in the inspector's naïve account. It had all the earmarks of one of those mean jokes which, amusing at first, ends by enraging its victims.

The inspector, who wanted to please M. Moncharmin, who was smiling, believed he too ought to smile. Unfortunate smile! Richard withered the employee with a look. The inspector tried at once to assume a look of appropriate dismay.

"Was there, in fact, no one present in the box?" the implacable Richard said reprovingly.

"No one, sir. No one. Not in the box on the right or the one on the left. I swear it. I'd stake my life on it. All of which proves that this is nothing but a joke."

"And the box keeper? What did she say?"

"Oh, as for her, that's simple enough. She says it's the Phantom of the Opera. Well . . ." and the inspector sneered. But once again, he realized that laughter was a mistake, because he had no sooner pronounced the words, "She says it's the Phantom of the Opera" when Richard's expression, already somber, turned positively fierce.

"Somebody get the box attendant," he commanded. "Now! Bring her to me. And get these people out of here."

The inspector wanted to object, but Richard shut him up with a formidable "Be quiet." Then, when the lips of the unhappy underling seemed to be sealed forever, the director ordered him to open them once more. "What is this Phantom of the Opera?" he rasped.

This time, the inspector was incapable of saying a word. He made it clear, with a desperate gesture, that he knew nothing about it—or, better, that he wished to know nothing about it.

"And you. Have you seen the Phantom of the Opera?"

With an energetic shake of the head, the inspector denied ever having seen him.

"Too bad," Richard said coldly.

The inspector's eyes widened and seemed to start from their sockets as he asked why the director had uttered his sinister "Too bad."

"Because I'll settle the account of anyone who hasn't seen him," explained the director. "Since he's everywhere, it is intolerable for him not to be seen anywhere. I want people who work for me to work."

Chapter V

CONTINUATION OF "BOX NUMBER FIVE"

Having said that, M. Richard paid no further attention to the inspector and dealt with various matters with the administrator, who came in just then. The inspector, thinking that he could go, went slowly—slowly, oh how slowly—toward the door when M. Richard, seeing what he was up to, stopped him in his tracks, thundering, "Don't you budge."

At the insistence of M. Remy, the box attendant, who was also the concierge on the Rue de Provence[1] a few steps from the Opera, was sent for. She showed up moments later.

"What's your name?"

"Mme. Giry. You know me well, director, sir. I'm the mother of little Giry. Little Meg, you know." This was said in a brusque but solemn manner that impressed M. Richard for a moment. He looked at Mme. Giry (faded shawl, worn slippers, old taffeta dress, and soot-colored hat). It was clear from every indication, that the director neither knew nor had any memory of knowing Mme. Giry, nor little Giry, nor little Meg. But Mme.

---

[1] "Rue de Provence"

The Rue de Provence, in the VIIIth Arrondissement, begins with the Rue du Faugourg-Montmartre and ends at the Rue de Rome. At one time, Balzac lived at Number 24 Rue de Provence and the composer Berlioz at Number 41.

Giry's pride was of the sort that made her imagine she was known to everyone. I believe, with reason, that it is from her name the theatrical slang "to Giry" is derived, as when one dancer reproaches another for gossiping and chattering by saying, "That's so much fussing and whining."[2]

"I don't know anyone," announced the manager. "Just the same, Mme. Giry, I'd like to know what happened to you yesterday evening that compelled you and the inspector to call the police."

"I was just coming to talk to you about that, director sir. Just so that you wouldn't have the same problems as those that Messrs. Debienne and Poligny had. They, too, wouldn't believe me at first."

"I'm not asking you about that. I want to know what happened last night."

Mme. Giry turned red with indignation. No one had ever talked to her in such a tone. Gathering up the folds of her skirt and giving her soot-colored hat a dignified shake, she rose as if to go. Then, rethinking the matter, she resumed her seat and, in a superior voice, said, "What's happened is that someone has irritated the Phantom again."

Here, since M. Richard was about to explode again, M. Moncharmin interposed and took up the questioning. As a result, it was learned that Mme. Giry thought it was entirely natural for a voice to have proclaimed that there was someone in a box that was empty. She could not explain the phenomenon that she had discovered except by supposing that it was the Phantom who, though no one had seen him in the box, had been heard by everyone. She herself had heard him often, and this had to be true because everyone knew that she never lied. They could ask Messrs. Debienne and Poligny and everyone else who knew her, as well as M. Isidore Sack, whose leg the Phantom had broken.

"Oh?" Moncharmin interrupted. "The Phantom has broken poor Isidore Sack's leg?"

Mme. Giry's eyes widened. One could read in them the astonishment she felt in the presence of so much ignorance. Finally, she condescended to instruct these two unfortunate innocents. It had happened during the tenure of Messrs. Debienne and Poligny and, again, in Box Number Five during a performance of *Faust*.

Mme. Giry coughs, clears her throat, begins . . . one might say that she is readying herself to sing an excerpt from Gounod.[3] "Well then, sir,

[2] "to Giry"
  The French word *giries* refers to complaints or querulous whining.
[3] Notice that Levoux uses the present tense here, and elsewhere in *The Phantom* (see especially Chapter

in the first row that evening there were M. Maniera and his wife, the jewelers from Mogador Street. Behind Mme. Maniera there sat their close friend M. Isidore Sack. Mephisto sang [Mme. Giry sings]:

'You who here
Are soundly sleeping.'⁴

And it's then that M. Maniera hears in his right ear—his wife is sitting at his left—a voice that says, 'Ah, it's not Julie who's soundly sleeping.' (His wife's name is Julie.) M. Maniera turns to his right to see who's speaking. No one! He rubs his ear and says to himself, 'Am I dreaming?' Meanwhile Mephistopheles is singing. Am I boring you?"

"No, no. Go on."

"You are too kind, sirs." She grimaces. "Well, Mephisto continues to sing. [Mme. Giry sings]:

'Catherine whom I adore
Why do you refuse a lover
Who implores
You for one sweet kiss?'⁵

This time, M. Maniera hears a voice, still in his right ear, saying, 'Ah, ah, it isn't Julie who will refuse Isidore a kiss.'

"At this point, M. Maniera turns, but this time it is in the direction of his wife and Isidore. And what does he see? Isidore has taken Mme. Maniera's hand from behind and is covering it with kisses where the glove opens up. Like this, gentlemen, [and here Mme. Giry covers with kisses the back of her hand where the flesh is exposed to view and where her knit glove opens up]. Well, you can imagine that that isn't taken lightly. Slam, bang. M. Maniera who is large and strong—like you, M. Richard— gives M. Stack, who, with all due respect, is weak and slim—like you M. Moncharmin—a couple of blows. What a scandal. Throughout the hall,

---

VI), as a sort of cinematic quality, akin to his use of italics. This present translation is the only one in the English language which remains true to the original text in this manner.

⁴ "You who here"
   The lines are from a song Mephistopheles sings in Act IV, Scene 5 of Gounòd's *Faust*.

⁵ "Catherine whom I adore"
   The lines are from the same song as above.

there are cries of, 'Enough, enough. He's going to kill him.' Finally, M. Sack is able to escape.''

"So the Phantom didn't break his leg?'' asked M. Moncharmin, a bit irritated that his physique had made so little impression on Mme. Giry.

Mme. Giry, who understood Moncharmin's drift, said haughtily, "He broke it, sir. He broke it, clean and clear, on the grand staircase down which M. Isidore was going so hastily. Broke it so well that the poor fellow won't be coming up those stairs any time soon.''

"Was it the Phantom who told you what he whispered into M. Maniera's right ear?'' M. Moncharmin asked with the seriousness of a judge, though the matter seemed to be becoming increasingly more humorous.

"No, Monsieur. It is M. Maniera himself who told me. So . . .''

"What about you? Have you spoken to the Phantom, my good woman?''

"As clearly as I speak to you, dear sir.''

"And when he talks to you, what does he say?''

"Oh, he tells me to bring him a little footstool.''

At these words, spoken so solemnly, Mme. Giry's face turned to marble—yellow marble veined with red streaks, the kind that's called sarancolin. The kind that supports the grand staircase.

This time, Richard began to laugh, along with Moncharmin and M. Rémy, the secretary. The inspector, made wary by experience, did not laugh again. Leaning against the wall, he feverishly fingered the keys in his pocket and asked himself how this tale would end. And the haughtier Mme. Giry's tone became, the more he feared a renewal of the manager's anger. Now, in the presence of the manager's hilarity, she dared to be threatening. Truly threatening.

"Instead of laughing at the Phantom,'' she cried, offended, "you would do better to be like M. Poligny, who realized it for himself.''

"Realized what?'' asks Moncharmin, who had never been so amused.

"About the Phantom. Because I'm telling you. Take this—'' Abruptly she turned calm, realizing the seriousness of the moment. "Listen. I remember it as if it were yesterday. This time, they were performing *La Juive*.[6]

<hr/>

[6] "La Juive"

La Juive'' ("The Jewess''), an opera by Jacques-François-Fromental-Elie Halévy, with a libretto by Eugène Scribe, was performed first at the Paris Opera on February 23, 1835. By 1886, in the decade in which the action of *The Phantom* is presumed to take place, *La Juive* had been performed five hundred times. Halévy, a professor of composition at the conservatory, numbered Gounod and Bizet among his students.

The story of *La Juive* turns on misperceived or secret identities. Eleazar is a Jewish goldsmith living in the city of Constance. His daughter is Rachel, who is in love with Leopold, who, she supposes, is

M. Poligny had wanted to watch the performance alone in the Phantom's box. Mme. Krauss had been such a smash success. She had just sung that thing from the second act [Mme. Giry sings softly]:

'Beside the one I love
I want to live and die,
And death itself
Cannot part us.' "[7]

"All right, all right. I get it," M. Moncharmin interrupted with a discouraging smile. But Mme. Giry continues to sing while balancing the feather in her soot-colored hat:

"Away, away. Here, below the heavens.
The same destiny awaits us both."

"Yes, yes, we know that," repeated Richard, impatient once more.

"Well, then. It was at the moment when Leopold cries, 'Let us escape?' All right? And Eleazer stops them and asks, 'Where's your hurry?' It was just then that M. Poligny, whom I was watching from the back of a nearby box, stood up suddenly and left, walking as stiffly as a statue. I had only time enough to ask him, like Eleazer, 'Where are you off to?' But he made no reply. He was paler than a corpse. I watched him as he went down the stairs. But it wasn't he who broke a leg, though he walked as in a dream, a bad dream—and could not find his way out—he who was well paid for knowing the Opera well."

That, then, is what Mme. Giry said. She stopped talking to see what sort of impression she had made. The story of Poligny had made Moncharmin shake his head.

---

a Jew when in fact he is a noble Christian warrior just returned from a campaign against the Husites. To complicate the plot, Leopold has a loving wife named Eudossia and Eleazar has a mortal enemy, Cardinal Brogni, who harasses the Jews. In the climactic scene of the opera, when all is revealed too late, the vengeful Eleazar tells Cardinal Brogni that Rachel, a heretic, who has just been flung into a caldron of burning oil, is in fact Brogni's long lost daughter.

[7] "Beside the one I love . . .

"Where's your hurry?"

The snatches of text Madame Giry is quoting are from Act II, Scene 4 of La Juive. It is the scene in which the noble Leopold, having confessed to Rachel that he is a Christian, begs her to run away with him. As they start off, Eliezar, Rachel's "father" appears and accosts the lovers.

75

"None of that tells me anything about the circumstances or the way in which the Phantom asked you for a footstool," he insisted, staring fixedly at Mme. Giry, "under four eyes," as they say.

"Well, since that evening . . . because it was after that evening that they left our Phantom alone . . . nobody tried to deprive him of his box. Messrs. Debienne and Poligny gave orders that it be reserved for him at every performance. So, when he comes, he always asks me for his little stool."

"Uh-huh. A phantom who asks for a footstool. Is your phantom a woman, then?" Moncharmin inquired.

"No, the Phantom is a man."

"How do you know?"

"He has a man's voice. A man's beautiful voice. Here's how it happens: when he comes to the Opera, he usually arrives in the middle of the first act and knocks three times lightly at the door to Box Number 5. The first time I heard those three knocks—since I knew that there was no one in the box, you can imagine that I was curious. I open the door. I listen. I look. No one. Then I hear a voice that says, 'Mme. Jules (that was my dead husband's name), a footstool, if you please.' I turned, if you'll excuse the expression, tomato red. But the voice went on, 'Don't be frightened, Mme. Jules. It's me, the Phantom of the Opera.' I looked toward where the voice was coming from—a voice so kind, so welcoming, that I almost stopped being afraid. Sir, *the voice was sitting in the first chair of the first row on the right.* Except that there was no one to be seen sitting in the chair, one would have sworn that someone was there, someone who spoke—very politely, indeed."

"Was the box to the right of Number Five occupied?" asked M. Montcharmin.

"No. Box Number 7, like Box Number 3 on the left, was not yet occupied. It was still the beginning of the performance."

"And what did you do?"

"I brought the footstool. Evidently, the footstool he asked for was for his lady and not for him. As for her, I never saw nor heard her."[8]

"What? Now the Phantom has a wife?" Moncharmin and Richard shifted their gaze from Mme. Giry to the inspector standing behind her, who was waving his hands to get his employers' attention. He was tapping

---

[8] "for his lady"

This is an intriguing detail this early in our fiction. Though her mention raises all sorts of questions about the Phantom's private life, we will never hear of this "lady" again.

his finger against his forehead, desperate to convey to them that Mme. Giry was crazy. The pantomime determined M. Richard to get rid of an inspector who kept a lunatic in his service. The good woman, still engrossed in her Phantom, was now praising his generosity. "At the end of the performance, he always gave me a forty-sou piece. Sometimes a hundred sous. Sometimes, when he had not been there for several days, he would give me ten francs. But now that they've started to bother him, he hasn't given me anything."

"Pardon me, my good woman," (in the presence of such tenacious familiarity there was again a protesting movement of the feather in the soot-colored hat), "but how does the Phantom manage to give you your forty sous?" asked Moncharmin, who was born curious.

"Well, he leaves it on the railing of the box. I find it as well as the program I always bring him. Some evenings I even find flowers in my box—a rose that must have fallen from a woman's corsage. He must sometimes have come with a lady, because once I found a fan they left behind."

"Ah-hah. So the Phantom left a fan behind. And what did you do with it?"

"I brought it back to him the next time he came."

At this point, the inspector's voice was heard. "Then you haven't followed the rules, Mme. Giry. I'll have to fine you."

"Shut up, you fool." (*The bass voice of M. Firmin Richard.*)

"So you brought back the fan. Then what?"

"Then they took it away with them. I didn't find it after the performance. Instead, they left a box of the English candies I like so much, M. Manager, sir. It is one of the Phantom's courtesies."

"That's fine, Mme. Giry. You can go now."

When Mme. Giry left, having bowed to the two managers, not without a certain dignity that never abandoned her, they told the inspector that they had decided from here on to do without the services of the old fool. Then they bade the inspector to take his leave.

When the inspector, having protested his devotion to the Opera, had gone, in his turn, the managers informed the administrator that they wanted the inspector removed from the payroll. When the two managers were left alone, each informed the other of the same thought that had occurred to them simultaneously—that, together, they should take a quick look at Box Number Five.

We will follow them shortly.

Chapter VI

⇒❈⇐

THE ENCHANTED VIOLIN

Christine Daaé, victim of intrigues about which we will have more to say later, did not immediately repeat the triumph she had achieved on that famous gala evening. Just the same, she had occasion to be heard in town at the home of the Duchess of Zurich, where she sang the most beautiful segments of her repertoire; and this is how the great critic, X.Y.Z., who was among the guests, expressed himself:

"When one has heard her in *Hamlet,*[1] one asks oneself whether Shakespeare has returned from the Elysian Fields to have her rehearse *Ophelia*. . . . It's true that when she has put on the queen of the night's diadem of stars, Mozart has to leave his eternal home to come hear her. But no, he doesn't have to trouble, because the keen and vibrant voice of her magic interpretation of his *Magic Flute* scaled the heavens to find him with the same ease with which she passed effortlessly from her cottage in the village of Sckoteloff[2] to the gold and marble palace built by M. Garnier."

[1] *"Hamlet"*
This opera by Ambroise Thomas, with a libretto by J. Barbier and M. Carrée, was first performed at the Paris Opera on March 9, 1868. The love duet between Hamlet and Ophelia is considered to be especially beautiful.

But after that evening at the Duchess of Zurich's, Christine did not sing again in public. The fact is that during that epoch Christine refused all invitations, all fees. Without giving any plausible explanation she chose not to appear at a charity festival for which she had previously promised her participation. She behaved like someone who is no longer the mistress of her own destiny; as if she was afraid of a new triumph.

She knew that the Count de Chagny, to please his brother, had approached M. Richard on her behalf. She wrote to thank him and to beg him not to say anything more about her to the managers. What could possibly have been the reasons for such a strange attitude? There were some who claimed that it was an overweening pride; others spoke of a divine modesty. But in the theater no one is ever that modest. To be truthful, I wonder if I ought not to write simply this one word: fear. Yes, I really believe that Christine Daaé was frightened by what had happened to her and was as stunned by it as everyone around her. Stunned? Well, let's see. I have one of Christine's letters here (from the Persian's collection) that relates to the events of that period. Well then, having reread it, I would not write that she was stunned or even frightened by her triumph. Horrified! Yes, yes. Horrified! "When I sing," she says, "I no longer recognize myself."

The poor, sweet, pure child.

She did not show herself anywhere, and the Viscount de Chagny tried in vain to find some trace of her. He wrote to ask permission to visit her. He was losing hope of getting a reply when, one morning, she sent him the following note:

Monsieur, I have not forgotten the little boy who went into the sea to get my scarf. I cannot keep myself from writing this to you today as I am leaving for Perros compelled by a sacred duty. Tomorrow is the anniversary of the death of my poor father, whom you knew and who loved you. He is buried there with his violin in the cemetery that surrounds the little church at the foot of the hill where, when we were very small, we so often played; and where, beside the road, when we were a bit older, we bade each other farewell for a final time.

When he received this note from Christine Daaé, the Viscount de Chagny snatched up a railway timetable, dressed in haste, wrote a few lines

---

[2] "Skoteloff"
I have been unable to find Skoteloff in any of the atlases I have consulted.

which his valet was to give to his brother, and threw himself into a cab, which left him at the platform of the Montparnasse Station too late for him to catch the morning train he had counted on.

Raoul passed a dreary day and did not recover his good spirits until nearly evening when he was settled into his compartment. Throughout the long voyage, he reread Christine's note, breathed its perfume, and called up sweet images of his younger years. He passed that entire abominable night on the train in a feverish dream which began and ended with Christine Daaé. Dawn was beginning to break when he got off at Lannion.[3]

He hurried to catch the diligence to Perros-Guirec[4] on which he was the only passenger. He questioned the driver, from whom he learned that on the evening of the previous day, a young woman who seemed to be a Parisian had been driven to Perros, where she had gotten off at the Inn of the Setting Sun. That could not be anyone but Christine. She had come alone. Raoul heaved a deep sigh. Soon, in this solitary place he would be able to speak to her without interruption. His love for her left him breathless. This tall youth, who had traveled the world over, was as pure as a virgin who had never left his mother's home.[5]

As he came nearer and nearer to her, he fondly recalled the story of the little Swedish singer. Most people still don't know any of those details.

Once upon a time in a little town near Upsala,[6] there lived a peasant and his family. He tilled the soil during the week and sang in the choir on Sundays. This peasant had a little daughter to whom (even before she could read) he had taught the musical alphabet. It may be that the elder Daaé was, without himself being aware of it, a great musician. He played the violin and was considered the best wedding fiddler in all of Scandinavia. His reputation spread widely through the district, and he was always called upon to play at weddings and banquets. Daaé's mother, an invalid, died when the little girl was just entering her sixth year. The father, whose only

---

[3]   "Lannion"

    A port town in northwestern France. Also, the arrondissement of the same name.

[4]   "Perros-Guirec"

    A fishing and resort village on the bay of Perros in the Lannion arrondissement. The town boasts a church that may date back to the twelfth century.

[5]   "as a Virgin . . . never left his mother's home"

    A reader will by now have noticed that Leroux is positioning Raoul for the role of the sexless lover, in the tradition of Gothic fiction, which often has an erotically unthreatening protagonist and a dynamic, dark, and sexually threatening antagonist.

[6]   "near Upsala"

    Presumably the town is Skoteloff. Upsala is a Swedish town situated on both banks of the Fyrisän River, some sixty-six kilometers from Stockholm. The town boasts both a remarkable cathedral and a famous university—one of the oldest in Europe, founded in 1477.

loves were his daughter and his music, immediately sold his bit of land and left to seek fame in Upsala. What he found there was poverty.

Back he went, then, to the countryside, going from fair to fair, strumming his Scandinavian melodies, while his child, who never left him, listened ecstatically, or accompanied him with her songs. One day, at the Limby fair, Professor Valerius[7] heard the two of them and brought them to Gothenburg.[8] He asserted that the father was the finest violinist in the world, and that the daughter had the makings of a great artist. He provided for her education and instruction. Wherever she went, people marveled at her beauty, her grace, and her eagerness to speak and to behave well. Her progress was rapid. When Professor Valerius and his wife had to move to France, they took the Daaés with them. Madame Valerius treated Christine as if she were her daughter. As for her father, who suffered from homesickness, he began to wither away. In Paris, he never went out. He lived in a sort of dream that he maintained by means of his violin. He shut himself into his room with his daughter where they could be heard for hours on end playing the violin and singing very softly, very softly. Sometimes Madame Valerius would come and listen at the door. She would sigh and wipe the tears from her eyes, then tiptoe away. She, too, was nostalgic for the Scandinavian sky.

The elder Daaé seemed unable to recover his strength until the summer, when the entire family went on a holiday to Perros-Guirec, in a corner of Brittany which, in those days, was practically unknown to Parisians. He loved the sea there, saying that it had the same color as the one in his homeland; often, at the beach, he would play his most poignant melodies, saying that the sea grew calm to hear them.

Then, after he had pleaded with Mme. Valerius, she consented to indulge a new whim of the fiddler's. During the season of the "pardons" [Breton pilgrimages], festivals, and dances, he went, as formerly, with his violin, and he was allowed to take his daughter with him for eight days. No one tired of hearing them. Into the tiniest of villages, they poured out enough music to last for an entire year. Refusing beds in an inn, they slept at night in barns, where they lay beside each other on the straw as they had done in those days in Sweden when they were so poor.

Meanwhile, they were properly dressed. They refused the money they

---

[7] "Professor Valerius"

Leroux's choice of a name for the benign Valerius couple may be purely accidental. On the other hand, he may have been thinking of Caius Flaccus Valerius, the Roman poet who lived in the first century A.D. and who died young. Valerius is the author of "Argonautica," an uncompleted epic poem about the tragic and violent love affair between Jason and Medea.

[8] "Gothenburg" (Swedish, Göteborg)

Gothenburg is the second largest city in Sweden and is perhaps Sweden's most important commercial center. In 1884, it was a center for the export of iron, wood, butter, and fish.

From *The Phantom of the Opera* (1943)

were offered, nor would they take up a collection. People who followed them from village to village did not understand the conduct of the violinist who traveled their roads with a beautiful child who sang so well that one might have thought her to be an angel out of paradise.

One day, a city boy who was out with his governess made her take a very long route because he could not stop following the little girl whose sweet, pure voice seemed to have enchanted him. They arrived thus at the banks of an inlet that is still called Trestraou. In those days there was nothing there but the sea and the sky and the golden shore. On that day, there was a high wind that blew Christine's scarf into the sea. She uttered a cry and reached her arms out, but the scarf was already some distance into the waves. Then she heard a voice saying, "Don't be upset. I'll bring your scarf back from the sea."

And she saw a little boy running and running despite the protesting cries of a lady garbed entirely in black. All dressed as he was, the little boy ran into the water and brought back the scarf. The boy and the scarf were a mess! The woman in black was unable to calm herself, but Christine laughed with all her heart and kissed the little boy. It was the Viscount Raoul de Chagny who, at that time, was living with his aunt in Lannion. During the season the children saw each other almost every day and played together. At the aunt's request, and at the urging of Professor Valerius, the elder Daaé agreed to give the young viscount violin lessons. Thus it was that Raoul learned to love the same melodies as those that had enchanted Christine when she was a child.

Each of them had the calm, dreamy soul of a dreamer. Their chief game was to ask for old Breton folktales at people's doorsteps, like beggars. "Madame—or, my dear good sir—do you have a little story to tell us, please?" It was rare that they weren't "given" one. What old Breton grandmother had not once in her lifetime at least seen goblins dancing on the heath in the moonlight?

But their greatest delight came in the great calm peace of dusk after the sun had set in the sea. Then father Daaé came to sit beside them at the road's edge and in a low voice (as if he feared disturbing the ghosts he would evoke) told them the beautiful, sweet, and terrible legends of the land of the north. Some were as beautiful as the tales of Andersen,[9] while others were as sad as the lyrics of the great poet Runeberg.[10] When he stopped, the two children would cry, "Again."

There was one story that began, "There was a king sitting in a little skiff on one of those tranquil and deep waters that open like a brilliant eye in the midst of the mountains of Norway . . ."

And another, "Little Lotte would think about everything and about nothing. As a summer bird, she soared in the sun's rays, wearing a springtime crown on her blond curls. Her soul was as clear and as blue as her eyes. She was affectionate to her mother, loyal to her doll, and was very

---

[9] "tales of Andersen"

Hans Christian Andersen (1805–1875), the Danish novelist and poet, was born atop a second-hand catafalque, the only piece of furniture his impoverished shoemaker father could afford to provide for his wife when she went into labor.

Andersen is best known for his sprightly retelling, in three volumes, of traditional fairy tales. When his complete works were published in 1848, they amounted to thirty-five volumes.

[10] "Runeberg"

Johan-Ludvig Runeberg, a Finnish poet (1804–1877) was best known for his *Faenrik Stols Saegner* (*The Narratives of Ensign Sol*), within which are incorporated a number of popular Finnish folktales, among them "Cloud Brother," "The Two Dragons," and "The Village Daughter." Characteristically simple, straightforward, and lyric, the poems are said to reflect the special beauty of the northern landscape, with its dense forests and long starlit nights.

careful of her dress, her red shoes, and her violin. But more than anything else, she loved to hear the Angel of Music as she was falling asleep.''

While the elder Daaé was saying these things, Raoul gazed at Christine's blue eyes and golden hair, and Christine would think that little Lotte was very lucky to be hearing the Angel of Music as she was falling asleep. There was hardly a story of old Daaé's in which the Angel of Music did not play a part, and the children endlessly asked questions about him. Daaé claimed that all great musicians, all great performers, once in their lives received a visit from the Angel of Music. Sometimes he leaned over their cradles, as had happened to little Lotte. This is why young prodigies of six can play the violin better than fifty-year-old men, which, you will admit, is absolutely extraordinary. Sometimes, the Angel of Music will come much later on if the children are not well behaved, won't learn their lessons, or practice their scales. Sometimes the Angel doesn't come at all if the children have impure hearts or unquiet consciences. No one ever sees the Angel, but he can be heard by those predestined to hear him. He often comes at a moment when those souls least expect it—when they are sad or discouraged. It is then that they suddenly hear celestial harmonies, a divine voice which they will remember for a lifetime. Those who are visited by the Angel are left with an interior glow, stirred by a sensation unknown to other mortals. And they are privileged in that they will never again take up an instrument or open their mouths to sing without making sounds whose beauty puts all other human sounds to shame. Those who do not know that the Angel has visited these people say of them that they have talent or genius.

Little Christine asked her father if he had heard the Angel, but old Daaé shook his head sadly. His eyes shining, he gazed at his daughter and said, "You will hear him one day, my child. When I am in heaven, I will send him to you. I promise."

It was about this time that old Daaé began to cough.[11]

With the coming of autumn, Raoul and Christine were separated.

Three years later, they saw each other again. They were no longer children. This was in Perros once again, and the impression of that meeting stayed with Raoul ever after. Professor Valerius had died, but his widow stayed in France to look after her financial interests. Old Daaé and Christine, still playing and singing, lived with her, bringing into their harmonious dream their dear protectress, who seemed now to live only on music.

The young man had come to Perros entirely by chance and, also by

---

[11] "began to cough"
Afflicted, no doubt, with tuberculosis.

chance, visited the house in which his little friend lived. First, he saw old Daaé who, with tears in his eyes, rose from his chair and hugged him, telling him that they had remembered him faithfully. That, in fact, not a day had passed when Christine had not spoken about Raoul. The old man was still speaking when the door opened and the charming, attentive young woman entered carrying the steaming tea on a tray. As she put her burden down, she recognized Raoul. A faint flush passed over her face. She remained hesitant, not speaking. Her father watched the two of them. Raoul approached Christine and gave her a kiss that she did not avoid. She asked him a few questions, did her duty as a hostess nicely, picked up the tray, and left the room. Then she went to take refuge on a bench in the solitude of the garden. She was experiencing feelings that agitated her adolescent heart for the first time. Raoul came to join her and they talked awkwardly together until evening. They had completely changed and hardly recognized each other, though each felt that the other had acquired a new importance. Like diplomats, they were cautious with each other and told each other things that had nothing to do with their emerging feelings. When they parted company at the edge of the road, Raoul, placing a respectable kiss on Christine's trembling hand, said, "Mademoiselle, I will never forget you." And he went away, regretting this impetuous statement because he knew very well that Christine Daaé could never be the wife of the Viscount de Chagny.

As for Christine, she went to find her father, to whom she said, "Don't you think Raoul is not as nice as he used to be? I don't like him anymore." And she tried not to think of him again. But that was hard for her to do, so she flung herself into her work, which consumed every moment of her time. She made amazing progress. Those who heard her predicted that she would become the greatest singer in the world. But at that point, her father died, and as a result of the blow, she felt that she had lost both her soul and her genius. She retained just enough of both to be admitted to the conservatory. She did not distinguish herself in any fashion, but took the courses without enthusiasm and brought home a prize solely for the sake of old Mme. Valerius, with whom she continued to live. The first time that Raoul saw Christine at the Opera, he was charmed by the young woman's beauty and by the memories of an earlier time that it evoked, but it was the negative side of her art that surprised him more. She seemed removed from it all. He came back to hear her again. He went backstage and waited for her beside a flat. He tried to attract her attention. More than once he went after her to the door of her dressing room, but she did not see him. In fact, she did not seem to see anyone. She was the personification of indifference. That hurt Raoul because she was so beautiful. He was shy and did not dare to admit to himself that he loved her. And then there had come the thunderbolt on the evening of the gala. The heavens burst open and an angelic voice came down to earth to enrapture people and consume their hearts.

And then, and then, there had been that man's voice behind the door: "You must love me." And nobody there in the dressing room.

Why, at the moment that she opened her eyes after she fainted, had she laughed when he said, "I am the little boy who brought your scarf back from the sea"? Why had she not recognized him? And why had she written to him?

What a long, long hill it was. Here is the crucifix at the crossroads. Here the deserted moor, the frozen heather, the immobile landscape under a white sky. The tinkling windowpanes that seemed about to break. The coach making more noise than progress. He recognized the cottages, the enclosures, the embankments, the roadside trees. Here is the last turn in the road, then a swift descent and there would be the sea, the great bay of Perros.

So then, she got out at the Inn of the Setting Sun. Indeed, there is no other inn. And then, it is very comfortable. He remembers that in the old days good stories were told here. How his heart beats. What will she say when she sees him?

The first person he sees as he comes into the smoky old dining hall is Mme. Tricard. She recognizes him, greets him, and asks what brings him here. He blushes, saying that, having come to Lannion on business, he had decided to come on there to say hello. She wants to serve him lunch, but he says, "In a little while." He seems to be waiting for something or someone. The door opens. He gets up. He is not mistaken: it is she! He wants to speak, but falls back into his seat. She stands before him smiling, not in the least surprised. She is fresh-faced and as flushed as a shade-grown strawberry. No doubt she is excited from having walked briskly. Her bosom, enclosing a sincere heart, rises and falls gently with her breathing. Her eyes, clear, pale blue mirrors, are the color of still lakes dreaming in the north—her eyes gave him back a reflection of her own innocent soul. Her fur coat is partly open, revealing the harmonious lines of her young, graceful figure and her supple waist. Mme. Tricard smiles and discreetly steals away. Finally Christine says, "'You've come and that doesn't surprise me at all. I had a premonition that I would find you here when I came back from mass. *Someone* there told me. Yes, I was told of your arrival."

"Who told you?" Raoul asks, taking her small hand into his own. Christine did not draw it away.

"Why, my poor father, who is dead."

There was a silence between the two young people.

Again, Raoul speaks. "Did your father tell you that I love you, Christine, and that I cannot live without you?"

Christine blushes to the roots of her hair and turns her head away. Her voice trembling, she says, "Me? You must be mad, my friend."

Then, to put herself in countenance, as they say, she laughed.

"Don't laugh, Christine. This is very serious."

Gravely, she replies, "I did not make you come so that you would tell me such things."

"You have 'made me come,' Christine. You guessed that your letter would not leave me indifferent, and that I would hurry to Perros. How could you have thought that, if you had not also known that I loved you?"

"I thought that you would remember our childhood games in which my father so often joined. Really . . . I don't really know what I thought. Maybe I was wrong to write to you.[12] Your sudden appearance in my dressing room that night carried me far far back into the past, and I wrote to you like the little girl I once was and who, in a moment of sadness and loneliness, would be happy to see her little comrade beside her once again."

For a moment they were both still. Without his being able to pinpoint exactly what it was, there was something in Christine's attitude that Raoul did not find natural. However, he did not feel it to be hostile. Far from it. The regretful tenderness of her eyes let him know that. But what caused that regretful tenderness? Maybe that's what was disturbing the young man and what he needed to know.

"When you saw me in your dressing room, was that the first time you saw me, Christine?"

She did not know how to lie. She said, "No. I had already noticed you several times in your brother's box. And on the stage, too."

"I thought as much," said Raoul, pursing his lips. "Then why, when

---

[12] "wrong to write to you"

From the point of view of nineteenth-century good breeding, she certainly was wrong. A single young woman writes to a young man and lets him know that she will be alone in a small hotel in an isolated village on the Breton coast. He takes his cue and hurries after her. Now, with extraordinary disingenuousness, she tells him that she "wrote like the little girl I once was and who, in a moment of sadness and loneliness, would be happy to see her little comrade beside her once again."

If we add to all this what Raoul overheard through the door of her dressing room, we can hardly wonder that Raoul is perplexed and suspicious. And yet, as we will read later, "Raoul never for a moment doubted Christine's purity."

you saw me at your box, at your knees, reminding you that I had saved your scarf from the sea, then why did you respond as if you didn't know me? And why did you laugh?''

The tone of these questions is so harsh that a stunned Christine simply looks at Raoul and does not reply. The young man, too, is astounded by this sudden quarrel he dared to provoke at the very moment when he had promised himself to offer Christine words of gentleness, of love, and of submission. A husband, or a lover with acknowledged rights, would not have spoken differently to the wife or the mistress who had offended him. But being in the wrong only irritates him the more, and thinking himself stupid, he can find no other way out of his ridiculous situation than by making the fierce decision to be hateful.

"You won't answer me," he says, at once miserable and angry. "Very well, then. I'll answer for you. It's because there was someone in your dressing room whose presence troubled you, and you didn't want him to know that you could be interested in anyone but himself.''

"If there was anyone troubling me that evening," interrupted Christine icily, "it was you, because I had to put you out.''

"Yes, so you could be alone with the other man.''

"What are you saying?" gasps the young woman. "What other man are you talking about now?''

"The one to whom you said, 'I sing only for you. I've given you my soul this evening, and I'm dead.' ''

Christine seized Raoul's arm. She gripped it with a force one would not have expected from a being as fragile as she was.

"You were listening at the door?''

"Yes, because I love you. And I heard everything.''

"What did you hear?" And the young woman, turning strangely calm, released Raoul's arm.

"He said, 'You must love me.' ''

At these words, a pallor like death's spread over Christine's face and dark rings formed around her eyes. She staggers and is about to fall. Raoul, his arms outstretched, runs toward her, but Christine has overcome her temporary dizziness and, in a soft, almost inaudible voice, says, "Go on, what else? Tell me all that you heard.''

Raoul gazed at her and hesitated, unable to understand what was happening.

"Go on, then. Surely you can see that you're killing me.''

"I also heard what he replied when you told him that you had given

89

him your soul: 'You have a beautiful soul, and I thank you for it. There isn't an emperor in the world who has received a similar gift. This evening, the angels wept.' ''

Christine put her hand to her heart. Overcome with an indescribable emotion, she looks at Raoul. Her gaze has the narrow, fixed look of a madwoman. Raoul is horrified, but then Christine's eyes grow moist and two heavy tears, like a couple of pearls, slide down her ivory cheeks.

''Christine!''

''Raoul!''

The young man wants to embrace her, but she slips out of his arms and runs off in great disorder.

While Christine stayed shut up in her room, Raoul reproached himself a thousand times for his brutality, but then jealousy resumed its galloping pace through his feverish veins. For a young woman to have shown so much feeling when she learned that her secret had been discovered was an indication of just how important that secret was. Despite what he had heard, Raoul never for a moment doubted Christine's purity. He knew very well that she was widely reputed to be virtuous, and he was not so naïve as not to know that a performer is sometimes forced to hear declarations of love. She had replied well by saying that she had given her soul. Evidently, then, nothing more was involved here than music and song. Evidently? Then why so much emotion just now? Good Lord, how unhappy he was. Had he been able to seize the man, the man whose voice was all he knew, he would have demanded precise explanations from him.

Why had Christine run away? Why did she not come down again?

He refused to have lunch. He was very upset and he grieved to see himself far away from his young Swede during those hours he had so looked forward to passing sweetly with her. And why, since she seemed to have nothing more to do in Perros—and, in fact, was doing nothing there—why did she not take the road back to Paris at once? He had learned that that morning she had caused a mass to be said for the eternal repose of her father's soul, and that she had spent long hours in prayer in the little church and beside the fiddler's tomb.

Sad, discouraged, Raoul went toward the cemetery that surrounded the church. He pushed its door open. He wandered alone among the tombs, deciphering the inscriptions, but when he came behind the apse he was suddenly made aware of the tomb he was seeking by the dazzling colors of the flowers resting on the granite headstone and overflowing onto the white earth. They perfumed this entire chilly corner in a Breton winter. There were miraculous red roses, which seemed to have bloomed that morning in the snow. It was a bit of life in the midst of death—because here, death was everywhere. It obtruded from the soil, which had rejected its excess of corpses. Skeletons and skulls by the hundreds were piled up against the wall of the church, held there only by a thin network of iron wires which allowed the macabre edifice to be seen in its entirety. The piled-up heads were aligned like bricks mortared together by cleanly whitened bones that seemed to form the first foundation on which the walls of the sacristy had been built. The door to this sacristy opened onto the ossuary. Such sights can frequently be seen in old Breton churches.

Raoul prayed for Christine's father. Then, made melancholy by the eternal grinning of the skulls, he left the cemetery, climbed the hill, and seated himself at the edge of the moor overlooking the sea. The wind rushed fiercely across the beaches, pursuing with a howl the last poor meek light of day, which finally yielded to become no more than a pallid ray on the horizon. Then the wind subsided. It was evening. Raoul was enveloped in chill shadows, but he did not feel the cold. All of his thoughts were wandering over the deserted and desolate moor, along with his memories. It was here, to this place, that he had often come at evening with little Christine to see the goblins dancing just as the moon rose. He, for his part, had never seen them, though he had good sight. Christine, on the other hand, who was a bit short-sighted, claimed to have seen many of them. He smiled at the idea, then shuddered suddenly. A shape, a precise form which had come there without his knowledge, without having made the slightest sound to warn him, was standing at his side and saying, "Do you think the goblins will come out tonight?"

It was Christine. He wanted to speak. She put her gloved hand over his mouth. "Listen to me, Raoul. I want to tell you something important. Very important." Her voice trembled. He waited. She went on, her breathing troubled. "Do you remember the story of the Angel of Music?"

"Do I remember!" he said. "I think it was here that your father told us the story for the first time."

"It's also here that he told me, 'When I'm in Heaven, my child, I'll send him to you.' Well, Raoul, my father is in heaven, and I have had the visit from the Angel of Music."

"I don't doubt it," replied the young man gravely, because he believed he understood how, in his friend's pious thoughts, she might have mingled the memory of her father with that of her recent brilliant triumph.

Christine seemed a bit astonished by the coolness with which the Viscount de Chagny learned that she had had a visit from the Angel of Music.

"How do you understand that?" she said, leaning toward him so closely

91

that the young man might have believed that Christine was going to kiss him, though what she really wanted was to look into his eyes, despite the darkness.

"I understand," he replied, "that a human being does not sing the way you sang the other night without miraculous intervention, without Heaven being involved in some way. There is no earthly teacher who could teach you such accents. You heard the Angel of Music, Christine."

"Yes," she said. "In my dressing room. That's where he comes to give me my daily lessons."

The tone with which she said that was so edged and so remarkable that Raoul looked at her as one might look at someone who has said something outrageous, or who asserts some mad vision in which she believes with all the power of her poor sick brain. But she had drawn back and was no longer more than a bit of motionless shadow in the night.

"In your dressing room?" he repeated like a stupid echo.

"Yes, it was there that I heard him, and I wasn't the only one."

"Who else heard him, Christine?"

"You, my friend."

"Me? I've heard the Angel of Music?"

"Yes, the other evening. It was he who was speaking when you were listening at the door of my dressing room. It was he who said, 'You must love me.' But I thought I was the only one to hear his voice. So you can imagine my astonishment when I learned, this morning, that you could hear him, too."

Raoul burst out laughing. Just then night spread over the deserted moor and the first rays of the moon came to envelope the young people. An angry Christine turned toward Raoul. Her eyes, usually so kind, flashed lightning. "Why are you laughing? Perhaps you think you heard a man's voice?"

"Certainly," replied the young man, whose thoughts, given Christine's warlike attitude, were getting confused.

"You, Raoul! It's you saying that? My childhood friend. My father's friend. I don't recognize you anymore. But, what is it you think? I'm a virtuous woman, M. Viscount de Chagny, and I do not lock myself into my dressing room with men's voices. If you had opened the door, you would have seen that there was no one there."

"That's true. When you left, I opened that door and I didn't find anyone in the dressing room."

"So you see."

The viscount called upon all his courage. "Well, Christine. I think someone's playing a trick on you."

She cried out and fled. He ran after her. Fiercely angry, she flung out, "Leave me alone. Leave me alone." Then she disappeared. Raoul went back to the inn, very tired, very discouraged, very sad.

He learned that Christine had just gone up to her room and announced that she would not come down for dinner. The young man asked whether she was ill. The good landlady replied ambiguously that, if she was ill, it would have to be the kind of illness which was not so very serious and, since she believed it to be a lovers' quarrel, she left the room shrugging her shoulders and expressing, sotto voce, the pity she felt for young people who wasted the hours the good Lord gave them to spend on earth in vain quarrels. Raoul dined alone in a corner of the hearth and, as you may suppose, in a very gloomy mood. Then, in his room, he tried to read, then in his bed, he tried falling asleep. No sound could be heard from the room next to his. What was Christine doing? Was she sleeping? And, if she was not asleep, what was she thinking? And he! What were his thoughts? It would be hard for him to say. The strange conversation he had had with Christine troubled him terribly. He was thinking less about Christine herself than "around" her, and that "around" was so diffuse, so vague, so ungraspable that he experienced a very strange and agonizing malaise.

And so the hours passed slowly. It might have been eleven thirty at night when he distinctly heard footsteps in the room next to his. It was a light, furtive step. Then Christine had not gone to bed. Without a thought of what he was doing, the young man dressed hurriedly, being careful not to make any noise. Then, ready for any event, he waited. Ready for what? Did he know? His heart leaped when he heard Christine's door turning on its hinges. Where was she going at this hour, when everyone in Perros was asleep? Gently, he opened his door a bit, and in a ray of moonlight, he saw Christine's pale form moving carefully through the hallway. She reached the staircase; she descended, and he, above her, leaned over the rail. Suddenly he heard two voices in rapid conversation. One phrase reached him: "Don't lose the key." It was the landlady's voice. Below, the door leading to the waterfront opened, then closed. Then there was silence once again. Raoul returned to his room at once and hurried to open the window. Christine's white form stood on the deserted quay.

The second floor of the Setting Sun Inn was not very high up, and there was a tree trained to grow flat against the wall whose branches, reaching to Raoul's impatient arms, permitted him to leave his room without the landlady being aware of his absence. Then, what was the good woman's surprise the next morning when the young man was brought to her, half frozen, more dead than alive, and she was informed that he had been found stretched out at full length on one of the steps of the high altar of the little church of Perros. She hurried to inform Christine of the news. Christine descended hurriedly and, with the landlady's help, anxiously tended the young man who, not much later, recovered completely when, on opening his eyes, he saw the charming face of his friend bending over him.

So, just what had happened?

Several weeks later, when the tragedy at the Opera required action, the public prosecutor, Monsieur Mifroid the superintendent of police,[13] had occasion to interrogate the Viscount de Chagny about the events of that night in Perros, and here is what was transcribed in the dossier of the investigation (Document 150).

Question: "Mademoiselle Daaé did not see you descend from your room by the strange route that you chose?"
Answer: "No, sir. No. No. However, I followed her, but I neglected to muffle my steps. I only wanted one thing: that she should turn and see me, and that she should know it was I. In fact, I had just told myself that it was wrong of me to follow her, and that this form of spying in which I was indulging was unworthy of me. But she seemed not to hear me, and in fact, she behaved as if I was not there. She left the quay calmly, and then turned abruptly and went back up the road. The church clock had just rung a quarter to midnight, and it seemed to me that the sound of the chimes caused her to hurry her pace, almost to a run. That's how she arrived at the cemetery gate."
Question: "Was the cemetery gate open?"
Answer: "Yes, sir, and that surprised me, but it seemed not to surprise Mlle. Daaé at all."
Question: "There was no one in the cemetery?"
Answer: "I saw no one. If there had been, I would have seen him. The snow covering the earth reflected the dazzling moonlight, making the night even brighter."
Question: "No one could hide behind the tombs?"
Answer: "No, sir. They were poor, small headstones that disappeared under their covering of snow so that only their crosses could be seen above the

---

[13] "Superintendent of Police"
The *Commissaire de Police* is an executive officer of the judicial branch of the French government.

ground. The only shadows were those of the crosses and those of the two of us. The church was resplendently bright. I never saw a night so bright before. It was very beautiful, very clear, and very cold. I had never been to a cemetery at night and did not know that one could see such light—'a light that had no weight.' "

Question: "Are you superstitious?"

Answer: "No, sir. I'm a believing Catholic."

Question: "What was your state of mind?"

Answer: "Very sane, very calm, I assure you. Certainly I had been troubled by Mlle. Daaé's strange exit from the inn, but as soon as I saw her go into the cemetery I said to myself that she had gone there to accomplish a vow of some sort at her father's tomb, and I thought that that was so utterly natural I regained my calm. I was simply astonished, however, that she had not heard me walking behind her, because the snow crackled under my feet. But, no doubt, she had been completely absorbed in her pious thoughts. I decided not to trouble her. And when she reached her father's tomb, I stayed several paces behind her. She knelt down in the snow, made the sign of the cross, and began to pray. At that moment, the clock struck midnight. The twelfth stroke still sounded in my ear when I saw the young woman suddenly look up, her gaze fixed on the vault of heaven, her arms extended toward the moon. She seemed to be in an ecstasy, and I asked myself again what the sudden determining reason might be for that ecstasy when I, too, lifted my head and cast a troubled look around me, as I felt my whole being drawn to the Invisible—*the Invisible that was now playing music for us*. And what music! We already knew it. Christine and I had heard it in our childhood. But it had never been expressed with an art so divine on father Daaé's violin. I could do no more just then than to remember all that Christine had told me about the Angel of Music, and all I could think of were the unforgettable sounds which, if they were not descended from Heaven, gave no indication of what their earthly origin might be. There was no instrument there, nor any hand to guide the bow. Oh, I remembered that astonishing melody. It was "The Resurrection of Lazarus,"[14] which father Daaé had played for us in his hours of sadness and

[14] "Resurrection of Lazarus"

The story of Lazarus' death and his resurrection by Jesus is told in the Gospel of St. John, 11:38–44. According to tradition, Lazarus, a native of Bethany, was thirty years old when he died and was restored to life. He was the brother of Mary Magdalene and her sister Martha.

The musical composition Leroux may have in mind is Schubert's "Lazarus, or the Feast of the Resurrection." The *New College Encyclopedia of Music*, p. 317, says that it is "an unfinished cantata . . . based on a sacred drama in three parts by August Niemeyer, pastor, theological poet from Halle. Though Schubert called the work an Easter cantata, it is really a hybrid half-oratorio, half opera. He failed to write part three." The work was performed after the composer's death (1828) but the score was not published until 1892.

faith. If Christine's Angel existed, he could not have played better for us that night on the late wandering musician's violin. The Invocation to Jesus exalted us above the earth and, in faith, I almost expected to see her father's tombstone rise into the air. It occurred to me that old Daaé had been buried with his violin and, in truth, I did not know at that funereal and brilliant moment in the depths of that hidden little provincial cemetery beside the skulls grinning at us with their immobile mouths . . . no, I did not know just where my imagination might have gone nor where it would have stopped.

"But the music stopped and I came back to my senses. I seemed to hear a sound near the skulls in the ossuary."

Question: "Ah! ah! You heard a sound near the ossuary?"

Answer: "Yes, it seemed to me that the skulls were laughing at us now, and I could not help shuddering."

Question: "It did not occur to you at once that the celestial musician who had so charmed you could be hidden behind the ossuary?"

Answer: "I thought that so intensely I could think of nothing else, Monsieur Commissioner, and I forgot to follow Mlle. Daaé, who rose and went quietly to the cemetery gate. As for her, she was so absorbed that it is not at all surprising that she did not notice me. My eyes fixed on the ossuary, I did not budge, having decided to follow this incredible adventure to its end and find what lay behind it."

Question: "Well then, what happened so that you were found in the morning stretched out half dead on the steps of the high altar?"

Answer: "It happened very quickly. A skull rolled to my feet. Then another, then another. One might have said that I was the target of a macabre game of boules.[15] I imagined that some false move had upset the balance of the structure behind which our musician was hiding. This notion seemed even more reasonable when a shadow slipped over the shining wall of the sacristy.

"I leaped forward. The shadow, having pushed open the door, had already entered the church. I moved as if with wings; the shadow wore a cloak. I was quick enough to seize a corner of the shadow's cloak. At that moment, the shadow and I were directly in front of the high altar and the moon's rays coming through the stained glass window of the apse fell directly in front of us. Since I did not loosen my hold on his cloak, the

---

[15] "boules"

A form of lawn bowling played in Italy and in the south of France.

The section of this chapter set in Perros-Guirec is remarkable, first because it is the longest sequence in the novel with an outdoor setting, and second because of its intense lyricism. We note however that Leroux does not hesitate to risk marring the lyricism by the intrusion of this macabre detail of the rolling skulls.

shadow turned, the cloak opened a little and I saw—as clearly as I see you—I saw a fearful skull which sent me a look that blazed with the fires of hell. I believed I was dealing with Satan himself and, in the presence of that apparition from beyond the grave, my heart quailed, despite my courage, and I have no further memory of anything until I woke in my little room in the Inn of the Setting Sun.''

Chapter VII

A Visit to Box Five

We left Messrs. Firmin Richard and Armand Moncharmin at the moment when they decided to pay a little visit to Box Number Five in the first tier.

They had left behind them the large staircase which leads from the administrative vestibule to the stage and its dependencies; they had crossed the stage and entered the theater through the subscribers' entrance, then into the auditorium through the first hallway on the left. They then passed between the first rows of orchestra chairs and looked at Box Number Five in the first tier. They could not see it well because it was half-hidden in darkness and enormous dust covers had been thrown over the red velvet railings.

At this moment, they were practically alone, surrounded by a great silence in the immense gloomy structure. It was the quiet hour when the stagehands go out for a drink.

The team of workers had just left the stage, leaving half of the set in place. Some rays of light (a sinister glow that seemed to have been stolen from a dying star) was seeping in from who knows what opening and fell upon an old tower that raised its cardboard crenellations above the stage. Everything on this artificial night,[1] or rather, on this deceitful day, took on a strange form. The cloth covering the orchestra seats had the appearance of an infuriated sea whose blue-green waves had been instantly mobilized by the secret command of the storm—a giant whose name, as everyone knows, is Adamastor.[2] Moncharmin and Richard were the shipwrecked survivors of this congealed upheaval of a sea of painted cloth. They moved toward the boxes on the left with their hands out, like sailors who, having abandoned their ship, are seeking their way to shore. The eight great columns of polished stone stood in the shadows like so many prodigious piles destined to support the menacing, crumbling, projecting cliff whose foundation was represented by the circular, parallel, and bowed lines of the balconies of the first, second, and third tiers. High up, at the very top of the cliff, lost in M. Lenepveu's copper sky, faces grimaced, sniggered, mocked, and sneered at Moncharmin and Richard's anxiety.[3] Ordinarily, they were pretty serious faces. They were named, Isis,[4] Amphitrite,[5] Hebe,[6] Flora,[7]

---

[1] "this artificial night"

This entire paragraph serves Leroux's developing theme of the relationship between human suffering and the creation of art. In the opera, artifice is in the service of the humanly created sublime. Tinsel, canvas, paint, timbers, and pulleys combine to create the nourishing illusions for which one turns to art.

[2] "Adamastor"

The storm spirit that presides over the Cape of Good Hope. In Camoëns' The Lusiads, he is described as a hideous phantom.

[3] "Lenepveu's copper sky"

On the dome of Garnier's opera house, Jules Eugene Lenepveu (1819–1898) painted a vast scene representing all of the hours of the day and night. Garnier described the scene as follows: ". . . figures mounting and descending like clouds of birds; some rising almost perpendicularly; others, on the contrary . . . seem to be leaving the sky to approach the earth . . . and the light of the sun rising in a scarlet burst . . . and the light of the pale silvery moon . . . and the passions strewing flowers, and the muses intertwined joyously; all of that quivering, in flight, whirling in the air . . ." (Duault, p. 55.)

Unfortunately, none of the Lenepveu paintings are visible now, because in 1962, André Malraux, then France's culture minister, commissioned Marc Chagall to create a painting of his own which, painted on canvas and attached to a plastic dome, now hangs just ten centimeters below the Lenepveu work. Chagall's dome was installed in 1964. Alain Duault writes, "Without calling the talent of the great artist Chagall's into question, one cannot but deplore the total rupture of the auditorium's harmony by the harsh colors, characteristic of his style, but profoundly contradicting Garnier's conception." (Duault, p. 56.)

A model of the Lenepveu dome can be seen in Paris' Musée d'Orsay.

[4] "Isis"

An Egyptian deity, the sister and spouse of Osiris, she was regarded as a goddess of fecundity. She has been sometimes represented as a horned goddess and sometimes, as with Diana of Ephesus, as a many-breasted earth mother.

[5] "Amphitrite"

The daughter of Nereus, a sea deity, and Doris, an ocean nymph. Amphitrite was the wife of Neptune by whom she bore a son, Triton, who became his father's trumpeter.

[6] "Hebe"

The goddess of youth, Hebe was the daughter of Jupiter and Juno. She is called the cup-bearer to the gods on Olympus, where she was given a variety of helping tasks. She is represented as a young girl with a dress adorned with roses, holding aloft her cup of nectar while an eagle stands at her side.

[7] "Flora"

The Roman goddess of flowers. Her festival was celebrated for eight days at the end of April and the beginning of May.

Pandora,[8] Psyche,[9] Thetis,[10] Pomona,[11] Daphne,[12] Clythie,[13] Galatea,[14] Arethusa.[15] Yes, Arethusa herself, and Pandora—whom all the world knows because of her box—looked down at the directors, who had ended by leaning against a piece of wreckage and who, from there, were silently studying Box Number Five of the first tier. I have said that they were

---

[8] "Pandora"

In Greek mythology, Pandora is the first created woman, but her creation was an act of vengeance on the part of Jupiter, who contrived her creation as an act of vengeance against mankind for receiving the gift of fire stolen from the gods by Prometheus. Jupiter ordered Vulcan to make a female being out of earth and water. Minerva endowed the creature with creativity and knowledge; Venus gave her her beauty; Mercury gave her her slyness. The Seasons and the Graces clothed her. As a consequence of all these gifts she was called Pandora, "all gifted."

She was then sent down to earth, where Prometheus' brother, Epimetheus, married her. In Epimetheus' home there stood a closed jar that he had been forbidden to open. As we know, Pandora opened it, and all the evils that plague the world escaped from it. When Pandora managed to close the lid of the jar again, all that was left in it was Hope.

[9] "Psyche"

The story of Psyche has particular relevance for the readers of The Phantom of the Opera, containing as it does elements of the Beauty and the Beast story and the theme of the redemptive power of love.

Psyche was the most beautiful of the three daughters of a king. Beautiful though she was, she remained unmarried, though her two sisters found husbands. When Psyche's father consulted the oracle, he was told to expose her on a rock from which a monster would carry her away. The father did as he was told. Psyche was exposed. But instead of a monster, a zephyr, sent by Cupid, carried her away to a magnificent palace where she was waited on by invisible servants. When she retired to her bed, an unseen youth spoke gently to her and she became his bride.

Later, egged on by her sisters, who told her that her invisible husband was a serpent, she armed herself with a lamp and a razor—the first so that she could see what he looked like, and to kill him with the second. What she saw was Cupid in all his beauty. When a drop of oil from her lamp fell on the sleeping god's shoulder, he woke and flew away.

What followed was a long penitential period during which Psyche hunted for her husband. In the end, Cupid found her and their story ended happily with their marriage in the skies.

[10] "Thetis"

Thetis is a sea goddess, the daughter of Nereus and Doris. She became the wife of the mortal Peleus and was the mother of Achilles whom, to make him immortal, she dipped into the River Styx. His body thus became invulnerable everywhere but at his heel, where she held him.

[11] "Pomona"

As a maiden Hamadryad, she was courted by a number of the gods, among them Vertumnus, but she resisted them all and refused to marry. Vertumnus came to her in a variety of guises (as a reaper, a hay-maker, a plowman), but she continued to spurn him. Then he assumed the guise of an old woman and described the evils of single life and the joys of matrimony (dwelling, incidentally, on the charms of Vertumnus) so well that she was persuaded to marry him.

[12] "Daphne"

The story of Daphne, the daughter of the river god, Peneus, is a sad one.

First, we have to know that the love god, Cupid, irritated by some scoffing words about him spoken by Phoebus Apollo, took his revenge by shooting a golden arrow of love into Phoebus' heart and then by shooting a leaden arrow of aversion into the heart of Daphne. Then, the enamored Phoebus pursued Daphne, who loved only hunting and wanted nothing to do with him. Phoebus, however, was both assiduous and powerful and overtook the exhausted Daphne on the banks of her father's river. In despair, Daphne called on Peneus for help. He heard her and turned her into a bay tree, which then became Apollo's favorite tree, whose branches (as laurel wreathes) are used to crown poets.

[13] "Clythie"

Clythie, a nymph, fell in love with the sun god, Apollo, and he with her. But the inconstant Apollo soon tired of the nymph and abandoned her. Heartbroken, she spent nine day gazing mournfully at the chariot of the sun as it made its daily trajectory across the sky. The gods, taking pity on her, turned her into a heliotrope.

101

anxious. At least, I presume so. In any case, Moncharmin admits that he was upset. He says, and I quote: "This seesaw of the Phantom's (some prose style!), on which we have so politely been seated from the time that we first took over from Messrs. Poligny and Debienne, has no doubt upset the balance of my imaginative faculties and, all things considered, my visual faculties, as well. Perhaps it was the extraordinary setting (through which we were moving through an incredible silence) that so impressed us at that point. Were we the plaything of a sort of hallucination made possible by the semidarkness of the room and the half-light in which Box Number Five was bathed? Because at the same instant, Richard and I both saw a figure in Box Number Five. Richard said nothing, and in fact, neither did I. But we reached for each other's hand simultaneously. Then, for a few minutes, we waited without making a move, our eyes fixed on the same point. But the form had disappeared. Then we left and in the hallway we shared each other's impressions and spoke about the 'shape.' Unhappily, my shape in no way resembled Richard's. I myself had seen something that resembled a skull at the railing of the box, while Richard had seen the shape of an old woman who looked like Mother Giry. We could see then that we had truly been victims of an illusion and we ran, laughing madly, toward Box Number Five, which we entered but in which there was no longer any 'shape.' "

And now, here we are, in Box Number Five.

It is a box like all the others in the first tier. In truth, nothing distinguishes it from any of its neighbors.

Visibly amused and laughing at each other, Moncharmin and Richard moved the furniture in the box, lifted the dust covers and the chairs, and examined in particular the one in which *the voice habitually sat*. But they saw that it was an honest chair, with nothing magical about it. To sum up, the box was the most ordinary of boxes, with its red wall hangings, its chairs, its rug, its red velvet armrests. After they had, in perfect seriousness, felt the rug and found nothing special there or anywhere else, they went down to the box below that corresponded on that level with Box Number

---

[14]   "Galatea"

Another of the daughters of Nereus and Doris. Galatea loved Acis, a Sicilian shepherd, and spurned the love of the one-eyed giant, Polyphemus. Polyphemus had his revenge. He rolled a rock off a cliff, crushing Acis. Galatea, unable to restore the shepherd to life, turned him into a flowing stream.

[15]   "Arethusa"

A nymph, the daughter of Oceanus and one of Diana's attendants. One day, tired after a long hunt, she decided to bathe in the cool waters of the River Alpheus, but the god of the river, catching sight of her, was overcome by lust and pursued her. As her strength gave out, Arethusa prayed to the goddess Diana, who turned her into a fountain.

Five. On that floor, Box Number Five is just at the corner of the first exit to the left of the orchestra seats. There, too, they found nothing of note.

Finally, Firmin Richard cried, "All these people are poking fun at us. On Saturday, they're doing *Faust*. We will both watch the performance from Box Number Five in the first tier."

Chapter VIII

❖❖

IN WHICH MESSRS. FIRMIN RICHARD AND ARMAND MONCHARMIN HAVE THE AUDACITY TO PRESENT *FAUST* IN AN AUDITORIUM THAT HAS BEEN CURSED, AND THE FRIGHTFUL EVENT THAT FOLLOWED THEREUPON.

But Saturday morning, on arriving at their office, the directors found a letter jointly addressed to them from the Phantom of the Opera, as follows:

My dear directors,

Then it's war?

If you still care about peace, here is my ultimatum. There are four conditions, as follows:

1. Give me back my box. And I want it to be at my disposition, as of now.

2. The role of "Margaret" will be sung tonight by Christine Daaé. Don't bother about Carlotta; she will be ill.

3. I insist absolutely on the good and loyal service of Mme. Giry, my box attendant, whom you will immediately reengage in her duties.

4. Let me know, by a letter given to Mme. Giry, who will deliver it to me, that, like your predecessors, you will accept the conditions set down in my rule book relating to my monthly allowance. Later, I will let you know in what manner it will be paid to me.

Otherwise, this evening you will put on "Faust" in an auditorium that has a curse upon it.

To a better understanding! Farewell.

Ph. of the O.

"Oh, he annoys me . . . he annoys me!" Richard shouted, pounding his office table noisily with his fists. At this, Mercier, the administrator came in. He said, "Lachenal wants to see one of you. It appears that the matter is urgent. The man seems to be terribly upset."

"Who is Lachenal?," asked Richard.

"He's your stable master."[1]

"What do you mean, my stable master?"

"Yes, of course," Mercier explained. "The opera house has several stablemen, and Monsieur Lachenal is in charge of them."

"And what does this stable master do?"

"He looks after the stable."

"Which stable?"

"Why, yours, sir. The Opera's stable."

"There's a stable in the Opera? My Lord, I had no idea. And where may it be?"

"In the lower level, next to the rotunda. It's a very important task. We have twelve horses."

"Twelve horses? What for, for God's sake?"

"Why, for the processions in *La Juive, The Prophet,*[2] and so on. The horses must be trained to 'tread the boards.' The job of the stablemen is to teach them. M. Lachenal is very skillful. He's the former director of the Franconi stables."[3]

---

[1] "stable master"

Live horses were used in French musical theater. At a performance of Corneille's *Bellerophon* at the Académie Royale de Musique in the Salle de Jeu de Paume de Bel Air, a real horse in the role of Pegasus seemed actually to fly. The trick was accomplished by making the horse fast for a day then, when it was hoisted into the air, it was stimulated to move its legs as if it was running by the sound of oats being winnowed offstage. (Alphonse Royer, *Histoire de l'Opéra,* pp. 29–30.)

In 1878, when horses were needed for a performance of Gounod's *Polyeucte,* they were rented from a Paris funeral home. (Frederique Patureau, *Le Palais Garnier dans la Societé Parisienne.* Paris: Mardaga, p. 165.) The horses were hoisted on stage by means of an elevator.

[2] "The Prophet"

An opera by Giacomo Meyerbeer and a libretto with an extraordinarily entangled plot by Eugène Scribe. It had its first performance at the Paris Opera in 1849. The opera is based on events in the life of the sixteenth-century Anabaptist leader, John of Leyden. The opera, with its subtheme of popular revolution, had a special resonance for audiences at the end of the 1840s, when revolution was endemic in Europe.

"Very well, but what is it he wants?"

"I have no idea. I have never seen him in such a state."

"Let him come in."

M. Lachenal comes in. He has a riding crop in his hand and slaps nervously at one of his boots with it.

"Good day," said the distressed Richard. "What occasions the honor of your visit?"

"Sir, I've come to ask you to get rid of the entire stable."

"What? You want to get rid of the entire stable?"

"It has nothing to do with the horses, but with the grooms."

"How many grooms do you have, M. Lachenal?"

"Six."

"Six grooms! That's at least two too many."

"These are jobs," interrupted Mercier, "that have been created, and that have been imposed on us by the Undersecretary of Fine Arts. They are held by protégés of the government, and if I may be permitted to say—"

"The government! I don't give a damn about the government," Richard said energetically. "We don't need more than four grooms for twelve horses."

"Eleven!" corrected the chief stableman.

"Twelve," repeated Richard.

"Eleven," repeated Lachenal.

"Oh. The administrator told me that you had twelve horses."

"I did have twelve, but I have no more than eleven ever since César was stolen." And M. Lachenal slapped hard at his boot with his riding crop.

"Someone's stolen César?" cried the administrator. "César, the white horse in *The Prophet?*

"We don't have two Césars," said the head stableman dryly. "I spent ten years with Franconi, and I've seen a good many horses. Well, there's only one César, and he's been stolen."

"How did that happen?"

"Oh, I have no idea. Nobody knows anything about it. And that's why I've come to you, to ask you to get rid of the entire stable."

---

[3] "Franconi"

The Franconis were a celebrated family of Parisian riding masters. Antonio (1738–1836), the first of the Franconis to come to France, fled there to avoid prosecution for having killed his antagonist in a duel. For more than a century the Franconis, from father to son, carried on the tradition of superb equitation. Henri-Adolphe Franconi, the son of Jean-Gérard-Henri, fused equitation skills with theatrical spectacles in which military dramas were acted out. The mixture, at the Cirque Olympique, proved wildly popular.

"What do your grooms say?"

"Stupidities. Some accuse the extras. Others claim that it's the administration's concierge."

"Our concierge? I trust him as I would myself," Mercier protested.

"But finally, M. Stable Master," Richard cried, "you must have some idea . . ."

"Well, yes. I do. I have one," M. Lachenal said abruptly, "and I'll tell you what it is. As for me, I'm absolutely convinced of it." The stable master approached the directors and whispered in their ears, *It's the Phantom who pulled it off.*

Richard gave a start. "Oh, you too. You too."

"What, me too? It's the most natural thing in the world . . ."

"But how, M. Lachenal! How, M. Stable Master?"

"Let me tell you what I think, based on what I saw."

"And what did you see, M. Lachenal?"

"I saw—just as I see you—I saw a black shadow mounting a white horse that resembled César the way two drops of water resemble each other."

"And you didn't chase the white horse and the black shadow?"

"I ran and I called, M. Director, but they fled with disconcerting speed and disappeared into the darkness of the gallery."

M. Richard got to his feet. "Very well, M. Lachenal. You may leave. We'll file a complaint against the Phantom."

"And you'll fire my stablemen?"

"That's understood. Good-bye, sir."

Richard was frothing at the mouth. "You're going to settle this imbecile's account?"

"He's a friend of the government commissioner," Mercier risked saying.

"And he takes his apéritif at Tortoni's with Lagréne, Scholl, and Pertuiset,[4] the lion killer," Moncharmin added. "We'll have the entire press yapping at our heels. They'll tell the story of the Phantom and everyone will be amused at our expense. The very minute we appear ridiculous, we're dead."

"Very well, let's not talk about it anymore," conceded Richard, who was already thinking about something else.

---

4 "Pertuiset"

One of Leroux's drinking companions. In *Balaoo,* the novel that followed *The Phantom,* Leroux speaks of a lion killer named Barthuiset. (Francis Lacassin, ed. *Les Aventures Extraordinaires de Rouletabille.* Paris: Lafont, 1988, p. 877.)

At this point, the door opened. Evidently, it was not being guarded by its usual doorkeeper, because suddenly Mme. Giry appeared, a letter in her hand, and said hurriedly, "Pardon me, excuse me, sirs, but this morning I received a letter from the Phantom of the Opera. It told me to come see you because, evidently, you have something for m—"

She did not finish her sentence. She saw M. Firmin's face, and it was fierce. The honorable director of the Opera was ready to burst. The fury agitating him had not yet manifested itself, except for the scarlet color that suffused his face and the lightning flashing from his blazing eyes. He did not say a word. He could not speak. Then all of a sudden he went into action, seizing the colorless Mme. Giry first with his left hand, making her spin in a half-circle, a pirouette that was so unexpected, so swift, that she uttered a desperate cry. Then, it was his right foot, the right foot of the same honorable director, who then stamped the imprint of the sole of his shoe on the black taffeta of her skirt which, certainly, had never before been subjected in that place to such an outrage.

It all happened so quickly that Mme. Giry, when she found herself in the hallway, stood there, still dumbfounded, as if she did not understand. Then all at once, she realized what had happened, and the Opera resounded with her indignant cries, her ferocious protests, her threats of death. It required three lads to drag her down to the courtyard and two policemen to carry her into the street.

At almost the same time, Carlotta, who lived in a small hotel on the Rue du Faubourg Saint-Honoré,[5] rang for her chambermaid and had her mail brought to her bed. In that bundle of mail, she found an anonymous letter that said, "If you sing tonight, be warned of a great disaster that will befall you as you begin to sing—a calamity worse than death." This threat had been scrawled in red ink in a wivvery and ragged handwriting.

Having read the letter, Carlotta lost her appetite for breakfast. She pushed the tray back on which the chambermaid had brought her the steaming chocolate. She sat up in bed deeply engrossed in thought. This was not the first letter of this kind that she had received. But never before had there been one as threatening.

At that moment, she believed herself to be the target of a thousand acts of jealousy and would often say that she had a secret enemy who had sworn to ruin her. She claimed that he was devising a wicked plot against

---

[5] "Faubourg Saint-Honoré [Rue]"

This street in the VIIIth Arrondissement begins at the Rue Royale and ends at the Place des Ternes. Once a road leading from Paris to the village of Roule, it received its present name in the early eighteenth century. The author of "La Marseillaise," Rouget de l'Isle, lived at Number 96.

her, some sort of cabal that would one day be revealed. But, she added, she was not a woman who was easily intimidated.

The truth was that, if there were a cabal, it was the one Carlotta herself had directed against poor Christine, who was unaware of it. Carlotta had not forgiven Christine the triumph she had achieved when she had substituted for her at the last moment.

When she was told of the extraordinary reception her replacement had achieved, Carlotta had been instantly cured of an incipient bronchitis and of a fit of sulking against the administration, and she no longer showed the slightest desire to leave her job at the Opera. Since then, she had worked with all of her might to thwart her rival and to get her powerful friends to influence the directors so that they would not give Christine a chance for another triumph. Certain newspapers, which had begun by praising Christine's talents, later talked about nothing but the glorious Carlotta. Finally, in the theater itself, the famous diva[6] spoke of Christine in the most outrageous fashion and did what she could to cause her a thousand little annoyances.

Carlotta had neither heart nor soul. She was nothing more than an instrument. A marvelous instrument, certainly. Her repertory included all that could excite the ambition of a great artist, including the German, the Italian, and the French masters. No one, to this day, had ever heard Carlotta sound a false note, and she did not lack the volume necessary for the interpretation of any passage in her immense repertory. In short, as an instrument she was wide-ranging, powerful, and admirably precise. But no one could say to Carlotta what Rossini[7] said to Krauss[8] after she had sung "Dark Forests" for him in German, "You sing with your soul, dear girl, and your soul is beautiful." Where was your soul, Carlotta, when you danced in the low taverns of Barcelona? And where was it later when you sang your cynical bacchanalian couplets on the sad stages of Paris' music halls? Where was your soul when, before the masters assembled at the home of one of your lovers, you made resound that docile instrument of

---

[6] "diva"

   From the Italian, *diva,* meaning goddess.

   The term came into vogue at the beginning of the twentieth century and is used usually to refer to a famous female singer or actress. Note that there was a famous diva named Lyda Borelli, whose name may well have prompted Leroux to name his diva Sorelli.

[7] "Rossini"

   Gioacchino Rossini (1792–1868), an Italian composer of operas including *Tancred* (1813), *The Barber of Seville* (1816) and *William Tell* (1829).

[8] "Krauss"

   See Chapter II, Note 8, page 40.

your voice whose marvel is that it sings indifferently and with the same perfection of the sublimity of love, or of the most abysmal debauchery. Oh, Carlotta, if you ever had a soul and lost it, you would have found it again when you became Juliette, when you were Elvira[9] and Ophelia and Marguerite!

Because there have been others who have climbed up from depths lower than your own, who were purified by art and the help of love.

In truth, when I think of all the pettiness and vile behavior that Christine Daaé had to endure at that time from Carlotta, I can't restrain my anger, and I'm not at all surprised that my indignation manifests itself in these truisms on art in general and vocal art in particular, regarding which Carlotta's admirers will certainly not get their due.

When Carlotta had finished thinking about the threat contained in the strange letter she had received, she got up. "We'll just see," she said, and uttered several oaths in Spanish with a resolute air.

The first thing she saw when she looked out of her window was a hearse. The hearse and the letter convinced her that she risked serious danger that evening. She gathered every last one of her friends in her home and told them that Christine Daaé had organized a cabal against her at the evening's performance and declared that they must teach her a lesson by filling the auditorium with her own admirers—of whom she had a great many, wasn't that so? She counted on them to be ready for any eventuality and to suppress any disturbance if, as she feared, the plotters created one.

M. Richard's private secretary, having come to ask about the diva's health, returned with the assurance that her health was sound and that, even were she to be *at death's door* that evening she would sing the role of Marguerite. Since the secretary, speaking for his employer, had urged her to be careful, to stay indoors and avoid drafts, Carlotta, after he left, could not help comparing those remarkable and unexpected recommendations with the threats contained in the letter.

It was five o'clock when the mail brought her another anonymous letter with the same handwriting as the first. It was brief. It said simply, "You have a cold. If you were sensible, you would understand that it is madness for you to sing tonight."

Carlotta smiled contemptuously and shrugged her shoulders (which were magnificent) and sang two or three notes that reassured her.

---

[9] "Elvira"
   Don Giovanni's long-suffering wife.

Her friends kept their word. They were all at the opera that evening, but they looked around in vain for the fierce conspirators they were meant to fight. If one excepted several ordinary, honest bourgeois whose placid faces reflected no other intent than to hear once again music to which, long ago, they had given their approbation, the only other habitués were those whose elegant, peaceful, and appropriate manners made it impossible to associate them with any thought of a disturbance. The only thing that appeared to be abnormal was the presence in Loge Number Five of Messrs. Richard and Moncharmin. Carlotta's friends thought that the directors, for their part, had gotten wind of a threatened disturbance and had determined to be in the auditorium to stop it the moment it began. But, as you know, this was an unjustified suspicion, because Messrs. Richard and Moncharmin were thinking only of the Phantom.

"Nothing? . . . In vigil passionate,
I ask a consoling word
From Nature and the Creator
But not a voice is heard."[10]

The famous baritone Carolus Fonta[11] had just begun Dr. Faust's first appeal to the powers of hell, when M. Firmin, who was seated on the Phantom's own chair—the chair on the right in the first row—leaned toward his associate and, in the best of humors, said, "And what about you, has there been a word in your ear yet?"

"Let's listen. Let's not be in too much of a hurry," replied M. Armand in an equally pleasant tone. "The performance has just begun and you know very well that the Phantom doesn't get here until the middle of the first act."

The first act went by without incident, which did not surprise Carlotta's friends, since Marguerite does not sing at all in that act. As for the two directors, when the curtain went down, they smiled at each other. "One down," said Moncharmin.

---

[10] "Nothing? . . ."

These are the opening words of the opera. Faust is in his study. The stage directions read, "Faust, alone. His lamp is about to go out. He is seated before a table loaded with parchment scrolls. There is a book open before him."

[11] "Carolus Fonta"

This singer's name does not appear in any of the lists I consulted of male singers who performed at the opera in the nineteenth century.

"Yes, the Phantom is late," declared Firmin Richard.

Moncharmin, still joking, replied, "It's not a bad turnout for *a house that has a curse on it.*"

Richard deigned to smile. To his colleague, he indicated a heavyset, somewhat common-looking woman dressed in black sitting in a seat in the middle of the auditorium between two rough-looking men in broadcloth frock coats.

"What do you make of 'that'?" Moncharmin inquired.

"That, my dear fellow is my concierge, her brother, and her husband."

"You gave them tickets?"

"Indeed, yes. My concierge has never been to the Opera. It's her first time. And, since she's going to be coming every evening from now on, I wanted her to have a good seat before she spent her time seating others."

Moncharmin asked for an explanation, and Richard told him that he had decided to have his concierge, in whom he had the greatest confidence, take Mme. Giry's place.

"Speaking of Mme. Giry," Moncharmin said. "You know that she's going to file charges against you."

"With whom? With the Phantom?"

The Phantom! Moncharmin had almost forgotten him. Thus far, the mysterious being had done nothing that would remind the directors of him.

Suddenly the door of their box was abruptly pushed open by an alarmed stage manager.

"What's the matter?" they asked, amazed to see him there at that particular moment.

"What's wrong is that there is a cabal against Carlotta organized by Christine Daaé's friends. Carlotta is furious."

"What do you mean?" Richard said, knitting his eyebrows.

But the curtain went up and the director motioned for the stage manager to leave.

When he was gone, Moncharmin leaned over and whispered to Richard and asked, "Then Daaé has friends?"

"Yes," Richard said, "she has."

"Who?"

Richard, with a look, indicated a box on the first tier in which there were two men.

"The Count de Chagny?"

"Yes. He recommended her to me so warmly that, if I had not known that he was a friend of Sorelli's . . ."

"Ah . . . ah . ." Moncharmin murmured. "And who is the pale young man sitting beside him?"

"It's his brother. The viscount."

"He ought to go to bed. He looks ill."

The stage resounded with joyous song. Intoxicating music. The goblet triumphant.

"Wine or beer,
Beer or wine,
Keep my glass full
And I'll be fine."[12]

Students, citizens, soldiers, girls, and women swirled about before the tavern whose sign showed the god Bacchus.[13] Siebel made his entrance.

Christine Daaé was charming dressed as a youth.[14] Her fresh youth, her melancholy grace was immediately seductive. Carlotta's friends thought that she would be greeted by an ovation, which would have let them know what Christine's supporters intended. Such an indiscreet ovation would have been a signal mistake. But it did not take place.

On the contrary, when Marguerite crossed the stage, and when she sang the only two verses of her role in the second act:

"No, sirs, I am neither a lady nor beautiful
And I have no need to take anyone's arm."[15]

an outburst of applause greeted Carlotta. It was so unexpected, and so pointless, that those who were not in the know looked at each other, wondering what was going on, and the act finished without further incident.

---

[12] "Wine or beer"
The opening lines of Act II, Scene 1, of Gounod's *Faust*.
[13] "Bacchus"
Act II, Scene 3, in Gounod's *Faust*. Mephisto magically brings forth wine from a cask on which is printed the image of Bacchus, the Greek god of wine. It serves as a sign to the inn at which Faust and Valentine, Marguerite's brother, meet.
[14] "dressed as a youth"
In the scene above, Christine plays the part of Siebel, Faust's overmatched rival for Marguerite's affections. Her masculine garb gives a strange ambiguity to the uncertain look that Christine sends Raoul as she sings.
[15] "No, sirs, . . ."
Gounod's *Faust*, Act II, scene 5, p. 12

Everyone said, "Evidently, it's going to happen in the next act." There were some who, it would appear, were better informed than the others, and who said that the row would begin with "the King of Thule's gold cup,"[16] and they started toward the subscribers' entrance to warn Carlotta.

The directors left their box during the *entr'acte* to investigate the story of the cabal about which they had been told by the stage manager, but they soon resumed their places, shrugging their shoulders and treating the whole affair as foolishness. The first thing they saw when they returned was a box of English candy on the railing. But who had brought it there? They questioned the box attendants, but no one could give them any information. When they turned back again to the railing, they saw a pair of opera glasses beside the box of candy. They looked at each other. They had not the slightest desire to laugh as they remembered all that they had heard from Mme. Giry . . . and then . . . it seemed as if there was a strange air current. They sat down in silence, profoundly affected.

Marguerite's garden was now to be seen on stage.

"Give her my greetings
Take my vows to her . . ."[17]

As she sang these first two verses, her bouquet of roses and lilacs in her hand, Christine looked up and saw the Viscount de Chagny in his box, and it seemed to all who heard her that her voice was a little less assured, less pure, less crystalline than usual. Some unknown thing was muffling, oppressing her singing, giving it a fearful tremolo.

"Strange girl," a friend of Carlotta's in the orchestra seats said almost aloud, "the other night, she was divine, and now look at her—she's bleating. No experience. No method."

"My faith is in you,
Speak thou for me."[18]

---

[16] "King of Thule's gold cup"
Act III, Scene 1, of Gounod's *Faust* begins as follows:
"Once there was a king in Thulé
Who was until death always faithful.
And in memory of his loved one
Caused a cup of gold to be made . . .
And always when he drank from it,
His eyes with tears would be o'erflowing."
[17] "Give her her my greetings . . ."
Gounod's *Faust*, Act III, scene 1, p. 12

The viscount covered his face with his hands. He wept. Behind him, the count gnawed violently at a corner of his mustache, shrugged his shoulders, and frowned. The count, ordinarily so correct and so cold, must have been furious to have given such outward signs of his intimate feelings. Indeed, he was. He had seen his brother return from a rapid and mysterious trip in an alarming state of health. No doubt the explanations that had followed had not had the good effect of calming the count who, desiring to know more of what had happened, had asked for a meeting with Christine. She had had the audacity to reply that she could see neither him nor his brother. He had thought that to be an abominably calculating move. He did not forgive Christine for making Raoul suffer, but above all he did not forgive his brother for suffering on her account. Ah, he had been wrong to interest himself, even for an instant, in the young girl whose triumph on a single evening remained incomprehensible to everyone.

"May the flower at her lips
At least know how to give
A sweet kiss."[19]

"Sly little minx," grumbled the count. And he wondered what she wanted. What she could be hoping for. She was chaste, said to be without a lover, without a protector of any kind. This Nordic angel must be wily.

Raoul, whose hands before his face formed a curtain that hid his childish tears, could think of nothing but the letter he had received upon his return to Paris, where Christine had arrived before him, having fled Perros like a thief.

My dear little friend of long ago, you must have courage enough not to see me again, to talk to me again. If you love me a little, do that for me; for me, who will never forget you, my dear Raoul. Above all, do not ever come to my dressing room. My life depends upon it. Yours does, too. Your little Christine.

---

[18] "My faith is in you . . ."
    Gounod's *Faust*, Act III, scene 2, p. 13
[19] "May the flower at her lips . . ."
    Gounod's *Faust*, Act III, scene 2, p. 13

A thunderous ovation. It was Carlotta making her entrance. The garden act unfolded with its customary vicissitudes.

When Marguerite had finished singing the King of Thule melody, she was applauded. She was applauded again when she had finished the melody of the jewels.

"Oh, I laugh when I see
In the mirror
The beauty that's me."[20]

From then on, sure of herself, sure of her friends in the auditorium, sure of her voice and of her success, and afraid of nothing, Carlotta, intoxicatated, gave of herself utterly, enthusiastically, passionately. Her performance was entirely unrestrained and shameless. She was no longer Marguerite, but Carmen.[21] The applause was even greater, and her duo with Faust seemed to be preparing her for yet another success when, all of a sudden, something atrocious happened.

Faust was on his knees.

"Let me, let me contemplate your face
Beneath the pale clarity
Of the night star shaded by cloud,
Let me caress your beauty."[22]

And Marguerite replied,

"Ah, silence. Ah happiness, ineffable mystery!
Intoxicating languorous! I hear
And understand this solitary voice that speaks to me,
Singing in my heart."[23]

---

[20] "Oh I laugh when I see . . ."
Gounod's *Faust*, Act III, scene 6, p. 16
[21] "she was Carmen"
Georges Bizet's opera, with a libretto by Henri Meilhac and Ludovic Halévy, was first performed at the Paris Opéra Comique on March 3, 1875
[22] "Let me, let me . . ."
Gounod's *Faust*, Act III, scene 10, p. 20
[23] "Ah silence. Ah, happiness . . ."
Gounod's *Faust*, Act III, scene 10, p. 20.

At this moment . . . at precisely this moment . . . something happened. . . . Something, as I've said, atrocious.

The audience, in a single movement, stood up. The directors, in their box, cannot repress an exclamation of horror. The spectators, men and women, look at each other as if asking for an explanation of the unexpected phenomenon. On Carlotta's face there is now an expression of the most dreadful grief and in her eyes there is a haunted look of madness. The poor woman stood, her mouth still half open from having sung,

"This solitary voice that speaks to me,
Singing in my heart."

But that mouth no longer sang. She did not dare to speak another word, to make another sound.

Because that mouth, created for harmony, that flexible instrument that had never failed her, that magnificent organ that could generate the most magnificent resonances and could sound the most difficult chords, the smoothest modulations, the most ardent rhythms, that sublime human mechanism which only lacked heavenly fire to be divine—that fire which alone gives true emotions and uplifts the soul—that mouth had uttered . . .

From that mouth there had escaped . . .

A toad!

Ah! A frightful, hideous, scaly, venomous, frothing, foaming, croaking toad!

From where had it come? How had it crouched at the tip of her tongue? Its hind legs folded in order to jump higher and farther, it had come sneakily out of her larynx and—croak.

Croak! Croak! Ah! that terrible croak!

But you must clearly understand that one speaks of a toad here only figuratively. No one could see it, but, the devil take it, it could be heard. Croak.

The audience was splattered by it. No reptile on the banks of a noisy marsh had ever rent the night with a more frightful croak.

You may be sure that it was utterly unexpected by anyone. Carlotta could not believe her throat or her ears. Lightning striking at her feet would have surprised her less than this croaking toad that had just come out of her mouth. . . . And lightning would not have dishonored her, while it is well known that a toad huddled against a tongue always dishonors a singer. There are those who have died of it.

My God! Who would have believed it? She sang so tranquilly, "And I understand this solitary voice that sings in my heart." She sang effortlessly, as always, with the same ease with which one might say, "Hello, madame. How are you?"

One can not deny that there are presumptuous singers who make the mistake of underestimating their capacity and who, in their pride, with the feeble voice heaven gave them, want to achieve exceptional effects by singing notes forbidden to them by the voices they were born with. And it is then that heaven, without their being aware of it, sends a toad into their mouths to punish them—a toad that goes "croak." Everyone knows that. But no one could admit that Carlotta, who had a range of at least two octaves, could also have a toad.

No one there could have forgotten her strident high notes, her incredible staccati[24] in *The Magic Flute*.[25] They remembered *Don Giovanni*[26] in which she played Elvira and in which she brought off a stunning triumph one evening when she sang the G-flat that her colleague Dona Anna was unable

---

[24] "staccati"

A musical notation to indicate interruption, separation. It is the opposite of *legato,* which suggests connection, linking.

[25] "*The Magic Flute*"

Mozart's *The Magic Flute* (*Die Zauberflöte*) was his last opera. It had its premiere performance in Vienna in 1791.

[26] "*Don Giovanni*"

Mozart's' *Don Giovanni,* with a libretto by Lorenzo Da Ponte, was first performed publicly in Prague, on October 29, 1787. The influence of the opera on Leroux's imagination can hardly be overstated.

We will recall that in Da Ponte's libretto, Don Giovanni is a heartless rapist and murderer, an impelled and impenitent seducer of an endless number of women. As his servant Leporello boasts for him, there were 640 in Italy, 231 in Germany, 100 in France, 91 in Turkey, and 1,003 in Spain. As the opera comes to a close, the statue of the Commendatore, father of the ravished Donna Anna, appears in Don Giovanni's rooms and, like Donna Elvira, urges him to repent, but Don Giovanni refuses. The Commendatore then sends him headlong down to hell where flames await him.

Leroux turns the Don Giovanni story upside down. His phantom, the grotesquely ugly Erik, already lives in the hell of lovelessness. But, transformed by love, he climbs upward toward the sublime. Both he and Don Giovanni employ disguises, but Erik's disguise as the Angel of Music has at least the truth of his musicianship which, with his experience of pain, elicits Christine's compassion.

Where love is concerned, Don Giovanni starts as an empty vessel that is never filled. Women, for Don Giovanni, represent irresistible—and damnable—temptation. For Erik, who is drawn to her first because of her beauty, Christine becomes finally a means for his own moral redemption. Unlike Don Giovanni, who ends in the bottomless pit, Erik will have climbed out of his abyss. The music he plays as his story comes to its end is aptly -named, "Don Giovanni Triumphant."

In addition to the reversal of the *Don Giovanni* theme, one notes that in both works, a crucial scene takes place at a masked ball. Masks or spurious facial features are frequently reiterated elements in Leroux's fictions. (See *Chéri-Bibi, La Double Vie de Théophraste Longuet, Balaoo, Le Parfum de la Dame en Noir.*)

to sing. Well, then, what could the croak mean at the end of that tranquil, peaceful, tiny little "solitary voice that sings in my heart"?

It was unnatural. There was sorcery behind it. The smell of hellfire behind that toad. Poor, miserable, desperate, overwhelmed Carlotta. . . .

In the auditorium, there was a growing rumble. Had such an adventure befallen anyone but Carlotta, the audience would have booed. But with her, whose perfect voice was well known, the audience showed not anger but consternation and fear. Those people—if there were any—who witnessed the catastrophe in which the Venus de Milo's arms were broken, must have felt the same sort of horror. But then they would have seen the blow and understood it.

But now! This toad was incomprehensible.

So much so that, after several seconds spent wondering whether she had herself really heard that note coming out of her mouth—was that sound really a note? Could one call it a sound? A sound was still music—she wanted to persuade herself that she had not heard this infernal noise; that nothing had happened; that, for an instant she had had an auricular illusion, not a criminal treason of her vocal chords.

Frantically, she looked around as if seeking a refuge, some protection, or the spontaneous reassurance of the innocence of her voice. She put her rigid fingers to her throat in a gesture of defense and protest. No, no. That croak was not hers. And it would seem that Carolus Fonta, who was close to her, who had not left her, and who was looking at her with childish amazement, agreed with her. Perhaps he could explain how such a thing could have happened. But no, he could not. His eyes were stupidly riveted on Carlotta's mouth like the eyes of very young children gazing at a magician's bottomless hat. How could such a small mouth contain so large a croak?

All of it—toad, croak, emotion, terror, noise in the theater, confusion on stage and in the wings . . . the terrified looks on the faces of extras— all that I have described in detail lasted a few seconds.

A few frightful seconds that seemed particularly endless to the two directors up there in Box Number Five. Moncharmin and Richard were very pale. This unheard-of and as yet inexplicable episode filled them with an anguish that was all the more mysterious because now, for a little while, they had been directly under the Phantom's influence.

They had felt his breath and its touch caused several of Moncharmin's hairs to stand on end. And Richard had wiped his moist brow with his handkerchief. Yes, he was there around them, behind them, beside them.

Without seeing him, they felt his presence. They heard him breathing, so close to them. So close to them. One can tell when someone is there, and they could tell it now. They were sure that there were three people in the box. They trembled, they thought of running away, but didn't dare to make a move, or exchange a word that might let the Phantom know that they knew he was there. What was going to happen? What?

The croak happened. Their simultaneous exclamation of horror could be heard above every sound in the auditorium. *They could feel the Phantom's blows.* Leaning over the railing of the box, they looked toward Carlotta without recognizing her. The croak of that daughter of darkness seemed to be the signal for a catastrophe. It was the catastrophe they had been waiting for. The Phantom had promised it. The auditorium was under a curse. The two directorial bosoms heaved under the weight of that catastrophe. Richard's strangled cry was heard calling to Carlotta, "Well, go on."

No, Carlotta did not go on. Bravely, heroically, she started again the fatal verse at whose end the croak had appeared.

A frightful silence ensued. Only Carlotta's voice filled the auditorium again.

"I hear . . ."

The audience also heard,

"And I understand the solitary voice (croak)
Croak. Which sings in my (croak)"

The toad, too, began again.

There was a tremendous tumult in the auditorium.

The audience erupted in a prodigious uproar. The two directors, having fallen back into their seats, did not dare to turn. They hadn't the strength. The Phantom was laughing behind them. And then, at last, they distinctly heard his voice in their right ears, that impossible voice that no mouth uttered, the voice that said, "Tonight, her singing will bring down the chandelier."

Moving in unison, the two directors looked up to the ceiling and uttered a dreadful cry. As if in response to that satanic voice, the enormous mass of the dislodged chandelier was sliding down toward them. It plunged from the heights of the auditorium and crashed into the middle of the orchestra amid shouts and screams. There was a general panic, a tumultuous "every man for himself." I have no intention of reproducing again that historic moment. Anyone who is curious about it has only to open a newspaper of that period. Many were hurt, and one person died.

The chandelier had fallen onto the head of that unfortunate person who, that night, had come to the Opera for the first time in her life—the person whom M. Richard had chosen to take over Mme. Giry's duties as the Phantom's box attendant. The impact killed her, and the next morning there was this headline in a newspaper, "200,000 kilos land on a concierge's head."[27] It was the only funeral oration she received.

---

[27] "concierge's head"

Two hundred thousand kilos is clearly excessive. That would amount to 440,000 pounds or 220 tons. Its actual weight, says Alain Duault, was "some seven tons." Initially, the chandelier was equipped to burn gas.

On November 22, 1888, a man named Obrech was killed at a performance of a play called *If I were King* when the chandelier at the Theatre Lyrique fell and smashed his skull (Chadwyck-Healey, p. 5). The *Times* for that date reports that "the performance was continued by desire of the audience."

Chapter IX

THE MYSTERIOUS BROUGHAM

That tragic evening was bad for everyone. Carlotta fell ill. As for Christine Daaé, she disappeared after the performance. Two weeks passed and she still had not been seen in or out of the theater.

One ought not to confuse this first disappearance, which happened without an uproar, with the famous abduction which, some time later, would take place under such inexplicable and tragic conditions.

Naturally enough, Raoul was the first to be perplexed by the diva's absence. He wrote to her in care of Mme. Valerius and got no reply. At first he was not especially surprised, knowing Christine's state of mind and the decision she had made to break off all contact with him—though he was still unable to guess her reasons for doing so.

And so it was that his unhappiness only intensified and he grew uneasy at not seeing her name on any program. *Faust* was played without her.

One afternoon, at about five o'clock, he asked the management of the Opera to tell him the reasons for her absence. He found the directors very preoccupied. Their own friends could hardly recognize them. They had lost all their gaiety, their liveliness. They could be seen walking through the theater, their heads lowered, brows furrowed, their cheeks pale, as if they were being dogged by some sort of dreadful thought, or were in the grip of an evil fate that would not loosen its hold.

The fall of the chandelier had produced serious consequences, but it was hard to get the directors to offer any explanation of the matter. The inquest had ruled that it was an accident caused by the deterioration of the suspension cables and that it should have been the duty of the former directors, as well as of the present ones, to be aware of that deterioration, and to have repaired it before it produced a catastrophe.

And I must say that Messrs. Richard and Moncharmin seemed at that time to be so changed, so distant, so mysterious, so incomprehensible, that there were many subscribers who thought that there was something in addition to the fall of the chandelier that had so altered their temperaments.

They showed themselves extremely impatient in their daily relationships with everyone except Mme. Giry, whom they had reinstated in her duties. One can guess then how they received the Viscount de Chagny when he came to ask for news of Christine. They said only that she was on leave of absence. He asked how long her leave was to last. He was told, dryly enough, that it was indeterminate. Christine Daaé had applied for it—for health reasons.

"So then, she is ill?" he cried. "What's the matter with her?"

"We have no idea."

"You mean you haven't sent the theater's doctor to see her?"

"No, she made no such request, and since we trust her, we took her at her word."

The whole affair seemed unnatural to Raoul, who left the Opera prey to very dark thoughts. He decided that, at all events, he would go to Mme. Valerius' home for news.

No doubt he recalled the stern terms of Christine's letter in which she had forbidden any attempt on his part to see her. But what he had seen at Porros and what he had heard behind the dressing room door, and the conversation he had had with Christine at the edge of the moor, made him suspect a machination of some kind that, though it had a little of the demonic about it, was nevertheless still human. The young woman's highly strung imagination, her delicate mind, her primitive education which had enclosed her in a circle of legends when she was young and the constant thoughts of her dead father—and above all, the sublime ecstasy into which music plunged her when, under exceptional circumstances, it manifested itself to her, as Raoul himself had been able to judge in the course of that scene in the cemetery—all this, it seemed to him, would appear to constitute a propitious ground for the wicked endeavors of some mysterious and unscrupulous person. Of whom was Christine Daaé a victim? That was the sensible question Raoul asked himself as he hastened to the home of Mama Valerius.

Because the viscount had the sanest of minds. Though he was a poet and loved music in its most ethereal forms, and was, as well, a lover of old Breton stories in which goblins dance—and though he was in love with that little sprite of the North, Christine Daaé—still, he did not believe in the supernatural, except in religious matters, and not even the most uncanny story in the world would make him forget that two plus two equals four.

What would he learn at Mama Valerius' house? He trembled to think of it as he rang the doorbell of the little apartment on the Rue Notre Dame-des-Victoires.[1]

The same maid who, at the Opera, had left Christine's dressing room before him, opened the door. He asked if he might see Mme. Valerius. He was told that she was unwell, in bed, and unwell to "receive."

"Give her my card, please," he said.

He did not have long to wait. The maid returned and showed him to a small, dark, and sparsely furnished sitting room where the two portraits of the elder Daaé and Professor Valerius faced each other.

"Madame apologizes to the viscount," said the servant. "She cannot receive anywhere but in her bedroom because her poor legs can no longer support her."

Five minutes later, Raoul was shown into a nearly dark room where, in the half-light of an alcove, he immediately discerned the kindly face of Christine's benefactress. Mme. Valerius' hair was now entirely white, but her eyes had not grown old. On the contrary, her gaze had never been so pure, so clear, or so childlike.

"M. de Chagny," she said, delighted, as she put out both hands to her visitor. "Ah, Heaven itself has sent you. Now the two of us can talk about *her*."

That last sentence had an ominous ring to it. He asked at once, "Where is Christine?"

The old woman calmly replied, "Why, she is with her 'good spirit.' "

"What good spirit?" poor Raoul exclaimed.

"The Angel of Music."

---

[1] "Notre Dame-des-Victoires"

The street that begins at 2 Place des Petit Peres and ends at the intersection of Rue Montmartre and Rue Feydeau. It takes its name from the church along whose eastern side it passes.

Dismayed, the Viscount de Chagny sank into a chair. Christine was with the Angel of Music? And Mama Valerius in her bed smiled as she put a finger to her lips to urge his silence. She added, "Don't repeat that to anyone."

"You can count on me," replied Raoul without properly knowing what he said, because his thoughts about Christine—already extremely troubled—were increasingly muddled and it seemed to him that everything was beginning to spin around him, around the room, around this extraordinary good woman with white hair, with eyes like the color of a pale blue and empty sky—with eyes like an empty sky. "You can count on me."

"I know. I know," she said happily. "But come closer to me—the way you used to when you were small. Give me your hands, the way you used to when you told me the story of little Lotte as you heard it from Christine's father. You know, M. Raoul, I like you so much. And Christine likes you very much, too."

"She likes me?" sighed the young man, who was having trouble collecting his thoughts about Mme. Valerius' "spirit" and the angel of whom Christine had spoken so strangely; and about the skull he had seen in a sort of nightmare on the steps of the altar in Perros; as well as about the *Phantom of the Opera* whose renown had reached him one evening when he lingered on the stage a few paces away from a group of stagehands who were reminiscing about Joseph Buquet's description of him as cadaverous just before Buquet's mysterious death by hanging.

"What makes you think Christine likes me?" he asked in a whisper.

"She talked to me about you every day."

"Really? And what did she say?"

"She said you declared that you loved her."

And the good woman burst out into a laugh that showed all of the teeth she had so carefully preserved.

A flushed Raoul, suffering terribly, got to his feet.

"Well, now. Where are you going? Be good enough to sit down. Do you think you're going to leave me just like that? You're angry because I laughed, for which I beg your pardon. After all, what's happened is in no way your fault. You didn't know. You're young. And you thought Christine was free."

"Is Christine engaged?" asked Raoul in a strangled voice.

"Oh, no. No. Surely you know that, even if she wanted to, Christine can't marry."

From *The Phantom of the Opera* (1925)

"What? No. I don't know anything. And why can't Christine marry, even if she wanted to?"

"Why, because of the Spirit of Music."

"Again?"

"He's forbidden it."

"He's forbidden it? The Guardian Spirit of Music has forbidden her to marry."

Raoul leaned toward Mama Valerius, his jaw thrust forward as if to bite her. Had he wanted to devour her, he could not have glared at her with more ferocious eyes. There are moments when too great an innocence of mind can appear so monstrous that it becomes hateful. Just then, Raoul thought Mme. Valerius was too innocent by far.[2]

She was not at all aware of the frightful look directed at her. She resumed her perfectly natural manner. "Oh, he has forbidden it without forbidding it. He simply told her that if she married, she would never hear him again. That's all! And that he would go away forever. Well, you can understand that she doesn't want him to leave her. It's only natural."

"Yes. Yes," Raoul agreed, almost under his breath. "It's only natural."

"But I would have thought that Christine told you all that when she found you at Perros where she went with her 'good guardian spirit.' "

"Ah, ah! So she went to Perros with her 'good guardian spirit'?"

"What I mean is that he arranged to meet her there in the cemetery at her father's tomb. He promised to play the 'Resurrection of Lazarus' for her on her father's violin."

Raoul de Chagny got to his feet. Speaking with great authority, he said, "Madame, you will tell me where this 'guardian spirit' lives."

The old woman did not seem surprised by this indiscreet question. Raising her eyes, she said, "In Heaven."

So much guilelessness disconcerted him. He was left stupefied by her perfect faith in a spirit which descended from Heaven every night to frequent the dressing rooms of Opera singers.

He understood now the state of mind a young girl could be in who had been raised by a superstitious fiddler and a good "spiritually enlightened" woman, and he shuddered at the consequences such an upbringing might have.

He could not help asking abruptly, "Is Christine still virtuous?"

"I swear it, as I hope for my share of Paradise," the old woman exclaimed, apparently outraged. "And if you doubt it, I don't know why you've come here."

Raoul pulled off his gloves. "How long has it been since she first met the 'spirit'?"

"About three months. Yes, it's about three months since he began giving her lessons."

The viscount raised his arms in a gesture of immense despair, then let them fall again, despondently. "The 'spirit' gives her lessons? And where might that be?"

"Now that she's gone away with him, I don't know. But two weeks

---

[2] "too innocent by far"

Mme. Valerius, one of Leroux's characters whom he seems to have felt no need to develop beyond giving her and her husband the joint role of a *deus ex machina*, does appear to be entirely too innocent to be true. Neither marriage nor travel seem to have given her any sense of the nature of the real world. She belongs to the never-never land world in which Christine's father enclosed Christine's childhood.

ago, they were given in Christine's dressing room. It would have been impossible here, in this small apartment. Everyone in the house would hear them. But there's no one at the Opera at eight o'clock in the morning. They wouldn't bother anyone. You understand."

"I understand, I understand," cried the viscount, bidding the old woman farewell so abruptly that she wondered—in an aside—whether he might not be a bit loony.

As he was crossing the sitting room, Raoul ran into the serving maid and, for a moment, considered questioning her, but he thought he detected a faint smile on her lips and it occurred to him that she might be making fun of him.[3] He fled.

Had he not learned enough? He had wanted information, now what more could he ask for?

In a pitiful state, he walked home to his brother's house.

He would have liked to punish himself, to bang his head against the wall. How could he have believed in so much innocence, so much purity? He had tried for a moment to explain everything by Christine's naïveté, by her simplicity of spirit and spotless candor. The Guardian Spirit of Music! He knew him now. He saw him. He was, beyond a doubt, some dreadful tenor who sang as he simpered. Raoul thought himself as humiliated and as unhappy as it was possible to be. Angrily, he thought, "Oh what a miserable, small, insignificant, silly young man is the Viscount de Chagny." As for her, what an audacious and devilishly cunning creature she was.

Still, this hurried walk through the streets had done him good and cooled the fire in his brain a bit. When he entered his room, all he could think of was that he would throw himself onto the bed to stifle his sobs. But his brother was there, and Raoul fell into his arms like a baby. The count, without asking for explanations, consoled him like a father. Besides, Raoul would have hesitated to tell him the story of the *Spirit of Music*. If there are some things one does not flaunt, there are others for which it is too humiliating to be pitied.

The count arranged to take his brother to dinner at a cabaret. With his despair fresh in mind, Raoul would have refused a dinner invitation that evening except that his brother, to encourage him to change his mind, told him that on the previous evening, the woman of his dreams had been seen

---

[3] "on her lips . . . making fun of him"

Here, in a lovely two-line portrait of the serving maid, Leroux's sense of irony peeps out at us from his pages. This young woman, Leroux is saying, has, like himself, a sound French head on her shoulders. Of course she is laughing at Raoul.

on an avenue in the Bois de Boulogne.[4] At first, the viscount did not want to believe it, but when he had been given precise details of the encounter, he no longer protested. After all, it was only normal. She had been seen in a brougham with its window down. She seemed to be taking in the chilly night air. The moonlight was superb, so she had been unmistakably recognized. As for her companion, one could only make out a vague silhouette in the shadows. The coach was moving along at a walking pace on a deserted avenue behind the grandstands of the Longchamps racetrack.[5]

Raoul dressed in feverish haste, ready to forget his unhappiness by throwing himself into a whirlwind of pleasure, as they say. Alas, he was but a poor dinner companion and, having left the count early, he found himself, at about ten that night, in a cruising cab behind the Longchamps grandstands.

It was a bitterly cold night. The road appeared deserted and the moonlight was bright. He ordered the driver to wait for him at a nearby little path and, stamping his feet against the cold, he hid himself as well as he could.

He had passed less than half an hour in this healthy exercise when a coach coming from Paris turned at the corner of the road and made its way slowly toward him.

His first thought was, "It's she." And his heart began to beat muffled beats like those he had felt in his chest once before when he stood behind her dressing room door listening to the man's voice. My God, how he loved her!

The coach was still advancing. He, for his part, had not moved. He was waiting. If it was she, he was determined to stop the horses by seizing their heads. He wanted, at all costs, to get an explanation from the Guardian Angel of Music.

A few more steps and the brougham would reach him.[6] He did not doubt that it was Christine. Indeed, there was a woman leaning her head

---

[4] "Bois de Boulogne"

Bois de Boulogne, a park in the northwest section of Paris, famous as the preferred place where fashionable Parisians displayed themselves and their wealth.

For a brother who, Leroux has asserted, is doting and fatherly to his twenty years younger sibling, this is a singularly cruel bit of gossip to pass on to his suffering brother.

[5] "Longchamps racetrack"

The racetrack was inaugurated in 1857 as part of the monumental rebuilding of the city of Paris undertaken by the city planner, Georges Haussmann (1809–1891).

[6] "would reach him"

Leroux is unembarrassed by what contemporary readers of fiction may find a glib use of coincidence. Only a few hours ago, Raoul learned that his beloved had been seen in a brougham in the Bois de Boulogne. Now, there she is in a brougham with a curtained window.

out of the curtained window. All at once, the moon's pale aureole illuminated her face. "Christine."

The sacred name of his beloved burst from his lips and from his heart. He could not repress it. He leaped forward to catch at the coach, because that name, flung into the night had, like an expected signal, served to send the horses off at a furious gallop. The carriage swept by him without giving him time to stop it. The curtained window had been raised; the face of the young woman had disappeared. And the brougham he was chasing was no more than a black spot on the white road.

He called again, "Christine!" There was no reply. He stopped, enfolded in silence.

In despair, he looked up at the sky, at the stars. He struck at his inflamed heart with his fist. He loved, and he was not loved.

He looked gloomily around at the desolate, cold road, at the night as still as death. There was nothing colder or deader than his heart. He had loved an angel and now he despised a woman.

"Oh, how she has deceived you, Raoul, that little northern sprite. What's the good, what's the good of having such fresh cheeks, such a timid brow ready at every moment to cover itself in the pink veil of modesty, if it's only in order to go out into the deserted night seated in the back of a luxurious brougham, in the company of a mysterious lover? Should there not be some sacred limits to hypocrisy and to falsehood? And shouldn't it be forbidden to have the lucid eyes of a child when one has the soul of a courtesan?"

She had passed by with no response to his cry.

But then, why had he put himself in her way?

And what gave him the right to reproach her with his presence when all she has asked of him was to forget her?

"Go away. Disappear. You don't count."

He was twenty years old[7] and he thought of dying.

His servant found him in the morning, seated on his bed. He had not undressed and the valet, seeing the ghastly look on his face, feared some disaster. Raoul, seeing the mail the valet had brought, snatched it from his hand. He had recognized a letter, the paper, the handwriting.

Christine said,

---

[7] "twenty years old"

In Chapter II, we were told that the Count de Chagny was "precisely forty-one years old." On page 44, Raoul was said to have been born twenty years after his older brother. That should make Raoul twenty-one years old.

My friend,

Be at the masked ball at the Opera tomorrow at midnight in the little sitting room behind the great hall; stand near the door that leads into the rotunda. Don't tell anyone about this meeting. Wear a white domino[8] that masks you well. If you would save my life, let no one recognize you. Christine.

---

[8] "domino"
A loose, lightweight cloak with a hood that incorporates a half-mask.

Chapter X

AT THE MASKED BALL

The envelope, all splattered with mud, had no stamp on it. It read, "To be given to M. the Viscount Raoul de Chagny," and it bore a penciled address. Clearly, it had been thrown out in the hope that a passerby would pick it up and bring it to Raoul's home—as had happened. The note had been found on a sidewalk in the *Place de l'Opéra*. Raoul read it feverishly.

It was all he needed to revive his hope. The dark image he had for himself for a while created of a Christine forgetful of her responsibilities to herself yielded to the first image he had had of her as an unhappy innocent who was a victim of her own imprudence and hypersensitivity. Even now, to what degree was she actually a victim? Whose prisoner was she? Into what abyss had she been dragged? He asked himself all this with cruel anguish, but even that pain seemed bearable when set against the idea that Christine might be a liar and a hypocrite. What had happened? To what influence had she been subjected? What monster had abducted her, and with what weapons?

What weapons, indeed, if not those of music? Yes, yes, the more he thought about it, the more he convinced himself that it was there he would discover the truth. Had he forgotten the tone in which she had told him that she had received a visit from a celestial messenger? And Christine's own recent history—should it not help to shed light on the shadows he was fighting? Had he not known the despair that had enveloped her after the death of her father, and the aversion she had had for everything life has to offer—even for her art? At the conservatory, she had performed more like a soulless singing machine. Then, suddenly, she had awakened, as if inspired by divine intervention. The Guardian Angel of Music had come! She sang Marguerite in *Faust* and triumphed. The Angel of Music had come! Who was it, who was it who passed himself off as a marvelous spirit? Who, knowing the legend that she was so dear to old Daaé, made use of it with such skill that the young woman became in his hands a helpless instrument that he could play at will?

Considering the matter, Raoul could see that such an event was not so unlikely. He remembered what had happened to the Princess Belmonte, who had recently lost her husband and whose grief had paralyzed her. For a month, the princess had been unable to speak or to weep. This physical and psychological apathy was worsening day by day, weakening her reason, and was beginning slowly to endanger her life. She was brought into her garden each evening, but seemed not to know where she was.

Raff,[1] Germany's greatest singer, who was visiting Naples, wanted to see her gardens, which were famous for their beauty. One of the princess' attendants asked the great performer to sing for the princess from a hiding place in a grove near where she was resting. Raff agreed and sang a simple melody that the princess' husband had sung to her in the early days of their marriage. It was an expressive and touching song. The melody, the lyrics, the admirable voice of the singer, all combined to stir the princess' soul. Tears flowed from her eyes. She wept and was cured, and remained convinced that her husband had come down from heaven that evening to sing to her "their" song from long ago!

"Yes. That evening. A single evening," Raoul thought. "But that beautiful fantasy could not have been sustained repeatedly." Had the grieving and fanciful princess returned every evening for three months . . . she would have ended by discovering Raff hidden in the trees.

The Angel of Music had given Christine lessons for three months. . . . Oh, he was a meticulous teacher. And now he was squiring her about in the Bois.

---

[1] "Raff"

The only notable musical Raff I have been able to identify is Joseph Joachim Raff (1822–1882) a German composer of operas, symphonies, and other orchestral works. His early career was much advanced by the help of Mendelssohn and Liszt. In 1877 he was appointed director of the Frankfurt Hoch Conservatory, where Edward MacDowell, the American composer, was one of his pupils.

With stiffened fingers, Raoul clawed at his chest where his jealous heart pounded. Essentially inexperienced, Raoul wondered fearfully what the game was to which the young woman was inviting him at the masked ball. And just how far a girl from the Opera would go to play tricks on a young man who was new to love. What misery!

So it was that Raoul's thoughts swung between extremes. He no longer knew whether pity Christine or curse her, and so he pitied and cursed her by turns. Meanwhile, he provided himself with a white domino.

At last, it was time for the rendezvous. His face covered by a white mask trimmed with long, thick lace, and wearing a clown's white cloak, the viscount felt how ridiculous it was to have put on a costume fit for a romantic masquerade. A sophisticated man would not disguise himself to attend a ball at the Opera. It would just make people smile. One thought consoled him—he would certainly not be recognized. And then, this costume and this mask had another advantage: He would be able to move about comfortably in them as if he were at home with his sick heart and his disordered soul. He would have no need to pretend. He would not need to mask his feelings. He had a mask.

This ball was of a special sort, given just before Shroventide[3] in honor of the birthday of a famous artist, who sketched festivities in the old days, a follower of Gavarni,[4] whose pencil had immortalized the fashionable folk and the procession of merrymakers from the Courtille. It should, therefore, have had a gayer aspect, more noisy, more bohemian than masked balls usually have.

A number of artists had agreed to meet there, followed by an entire host of models and daubers who, around midnight, would begin to make a great racket.

Raoul went up the great staircase at five minutes to midnight, without pausing to look about him at the sight of the multicolored costumes deployed upon the marble stairs in one of the most sumptuous settings in the world. Nor would he permit himself to be waylaid by any of the masked merrymakers, or to respond to a pleasantry, and he brushed off the pushy

---

[2]   "Shrovetide"
      The three-day period immediately preceding Ash Wednesday.
[3]   "Gavarni"
      Guillaume Sulpice Chevallier (1804–1866) was a sketch artist famous for designing costumes for masked balls and the depiction of revealing crowds. "Gavarni," his pseudonym, was taken from the name of a circus, the Cirque Gavarni, that had profoundly impressed him. The Goncourt brothers admired his passionate devotion to "the real, the living, the contemporary. . . ." His energy and his output were phenomenal. At the time of his death he had produced eight thousand watercolors, sketches, and lithographs.

familiarities of several couples that were already too tipsy. Having crossed the lobby and escaped a group of dancers doing a farandole,[5] who would have surrounded him for a moment, he finally reached the room Christine's note had specified. Here, in a small space, there was a packed crowd, because this was the designated meeting point of all those who were going to eat in the rotunda or who were returning to have a glass of champagne. The tumult was warm and joyful. Raoul thought that Christine must have preferred his thronging spot for their mysterious meeting rather than a more isolated corner; here, and behind a mask, one could be better hidden.

He leaned against the door and waited. He did not wait long. A black domino passed by and lightly squeezed his fingertips. He understood that it was she.

He followed.

"Is that you, Christine?" he asked, hardly moving his lips. The domino turned around abruptly and lifted her finger to her lips, no doubt to urge him not to repeat her name.

Silently, Raoul continued to follow her.

He was afraid of losing her after having found her so strangely. He no longer felt hatred for her. As bizarre and inexplicable as her behavior had seemed, he no longer doubted that she "had nothing to be ashamed of." He was ready for any indulgence, any pardon, any lapse of conduct. He was in love, and of course the reason for her strange absence would soon be explained to him.

The black domino turned occasionally to see if the white one was still following.

As Raoul, moving behind his guide, was crossing the main lobby again, he could not help noticing that among the clusters of people endeavoring their best to be outrageous there was one group that was gathered around an individual whose disguise and way of walking, as well as his macabre appearance, were causing a sensation.

This person, dressed all in scarlet, had a death's-head over which he wore an immense feathered hat. Ah, what a remarkable imitation of a death's-head that was. The young art students around him fussed over him. They complimented him and asked him who his master was, and in what studio, frequented by Pluto,[6] he had had such a beautiful skull designed and painted. Old "Camarde" himself must have posed for it.

---

4 "farandole"
   A Provençal folk dance in which pairs of men and women form a chain and follow a leader.

136

The man with the skull, the feathers, and the scarlet garb trailed an immense red velvet cloak behind him, whose train spread out royally on the floor. Embroidered on that cloak was a sentence in gold letters that everyone read and repeated aloud: "Touch me not. I am Red Death passing by."[7] Someone wanted to touch him, but a skeletal hand coming out of a purple sleeve brutally seized the wrist of the imprudent man who, having felt the grip of those bones, the maniacal clutch of Death which seemed as if he would never let go, screamed with pain and terror. When the Red Death finally released him, he fled like a madman, followed by the jeers of the crowd. It was at this moment that Raoul passed in front of the funereal creature who, in fact, had just turned to face him. Raoul almost cried out, "The Perros skull." He wanted to accost him, forgetting Christine for the moment, but the black domino, who seemed also to be in the grip of a singular emotion, had seized his arm and was dragging him . . . dragging him far from the lobby, away from the demonic crowd among whom the Red Death was passing.

---

5 "Pluto"

The brother of Jupiter and Neptune, Pluto, in Roman mythology was the king of Hell and the God of the dead. His realm, Hades, or Erebus, is dreary, dark and cheerless. He is described as being inexorable and deaf to supplication—for from his realms there is no return. His name is associated with wealth because of ore that comes from the bowels of the earth.

There is a special relevance to this reference to Pluto, since Pluto, like Erik, abducted his love, Persephone, and carried her off to his dark netherworld.

6 "I am Red Death passing by"

Clearly, Leroux borrowed his Red Death from Edgar Allan Poe's "The Masque of the Red Death," a short story that appeared in *Graham's Magazine* in 1842. In that story, in which the Prince Prospero and his thousand riotous good friends have immured themselves in a castle to avoid the plague of the Red Death raging in the countryside, the tale's central event takes place at a masked ball where the Red Death appears.

Poe writes, ". . . before the last echoes of the last chime had utterly sunk into silence, there were many individuals in the crowd who had found leisure to become aware of the presence of a masked figure . . . The figure was tall and gaunt, and shrouded from head to foot in the habiliments of the grave. The mask which concealed the visage was made so nearly to resemble the countenance of a stiffened corpse that the closest scrutiny must have had difficulty in detecting the cheat . . . The mummer had gone so far as to assume the type of the Red Death. His vesture was dabbled in *blood*—and his brow, with all the features of the face, was besprinkled with the scarlet horror." (Stephen Peithman, ed., *The Annotated Tales of Edgar Allan Poe.* New York: Doubleday, 1981, pp. 117–118.)

Poe's tale, evidently, was suggested to him by the following story in the *New York Mirror* of June 2, 1832: Nathaniel Wills describes a masked ball he attended in Paris during a cholera epidemic. "I was at a masque ball at the *Théâtre des Variétés* a night or two since, at the celebration of *Mi-carême* or half-Lent. There were some two thousand people, I should think, in fancy dresses, most of them grotesque and satirical, and the ball was kept up till seven in the morning, with all the extravagant gayety, noise, and fun, with which the French people manage such matters. There was a *cholera-waltz* and a *cholera-galopade* and one man, immensely tall, dressed as a personification of the Cholera itself, with skeleton armor, bloodshot eyes, and other horrible appurtenances of a walking pestilence. It was the burden of all the jokes, and all the cries of the hawker, and all the conversation; and yet, probably, nineteen out of twenty of those present lived in the quarters most ravaged by the disease, and knew perfectly its deadly character" (p. 115).

At intervals, the black domino turned and—Raoul was certain of this—twice it seemed to have seen something that frightened it, because it hurried its pace and Raoul's as if they were being pursued.

They went up two flights of steps in this fashion. There, the stairways and the corridors were nearly deserted. The black domino pushed open the door of a box and gestured to the white domino to follow it in. Christine (for it was indeed she—he recognized her by her voice), Christine closed the door of the box at once as she urged him in a whisper to stay well back inside the box to avoid being seen. Raoul took his mask off. Christine kept hers on. And, as he was about to ask her to remove it, he was surprised to see her leaning toward the partition to listen attentively to what was going on in the next box. Then she opened the door and looked into the corridor as she said in a hushed whisper, "He must have gone upstairs to the Box of the Blind." Suddenly she exclaimed, "He's coming back down!"

She wanted to close the door again, but Raoul wouldn't let her because he had seen *a red foot* and then another stepping onto the topmost step of the staircase leading to the floor above. Slowly, majestically, the Red Death's entire scarlet garment descended. Once again, Raoul saw the skull from Perros.

"It's he," he cried. "This time, he won't escape me."

But Christine had shut the door the moment Raoul started forward. He tried to thrust her aside.

"Who is *he*?" she asked in a totally altered voice. "Who will not escape you?"

Brutally, Raoul tried to overcome her resistance, but she pushed him away with unexpected strength. He understood—or supposed he understood, and was immediately furious. "Who, then?" he said, enraged. "*Him.* The man hiding behind that hideous image of death. The evil spirit of the Perros graveyard. The Red Death. And, finally, madame, your friend. *Your Guardian Angel of Music.* But I'll tear his mask off as I've taken off my own, and we will look each other in the face this time, without veils or lies, and I'll learn whom it is you love and who loves you."

He burst into crazed laughter while Christine, behind her mask, moaned miserably. She put her arms out in a tragic gesture, making a barrier of white flesh before the doorway. "In the name of our love, Raoul, don't go."

He stopped. What had she said? In the name of their love? But she had never, never said that she loved him. And yet, there had been no lack of opportunity. She had seen him unhappy to the point of tears, begging her for a gentle word of hope that had not been spoken. She had seen him sick, nearly dead with terror and cold after the night in the graveyard at Perros. Had she stayed with him at the moment when he most needed her care? No! She had run away. And now she said that she loved him! She said, "in the name of our love." Come! She had no other goal but to detain him for a few seconds to give the Red Death time to escape. Their love! She was lying!

And he told her so, in a tone of infantile hatred. "You're lying, madame. Because you don't love me and you never loved me! One would have to be a poor miserable young man like me to allow oneself to be toyed with and deceived as I have been. Why was it that, by your behavior, by your look of happiness, even by your silence, that you gave me so much hope at the time of our first meeting at Perros? Honorable hope, madame, for I am an honorable man and I believe you to be an honorable woman. But all you wanted was to deceive me. Alas! You have deceived everyone! You have even taken shameful advantage of your benefactor's innocent heart. She continues to believe in your sincerity while you go to an Opera ball with the Red Death. I despise you."

And he wept. She permitted his insults. She thought of one thing only—to detain him. "One day you will ask me to forgive you for your cruel words, Raoul, and I will forgive you."

He shook his head. "No! No. You've driven me mad. When I think that I had no other goal in life than to give my name to an Opera girl!"

"Raoul! You're making me miserable."

"I'll die of shame."

"Live, my friend," said Christine in a gravely altered voice. "And good-bye."

"Good-bye, Christine."

"Good-bye, Raoul."

The young man took a trembling step toward her. He risked a final sarcasm, "Oh, will you let me come to applaud you again from time to time?"

"I'll never sing again, Raoul!"

"Really," he added, even more ironically. "So you're going to have leisure. Congratulations. But, one of these nights, we'll see each other at the Bois de Boulogne."

"No, Raoul. You will see me neither at the Bois, nor anywhere else."

"May I at least know into what shadows you are going to return? Mysterious lady, into what hell are you going? Or to what heaven?"

"That's what I had come to tell you, my friend. But there's nothing more I can say. You wouldn't believe me. You've lost faith in me. It's over, Raoul."

"It's over" was spoken in a tone so desperate that the young man trembled to hear it, and remorse for his cruelty began to trouble his soul.

"Come now, won't you tell me what all of this means? You are free, unencumbered. You move about the city. You put on a mask to hurry to a ball. Why haven't you gone home? What have you been doing for the past two weeks? What is all this nonsense about a Guardian Angel of Music that you've been telling Mme. Valerius? Someone's been deceiving you, taking advantage of your credulity. I saw it for myself at Perros. But now you know what to watch out for. You seem very sensible to me, Christine. You know what you're doing. And meanwhile, Mme. Valerius continues to wait for you and speaks of your 'good spirit.' Explain yourself, Christine! I beg you. Anyone might have been taken in, as I was. What's the point of this farce?"

Christine simply removed her mask and said, "It's a tragedy, my friend."

Raoul then saw her face and could not restrain an exclamation of fear and surprise. Her former fresh complexion had disappeared. A mortal pallor covered the features he had known as so charming and sweet, reflecting a calm grace and an unconflicted conscience. How tormented her face was now. Pain had mercilessly furrowed her cheeks, and Christine's beautiful pale blue eyes, previously as limpid as the lakes that could be seen in little Lotte's eyes, ringed as they were by a frightfully sad shadow, appeared now to have dark, mysterious and unfathomable depths.

"My dear! My dear!" he said, trembling as he held out his arms. "You promised to forgive me."

"Perhaps someday," she said, replacing her mask. Then she went, forbidding him to follow her with a stern gesture. He started after her, but she turned and repeated her parting gesture with such sovereign authority that he dared not take another step.

He watched her receding. Then he, in turn, returned to the crowd, not knowing exactly what he was doing. The veins in his temple throbbed and his heart was broken. As he crossed the lobby, he asked whether anyone had seen the Red Death go by. They replied, "Who is the Red

Death?" and he answered, "It's a man whose disguise includes a skull and large red cape." He was told that the Red Death had just passed by, but he could not find him anywhere. At two o'clock in the morning, he returned backstage to the corridor that led to Christine's dressing room.

His wandering footsteps had brought him to this place where his sufferings had begun. He knocked at the door. There was no reply. He went in as he had done when he was searching for *a man's voice*. The dressing room was empty. A gas jet burned dimly. There was a pad of letter paper on a small table. He thought of writing to Christine, but he heard footsteps in the corridor. He only had time enough to hide himself in the boudoir that was separated from the dressing room by nothing more than a curtain. A hand pushed open the dressing room door. It was Christine!

He held his breath. He wanted to see! He wanted to know! Something told him that he was about to be a witness to a part of the mystery and that, perhaps, he might begin to understand.

Christine came in, took her mask off with a weary gesture, and threw it onto the table. She sighed and buried her face between her hands. What was she thinking? Of Raoul? No! No, because Raoul heard her murmuring, "Poor Erik."[8]

At first he thought he had misunderstood. Because, after all, if anyone was to be pitied, surely it was he, Raoul. What, finally, would have been more natural after what had passed between them than that she should sigh, "Poor Raoul." But, shaking her head, she repeated, "Poor Erik." Why was this Erik the target of Christine's sighs? And why was this little northern sprite pitying him when it was Raoul who was so miserable?

Christine began to write, deliberately, calmly, and so peaceably that Raoul, who was still trembling from the dramatic scene that had separated them, was singularly and most unpleasantly upset. "Such composure!" he said to himself. She wrote on, filling up two, three, four sheets of paper. Suddenly, she lifted her head and thrust the papers into her bosom. She seemed to be listening. Raoul, too, listened. Whence did that strange sound

---

[7] "Erik"

Since, as I have argued, there are truly only two protagonists in this book, Erik and Christine, it is worth our while to look closely at their names.

Both syllables of Erik's name are significant: the first has the meaning of the archaic English word *aye* or the Latin *e* in *oevum,* meaning, in both cases "ever" or "forever." The second syllable, *rik,* means "king." And so, Erik stands for "ever king," or "eternal king," a name appropriate enough for our Erik who is the ruler of his underground domain.

Christine's name derives from *Christ* which in turn comes from the Greek *Kristos,* meaning "the anointed one." By extension, the name "Christ" has taken on the meaning of "redeemer" and, as we will see, Christine's role is that of one who redeems by love.

come from? That faraway rhythm? A muffled song seemed to rise out of the walls. Yes, one would have said that the walls were singing! The song became clear. The words distinguishable. One could distinctly hear a voice, a very beautiful and very sweet, captivating voice. But the sweetness retained its masculinity and one could tell that the voice did not belong to a woman. The voice came nearer. It passed through the walls and was there, "in the room" in front of Christine. She got up and spoke to it as she might have spoken to someone standing beside her.

"Here I am, Erik," she said. "I am ready. It is you who are late, my friend."

Raoul, who was watching carefully from behind his curtain, could not believe his eyes which showed him—no one. Christine's face lighted up. There was a happy smile on her pale lips, the kind of smile that one sees on convalescents when they begin to hope that they will not die of the illness that has attacked them.

The bodiless voice resumed its song and Raoul, certainly, had never heard anything in the world like it. A voice which, at the same time, and in the same breath, united all the extremes: broadly and heroically smooth, victoriously insidious, delicately strong and strongly delicate, and finally, irresistibly triumphant. In it one could hear distinctive strains sung with a mastery that could, by mere virtue of their being heard, rouse lofty strains in mortals who love, who feel, and who interpret music. It was a tranquil stream of pure harmony at which the faithful could drink devotedly and with the certainty that they were imbibing musical grace. And their art, having suddenly touched the divine, would be transformed by it.

Raoul listened feverishly to this voice and began to understand how Christine Daaé had, on one night, been able to appear before the public and stun it with her superhuman exaltation and the strains of a beauty never heard before, when she was undoubtedly under the influence of this mysterious and invisible master. He was also able to understand that considerable event as he listened to this exceptional voice singing what was by no means exceptional: turning mud into blue sky. The banality of the verses, and the facile, almost vulgar popularity of the melody seemed to have been transformed into greater beauty by a breath that elevated them, carrying them right to the heavens on the wings of passion. For this angelic voice was glorifying a pagan hymn. It was singing "the wedding night" from *Romeo and Juliette*.

Raoul watched as Christine extended her arms toward the voice, as she had done in the cemetery at Perros, toward the invisible violin that had played "The Resurrection of Lazarus."

Nothing can convey the passion with which the voice said, "Fate chains you to me. There is no going back."

Raoul felt his heart pierced, and struggling against the magic that seemed to deprive him of his will, of his energy, and of almost all of the lucidity which, at the moment, he needed most, he managed to pull back the curtain that hid him and started toward Christine. She was walking toward the rear of the dressing room whose wall was covered by a large mirror that, though it reflected her image, did not show Raoul because he was right behind her, concealed by her form.

"Fate chains you to me. There is no going back."

Christine was advancing toward her image and her image was moving toward her. The two Christines—the body and its image—touched, combined, and Raoul extended his arm to seize them both in a single movement.

But then, there occurred a dazzling miracle that made Raoul stagger. He was flung backward while an icy wind swept across his face. He no longer saw two, but four, eight, twenty Christines, who spun around him laughing at him and fleeing so quickly that he could not touch them with his hand. Finally, everything was still again and he saw himself in the mirror, but Christine had disappeared.

He rushed to the mirror. He threw himself against the walls. No one. And yet, the dressing room still resounded with the distant, impassioned rhythm,

"Fate chains you to me. There is no going back. . . ."

His hands pressed against his sweating forehead, he felt his awakened flesh, then groped in the shadows and turned the gas jet on to full power. He was certain that he was not dreaming. He was at the center of a formidable physical and mental game about which he had no clue and which might crush him. He felt a little like an adventurous prince who has crossed over a forbidden boundary in a fairy tale and who has no right to be surprised if he becomes the prey of magic phenomena which, without thinking, he has defied and unleashed for the sake of love.

Where? Where had Christine gone?

How would she return?

Would she return? Alas, had she not said that it was all over between them? And had not the wall repeated:

"*There is no turning back, fate chains you to me. . . .*" To me? To whom?

Then, exhausted, vanquished, his mind confused, he sat down in the very place where Christine had been sitting. Like her, he put his head between his hands. When he looked up, tears trickled abundantly down his young face. Heavy tears, real tears like those that jealous children shed; tears shed for a sorrow that was by no means imagined but which is shared by all the lovers on earth. He said it explicitly, aloud, "Who is Erik?"

Chapter XI

⤜❧❧⤛

THE NAME OF *THE MAN'S VOICE* MUST BE FORGOTTEN

The day after Christine had disappeared before his very eyes in some sort of dazzling manner which still made him doubt his senses, the Viscount de Chagny went to Mme. Valerius' house to get news of her. He stumbled upon a charming tableau. The old woman was sitting up in her bed knitting while Christine, at her bedside, was making lace. There had never been a lovelier oval face, a purer forehead, or a sweeter look arched over a maiden's work. Fresh coloring had returned to Christine's cheeks. The bluish circles around her lucid eyes had disappeared. Raoul no longer recognized the tragic face of the previous night. If the melancholy veil that had spread over her adorable features had not seemed to the young man like the last vestige of an unbelievable drama in which this mysterious child was embroiled, he might have thought she was not the enigmatic heroine of this story.

As he came near, she rose and extended her hand to him with no apparent show of emotion. But Raoul was so stupefied that he stood there, overwhelmed, without a word or gesture.

"Well, well, M. de Chagny," exclaimed old Mme. Valerius, "don't you recognize our Christine anymore? Her 'good spirit' has returned her to us."

"Mama," interrupted the young woman a bit curtly, as a blush spread over her face. "Mama, I thought that there would be no mention of that again. You know very well that there is no 'spirit of music.' "

"Just the same, he gave you lessons for three months."

"Mama, I promised to explain everything to you one day. I hope to, but you promised to be silent until then and not to ask me any more questions."

"If you promised never to leave me again. Did you make that promise, Christine?"

"Mama, none of this could possibly be of any interest to M. de Chagny."

"That's where you're wrong, mademoiselle," interrupted the young man in a voice he was trying to make firm and brave, but which was not much more than a quiver. "Everything that concerns you interests me to a degree that you will understand one day. I won't hide from you the fact that my surprise equals my delight at finding you here at the side of your foster mother; or that what passed between us yesterday—both what you said and what I have guessed—could have made me expect such a speedy return. I would be the first to be pleased by all this if you were not so stubborn about keeping it a secret that may turn out to be harmful to you. And I've been your friend far too long not to share, with Mme. Valerius, concern about a deadly adventure that will remain dangerous to you so long as we don't untangle its web."

At these words Mme. Valerius stirred restlessly in her bed. "What are you saying?" she asked. "Is Christine, then, in danger?"

"Yes, madame," declared Raoul courageously as he ignored Christine's signaling.

"My God," gasped the naïve and good old woman. "You must tell me everything, Christine. Why did you reassure me? And what kind of danger are you talking about, M. de Chagny?"

"There's an imposter who's taking advantage of her good faith."

The 'Guardian Angel of Music' is an impostor?"

"She told you herself that there is no 'Guardian Angel of Music.' "

"Then, in God's name, what's going on?" implored the invalid. "You'll be the death of me."

"Madame, there is an earthly mystery surrounding you, and surrounding Christine, which is more to be feared than any phantom or spirit."

Mme. Valerius turned her terrified face toward Christine, but she had already flung her arms about her foster mother and was holding her close.

"Don't believe him, Mama. Don't believe him," she repeated, trying with her caresses to comfort the old woman, whose sighs were heartbreaking.

"Then tell me that you won't leave me again," implored the professor's widow.

Christine said nothing. Raoul went on, "That's what you must promise, Christine. It's the one thing that can reassure us, your mother and me. We'll agree not to ask you any more questions about the past if you'll promise us to remain under our protection in the future."

"It's an agreement I don't ask of you, and it's a promise I will not make," the young woman said proudly. "My actions are my own, M. de Chagny. You have no right to control them. And I beg you to desist from doing so from now on. As for what I was doing for the last two weeks, there is only one man in the world who can have the right to ask that I tell him about it: my husband! Well, I have no husband, and I will never marry!"

Having said that with some force, she put her hand out toward Raoul as if to add solemnity to her words. Raoul turned pale, not only because of what he had just heard, but because he noticed a gold ring on Christine's finger.

"You have no husband, and yet you are wearing a wedding band." He would have reached for her hand, but Christine snatched it away.

"It's a gift," she said, blushing even more and trying in vain to hide her embarrassment.

"Christine, since you have no husband, that ring can only have been given to you by someone who hopes to marry you. Why do you continue to deceive us? Why torture me even more? That ring is a promise and the promise has been accepted."

"It's what I told her," cried the old woman.

"And what was her reply, madame?"

"Whatever I wanted to reply," said Christine, exasperated. "Don't you think, sir, that this questioning has gone on long enough? As for me—"

Raoul, very much moved, was afraid to let her speak words that would produce a final break between them. He interrupted. "Pardon me for having spoken to you that way, mademoiselle. You know very well what the honorable feeling is that has prompted me to involve myself in matters which, no doubt, are not my business. But let me tell you what I saw . . . and I saw more than you think I did, Christine. Or what I thought I saw, because, in truth, in this adventure one doubts the testimony of one's own eyes."

"What, sir, what did you see—or believe that you saw?"

"I saw you ecstatic at the sound of his voice, Christine. The voice that rose out of the wall, or from the box, or from a room next door. Yes, you were ecstatic. And that's what terrified me for you. You are under the most dangerous of spells. And it would appear that you know that you are being deceived, since you said today that 'there is no Guardian Spirit of Music.' That being the case, why have you followed him again? Why did you get up, your face radiant as if you were really hearing angels? Oh! That's a very dangerous voice, Christine. I myself, when I heard it, was so delighted by it that I could not tell how it was that you disappeared from my sight. Christine! Christine! In Heaven's name, in the name of your father who is in heaven and who loved you so—and who loved me . . . Christine, you must tell me and your benefactress to whom this voice belongs. And in spite of you, we will save you. Come now, the name of the man, Christine? The name of the man who has had the audacity to place a gold ring on your finger."

Coldly, the young woman said, "M. de Chagny, you will never know it."

Seeing with what hostility her ward had just spoken to the viscount, Mme. Valerius said sharply, "M. Viscount, if she loves that man, it's not any of your business."[1]

"Alas, madame," Raoul replied humbly, unable to restrain his tears, "alas, I believe indeed that Christine loves him. Everything proves it to me, but that's not all that makes me despair. It's because I'm not sure, madame, that the man she loves is worthy of her love."

"Only I can be the judge of that, sir!" said Christine, looking straight at Raoul with a supremely angry expression on her face.

Raoul, feeling his strength ebbing, said, "When one uses such romantic means to seduce a young girl . . ."

"In that case the man would have to be a scoundrel, or the girl a perfect fool."

"Christine!"

"Raoul, why do you condemn a man this way—a man whom you've never seen, whom nobody knows, and about whom you yourself know nothing?"

"Yes, Christine! Yes. I at least know the name of the man . . . the

---

[1] "it's not any of your business"

Here, in this moment of asperity, Mme. Valerius becomes a real woman instead of the fairy godmother that she has been throughout this fiction.

man you want to hide from me forever. Your 'Guardian Angel of Music,' mademoiselle, is called Erik.''

Christine betrayed herself at once. She turned as white as a sheet and stammered, "Who told you that?"

"You did, yourself."

"How was that?"

"While you were pitying him the other night, the night of the masked ball. When you came into your dressing room, didn't you say, 'Poor Erik'? Well, Christine, somewhere there, there was a poor Raoul who heard you."

"That's the second time you've listened at my door, M. de Chagny."

"I was not at your door. I was in the dressing room! In your boudoir, mademoiselle."

"Unhappy man," the young woman moaned, showing every sign of unspeakable fright. "Unhappy man! Do you want to be killed?"

"Perhaps."

Raoul uttered the word "perhaps" with such love and despair that Christine could not repress a sob. She took his hands and looked at him with the pure tenderness of which she was capable, while he, under her gaze, felt that his pain was already eased.

"Raoul," she said, "you must forget *the man's voice* and never recall his name, and you must never again try to fathom the mystery of *the man's voice.*"

"So the mystery is that dreadful?"

"Nothing on earth could be more horrible."

A silence interposed itself between the two young people. Raoul was overwhelmed.

"Swear to me that you'll do nothing 'to know it,' " she insisted. "Swear that you'll never again come into my dressing room unless I invite you in."

"Then you promise to invite me in sometimes, Christine?"

"I promise."

"When?"

"Tomorrow."

"All right then, I swear."

Those were the last words they spoke that day.

He kissed her hands and left, cursing Erik all the while and promising himself to be patient.

Chapter XII

ABOVE THE TRAPDOORS

The following day, he saw her again at the Opera. She still had the gold ring on her finger. She was sweet and kind. She discussed his plans, his future, and his career.

He told her that the departure of the polar expedition had been delayed for three weeks. In a month at the latest, he would be leaving France.

She suggested, almost gaily, that he should think of his voyage with pleasure, as a step in the direction of his future glory. And when he replied that in his eyes glory without love held no charm, she treated him like a child whose sorrows are ephemeral.

He told her: "Christine, how can you speak so lightly about such serious matters? We may never see each other again. I might die on this expedition."

"I, too, might die," she said simply. She was not smiling or joking any longer. She seemed to be thinking of something else that had occurred to her for the first time. The thought made her eyes glow.

"Christine, what are you thinking about?"

"I'm thinking that we will never see each other again."

"And that's what makes you so radiant?"

"And that in a month we'll have to say good-bye to each other . . . forever."

"Unless, Christine, we become engaged and promise to wait for each other—forever."

She put her hand over his lips. "Be still, Raoul! You know that's not what it is. We'll never be married. That's understood." She seemed to have trouble containing a boundless joy. She clapped her hands with childlike glee. Anxiously, Raoul watched her, unable to understand.

"But, but . . ." she said again, putting out both of her hands to the young man—or rather, giving them to him as if, suddenly, she had resolved to let him have them as a gift. "But if we can't be married, we can . . . we can be engaged! Nobody will know it except us, Raoul! There have been secret marriages! There can certainly be secret engagements![1] We are engaged for a month, my dear. In a month, you will leave, and I can be happy for a lifetime remembering that month."

The idea delighted her, then she became serious again. "That," she said, *"is a happiness that can do no one any harm."*

Raoul had understood. He leaped at the idea. He wanted to turn it into a reality at once. He bowed before her and, with incomparable humility, said, "Mademoiselle, I have the honor of asking for your hand."

"But you already have them both, my dear fiancé . . . Oh! Raoul, we're going to be so happy! We can play at being a future little husband and a future little wife."

Raoul said to himself, "The silly girl. A month from now, I will have had time to make her forget him—or to solve and destroy *the mystery of the man's voice.* And a month from now, Christine will agree to be my wife. And while we wait, we'll play!"

It was the most beautiful game in the world and it pleased them like the innocent children they were. Oh! What marvelous things they said to each other! And the eternal vows they exchanged! The idea that at the end of the month there would be no one to fulfill those vows troubled them and put them in a state of mingled delight and terror, between tears and laughter. They played "hearts" the way others play ball, but since it was real hearts they tossed back and forth, they needed to be very skillful in order to catch them without sustaining any harm. Raoul, whose heart was

---

[1] "secret engagements"

For the longest time, Christine's relationship to Raoul has had the character of childlike innocence and of romantic fantasy. The point is that in both instances there is no reality principle operating.

This gleaming little game of a one-month engagement is the sort of dream stuff that Emma Bovary might have doted on in her convent school. The reality of it all is, of course, emphasized by the fact that the game is played within the confines of the opera, the absolute realm of the fantastic.

Ironically enough, Erik's love for Christine, also played out within the confines of the opera, has real-world energy (see the Introduction).

aching, stopped the game on the eighth day with these wild words: "I'm not going to the North Pole."

Christine who, in her innocence, had not thought about this possibility, suddenly discovered how dangerous the game could be and reproached herself bitterly. Without a word to Raoul, she went back home.

This took place in the afternoon, in Christine's dressing room where she always met Raoul and where they enjoyed little tea parties of three cookies, two glasses of port wine, and a bouquet of violets.

She did not sing that night. And he did not get his usual letter from her, though they had given each other permission to write every day of their month. The next morning, he hurried to Mme. Valerius' house, where he learned that Christine had left the previous evening at five o'clock saying that she would be gone for two days. Raoul was dismayed. He hated Mme. Valerius, who had given him such news with such stunning calm. He tried "drawing her out," but it would appear that the old woman knew nothing. To the young man's frantic questions she replied only, "That's Christine's secret." It was said with touching gentleness and with a raised finger that seemed to recommend discretion at the same time as it appeared to be reassuring.

"Ah!" exclaimed Raoul angrily as he raced madly down the stairs. "Ah, these young women are well guarded by such Madame Valeriuses."

Where could Christine be? Two days! Two days out of their all too short happiness. And it was his fault. Hadn't it been understood that he would leave? And if it had been his firm intention *not* to leave, why had he spoken so soon? He blamed himself for this blunder and for the next forty-eight hours was the most miserable of men until, at the end of that time, Christine reappeared.

She reappeared in triumph. For a second time, she achieved an incredible success like that of the evening of the gala. Since the episode of "the toad," Carlotta had been unable to appear on stage. Fear of a second "croak" filled her heart and vitiated all of her powers; the scenes that had witnessed her incomprehensible defeat had become hateful to her. She found a way to break her contract. Daaé was immediately asked to take the vacated position. She was greeted with truly delirious applause for her role in *La Juive*.[2]

---

[2] "her role in *La Juive*"

Presumably, Christine played the role of Rachel, the Jewess who, as the opera ends, is flung into a caldron of boiling oil as a consequence of a series of confusions of identity and racial prejudice (see page 74, Note 6).

Naturally, the viscount was present that evening, but he was the only one who suffered as he heard the echoing of the tumultuous applause for this new triumph. Because he saw that Christine was still wearing her gold ring. A distant voice murmured in the young man's ear, "She still has the gold ring tonight, and you didn't give it to her. She has given her soul again tonight, but not to you." And the voice went on, "If she won't tell you what she has been doing for the last two days . . . if she conceals where she was, you must ask Erik."

He hurried to the stage and stood where she would have to pass by. She saw him because she was looking for him. She said, "Quick, quick. Come." And she led him to her dressing room, paying no attention to the courtiers of her young glory who stood murmuring, "It's a scandal," before her closed door.[3]

Raoul was immediately on his knees. He swore to her that he would leave on the expedition and begged her not to diminish by a single hour the ideal happiness she had promised him from now on. Her tears flowed without constraint. They embraced each other like a desperate brother and sister who have been afflicted by a common loss and who have come together to weep for their dead.

Suddenly, she extricated herself from the young man's sweet and timid embrace and seemed to be listening to something he could not hear, then, with an abrupt gesture, she showed Raoul to the door. When he was at the threshold, she told him, so softly that the viscount guessed her words more than he heard them, "Tomorrow, my dear fiancé. And be happy, Raoul. I sang for you tonight."

And so, he came back. But alas, those two days of absence had broken the charm of their delightful lie. Their eyes mournful, they looked at each other in the dressing room without saying a word. Raoul kept himself from crying out, "I'm jealous. I'm jealous. I'm jealous." Just the same, she understood him.

She said, "Let's go for a walk, my friend. The fresh air will do us good."

Raoul thought she was going to propose some sort of country excursion far from the building he hated as if it were a prison and in which, he felt angrily, there was a jailer lurking in the walls . . . Erik, the jailer. . . . Instead, she led him onto the stage and made him sit on the wooden rim

---

[3] "It's a scandal"

Because Christine openly goes into her dressing room accompanied by a man, and closes the door.

A phantom of the Phantom of the Opera

of a fountain in the peace and doubtful coolness of a first scene set placed there for the next performance.

On another day, she wandered with him, hand in hand, down the abandoned paths of a garden whose climbing plants had been cut by the skilled hands of a set designer, as if the real skies, real flowers, and earth were forever forbidden to her and she was doomed never again to breathe any air except that of the theater. The young man hesitated to ask her even the smallest of questions, because it seemed clear to him at once that she would be unable to answer it in any way and he dreaded making her suffer unnecessarily. Sometimes a fireman would pass by and watch their melancholy idyll from a distance. There were times when she tried courageously to deceive both herself and him about the false beauty of a scene invented to produce illusions. Her always vivid imagination would adorn the scene with the liveliest of colors such as, she said, nature could not possibly match. She waxed enthusiastic while Raoul lightly pressed her feverish hand. She said, "See these walls, Raoul, these trees, these supports, these images of painted canvas—they have all seen the most sublime loves because they were invented here by poets who stand head and shoulders taller than other men. Tell me then, Raoul, that our love, too, is to be found here, since it has also been invented and that it, too, alas, is no more than an illusion.''

Distressed, he could not bring himself to reply. Then she said, ''Our love is too sad on earth. Let's bring it to the heavens. You'll see how easy it is to do that here.''

And she led him higher than the clouds into the magnificent disorder above the flies, where it pleased her to make him dizzy while running before him on the fragile bridges there among the thousands of rigging cords attached to pulleys, winches, and revolving drums in the midst of a veritable aerial forest of masts and yardarms. If he hesitated, she said, pouting adorably, ''And you're a sailor.''

And then they came back down to solid ground—that is to say, into a solid corridor which led them to laughter, to dancing youngsters being scolded by a severe voice, ''Warm up, girls. Watch your *pointe!*''[4] It is the children's class, those who had just turned seven or who were about to be nine or ten. They already wear low-cut blouses, light tutus, white trousers, and pink stockings. And they work. How they work with their aching little feet hoping to study quadrilles, to become ballerinas, or prima ballerinas loaded with diamonds. In the meantime, Christine gives them candy.

On another day, she made him come into a vast room of her palace that was entirely filled with spangled cloth, cast-off knight's clothing; with lances, bucklers, and plumes, where she inspected the immobile, dust-covered ghosts of knights. She spoke kindly to them, promising that they would see sparkling evenings again and musical processions before the brilliant footlights.

That was how she took him through her entire empire, which was artificial but immense, extending seventeen levels from the first floor all the way to the roof, and was inhabited by an army of subjects. She passed among them like a popular queen, encouraging their work, sitting in their workrooms, giving wise counsel to the workers whose hands hesitated to cut into the rich fabrics that were to clothe heroes. The inhabitants of this country worked at all kinds of crafts. There were cobblers and goldsmiths. All of them had learned to love her, because she cared about their problems and knew the foibles of them all. She knew the hidden places in the building where aged couples lived in secret.

She would knock at their doors and present Raoul to them as a Prince

---

[4] ''your *pointe''*
A ballet step achieved when a ballet dancer is perfectly balanced on the tip of his or her toes.

Charming who had asked for her hand in marriage; then they would both sit on some worm-eaten prop and listen to tales about the Opera the way that, in their childhood, they had listened to the old Breton legends. These old people had no memory of anything but the Opera. They had been living there for countless years. Former administrations had forgotten them. Palace revolutions had ignored them. On the outside, the history of France had taken place without their being aware of it, and nobody remembered them.[5]

In this manner, the precious days flowed away and Raoul and Christine, by the excessive interest they appeared to have in external matters, did their best to hide from each other the single thought that was in both their hearts. One thing was certain—Christine, who until then had appeared to be the stronger of the two, suddenly became indescribably nervous. In their wanderings she took to running without reason, then stopping abruptly, and her hand, turned suddenly cold, would restrain the young man. Sometimes her eyes seemed to be following imaginary shadows. She would cry, "This way," then "This way," then "This way," in a breathless laugh that often ended in tears. Raoul, despite his promises, wanted to speak to her, to question her, but before he could even formulate the question she would reply feverishly, "Nothing. I swear to you, it's nothing."

Once, when they were on the stage and passing an open trapdoor, Raoul leaned over the dark abyss and said, "You've had me visit the heights of your empire, Christine, but they tell strange stories about what is down below. Would you like us to go down there?" Hearing this, she put her arms around him as if she feared to see him disappear into the black hole, and said, her voice low and trembling, "Never! I forbid you to go there. Besides, it doesn't belong to me. *Everything under the earth belongs to him!*"

Looking deep into her eyes, Raoul said harshly, "So *he* lives down there?"

"I didn't say that. Where did you get such an idea? Let's go. There are times, Raoul, when I wonder if you aren't mad. You always hear impossible things. Come on. Come on." She tried, literally, to drag him away because he wanted stubbornly to stay there, beside the trapdoor. The hole seemed irresistibly attractive to him.

Suddenly the trapdoor closed. So suddenly that they were unable to

---

[5] "without their being aware of it, and nobody remembered them"

These forgotten underground dwellers call to mind the lost race of eyeless, red-snouted Frenchmen Leroux calls the Talpa in his first novel, *La Double Vie de Théophraste Longuet* (*The Double Life of Théophraste Longuet,* 1903).

see the hand that made it move. They stood there, stunned. "Maybe *he's* there," said Raoul finally.

She shrugged her shoulders but appeared in no way reassured. "No, no. It is 'the trapdoor closers' doing something. They open and close the traps for no reason at all. They have to have something to do. Like the 'door closers,' they need something to do to pass the time."

"But what if it was *he,* Christine?"

"No! No! *He's* shut himself up. He's working."

"Oh, really? *He's* working?"

"Yes. *He* can't open and close the trapdoors and work at the same time. We can rest easy." Saying that, she shivered.

"What's he working at?"

"Oh! A dreadful thing. . . . So, we can relax. When *he* works at that, *he* sees nothing. *He* doesn't eat or drink or breathe . . . for days and nights. *He* becomes a living corpse and *he* doesn't have time to play around with trapdoors." Again, she shivered and leaned attentively in the direction of the trapdoor. Raoul let her do and say what she liked. He was silent, fearful now that the sound of his voice would make her think, impeding, therefore, the still tentative movements she was making to confide in him.

She had not left him. She still had her arms around him. It was her turn to sigh, "What if it was *he?*"

"Are you afraid of *him?*"

"No, no. Of course not."

Without being aware of it, the young man assumed a pitying stance, as one might with an impressionable person who was still in the grip of a recent nightmare. He seemed to be saying, "But you know, I'll always be here." And that manner was almost involuntarily threatening. Christine, astonished, looked at him as one might look at a phenomenon of courage and virtue and seemed to be inwardly measuring its true value as so much useless and audacious chivalry. She kissed poor Raoul like a sister,[6] rewarding him with an access of tenderness because he had made a brotherly little fist to defend her against all of life's possible dangers.

Raoul understood and blushed with shame. He felt as weak as she. He

---

[6] "like a sister"

    See Note 1 in this chapter.

    There is a certain condescension in Christine's fondness for Raoul, "rewarding him with an access of tenderness because he had made a brotherly little fist to defend her . . ."

    This, plus the nervousness she displays as she looks about for, or senses, Erik's presence is more evidence, if we need it, that Raoul is the unthreatening—nonsexual—lover, while the dark and dynamic Erik touches her emotions deeply.

thought, "She's pretending not to be afraid, but she's trembling as she moves us away from the trapdoor."

It was true. The next day and the days thereafter, the ambience for their curious and chaste love was almost at the top of the building, far from any trapdoors. With each passing hour, Christine's agitation increased. When, finally one afternoon, she came very late, her face so pale, and her eyes so reddened by despair that Raoul determined to go to any length, such as blurting out as soon as he saw her that *he would not go on the expedition to the North Pole unless she confided to him the secret of the Man's Voice.*

"Hush! In Heaven's name, hush! Poor Raoul, what if *he* should hear you?" And the young woman cast a haggard look around her.

"I'll tell you what should happen. I'll take you out of reach of his power. And you'll never need to think of *him* again."

"Is it possible?"

Encouraged by this doubt, the young man allowed her to lead him to the highest level of the theater—in "the altitudes," where one was very far, very far from any trapdoors.

"I'll hide you in some unknown corner of the world where *he* can't come looking for you. You'll be saved and then I'll leave, since you've sworn that you will never marry."

Christine seized Raoul's hands convulsively and squeezed them with incredible rapture. But she grew anxious again and turned her head away. "Higher," she said, "still higher." And she led him toward the heights.

It was hard for him to follow her. Soon, they were beneath the roof, in a labyrinth of timbers. They wound their way between buttresses, rafters, joists, support beams, and ranks of lights. They ran from cross beam to cross beam as in a forest they might have run from one huge tree to another.

And, despite the care she had taken to look constantly behind her, she did not see the shadow that followed her like her own shadow, which stopped and started when she stopped or started, and made no more noise than a shadow can. Raoul noticed nothing because, with Christine before him, nothing that happened behind him interested him at all.

Chapter XIII

APOLLO'S LYRE

And that was how they reached the rooftops. She glided along them, light and familiar as a swallow. Their gaze took in the empty space between the three domes and the pediment. She breathed hard, looking down at the valley of Paris at work below. She looked confidently at Raoul. She called him to be near her and together, side by side, they walked on high over streets of zinc and on cast-iron avenues. Their twin forms were reflected in vast tanks[1] filled with motionless water where, in summer, some twenty of the boys of the corps de ballet learned to swim and dive. Behind them, the surging shadow still followed them faithfully past iron intersections, circling the ponds and silent skirting the domes, flattening itself against the roofs with the movement of its black wings. The unhappy youngsters were entirely unaware of its presence as they sat down confidently under the noble protection of Apollo who, with a gesture of bronze, raised his prodigious lyre toward the heart of the fiery sky.

They were surrounded by a dazzling springtime evening. The slowly

---

[1] "vast tanks"

In a theater that was still lit by open gas jets, the fear of fire was ever present. To cope with the threat there were firemen constantly on duty. There was an elaborate water system involving nearly 7,000 meters of lead and copper piping, employing 573 faucets. There were three holding tanks for water with a total of 105,000 liters (roughly 26,000 gallons).

passing clouds had just received their light robe of purple and gold from the setting sun and let it pass over the young people. Christine said, "Soon, we'll be going farther and faster than the clouds, to the end of the world, and then you'll abandon me. But if, when the time comes for you to take me away, I refuse to follow you, then, Raoul, take me anyway."

She spoke with an energy that seemed to be directed against herself as she pressed nervously against him. "Then you're afraid you'll change your mind, Christine?"

"I don't know," she said, shaking her head strangely. "He's a demon." And she shuddered. Moaning she pressed herself against him. "I'm afraid now—of returning to live with him underground."

"What forces you to go back, Christine?"

"If I don't go back to him, dreadful things may happen. But .. I can't take it anymore. I can't take it. I know that we're supposed to pity those who live 'underground' but this one is too horrible. Still, the time is nearing—do I have no more than a day? And if I don't come to him, he'll come looking for me with his voice. He'll drag me off to his house underground, and then he'll get down on his knees before me—with his death's-head. He'll tell me that it loves me! And he'll weep. Ah, those tears, Raoul. Those tears in the two black holes of the death's-head. I can't bear to see the flowing of those tears again."

She wrung her hands in agony, while Raoul, in the grip of the same contagious despair, pressed her to his heart. "No, no! You won't have to hear him tell you again that he loves you. Or see the flowing of his tears. Let's run away. Now, Christine." And he would have led her away, but she stopped him.

"No, no," she said, shaking her head sadly. "Not now! It would be too cruel. Let him hear me sing again tomorrow night for one last time. And then we'll go away. At midnight. You'll come get me in my dressing room at exactly midnight. He'll be waiting for me in the dining room by the lake. We'll be free and you can take me away. Even if I refuse—you must swear to that, Raoul. Because I feel that if I return there, I'll never come back. Never." And she added, "You can't understand." She sighed and it seemed to her that there was an answering sigh behind her. "Did you hear that?" Her teeth chattered.

"No," Raoul reassured her. "I haven't heard anything."

"It's too dreadful," she admitted, "to tremble like this all the time. And yet, we're not in any danger here. We're at home . . . in my home, in the sky, in the fresh air, in daylight. The sun is blazing and night birds don't like to look at the sun. I've never seen *him* by the light of day. It must be terrible," she stammered, turning a distraught look at Raoul. "Oh! The first time I saw *him,* I thought he was going to die."

"Why?" Raoul asked, truly frightened by the tone this strange and fearful confession was taking. "Why did you think that he would die?"

"BECAUSE I HAD LOOKED AT HIM!!!"

Here, Raoul and Christine turned together at the same time. "There's someone in pain," said Raoul. "Perhaps hurt. Did you hear?"

"I can't say," Christine admitted. "Even when he's not here, my ears are filled with his sighs. . . . Still, if you heard . . ." They got up and looked around them. They were all alone on the immense leaden roof. They sat down again.

Raoul asked, "How did you see him the first time?"

"For three months I heard him without seeing him. The first time I 'heard' him, I thought, as you did, that this wonderful voice that had suddenly begun to sing *at my side* was singing in an adjoining dressing room. I went out and looked everywhere. But as you know, Raoul, my dressing room is very isolated, and it was impossible for me to find the voice anywhere outside while it continued to sing inside. It was not only singing; it was speaking to me, responding to my questions in a man's real voice. With one difference! It was beautiful, like an angel's voice.[2] How to explain such an incredible phenomenon? I had never stopped thinking about the 'Guardian Angel of Music' that my poor father had promised to send me after his death. I don't mind telling you about such childishness, Raoul, because you knew my father, and he loved you and believed in the 'Angel of Music' at the same time as I did, when you were little, and I'm sure that you won't sneer or make fun of me. Oh, my dear, I still had the tender and credulous soul of little Lotte, and the company of Mme. Valerius did nothing to change that. I held my pure little soul in my naïve hands and held it out—offered it to the 'man's voice,' believing I was offering it to the angel. Certainly, a little of the fault lies with my adoptive mother from whom I hid nothing of this inexplicable phenomenon. She was the first to say, 'It must be the angel. In any case, ask him if he is.'

"That's what I did, and the Voice replied that in fact it was the voice of the angel I had been waiting for, the one my father on his deathbed had promised to send me. From that moment on, a great intimacy developed

---

[2] "like an angel's voice"

In Leroux's first novel, *La Double Vie de Théophraste Longuet,* the psychic surgeon, M. Eliphas de St. Elme de Taillebourge de la Nox, is described as having a singularly beautiful voice.

between the Voices and myself, and I had absolute confidence in it. It told me that it had come down to earth in order to have me experience the supreme pleasures of eternal art, and it asked my permission to give me lessons daily. I agreed enthusiastically, and from the first hour I missed none of the meetings it arranged for me in my dressing room when that part of the Opera was deserted. Ah, what those lessons were like? You, who have heard the Voice, can't possibly imagine them.''

"Evidently not. I don't have any idea,'' the young man agreed. "What was the accompaniment?''

"A music about which I knew nothing, and which came from behind the walls and was incomparably appropriate. And then, dear, one would have said that the Voice knew precisely at what point in my training my father had left me at his death and what had been the simple method he had used in teaching me.

"And thus, what with remembering the past lessons—or, better, with my own voice recalling them and combining them with the present ones, I made the kind of prodigious progress that, under other circumstances would have taken years. You know, my dear, that I'm fairly delicate and that my voice at first lacked character: my natural low notes were not yet developed, the high notes were fairly harsh and the middle range was not distinct.[3] My father had struggled against these defects and had triumphed over them briefly. And these are the faults the Voice overcame completely. Little by little I increased the volume of the sounds I could produce to a degree I could not have hoped for given my former weakness. I learned to let my breath expand to its widest range. But above all the Voice taught me the secret of combining chest sounds with the soprano voice. Finally, all of that was enclosed within the sacred fire of inspiration. It awakened within me an ardent, insatiable, and sublime life force. The virtue of the Voice was that, by making itself heard, it elevated me to its own level and linked me to its own superb flight. Its soul lived in my mouth, breathing harmony.

"At the end of a few weeks, I could no longer recognize myself when I sang. Indeed, I was horrified by it. For a while, I was afraid that there was some sort of magic behind it, but Mme. Valerius reassured me. She said that she knew me well and that I was too simple a girl to give the devil a hold on me.

"Obedient to the Voice's orders, my progress remained a secret be-

---

[3] "not distinct"

With so many defects in her voice, one wonders how even an inspired teacher could get Christine to overcome them.

tween him, Mme. Valerius, and me. Strangely enough, outside of the dress-ing room, I sang with my everyday voice and nobody noticed anything. I did everything the Voice wanted. It said, 'We have to wait. You'll see. We'll astonish Paris.' And I waited. I lived in a sort of ecstatic dream within which the Voice ruled. At that point, Raoul, I saw you in the audience one night. I was so delighted I didn't even think to hide my joy when I came back to my dressing room. Unfortunately for us, the Voice was already there and could tell by how I looked that something new had taken place. He asked me 'What happened?' and I saw no reason not to tell him our sweet story, nor to keep from him the knowledge of the place you had in my heart. The Voice was silent for a while. I called to it; it did not reply. In vain, I begged it to speak. I was out of my mind with the fear that it had left me forever. Would God that it had, dear.

"That evening, I reached home in a desperate state. I threw myself around Mme. Valerius' neck and told her, 'The Voice is gone! It may never come back.' She was as frightened as I was and asked me to explain. I told her everything. She said, 'Of course, the Voice is jealous.' It was this that made me realize that I loved you, dear."

Here, Christine paused for a while. She leaned her head against Raoul's chest and they stayed silently for a moment in each other's arms. The emotion that bound them together kept them from seeing—or, rather, feeling the presence of the rampant shadow a few paces away. A shadow with two large black wings was nearing them over the roof, coming so close it could have smothered them had it enclosed them with its wings.

"The next morning," continued Christine with a deep sigh, "I was thoughtful when I came back to my dressing room. The Voice was there. Oh, darling! It spoke so very sadly to me. It told me straight out that if I gave my heart to anyone on earth, it would have no recourse but to return to heaven. And it told me all this with such a tone of *human* pain that I ought to have known from that moment that I had strangely been the victim of my deceived senses. But my faith in that apparition, with which thoughts about my father were so intimately connected, was still whole. I feared nothing so much as no longer hearing him; on the other hand, I had thought about the feelings which had led me to you, and I evaluated the useless danger. I didn't even know whether you remembered me. No matter what happened, your rank in the world would prevent me from ever thinking of an honorable union with you. I swore to the Voice that you were nothing more to me than a brother, and that you would never be anything else, and that my heart was free from all earth-bound love.

And that, my dear, is why I turned my eyes away—on stage, or in the corridors—whenever you've tried to attract my attention; and that's why I didn't recognize you, or didn't see you. Meanwhile, the hours of my lessons with the Voice were passed in a divine delirium. The beauty of sound had never before possessed me to such an extent. One day the Voice said, 'Go, Christine. You're able now to give mankind a bit of Heaven's music.' "

"I don't know why Carlotta didn't show up at the theater on the night of the gala. Nor how it happened that I was called to replace her. I don't know. But I sang. I sang, transported, as I had never sung before. I felt as light as if I had been given wings; for a moment, I thought that my incandescent soul had left my body."

"Oh, Christine," said Raoul, whose eyes grew moist as he too remembered. "On that evening, my heart vibrated with every note you sang. I watched your tears flow down your pale cheeks and I wept with you. How could you sing and weep at once?"

"My strength abandoned me," said Christine. "I closed my eyes. When I opened them again, you were at my side! But the Voice was there, too, Raoul! I was afraid for you. So I did not want to show that I recognized you. I laughed when you reminded me that you had retrieved my scarf from the sea.

"Alas, one can't trick the Voice. It had recognized you and it was jealous. For the next two days, it made atrocious scenes. It said, 'If you didn't love him, you wouldn't be trying to escape him. He'd be an old friend whose hand you'd shake as with anyone else. If you didn't love him, you wouldn't be afraid to be alone with him and me in your dressing room. If you didn't love him, you wouldn't send him away.'

" 'Enough,' I said angrily. 'Tomorrow, I have to go to Perros to my father's tomb, and I'm going to ask M. Raoul de Chagny to come with me.'

" 'As you like,' it said, 'but you should know that I'll be there, too, because I'm everywhere that you are and, if you have been worthy of me, if you haven't lied, I'll play the "Resurrection of Lazarus"[4] on "the violin of death" beside your father's tomb at the stroke of midnight.'

"And that, my dear, is what led me to write you the letter that brought you to Perros. How could I have been deceived to such a degree? How was it, considering the personal nature of the Voice's concerns, that I suspected no deceit? Alas, I was no longer in command of myself. I had

---

[4] "Resurrection of Lazarus"
See Chapter VI, Note 14, page 95.

become his thing. And, given the techniques at his disposal, the Voice must have found it easy to take advantage of such a child as I was."[5]

At this point in Christine's narrative, when she was tearfully regretting the too perfect innocence of an insufficiently instructed mind, Raoul exclaimed, "But finally, you must have known the truth. Why didn't you leave that abominable nightmare at once?"

"Known the truth, Raoul? Leave the nightmare! But, poor wretch that I was, I hadn't entered the nightmare until the day that I learned the truth. Hush now! Hush! I've told you nothing. And now that we're going to come down to earth from heaven, pity me, Raoul. Pity me. One evening . . . one fatal evening . . . it was that evening of so many misfortunes . . . when Carlotta thought herself transformed into a toad on stage and began croaking as if she had spent all her life on the banks of marshes. On the evening when the theater was plunged into darkness, when the chandelier fell like a thunderbolt crashing to the floor. There were dead and wounded that evening and the theater resounded with unhappy cries.

"My first thought, Raoul, in the midst of the commotion, was simultaneously for you and for the Voice, because at that time you were the two equal halves of my heart.[6] I was reassured as far as you were concerned because I saw you in your brother's box and knew that you were in no danger. I was afraid for the Voice, because it had told me it would be at the performance. I was really afraid as if it were 'an ordinary living person who was able to die.' I thought, 'My God, maybe the chandelier has crushed the Voice.' I was then on stage and so panic-stricken that I was about to run into the auditorium to look for the Voice among the dead and wounded when it occurred to me that if nothing dreadful had happened to it, it must already be in my dressing room, where it would have gone to assure me. I rushed to my dressing room. The Voice was not there. I locked myself in, and with tears in my eyes, I begged it—if it was still alive—to show itself to me. The Voice did not reply, but all at once I heard a long, lovely moan that I knew well. It was the moan Lazarus makes when, at the sound of Jesus' voice, he raises his eyelids and sees again the light of day. It was

---

[5] "such a child as I was"

Christine's discovery that the Phantom is a mortal man contributes to her rapid personal growth. Already, her maturity manifests itself in sharp contrast to Raoul, who remains much the boy he has always been.

[6] "the equal halves of my heart"

This observation, at once disingenuous and profoundly sophisticated, is the purest statement of Christine's situation: she has a divided heart, one half of which is simple, innocent, romantic, childlike, and is involved with Raoul, while the other incorporates the dark creative energy represented by the Phantom.

the weeping of my father's violin. Raoul, I recognized my father's bowing style, the same bow that had kept us motionless long ago on the roads of Perros; the same one that 'charmed' us that night in the cemetery. And then, there it was again, in the invisible and triumphant instrument: the cry of life's happiness. The voice, making itself heard at last, began to sing the dominating, sovereign sentence, 'Come and believe in me. They that believe in me will live again. Walk! Those who believe in me will not know death.'[7] I can't tell you the feeling that music gave me, singing eternal life at the same moment as, not far away, the poor unfortunate people crushed by that fatal chandelier were yielding up their souls. It seemed to me that it was commanding me, too, to 'Come, rise and walk' toward it. It was receding; I followed it. 'Come and believe in me.' I believed in it; I went. And, strangely, my dressing room as I walked seemed to elongate, to elongate. Obviously it had to be a mirror effect, because I had the mirror in front of me. Then, all at once, and without my knowing how it had happened, I was outside my dressing room.''

Here, Raoul brusquely interrupted her. ''What? Without knowing how? Christine! Christine! You must try to stop dreaming.''

''Ah, poor dear, I wasn't dreaming! Without knowing how it had happened, I was outside my dressing room. You, who saw me disappear in my dressing room one evening, may be able to explain it, but I can't. I can only tell you one thing, and that is that as I was standing before my mirror I could no longer see anything in front of me, and when I looked behind me, there was no mirror and no dressing room to be seen. I was in a dark hallway. Terrified, I screamed.

''It was dark all around me. A feeble red glow in the distance illuminated a corner of the wall at an intersection. I cried out. Only my voice could be heard, because the violin's song had stopped. Then, all at once, in the dark, a hand rested on mine. Or rather, something cold and bony enclosed my wrist and would not let it go. I screamed. An arm encircled my waist. I was lifted up. Horrified, I struggled for a moment. My fingers slid over wet stones to which they could not cling. And then I stopped moving. I thought I would die of fright. I was carried toward the small red glow, which we entered, and then I saw that I was in the arms of a man wrapped in a large black cloak. A man who had a mask that hid his

---

[7] ''will live again . . . will not know death''

In the Gospel According to St. John 11:25, we read, ''Jesus said unto her [Martha], I am the resurrection, and the life; he that believeth in me, though he were dead, yet shall he live: And whosoever liveth and believeth in me shall never die.'' And later, in verse 43, we read ''And when he [Jesus] thus had spoken, he cried with a loud voice, Lazarus, come forth.'' (King James transl.)

whole face. I made a supreme effort. My limbs stiffened; I opened my mouth again to scream with fear, but a hand closed over it—an hand that, as it touched my lips, my skin, felt like death! I fainted.

"How long did I remain unconscious? I couldn't say. When I opened my eyes again, we were still—the man in black and I—enveloped in shadows. A dark lantern set on the ground illuminated the jet of a fountain. The water, spurting from a wall, disappeared almost at once into the ground on which I was lying. My head rested on the knee of the man in the black mask and cloak, and my silent companion was sponging my forehead with a care, an attention and delicacy that seemed even more dreadful to endure than the earlier brutal abduction. Gentle as his hands were, they still felt like death. I pushed them away, but without much force. In a weak voice I said, 'Who are you? Where is the Voice?' I was answered only by a sigh. Then suddenly, a warm breath passed across my face and, vaguely, in the dark, and beside the dark shape of the man, I made out a white shape. The dark form lifted me onto the white shape and, just as a joyful neigh reached my astonished ears, I murmured, 'César.' The horse trembled. Raoul, dear, I was half-lying on a saddle. I recognized the white horse from *The Prophet* to whom I had often given tidbits. There had been a widespread rumor in the theater that this animal had disappeared and that it had been stolen by the Phantom of the Opera. I, though I believed in the Voice, did not believe in the Phantom. Still, there I was wondering if I wasn't the Phantom's prisoner. From the bottom of my heart, I called to the Voice for help, because I could never have imagined that the Phantom and the Voice were one. Have you heard talk about the Phantom of the Opera, Raoul?"

"Yes," replied the young man. "But tell me, Christine, what happened to you when you were on the white horse from *The Prophet*?"

"I held still and let myself be carried. Little by little, a strange torpor succeeded the state of agonized terror into which my infernal adventure had thrown me. The black shape held on to me and I made no further move to escape. I felt a strange peace flowing through me, and I thought I was under the beneficent influence of some elixir. I had total possession of my senses. My eyes adjusted to the darkness, which, moreover, was broken here and there by brief flashes of light. I judged that we were in a narrow gallery which I imagined encircled the Opera, whose substructure is immense. Once, and once only, my dear, had I gone down into those prodigious cellars, but I had stopped at the third level, not daring to go farther down into the earth. And yet, two more levels opened beneath me, so vast that you could have housed a city in them. But the shapes I saw there frightened me away. There are demons in black before boilers using shovels and pitchforks to stir up fires and light them, and if you come too close, they threaten you by suddenly opening the furnace doors. While César was carrying me calmly on his back through that tenebrous nightmare, I could see, far, far away, as if through the wrong end of a binocular, the tiny, tiny black demons before the glowing embers in their furnaces. They would appear and disappear, then reappear depending on the bizarre turns we made. Finally, they disappeared completely. The man's form still held on to me, and César walked sure-footedly, without being guided. I could not tell you, even approximately, how long that nighttime journey took. I remember only that we turned and turned; that we descended, following an inflexible spiral to the very heart of the earth,[8] or was it perhaps my head that was turning—actually, I don't think so. No. I was incredibly lucid. César flared his nostrils for an instant, breathed in the air, and speeded his pace a bit. I felt damp air, and then César stopped. The darkness lessened. A bluish glow surrounded us.[9] I looked around and saw that we were at the border of a lake whose leaden waters disappeared into the distance, into the dark, but the bluish glow shed light on this bank, and I saw a little boat tied to an iron ring on the quay.

"I knew, of course, that all of that existed and that the sight of this lake and the boat underground had nothing in them of the supernatural.[10] But consider the unusual circumstances that had brought me to this shore. The souls of the dead could not have been more ill at ease when they reached the shores of the Styx, nor could Charon[11] have been gloomier or

---

[8] "heart of the earth"

Leroux is at great pains here to create for us the sense that Christine, like Persephone whom Pluto abducted, is entering the domain of another lord of a netherworld. The sight of the man with their pitchforks and the glimpses she has of burning fires remind us, of course, of Satan's realm.

[9] "a bluish glow surrounded us."

A blue flame or a blue glow is a fixture of the gothic novel and makes its appearance in the romances of Ann Radcliffe and "Monk" Lewis. In Bram Stoker's *Dracula*, Jonathan Harker is told peasants believe that buried treasure is often found in places over which a blue glow hovers. A usual rational explanation for such blue glows is that they are the phosphorescence seen over marshes which are sometimes called *ignis fatuus* or "foolish fire" or "will-o'-the-wisp." In any case, whether in gothic fiction or in marshes, the blue glow, when it appears, does not bode well.

[10] "this lake . . . nothing in them of the supernatural"

There was, and there is, an underground body of water beneath the opera, though it is hardly the grand expanse of water Leroux has imagined for us here.

In 1861, the first excavations made in preparation for building the opera house revealed what had been suspected—that the ground beneath where the stage of the theater was to be built was soggy. To insure that the projected subcellars twenty meters below the stage would be dry enough to safely store flats and other stage furniture, an elaborate drainage system was constructed. For more than seven months that water was drained into a vast tank that had been constructed to receive it. It is the water in this manmade pool over which Erik's boat is rowed.

more silent than the man who put me into the boat. Had the effects of the elixir worn off, or was the coolness of the place enough to restore me completely to myself? My torpor was vanishing, and I made several movements that indicated my fear was returning. My sinister companion must have noticed it, because, with a quick gesture, he sent César away. The horse ran off into the darkness of the tunnel, and I heard his iron-shod hooves striking the steps of the staircase. Then the man leaped into the boat, untied the rope from the ring, took up the oars, and rowed powerfully, swiftly away. His eyes, behind the mask, never left me. I felt the intent gaze of his pupils on me. The surrounding water made no sound. We glided through the blue light about which I've told you, and we were once again in absolute darkness. Then we arrived. The boat bumped against something hard. Again, he carried me in his arms. I had recovered enough strength to cry out. And I screamed. And then, abruptly, I stopped, stupefied by the light. Yes, a brilliant light in the midst of which I had been placed. I leaped to my feet. I had all my strength back. I was in the middle of a large drawing room which appeared to be adorned with flowers that were at once magnificent and ridiculous because of the silk ribbons by which they were tied to their baskets, the kind that are sold in the shops on the boulevards. The flowers were too civilized, like those I used to find in my dressing room after each opening night. And in the midst of those typically Parisian flowers stood the black form of the masked man. With his arms crossed, he said, 'Don't worry Christine. You are in no danger.'

"*It was the Voice.*

"I was both staggered and angry. I leaped for the mask and tried to tear it off, to see the face that went with the Voice. The man said, 'You are in no danger if you do not touch the mask.' And, seizing my hands gently, he made me sit down. Then he knelt before me and said nothing more.

"The humility of his gesture restored my courage. The light, by revealing everything around me, made life seem real again. As extraordinary as my adventure seemed, it was now surrounded by moral things that I could see and touch. The tapestries on the walls, the furniture, the torches, the vases, and even the flowers—I could almost identify what shop they came from in their golden baskets, and how much they had cost—all of these

---

¹¹ "Styx . . . Charon"
    The River Styx was said to wind nine times around Hades. It is the river that mortals must cross when they leave the land of the living for that of the dead. Charon is the ferryman to whom a coin must be given in payment for the one-way journey.

constrained my imagination within the limits of an ordinary sitting room like any other, which at least had the excuse that it was not situated in the bowels of the Opera. I was no doubt dealing with some frightful character who, mysteriously, lived in these basements, and who, like the others, had, out of need and with the silent complicity of the administration, found shelter in this modern Tower of Babel,[12] where they schemed and sang in all languages and made love in every dialect.

"And then there was *the Voice, the Voice* which I had recognized beneath the mask and that could not hide from me *and who was before me on his knees—a man*.

"I thought no longer about the horrible situation in which I found myself, nor did I wonder what was to become of me or what was the cold tyrannical design that had brought me to this living room to be incarcerated like a prisoner in a jail or a slave in a harem. 'No! No! No!' I said to myself. 'That's what the Voice is. It is a man!' and I began to cry.

"The man, still kneeling, evidently understood the meaning of my tears for he said, 'It's true, Christine! I am neither an angel nor a genie, nor a phantom. I am Erik.' "

Here, again, Christine's story was interrupted. It seemed to the young people that an echo behind them repeated "Erik." What echo? They turned and saw that night had come. Raoul made a movement as if to stand, but Christine kept him by her side, saying, "Stay. You need to know all—*here*."

"Why here, Christine? I'm afraid the night chill isn't good for you."

"We don't need to fear anything but the trapdoors, dear, and here we are away from the world of trapdoors. And I'm not allowed to see you away from the theater. This is no moment to cross him. Let's not rouse his suspicions."

"Christine, Christine! Something tells me that we are wrong to wait for tomorrow night and that we ought to get away tonight."

"I tell you that he'll be in agony if he doesn't hear me tomorrow night."

"If you run away from him forever, it will be hard not to cause Erik pain."

---

12 "Tower of Babel"

The story of the Tower of Babel is told in Genesis 11:1–9, where we learn that at one time all of mankind spoke the same language. But, in a prideful gesture, "they said, Go to, let us build us a city and a tower, whose top *may reach* unto heaven; and let us make us a name, lest we be scattered abroad upon the face of the whole earth. . . ." The Lord, seeing what they were up to said, "Go to, let us go down, and there confound their language, that they may not understand one another's speech." And that is why, to this day, there is such a multitude of languages spoken to this day. (King James transl.)

"You're right about that, Raoul. Because my flight will certainly kill him." In a muffled voice, she added, "But it's a balanced risk for both sides, because if we stay, he may kill us."

"He must really love you?"

"He would commit murder for me."

"But surely one can find where he lives. They can go looking for him. Now that we know that Erik is no phantom, he can be talked to and made to answer."

Christine shook her head. "No, no. There's nothing to be done against Erik, except to flee him."

"Then why, since you could run away, did you return to him?"

"Because it was necessary, and you'll understand that when you know how I got away from him."

"Ah, how I hate him," cried Raoul. "And you, Christine, I need to know so that I can keep myself calm as I hear the conclusion of this extraordinary love story—tell me, Christine, do you hate him?"

Christine replied simply, "No."

"And why so much talk? You must love him. All that fear and terror. All that is love of the most delectable kind. The kind one doesn't admit," said Raoul bitterly. "The kind that makes you shiver when you think about it. Just imagine, a man who lives in an underground palace," he sneered.

"Then you want me to go back there," Christine interrupted harshly. "Be careful, Raoul. I've told you. I'm never going back again."

A terrifying silence ensued among the three of them . . . the two who spoke and the shadow behind them who listened.

"Before I answer," Raoul said slowly, "I'd like to know what feeling you have about *him,* since you don't hate him."

"Horror," she said, flinging the word with such force that it drowned out the night's sighs. "What is dreadful," she began again increasingly feverish, "is that he horrified me, but I don't hate him. How can I hate him, Raoul? Imagine him at my feet in his home beside the underground lake. He blames himself, he curses himself, he implores my forgiveness!

"He admits his imposture. Tells me that he loves me. That he sets a great and tragic love at my feet. That he kidnapped me out of love. That he shut me in with him underground out of love. But he respects me. He grovels, he moans, he weeps. And when I get up, Raoul, when I tell him that I will only despise him unless he restores the freedom he took from me, why, incredibly, he offers me just that. I have only to leave. He's ready to show me the secret way. Only . . . only . . . he too is standing, and I am forced to recall that, if he is neither the Phantom nor a genie nor an angel, he is still the Voice. Because he sings. And I listen—and I stay.[13]

"That evening, we exchanged not a word. He took up a harp and began to sing with his man's voice, his angel's voice, the romance of Desdemona. He made me ashamed to remember that I, too, had sung it. My dear, there is a virtue in music that can make you feel that nothing of the external world exists except those sounds that strike the heart. Forgotten was my bizarre adventure. Only the voice existed, and intoxicated, I followed it on its harmonious voyage; I was one of Orpheus' flock.[14] The Voice led me through grief and joy, through martyrdom and despair, through delight, through death and triumphant marriages. I listened. It sang unknown fragments and made me hear new music that gave me a strange feeling of sweetness, of languor, of repose. . . . A music that, after it had exalted my soul, calmed it little by little and led it to the threshold of dreams. I fell asleep.

"When I woke, I was alone on a chaise longue in a small, simple room furnished with an ordinary mahogany bed. There were cretonne hangings on the wall. The room was lit by a lamp set on the marble top of an old Louis Philippe commode.[15]

---

[13] "and I stay"

We are now fully in the midst of what might be called the "spiritual testing" of Christine. And we notice that it is Erik's music, first, that persuades her to stay with him. Later, that music, by its transforming power, will help her to feel compassion for his ugliness.

[14] "Orpheus' flock"

This is a puzzling reference, since Orpheus is nowhere described as a shepherd. It perhaps refers to Orpheus' enchantment of the denizens in Hades; Christine is also fully enchanted here.

In some accounts, Orpheus is said to be the son of Apollo and Calliope, the muse of epic poetry. He was one of the original Argonauts, and his music was so powerful it literally moved their boat. It was also said to be capable of moving rocks and trees.

The part of his legend that is of special interest to us has to do with his wife Eurydice, who was bitten by a serpent and died. The grief-stricken Orpheus, armed with his lyre, descended into Hades, the netherworld. At the sound of his music, the wheel on which Ixion was stretched stopped its motion, Tantalus forgot his thirst, and the vulture desisted for a while from gnawing at Tityus' vitals (see Chapter IV, Note 3, page 62,). Pluto and Persephone, the king and queen of Hades, gave Orpheus permission to take his wife back to the land of the living, but on the condition that he not look back at her on their way up. Like Lot's wife, he did look back, and the result was equally fatal. Eurydice vanished at once and could not to be retrieved a second time.

The usual account of Orpheus' death is that he was torn to pieces by Thracian women at a Bacchic festival because, maddened by his second loss of Eurydice, he ignored the women in the throes of their passion. His limbs were scattered, but his head was thrown into the Hebrus River, where it floated down to the sea. From there it was cast ashore on the island of Lesbos, where it was buried.

[15] "Louis Philippe commode"

Louis Philippe decor was stylish during the reign of Louis Philippe (1830–48). The furniture and furnishings were highly decorative, but, says The Penguin Dictionary of Decorative Arts, it was "heavier, gaudier and distinctly more bourgeois" than the Restoration style that preceded it. (John Fleming and Hugh Honour, The Penguin Dictionary of Decorative Arts. London: A. Lane, 1977.)

"What was this new setting? I passed my hand across my forehead as if to chase away a bad dream. Alas. It was not long before I realized I had not been dreaming! I was a prisoner and could not leave except to go into a most comfortable bathroom—with hot and cold water at will. When I came back to my room, I found on the commode a note written in red ink which informed me completely about my sad situation and which, had I needed to be told, would have removed all my doubts about the reality of these events.

'My dear Christine [said the note]
Let me reassure you about your fate. You have no one in the world who is a better or more respectful friend than I am. For the moment, you are alone in this house which belongs to you. I have gone out to do some shopping for such linens as you may need.'

" 'Clearly, I've fallen into the hands of a madman,' I cried. 'What's to become of me? And how long does this unhappy man think he's going to keep me locked up in his underground prison?'

"I ran around the little apartment like a madwoman, trying unsuccessfully to find a way out. I blamed myself bitterly for having been stupidly superstitious, and I took a dreadful pleasure in railing at the perfect innocence with which I had welcomed the Voice as the Guardian Angel of Music when I heard him through the walls. When one is as stupid as I had been, one could expect the most incredible disasters and deserve them all. I wanted to kick myself; I started both to laugh at and then to cry for myself. It was in this condition that Erik found me.

"Having knocked three times sharply, he came quietly through a door that I had been unable to find, and that he had left open. He was carrying boxes and packages, which he hastily put down on my bed while I heaped insults on him and demanded that he take off his mask if he had any pretension of hiding behind it the face of an honorable man. He replied calmly, 'You will never see Erik's face.'

"And he scolded me for not having finished dressing so late in the day and deigned to inform me that it was two o'clock in the afternoon. He would give me half an hour in which to do it. Having said that, he took care to wind and reset my watch. After that, he invited me to go into the dining room, where, he said, an excellent lunch awaited us. I was very hungry. I shut the door in his face and went into the bathroom. I took a bath after placing a magnificent set of scissors nearby with which I had decided to kill myself if Erik, after having behaved like a madman, stopped conducting himself like a man of honor. The coolness of the water did me a world of good, and when I appeared again before Erik, I made the wise resolution not to offend him, or to ruffle his pride in any way, and to flatter him if necessary to get him to let me go soon. It was he who spoke to me first about his plans for me, explaining them to reassure me, he said. He liked my company too much to deprive himself of it so soon, as he had agreed to do on the previous evening when he had seen my expression of fear and indignation. He wanted me to now understand that I had no need to be frightened by his near presence. He loved me, but he wouldn't say that again without my permission. As for the rest of our time, that would be devoted to music.

" 'What do you mean by "the rest of our time?" ' I asked.

" 'Five days,' he said firmly.

" 'And I'll be free after that?'

" 'You will be free, Christine, because when those five days have gone by, you will have learned not to be afraid of me anymore, and then you'll come back to see poor Erik from time to time.'

"The tone in which he pronounced those last words moved me deeply. It seemed to me that I could detect such real, such pitiable despair in it that I looked up at the mask with a softened expression. Not being able to see the eyes behind it in no way diminished the strange feeling of discomfort I had putting questions to that strange bit of black silk. But, at the edge of the mask's beard, there appeared one, two, three, four tears. Silently, he pointed out a seat facing him beside a small table in the center of the room where, on the previous evening, he had played the harp for me. Very troubled, I sat down. Just the same, I ate with a good appetite:[16] a few crayfish, a chicken wing washed down with a bit of Tokay wine[17] that, he told me, he had himself bought at the Koenigsberg cellars, which had been frequented in the past by Falstaff.[18] As for him, he neither ate

---

[16] "I ate with good appetite"

Here is an endearing as well as an astonishing moment in our fiction. Christine has been kidnapped by an unknown masked man. She is his prisoner in an underground room, and she has just learned that he intends to keep her with him for five days. Just a few moments ago, she bathed, but took the precaution to have a pair of scissors nearby in case she needed to save her honor by committing suicide. Now, unphased by her terrifying experience, and with the healthy appetite of youth, she downs an excellent meal. The only meal in this novel, let it be said, about which we have any details.

[17] "Tokay wine"

A dark, gold-colored unfortified sweet dessert wine whose name comes from the town of Tokaj in Hungary.

[18] "Falstaff"

nor drank. I asked him what his nationality was and whether the name Erik did not indicate a Scandinavian origin. He replied that he had neither name nor country, and that he had taken the name Erik by chance. I asked him why, if he loved me, he could not have found some better way to let me know it than dragging me off and imprisoning me underground.

" 'It's very hard to make yourself loved in a tomb,' I said.

"In a strange tone he said, 'One makes what rendezvous one can.'

"Then he rose and put out his arm because, he said, he wanted to do the honors of his apartment for me, but I pulled my hand back and uttered a cry. What I had touched was both wet and bony, and I remembered that his hands smelled of death.

" 'Oh, I beg your pardon,' he groaned. And he opened a door in front of me. 'Here's my room,' he said. 'It's curious enough to deserve a visit. Would you like to see it?'

"I did not hesitate at all. His manners, his words—everything about him told me to trust him. Besides, I felt that I did not need to be afraid.

"I went in. It seemed to me that I had entered a room in a mortuary. The walls were hung in black, but instead of the white tears which ordinarily decorate such funereal ornaments, there was an enormous musical staff on which she repeated notes of the *Dies Irae*[19] were written. In the middle of the room there was a canopy over which red brocade curtains

---

Prince Hal's jolly, fat and roistering friend, the "tutor and the feeder of [his] riots" who appears in Shakespeare's *Henry IV, Parts 1 and 2,* and in *The Merry Wives of Windsor.* In a famous "I know thee not, old man" speech at the end of *Henry IV, Part 2,* Falstaff is spurned by the newly responsible Hal, who has just become King Henry.

The realism of this scene only emphasizes the fact that Christine, in Erik's presence, grows and matures in the here-and-now.

[19] *"Dies Irae"*

The Latin words mean "day of wrath," which is part of the Catholic Requiem Mass. The two opening stanzas read:

Dies irae, dies illa
Solvet saeclum in favilla:
Teste David cum Sibylla.

Quantus tremor est futurus,
Quando judex est venturus,
Cuncta stricte discussurus!

Day of wrath and terror looming,
Heaven and earth to ash consuming:
Seer's and Psalmist's true foredooming!

Ah, what agony of trembling,
When the Judge, mankind assembling,
Probeth all beyond dissembling

hung, and under the canopy there stood an open casket. At sight of it, I stepped back.

" 'I sleep in that,' said Erik. 'One has to get used to everything in this life, even to eternity.'

"The sight of the coffin made such a sinister impression on me that I turned my head away. What I saw then was the keyboard of an organ that occupied the entire length of a wall. On a music stand there was a notebook splattered all over with musical notes in red ink. I asked for permission to look at it, and I read the first page: *Don Juan Triumphant*.[20]

" 'Yes,' he said, "I compose sometimes. It's been twenty years since I began this work. When it's done, I'll take it with me into my coffin and will never wake again.'

" 'Then you should work at it as little as possible,' I said.

" 'I work at it sometimes for fifteen days and fifteen nights without respite, during which time I live on nothing but music. After that, I rest for years.'

" 'Will you play me something from your *Don Juan Triumphant*?' I asked, thinking to please him by showing that I had overcome my repugnance at being in this room of death.

" 'Never ask me to do that,' he replied somberly. 'This *Don Juan* was not written to go with the words of Don Lorenzo Da Ponte,[21] inspired by wine and the trivial loves and vices that God finally punishes. I'll play you Mozart, if you like, Christine, to start your lovely tears flowing and inspire you with honorable thoughts. But my *Don Juan* sears, Christine, and yet he is not struck down by the fires of Heaven."

"With that, we went back into the living room we had just left. I noticed that there were no mirrors anywhere in this apartment. I was going to comment on this, but Erik sat down at the piano just then. He said, 'You see, Christine, there is a music that is so horrifying that it consumes all those who come near it. Luckily for you, you have not yet experienced it, because it would make you lose your fresh coloring and no one would recognize you on your return to Paris. Let's sing opera songs, Christine Daaé.'

"He said, 'Let's sing opera songs' as if he were spewing insults at

---

[20] *"Don Juan Triumphant"*

See the discussion of *Don Giovanni* in Chapter VIII, Note 26, page 120, and in the Introduction.

[21] *"Don Lorenzo Da Ponte"*

Lorenzo Da Ponte (1749–1838), an Italian poet, wrote the libretto for Mozart's *Don Giovanni*. After working in Vienna, where he churned out libretti for other composers, his life took a sudden downward turn. He lived for a while in New York where, unsuccessfully, he sold tobacco and liquor. His last years were spent teaching Italian at Columbia College.

me.[22] But I had no time to dwell on his manner of speech. We at once began the duet from *Otello*[23] and were engrossed in its disaster. This time, he left Desdemona's role to me, and I sang it with a despair and real fear such as I had never achieved until then. Instead of annihilating me, the near presence of such a partner inspired me with a magnificent terror. The events of which I was the victim brought me strangely near to the thoughts of the poet, and I reached notes that would have dazzled the composer. As for Erik, his voices was like thunder. Each sound was affected by his vengeful soul, which frightfully augmented its power. Love, jealousy, hate, burst from us in narrowing cries. Erik's black mask made me think of the natural mask of the Moor of Venice. He was Othello himself. I believed that he would strike me and that I would fall beneath his blows. And yet, like the timid Desdemona, I made no effort to escape him to avoid his fury. On the contrary, I was fascinated and drawn near to him, finding it charming to die at the center of such passion, but before dying I wanted to know—so that I might carry it with me into death—the sublime image of those unknown features that the fires of eternal art must have transformed.[24] It was the face of *the Voice* that I wanted to see, and so, instinctively, and with a gesture that I did not control, my quick fingers plucked off the mask.

"Oh, horror! horror! horror!"

Here Christine paused, as if repelling with both trembling hands the memory of that sight while the night echoes, just as they had repeated Erik's name, repeated three times, "Horrror! Horror! Horror!" Raoul and Christine, more firmly united by the terror of her tale, lifted their eyes toward the stars shining in a pure calm sky. Raoul said, "It's strange, Christine, how a night as calm and sweet as this one can be filled with groans. It is as if the night were grieving for itself—and us."

---

[22] "as if he were spewing insults at me"

We get some sense of Erik's contempt for the contemporary opera-going public's taste by this sarcastic comment.

[23] "*Otello*"

We may have here another of Leroux's lapses. The music for this opera was written by Giuseppe Verdi, the libretto by Arigo Boito. It was performed in Garnier's opera on October 12, 1894. It had its first performance in Milan at the La Scala opera in 1887, six years *after* the time in which, as I have suggested in the Introduction, the action of this novel takes place.

[24] "the sublime image of those unknown features that the fires of eternal art must have transformed."

This entire, extraordinary paragraph stands at the thematic center of the novel. First, it is written at a pitch of exaltation unmatched anywhere else in the book, and then, in letters of fire, it reveals the passionate masochism of Christine's sensibility. She is a woman who would make no effort to avoid Othello's blows, but rather would "find it charming to die at the center of such passion." Finally, she believes, with Leroux, in the transforming power of art. The face she expects to see under the mask is sublime. In the face of such vehemence, what has poor Raoul to offer?

"Now that you're going to know the secret," she said, "your ears, like mine, will resound with lamentations." With a convulsive shudder, she seized Raoul's protective hands and went on, "Oh! If I were to live for a hundred years, I would still hear the superhuman cry he gave—that cry of pain and infernal rage, while what was to be seen appeared before my eyes, which were opened wide with horror, as was my mouth, which, though it was gaping, was unable to utter a sound.

"Oh Raoul, the thing that I saw. How can I not stop seeing it? If my ears are forever filled with his cries, my eyes are forever haunted by the sight of his face. What a sight! How can I stop seeing it and how can I make you see it? Raoul, you have seen skulls that have dried over centuries, and it may be, if you were not a victim of a dreadful nightmare, that you saw his skull that night at Perros. And you also saw the 'Red Death' walking about at the masked ball. But all those skulls were immobile and their mute horror was not alive. But imagine, if you can, the mask of Death with its four black holes that are its eyes and nose and mouth coming suddenly to life to express the sovereign anger of the devil. And no expression coming from its eye sockets for, as I later learned, his fiery eyes can only be seen in the dark. I must have been flattened against the wall by the very image of Horror, just as he represented all that is hideous.

"Then he came near me, frightfully gnashing his lipless teeth, and as I fell to my knees, he whispered hateful, incoherent things to me, disordered words, curses, delirious phrases. Who knows what he said? Who knows?

"Bent over me, he cried, 'Look! You wanted to see. See! Feast your eyes, make your soul drunk with my cursed ugliness. Look at Erik's face! Now you know. It was not enough for you to hear me. You wanted to know what I was made of? You women are so curious.' And he began to laugh as he repeated, 'You women are so curious.' A laugh that was menacing, hoarse, foaming with rage. He continued to say such things as, 'Are you satisfied? I'm handsome, eh? When a woman has seen me—as you have—she becomes mine. She loves me forever. I'm a real Don Juan.' And, straightening up, he put his hand on his hip, and with the hideous thing that was his head wobbling on his shoulders, he thundered, 'Look at me! *I'm Don Juan triumphant.*'

"And, as I turned my head away, pleading for mercy, he drew it brutally back to him by my hair, which he clutched with his dead fingers."

"Enough! Enough!" Raoul interrupted. "I'll kill him. I'll kill him. In God's name, Christine, tell me where that *dining room by the lake* is. I must kill him."

"Oh, Raoul. Hush, then, if you want to know."

"Ah, yes. I want to know how and why you went back to him. That's where the secret lies. Take care that there is no other.[25] But, in any case, I'll kill him."

"Oh, Raoul, listen, since you want to know. Listen. He dragged me by the hair and then . . . and then . . . oh, it's still more horrible."

"Well, then, tell me, now," said Raoul fiercely. "At once."

"Well, he whispered to me, 'What? I'm frightening you. Is that it? You think perhaps that I have another mask, eh? And that . . . that this head is a mask. Very well, then. Pull it off like the other one. Come on. Come on. Again, again. I want you to. Give me your hands. If they're not enough for you, I'll lend you mine, and we'll put them together to tear that mask off.' I rolled at his feet, but he seized my hands, Raoul . . . and pushed them onto the horror of his face. He scratched his flesh, that horrible dead flesh with my fingernails.

" 'Learn! Learn!' he shouted from the depths of a throat that panted like a bellows. 'Learn that I am made entirely of death. From head to toe. And that it's a cadaver that loves you, that adores you, and that will never leave you. Never, never. I'll enlarge the coffin, Christine. For later on, when we have come to the end of our loves. There, you see that I'm no longer laughing. I'm weeping for you, Christine, who tore off my mask, and who, therefore, will never be able to leave me. So long as you could believe me handsome, you would have come back to me. I know you would have come back. But now that you know me to be hideous, you will flee from me forever. I'll keep you!!! And then, why did you want to see me? Foolish, mad Christine, who wanted to see me . . . when my father himself never saw me, and when my mother, in order not to see me anymore, wept as she gave me a mask for my first present.'[26]

"He had finally let me go and was dragging himself across the floor, sobbing dreadfully. And then, writhing like a reptile, he crawled away to his own room, whose door closed behind him, and I remained alone, left with my horror and my reflections, but rid of the sight of the thing.

"A long silence, the silence of the tomb, followed on that tempest,

---

[25] "that there is no other"

With the scene still charged with the stupendous emotion generated by the tale Christine has just told, Raoul's threatening jealousy is as unseemly as it is trivial.

[26] "my mother . . . wept as she gave me a mask for my first present"

In the made-for-television film *The Phantom of the Opera,* starring Burt Lancaster as Erik's father, Erik's mother is said to have been so maternally love-besotted that she did not know her child was monstrous.

and I was able to consider the terrible consequences of the gesture that had plucked off the mask. The monster's last words had made them sufficiently clear. I had imprisoned myself forever and my curiosity would be the cause of all my sorrows. He had given me sufficient warning. He had said over and over again that I was in no danger as long as I did not touch the mask. And I had touched it. I cursed my imprudence, but I realized, shuddering, that the monster's reasoning was logical. Yes, I would have come back if I hadn't seen his face. I had already been moved by him. Because he had roused my interest in him and, with the tears he shed behind his mask, he had made me pity him, I would not have stayed insensitive to his plea. Finally, I was not an ingrate, and his impossible situation could not make me forget that he was the Voice and that it had awakened me with his genius. I would have come back! And now, if I got out of these catacombs, I would certainly not go back! One does not return to lock oneself in a tomb with a corpse that loves you.

"In certain of the deranged ways he had of looking at me, during that last scene, or rather, of turning the two black holes of his invisible gaze on me, I had been able to judge the savagery of his passion. In order to avoid taking me into his arms—though I could not have offered him any resistance—it had been necessary for the monster to play the role of an angel, which, to some small degree, he might have been. After all, he was the Guardian Angel of Music, and he might have been entirely an angel if God had clothed him in beauty instead of filth.

"Made frantic by the thought of the fate that awaited me, and terrified that I might see his door opening and see again the monster's unmasked face, I crept into my own room, where I seized a pair of scissors with which to put an end to my dreadful destiny, when I heard the sounds of an organ.

"It was then, dear, that I began to understand Erik's contemptuous words for what he called 'opera music'—a contempt that had stupefied me. What I heard now had nothing to do with the sort of music that had charmed me until that day. His *Don Juan Triumphant* (and there was no doubt in my mind that he had immersed himself in his masterpiece in order to forget the horror of the present); his *Don Juan Triumphant* seemed to me to be nothing but a long, terrible, and magnificent sob into which poor Erik had put all of his cursed misery.

"I saw again the notebook with its red notes, and it was easy for me to imagine that the notes had been written in blood. That music showed me martyrdom in every detail; it led me into every part of the abyss, the abyss in which *a loathsome man* lived. It showed me Erik beating his poor

182

hideous head against the funereal walls of that hell, and taking refuge there so that he could avoid terrifying men by the sight of him. I watched, devastated, gasping, pitying, and overwhelmed by the swelling of those gigantic chords where Sorrow had been deified. And then there were sounds that rose from the abyss and, gathered together, made a prodigious and menacing flight forming a whirling troop that seemed to mount upward toward heaven as the eagle rises to the sun. Such a triumphal symphony seemed to set the world ablaze so that I understood the work was finally finished and Ugliness, lifted on the winds of Love, had dared to look into the face of Beauty. It was as though I were drunk.

"The door that separated me from Erik yielded to my efforts and opened. He rose when he heard me come in, *but he did not dare to turn toward me.*

" 'Erik,' I cried, 'show me your face without fear. I swear to you that you are the unhappiest and the most sublime of men, and if Christine Daaé ever shudders again when she looks at you, it will be because she will be thinking of the splendor of your genius.'

"Then Erik turned around, for he believed me, and I did, too, alas. I had faith in myself. He raised his fleshless hands toward Destiny and fell at my knees with words of love.

"With words of love in that mouth of Death. And the music stopped.

"He kissed the hem of my robe; he did not see that my eyes were closed.

"What more can I tell you, dear? Now you know the tragedy. It was renewed daily, for fifteen days. Fifteen days during which I lied to him. My lie was as hideous as the monster who inspired it, and it was what I paid for my liberty. I burned his mask. And I succeeded so well that though he no longer sang, he risked begging for a look from me, the way a timid dog moves around his master. That's how he was around me, like a faithful slave surrounding me with a thousand attentions. Little by little I inspired him with so much confidence that he dared take me for walks along the banks of the Lake Avernus[27] and to row me in a boat upon its leaden waters. In the final days of my captivity, he took me at night through the gates that close the underground passage that leads to the Rue Scribe. There, a coach awaited us and drove us through the solitudes of the Bois de Boulogne.

---

[27] "Lake Avernus"

A lake believed by the Greeks to be the entrance to Hades because of the sulfurous fumes rising from it.

"The night on which we met you was nearly a tragic one for me, because he is terribly jealous of you. I could only fight it by assuring him that you were going to leave the country soon. Finally, after two weeks of this abominable captivity in the course of which, turn and turn about, I was filled with pity, enthusiasm, despair, and horror, he believed me when I told him, *'I will return.'*"

"And you did return," groaned Raoul.

"That's true, dear, and I must say it was not the frightful threats that accompanied my being set free which helped me to keep my word, but the heartbreaking sob that he gave on the threshold of his tomb.

"Yes, that sob," Christine repeated, shaking her head sadly, "bound me more to the unhappy man than I myself realized at the time of our good-byes. Poor Erik. Poor Erik!"

"Christine," said Raoul, getting up, "you say that you love me, but several hours went by after you recovered your freedom, and yet you went back to Erik. Remember the masked ball!"

"That's what we agreed to. . . . Remember, too, that I passed those few hours with you, at great peril to both of us."

"During those few hours I doubted that you loved me."

"Do you still have doubts, Raoul? Know then that each of my visits to Erik has only increased my horror of him. Because each of my visits, instead of appeasing him as I hoped, has made him fall even more madly in love. And I'm afraid! I'm afraid! I'm afraid!"

"You're afraid. But do you love me? If Erik were handsome, would you love me, Christine?"

"Unhappy man! Why do you tempt destiny? Why do you ask me about things that I hide deep in my conscience the way I would hide a sin."[28] She got to her feet and trembling, put her lovely arms around the young man, saying "Oh, my fiancé of a single day, if I did not love you, I would not give you my lips. For the first and last time, take them."

He took them, but the surrounding night was so violently ripped apart that they fled as if at the approach of a storm. Before they disappeared into the forest of timbers, their eyes, in which the dread of Erik dwelt, showed them a night bird that seemed to be perched on the strings of Apollo's lyre and looked down at them with glazing eyes.

---

[28] "hide a sin"

There is a sublimity in Christine's reply, both for what it shows about the depths of her self-knowledge and the courage it takes to acknowledge the truth to a man as emotionally immature as Raoul.

Chapter XIV

A Trapdoor Lover's Masterstroke

Raoul and Christine ran and ran, fleeing from the roof where were the fiery eyes that could only be seen in the dark of night, and they did not stop until they reached the eighth level, as they made their way toward the ground.

Because there was no performance that evening, the corridors of the Opera were deserted. Suddenly a bizarre silhouette rose before them, barring their path. "No. Not this way." And the silhouette pointed out another corridor that would take them to the winds. Raoul would have stopped to ask for an explanation. "Go, go quickly," commanded the vague form that was enveloped in a greatcoat and wore a peaked hat.

Christine, tugging at Raoul, forced him to keep running. "But who is that? Who is that fellow?" the young man asked.

And Christine replied, "It's the Persian."

"What's he doing there?" he said.

"Nobody knows. He's always in the Opera."

"What you're making me do is cowardly, Christine," said Raoul, who was profoundly upset. "You're making me run away for the first time in my life."

"I think," replied Christine, who was beginning to calm down, "that we're running away from an imagined shadow."

"If that really was Erik we saw, I should have nailed him to Apollo's lyre the way they nail owls to the wall on Breton farms, and that would have been the end of that."

"But first, dear Raoul, you would have had to climb to Apollo's lyre; and that's not an easy matter."

"The blazing eyes made it up there, all right."

"Now you're like me, ready to see him everywhere, and then later, thinking it over, you say, 'What I took to be his blazing eyes was nothing more, no doubt, than the golden points of two stars looking at the town through the strings of the lyre.'"

Christine descended another flight and Raoul followed. He said, "Since you've decided to leave, Christine, let me say it would be better to leave at once. Why wait until tomorrow? Perhaps he heard us tonight."

"Oh, no, no. I tell you again, he's working on his *Don Juan Triumphant* and he's not concerned with us."

"You're so unsure that you keep looking behind you."

"Let's go to my dressing room."

"Let's meet, rather, outside the Opera."

"No. Not until the very moment of our escape. Not keeping my word will only bring us trouble. I promised him that I would not see you anywhere but here."

"Lucky for me that he even allowed you that. Do you know," said Raoul bitterly, "that you were extremely audacious to play our engagement game."

"But darling, he knows about it. He said, 'I trust you, Christine. M. Raoul de Chagny is in love with you and should go away. Before he leaves, let him be as miserable as I am.'"

"And what, pray, does that mean?"

"I'm the one who should be asking you, dear. Is someone who is in love miserable?"

"Yes, Christine. When one loves and is not sure of being loved."

"Are you saying that on Erik's account?"

"On his and on my own," said the unhappy young man, shaking his head thoughtfully.

They reached Christine's room. "How can you believe yourself to be safer here than in the theater?" Raoul asked. "If you can hear him through the walls, then he can hear us."

"No. He gave me his word that he would not be behind the walls of my dressing room again, and I rely on Erik's word. My dressing room and my room in the *apartment beside the lake* are exclusively mine and sacred to him.''

"How were you able to get out of this dressing room so that you could be taken away through the dark corridor? Shall we try repeating your movements? Do you want to?''

"It's dangerous, dear, because the mirror might take me away again, and then, instead of running off with you, I'd have to go to the end of the secret passage that leads to the banks of the lake to call for Erik.''

"Would he hear you?''

"He'll hear me no matter where I am when I call. He himself told me so. He's an unusual genius. One shouldn't think, Raoul, that this is simply a man who amuses himself by living underground. He does things that no other man can do. He knows things that are unknown to the rest of the living world.''

"Be careful, Christine. You're turning him into a phantom again.''

"No, he's not a phantom. He's a man of heaven and earth, that's all.''

"A man of heaven and earth . . . that's all. Listen to you talk! And you're still determined to run away from him?''

"Yes, tomorrow.''

"Can I tell you why I would like to see you do it tonight?''

"Tell me, dear.''

"Because tomorrow you won't have your mind made up about anything.''

"Then, Raoul, you'll take me away by force. Isn't that understood?''

"Tomorrow night, then. Here. I'll be in your dressing room tomorrow night at midnight,'' the young man said solemnly. "Whatever happens, I'll keep my promise. You say that, after he's seen the performance, he'll wait for you in the *lake dining room*.''

"That's where he's arranged to meet me.''

"And how are you supposed to get there, Christine, if you don't know how to get out of your dressing room through the mirror?

"Why, by going directly to the lake.''

"Passing through all those levels. Through stairways and corridors that stagehands and workmen use. How could you get there secretly? Everyone would follow Christine Daaé, and she would arrive at the shore of the lake with a whole crowd behind her.''

Christine took an enormous key out of a jewel chest and showed it to Raoul.

"What's this?'' he said.

"It's the key to the underground gate on the Rue Scribe."

"I understand, Christine. It leads directly to the lake. Let me have the key, will you?"

"Never," she replied with conviction. "That would be a betrayal."

Suddenly Raoul saw that Christine had changed color. A deathly pallor spread over her face. "Oh, my God," she cried. "Erik! Erik! Have mercy on me."

"Hush," commanded Raoul. "Haven't you told me that he can hear you?"

But the singer's manner became more and more inexplicable. She twisted her fingers as she repeated distractedly, "Oh, my God. Oh, my God."

"But what is it? What is it?" Raoul implored.

"The ring."

"Which ring? Please, Christine, get a grip on yourself."

"The gold ring he gave me."

"Oh, he's the one who gave you the gold ring."

"You know that, Raoul! But what you don't know is what he told me when he gave it to me. He said, 'I'll give you back your freedom, Christine, but on condition that this ring be always on your finger. As long as you keep it, you will be safe from all danger and Erik will be your friend. But woe unto you if you ever part with it, Christine.' Oh, Raoul, Raoul. The ring isn't on my finger. This is dreadful for us both."

It was in vain that they searched for the ring. They did not find it. Christine could not calm down. "It was when I gave you that kiss, up there, beneath Apollo's lyre," she tried to explain, trembling. "The ring must have slipped from my finger and fallen into the street. How can we find it now? And what danger menaces us, Raoul? Ah, let's run away, away."

"At once," Raoul insisted again.

She hesitated. He thought she was going to say "Yes." Then, her clear eyes grew troubled, and she said, "No, tomorrow."

Completely disordered, she left him abruptly, still wringing her hands as if she hoped that the ring would thus reappear.

As for Raoul, he went back home, very worried by all that he had heard.

In his room, as he was getting ready for bed, he said aloud, "If I don't save her from the hands of this charlatan, she will be lost. But I will save her."

He extinguished the lamp and, in the dark, felt the need to hurt Erik. Three times he cried aloud, "Fraud! Fraud! Fraud!" But suddenly he raised himself up on an elbow; a cold sweat ran down his temples. Two eyes, burning like embers, had just glowed at the foot of his bed. They stared horribly at him in the dark.

Raoul was a brave young man, but just the same, he trembled. He reached his arm out, felt hesitantly, uncertainly around on his bedside table. When he found the box of matches, he lit one. The eyes disappeared.

Not reassured at all, he thought, "She said that his eyes could not be seen except in the dark. They disappeared when I struck a light. But *he* may still be here."

He got up and searched carefully, looking at everything. Like a child, he looked under his bed. And then he thought himself ridiculous. Aloud, he said, "What can I believe? What shall I *not* believe in this fairy tale? Where does reality end and fantasy begin?[1] What did she see? What did she believe she saw?" And, trembling, he added, "And me! What did I see? Did I really see those blazing eyes a while ago? Were they blazing only in my imagination? See how I'm no longer sure of anything. I would not swear to having seen those eyes."

He went back to bed. Again, it was dark. The eyes reappeared. "Oh," Raoul sighed.

He sat up and stared back at them as bravely as he could. After a silence spent restoring his courage, he called out suddenly, "Is it you, Erik? Man, genius, or phantom? Is it you?"

He thought a bit. "If it's he, he's on the balcony."

Still in his nightshirt, he ran to a little table on which he felt about and found his revolver. Armed, he opened the French windows. The night was extremely chilly. Raoul glanced quickly at the deserted balcony, then came back in, closing the door. Shivering, he went back to bed with the revolver within reach on the night table. Once again, he blew out the candle.

The eyes at the foot of his bed were still there. Were they between the bed and the glass in the window, or behind it—that is, on the balcony? That's what Raoul wanted to know. He wanted to know, too, whether those eyes belonged to a human being. He wanted to know everything.

---

[1] "Where does reality end and fantasy begin?"

Raoul is given a moment of self-consciousness about the relationship between being and perception which is one of the thematic threads that runs through this work. But Leroux's larger theme, as we find it more complexly developed in the relationship between Christine and Erik, is how being and perception are mediated by the creative imagination.

Then, patiently, coldly, without disturbing the night that surrounded him, the young man took his revolver and aimed.

He aimed at the two stars that continued to gaze at him with a singularly immobile brightness. He aimed a little bit above them. Certainly, if those stars were eyes, and if above them there was a forehead, and if Raoul was not too clumsy . . .

The explosion made a dreadful racket in the peacefully sleeping house. And, as steps could be heard in the hallways, Raoul, who sat up, his arm outstretched and ready to shoot again, saw . . . that this time, the two stars had disappeared.

There were lights and people. A dreadfully anxious Count Philippe asked, "What's going on, Raoul?"

"What's going on is that I must have been dreaming," the young man replied. "I shot at a couple of stars that kept me from getting to sleep."

"Are you out of your mind? Are you sick? I beg you, Raoul, tell me what happened," and he took possession of the revolver.

"No, no. I'm in my right mind. Beyond that, we'll find out." He got up, put on a robe and his slippers, took a light from a servant and, opening the French windows, went back out on the balcony.

The count had noticed that there was a bullet hole in the window at a man's height. Raoul, on the balcony, was bent over something with his candle. "Oh, oh," he said. "Blood . . . blood. Here, there. More blood.[2] So much the better. A phantom who bleeds is less dangerous." He laughed.

"Raoul, Raoul, Raoul." The count shook him as if he wanted to shake a sleepwalker out of a dangerous sleep.

Impatiently, Raoul protested, "But Philippe, I'm not asleep. You can see the blood, as anyone else can. I thought I was dreaming and shot at a couple of stars. They were Erik's eyes, and here you have his blood."

Suddenly anxious, he added, "Maybe I was wrong to shoot and Christine may not forgive me for it. None of this would have happened if I had taken the precaution of lowering the window curtain when I went to sleep."

"Raoul, have you suddenly gone mad? Wake up."

"Are you at it again? You'd do better, Philippe, to help me look for Erik. After all, a phantom who bleeds can be found."

The count's valet said, "It's true, sir. There's blood on the balcony."

A servant brought a lamp bright enough for them to examine every-

---

[2] "more blood"

We never learn whether this night visitor really was Erik or not. Certainly, if it was Erik, no mention is ever made of his having sustained a wound.

thing. The traces of blood followed the balcony rail to a drainpipe, then up the drainpipe. "It was a cat you shot, Raoul."

"The trouble is," Raoul said with a laugh that sounded sorrowful in his brother's ears, "that it's quite possible. With Erik, one never knows. Is it Erik? Is it a cat? Is it the Phantom? Is it flesh or shadow? No! No! With Erik, one never knows."

Raoul went on to make such bizarre remarks, which were intimately and logically related to what preoccupied his mind, and which followed naturally on the strange confidences—at once real and supernatural—that Christine had made. But such remarks had much to do with persuading many people that the young man's mind was deranged. The count, too, was affected by them, and on the police commissary's report, the examining magistrate came easily to the same conclusion. "Who is Erik?" the count inquired, pressing his brother's hand.

"He's my rival, and if he's not dead I'll be sorry." He sent the servants away with a wave of his hand. The door closed again on the brothers. But the departure of the servants was not so quick that the count's valet did not manage to hear Raoul saying clearly and forcefully, "I'm going to run off with Christine Daaé tonight." Later on, that sentence was repeated to the examining magistrate, Faure. But no one ever knew exactly what the brothers said to each other in the course of that encounter.

The servants said later that it wasn't the first quarrel they had behind locked doors. They spoke of shouts heard through the walls, and always the quarrel was over an actress named Christine Daaé.

At breakfast, which the count had served to him in his study, Philippe asked that his brother be sent for. Raoul came, gloomy and silent. The encounter was brief.

The COUNT: Read this.

(PHILIPPE hands his brother a newspaper, *L'Epoque*. He points to the following item.)

(The VISCOUNT reluctantly reads): The latest news in the suburbs: an engagement has been announced between Mlle. Christine Daaé, a singer, and the Viscount Raoul de Chagny. If the gossip in theater circles is to be believed, Count Philippe would have sworn that the de Chagnys, for the first time, would not honor a commitment. But, since love, at the Opera as well as elsewhere, is all powerful, one may ask just what means does the count have at his command to prevent the viscount, his brother, from conducting the "New Marguerite" to the altar. It is said that the brothers are very close, but the count is strangely mistaken if he hopes that fraternal affection will triumph over true love.

The COUNT: (sadly) Do you see, Raoul? You're making us look ridiculous. That little one has completely addled your brain with her ghost stories. (Evidently the viscount had told his brother Christine's story.)

The VISCOUNT: Good-bye, Philippe.

The COUNT: It's understood, then? You're leaving tonight? (The viscount does not reply) With her?: You're not going to do anything that stupid? (The viscount is silent.) I'll find a way to stop you.

The VISCOUNT: Good-bye, Philippe. (He goes.)

That scene was described to the examining magistrate by the count himself, who would not see his brother again except at the Opera a few minutes before Christine disappeared that evening.

Raoul had indeed devoted the entire day to preparations for their flight. The horses, the carriage, the necessary money, the route they would take— to throw the Phantom off the track, they would not take the train. All of that kept him busy until nine o'clock that night.

At nine o'clock, a sort of berlin with curtains drawn across heremetically sealed doors drew up in the line of carriages outside the rotunda. It was drawn by two sturdy horses that were driven by a coachman whose features were hard to make out, muffled as they were in the folds of a long scarf. There were three coaches ahead of the berlin. Later, the magistrate established that they belonged to Carlotta, who had suddenly come back to Paris; to Sorelli; and, the coach at the head of the line, to the Count de Chagny. No one stepped out of the berlin. The coachman stayed in his seat and the three other coachmen stayed likewise in theirs.

A shadow enveloped in a black greatcoat and wearing a black hat of soft felt passed by on the sidewalk between the rotunda and the coaches. The shadow seemed to consider the berlin with greater care. It approached the horses, then the coachman, then it left without saying a word. Later, the investigation concluded that this shadow was that of the Viscount Raoul de Chagny. As for me, I don't believe it, since on that evening, as on all the others, the Viscount de Chagny was wearing a top hat, which was later found. I think rather than the shadow belonged to the Phantom, who was informed of everything, as we will see shortly.

As it happened, they were playing *Faust* that evening before a most splendid audience. High society was magnificently represented. In those days, subscribers did not lend, or lease, or sublease, or share their boxes with financiers, businessmen, or foreigners. Nowadays in the box of the Marquis So-and-so, which is still called "The Box of the Marquis of So-and-so" because, according to the contract, the box is his—in that box, let us say, are sprawled a salt pork merchant and his family, which is the salt pork merchant's right because he has paid for the marquis' box. In the old days, such customs were practically unknown. Boxes at the Opera were salons where one was almost certain to meet or to see fashionable people, some of whom loved music.

All of the people in that glittering world knew each other without necessarily moving in the same social circles. But everyone knew the names that went with the assembled faces, and the Count de Chagny's face was known by them all.

The squib in the morning *L'Epoque* had already had a small effect, because all eyes were turned toward the box where Count Philippe sat alone with a look of careless indifference on his face. The feminine element in that brilliant audience seemed particularly intrigued, and the viscount's absence gave rise to whispers behind a hundred fans. Christine Daaé was received rather coldly. This particular audience could not forgive her for setting her sights so high.

The diva was aware that a part of the audience was ill-disposed toward her and was troubled by it. The regular opera-goers, who claimed to be *au courant* regarding the viscount's love affair, smiled at certain passages in Marguerite's part. This is why, ostensibly, they turned toward Philippe de Chagny's box when Christine sang the sentence,

"I'd dearly like to know who that young man is,
If he's a nobleman, and what his name might be."[3]

With his chin resting on his hand, the count seemed not to notice any of those manifestations. His eyes were fixed on the stage, but was he watching her? He seemed to be far away from everything.

Christine, meanwhile, was losing more and more of her self-confidence. She trembled and seemed headed for disaster. Carolus Fonta[4] wondered whether she might not be ill, whether she could sustain the role until the

---

[3] "I'd dearly like to know . . ."
  Gounod's *Faust*, Act III, Scene 6.
[4] "Carolus Fonta"
  See Chapter VIII, Note 11, page 112.

end of the act, which takes place in the garden. The audience remembered the misfortune that had overtaken Carlotta at the end of this act, and the historic "croak" that had temporarily ended her career in Paris.

Just then, Carlotta made her entrance into a box facing the stage—a sensational entrance. Poor Christine raised her eyes toward this new, distressful occasion. She recognized her rival and thought she saw her sneering, and that was what saved her. Christine forgot everything to triumph once again.

From that moment on, she sang with her whole soul. She undertook to surpass everything she had done until then, and she succeeded. In the last act, when she began to invoke the angels and to rise above the earth,[5] she led the entire quivering audience on a new flight until each of them believed they had wings.

At her superhuman call, a man at the center of the auditorium stood up and remained standing facing the actress as if, with a single movement, he would rise from the earth. It was Raoul.

"Holy angels, in heaven bless'd
My spirit longs with ye to rest!"

And Christine, her arms extended, her throat impassioned . . . Christine, enveloped in the glory of her unbound hair that descended to her bare shoulders, uttered the divine cry,

"Carry my soul to Heaven's bosom."[6]

It was then that a sudden darkness covered the theater. It was so rapid that the audience hardly had time to utter an astonished cry before the stage was lit once again.

But Christine was no longer there! What had become of her? What kind

---

[5] "to rise above the earth"

This was an intricate, beautiful, and expensive scene for the Paris Opera to mount. It required a vast coordination of canvas flats, steel springs, and steam to create a paradisal effect that included flights of angels, knots of blissful denizens, and a cloud-filled sky toward which puffs of incense were wafted. (Frédérique Patureau, Le Palais Garnier . . . , p. 165.)

[6] "Carry my soul to Heaven's bosom"

Gounod's Faust, Act V, Scene 2. This moment marks a masterful irony on Leroux's part. Christine, in her role as Marguerite, pleads with the angels to take her up to heaven, just as Erik, in his role as a demonic force, snatches her down to his netherworld.

194

of miracle was this? People looked at each other without comprehension and mounting excitement. The feeling was as intense on the stage as it was in the audience. From the wings, people hurried toward the spot where, an instant ago, Christine had been singing. The performance was interrupted in the midst of the greatest disorder.

Where, then, where had Christine gone? What magic spell had stolen her away from before thousands of enthusiastic spectators and out of Carolus Fonta's very arms? Indeed, one might ask whether the angels, while granting her passionate prayer, had not really "carried her to heaven's bosom," body and soul.

Raoul, still standing in the auditorium, uttered a cry. In his box, Count Philippe got to his feet. People looked toward the stage, toward his box, toward Raoul, and wondered whether what had happened was not in some way related to the article which had appeared that same morning in a newspaper. But Raoul hurriedly left his place; the count disappeared from his box, and as the curtain went down, the subscribers thronged to the entrance backstage. In the midst of an indescribable hubbub, the public waited for an announcement. Everyone spoke at once, and everyone tried to explain what had happened. Some said, "She fell through a trapdoor." Others, "She was lifted up into the flies. The poor thing may be a victim of some new contraption the management is trying out." Still others said, "It's a conspiracy planned in advance. The coincidence of the blackout with her disappearance is sufficient proof."

At last, the curtain was raised slowly and Carolus Fonta walked forward as far as the conductor's podium and, in a sad and serious voice, announced, "Ladies and gentlemen. An unprecedented event, and one which leaves us profoundly worried, has just occurred. Our colleague, Christine Daaé, has disappeared before our eyes without anyone knowing how."

Chapter XV

❊❊

THE REMARKABLE BEHAVIOR OF A SAFETY PIN

On stage, there is unspeakable turmoil.[1] Singers, stagehands, walk-ons, supernumeraries, choristers, subscribers all asking questions, calling out, jostling each other— "What's become of her?" "She's been ab-ducted—" "It's the Viscount de Chagny who ran off with her—" "No, it's the count—" "Ah, there's Carlotta! It's Carlotta who did it—" "No! It's the Phantom."

And there are some who laugh, especially after a close look at the floor boards and the trapdoors rules out any notion of an accident.

In that noisy crowd there is a notable group of three who speak in hushed tones and make despairing gestures: Gabriel, the choir master, Mer-cier, the administrator, and Rémy, the secretary. They have withdrawn to a corner of the lobby that connected the stage with a wide hallway of the dancers' lounge. There, behind enormous stage props, they carried on a discussion: "I knocked. They didn't answer. They may not be in the office anymore. Anyway, it's impossible to know because they took the keys."

That was the secretary, Rémy, speaking and there is no doubt he is talking about the messieurs, the directors. Those two had, during the last

---

[1] Note the use of the present tense throughout this section, bringing an immediacy to the scenes. (See Chapter V, Note 3, page 73.)

intermission, given orders that they must not be disturbed under any circumstances. They were "not in" for anyone.

"Just the same," Gabriel exclaimed, "it isn't every day that a singer is abducted from the stage."

"Did you make them understand that?"

"I'll try again," says Rémy, and disappears at a run.

At this point, the stage manager shows up. "Well then, Mr. Mercier. Are you coming? What are both of you doing here? We need you, Mr. Mercier."

"I don't want to do anything or know anything until the police superintendant comes," declares Mercier. "I sent for Mifroid.[2] When he gets here, we'll see."

"And I'm telling you that we must get down to the lighting controls at once."

"Not before the police superintendent comes."

"I've been down to the controls."

"Ah! And what did you see?"

"Actually, I didn't see anyone. Do you understand? No one."

"What do you want me to do?"

"Of course," says the stage manager, frantically brushing aside an unruly lock of his hair. "Of course. But if there were someone at the lighting controls, that someone might be able to tell us how the stage was so suddenly blacked out. Yet Mauclair is nowhere to be found. Do you understand?"

Mauclair was in charge of the lights that, as required, created day or night on stage. "Mauclair is nowhere to be found," a shaken Mercier says again.

"What about his helpers?"

"Neither Mauclair nor his helpers. I tell you, none of the lighting crew. Surely you understand that Christine didn't disappear by herself," says the stage manager loudly. "There is a plot here that must be uncovered. And the managers who aren't here! I've made the lighting controls

---

[2] "Mifroid"

Mifroid, whom we will meet soon, plays a key role in Leroux's novel *La Double Vie de Théophraste Longuet*, where, as a police official, he pursues Théophraste Longuet, whose criminality he suspects. As both men run, they fall together into a street repair hole and find themselves bricked up in the catacombs beneath the streets of Paris. There, they become fast friends, as they have the kinds of adventures one expects of characters in a Jules Verne novel (see the Introduction).

Mifroid, in that novel, is the discoverer of *"le bon bout de la raison"* (the right end of reason), which becomes the guiding principle of Rouletabille, the eighteen-year-old detective whose elaborate adventures through a series of books helped establish Leroux's career as a *feuilletoniste* (see the Introduction).

off limits and put a fireman on guard before the alcove housing them. Was that wrong of me?''

"No. That was well done. And now, let's wait for the police superintendent."

The stage manager goes off with an angry shrug of his shoulders, mouthing curses at those pusillanimous wet hens who cower quietly in a corner while the entire theater is turning topsy-turvy.

But Gabriel and Mercier were hardly calm. It was only that they had been given an order that paralyzed them. They were not to disturb the managers for any reason whatsoever. Rémy had violated that order without success.

And here he is, returned from his latest attempt with a strange look of fear on his face.

"Well? You've talked to them," Mercier inquires.

Rémy replies, "Moncharmin finally opened the door. His eyes were popping out of his head. I thought he was going to hit me. I couldn't get a word in edgewise. And do you know what he yelled at me? 'Do you have a safety pin?'

" 'No.'

" 'Well then, get the hell out of here.'

"I wanted to say that something unprecedented had happened in the theater, but he shouted, 'A safety pin! Get me a safety pin at once.' A boy from the office who had heard him—Moncharmin was shouting like a deaf man—ran up, bringing a safety pin, which he gave him at once. Moncharmin shut the door in my face. And that's it.''

"And couldn't you have said, 'Christine Daaé . . .' ''

"Ah, I'd like to have seen you do it. He was foaming. All he could think of was that safety pin. I think that if someone had not brought him that pin so quickly, he would have had a heart attack. Of course, none of this is natural, and the managers are going crazy."

M. Rémy, the secretary, is unhappy and shows it. "This can't go on. I'm not used to being treated this way."

Suddenly, Gabriel whispers, "It's another blow struck by the Phantom of the Opera." Rémy snickers. Mercier sighs and seems about to confide something, but seeing Gabriel's signal to be quiet, he stays silent. Mercier, who, as time goes by, feels that his responsibility is growing while the managers have not yet shown up, cannot keep silent any longer. "Ah! I'll go after them myself," he decides.

Gabriel, grown suddenly very serious, stops him. "Think what you're doing, Mercier. If they're in their office, it may be because it's necessary. The Phantom of the Opera has more than one trick up his sleeve."

But Mercier shakes his head. "Too bad. I'm going. If they had listened to me, they would long ago have told the police everything." And he leaves.

"What is *everything*?" Rémy promptly asks. "What was it they should have told the police? Ah, you're holding your tongue, Gabriel. You're in on this, too? You could do worse than to let me in on the secret to keep me from shouting that you're all crazy. Yes, crazy, and that's the truth."

Gabriel rolls his eyes stupidly and pretends not to understand the private secretary's embarrassing outburst. "What secret?" he murmurs. "I don't know what you're talking about."

Rémy is exasperated. "Tonight, right here, during the intermissions, both Richard and Moncharmin behaved like madmen."

"I didn't notice," Gabriel grumbles, very annoyed.

"Then you were the only one. Do you think I didn't see them? And that Mr. Parabise, the manager of Credit Central, did not notice anything? Or that Ambassador de la Borderie is blind? Let me tell you, Mr. Choir Director, all of the subscribers pointed at them—at our managers."

"What were our managers doing?" Gabriel asks with the air of a simpleton.

"What were they doing? But you know better than anyone else what it was they were doing. You were there. And you watched them, you and Mercier. And you were the only ones who did not laugh."

"I don't understand."

Very cold, "very aloof," Gabriel raised his arms and lets them fall, a gesture that evidently signifies that he is no longer interested in the matter.

Rémy goes on. "What is this new obsession of theirs? *They won't let anyone get near them.*"

"What? *They don't want anyone to come near them?*"

"*They won't let anyone touch them anymore.*"

"Really! You've observed *that they won't let anyone touch them?* That's certainly strange."

"Then you admit it. Not a minute too soon. *And they walk backward.*"

"Backward? You've seen our managers walking backward? I thought that only crabs walked backward."

"Don't laugh, Gabriel. Don't laugh."

"I'm not laughing," protests Gabriel, who tries to look as serious as a pope.

"Could you explain it to me, please? I beg you Gabriel, you who are

From *The Phantom of the Opera* (1962)

a close friend of the managers, tell me why, during the intermission after the garden scene, when I went to shake Richard's hand in the lobby, I heard M. Moncharmin suddenly whispering to me, 'Go away. Go away. Above all, don't touch M. Richard.' Do I have the plague?"

"Incredible."

"And a few minutes later, when the ambassador of the Borderie started toward M. Richard, didn't you see how Mr. Moncharmin threw himself between them, and didn't you hear him cry, 'Mr. Ambassador, I implore you. Don't touch Mr. Richard.' "

"Frightful. And what did Richard do all that while?"

"What was he doing? You saw him! He tuned halfway around and greeted someone *in front of him, though there was no one in front of him.* Then he moved away *backward!*"

"Backward?"

"And behind Richard, Moncharmin also turned halfway around, that is to say that he had made a half-circle behind Richard, then he too moved away *backward*. And they went off together like that, backward, all the way to the administration staircase. Backward. Backward. Well then, if they're not mad, you tell me what all that means."

"Maybe they were rehearsing a ballet turn," says Gabriel without conviction.

Rémy, the secretary, felt outraged by such a vulgar joke at so dramatic a time.[3] He frowned. He pursed his lips. Speaking into Gabriel's ear, he said, "Don't be clever, Gabriel. Things are happening here for which you and Mercier will have to share responsibility."

"Like what?" Gabriel asks.

"Christine Daaé is not the only one who has suddenly disappeared this evening."

"Oh, come on."

"There's no 'come on' about it. Can you explain why, when Mme. Giry went down into the lobby, Mercier took her by the hand and led her out of there posthaste?"

"So!" says Gabriel. "I didn't notice."

"You noticed it sufficiently well so that you followed Mercier and Mme. Giry all the way to Mercier's office. After that, you and Mercier were still in sight, but Mme. Giry was no longer to be seen."

"Do you think, then, that we might have eaten her?"

"No, but you've put her in the office behind lock and key, and when anyone passes by the door, do you know what they hear? 'Oh, the rogues. The rogues,' is what they hear."

At this moment, in the course of this strange conversation, Mercier arrives, completely out of breath.

"There it is," he says, his voice gloomy. "It's beyond anything. I called to them. I told them, 'It's a serious matter. Open up. It's me, Mercier.' I heard footsteps. The door opened and Moncharmin appeared. He was very pale. He said, 'What do you want?' I said, 'Christine Daaé has been kidnapped.' Can you believe what he replied? 'All the better for

---

[3] "vulgar joke at so dramatic a time"

Leroux, clearly, is aware that this chapter, coming so soon after the intensely lyric Chapter XIII and the cataclysmic end of Chapter XIV, risks being read as tasteless. But he cannot escape the temptation of the *feuilletoniste* to delay giving crucial information to achieve heightened dramatic suspense. Nor can he refrain offending our sensibilities by intruding low comedy at a moment when we are on the *qui vive* about Christine's fate. Depending on a reader's own judgment, Leroux is being either audacious or inexcusable. Or both.

her.' And he shut the door as he put this in my hand.'' Mercier opens his hand. Rémy and Gabriel look down.

"The safety pin," cries Rémy.

"Strange. Strange," intoned Gabriel softly, unable to repress a shudder.

Suddenly, all three of them turned at the sound of a voice, "Pardon me, sirs. Can you perhaps tell me where Christine Daaé is?"

Despite the gravity of the situation, they would undoubtedly have burst out laughing at such a question had they not been moved to pity by the sorrow they saw in the face of the man who asked it. It was the Viscount de Chagny.

Chapter XVI

≫⋘

CHRISTINE! CHRISTINE!

Raoul's first thought after the amazing disappearance of Christine Daaé had been to accuse Erik. He had no further doubts about the nearly supernatural power the Angel of Music possessed in the realm of the Opera house, where he had diabolically established his reign.

And Raoul, maddened by despair and love, had rushed to the stage. "Christine, Christine," he moaned, calling for her as she must have called to him from the depths of that dark gulf where the monster had taken her as his prey, still trembling from her divine exaltation, and clad in the white shroud in which she had offered herself to the angels in paradise.

"Christine, Christine," Raoul cried again, and it seemed to him that he could hear her cries through the thin boards that separated him from her. He leaned down; he listened; he wandered about the stage like a madman. Down, down, down into this pit of shadows whose entrances are all closed to him.

Ah, this fragile obstacle which usually slides aside so easily to let him see the gulf toward which all his desire leads him . . . these boards creaking under his step, resonating through the prodigious emptiness of the depths below—these boards are more than immovable tonight; they appear immutable. They look so solid, as if they had never moved. And these stairs which allow one to descend below the stage are forbidden to everyone.

"Christine, Christine!" People push him aside, smiling. They make fun of him. They think the poor fiancé is out of his mind.

By what desperate byways among corridors of night and mystery known only to him had Erik brought the pure young woman to his frightful lair, the Louis Phillipe room whose door opens onto the Lake of Hell? . . . "Christine! Christine! You don't reply. Are you still alive, Christine? Have you breathed your last in a moment of abominable horror under the fevered breath of the monster?"

Frightful thoughts pass, like bolts of lightning, through Raoul's congested brain.

Erik must have discovered their secret. What vengeance would he take knowing that he had been betrayed by Christine?

Toppled from the heights of his pride, what was there that the Angel of Music would not dare to do? Between the monster's all-powerful hands, Christine is lost.

And Raoul thinks again about the gold stars that came last night to wander over his balcony, and why it was that he had been powerless to shoot them with his pistol.

His eyes are certainly extraordinary for a man, dilating in the shadows and brightening like stars, or like the eyes of a cat. (Certain albinos[1] appear to have a rabbit's eyes by day and a cat's eyes at night. Everyone knows that!)

Yes, yes. Of course it was Erik at whom Raoul had shot. Why had he not killed him? The monster had escaped by means of the downspout, like cats or prisoners who—everyone knows that, too—can climb skyward by means of a drainpipe.

No doubt Erik was thinking of some decisive action against Raoul, but Erik had been wounded and, having escaped, had turned on poor Christine.

These are Raoul's cruel thoughts as he runs to the singer's dressing room.

"Christine, Christine." Bitter tears scald the young man's eyelids as he sees the clothes scattered about the furniture, the clothes his beautiful fiancée was to have worn when they ran off together. Ah, why had she

---

[1] "albinos"

Persons suffering from albinism have a genetic defect that makes their bodies unable to produce pigment, so that their skin usually has a milky cast, their hair is colorless, and their eyes show pink or blue irises. They do *not* have "cat's eyes" by night, though they may prefer that time because they experience eye discomfort in bright daylight.

In Leroux's novel *Balaoo*, two of the brigand triplets, who are the scourge of the countryside, are albinos.

not been willing to leave earlier? Why had she delayed so long? Why had she toyed with the menacing catastrophe, with the monster's heart? Why, in a gesture of supreme pity, had she flung this final nourishing, celestial song to the demon's soul.

"Radiant angels, angels blessed,
Take my soul to its heavenly rest."[2]

Raoul, uttering sobs, oaths, and curses, feels with unskillful hands the great mirror that had opened before him one evening, permitting Christine to descend for her sojourn in that dark abode. He pushes, he presses, he taps, but the glass, it seems, obeys only Erik. Perhaps action is useless with a mirror like this one. Perhaps certain words need to be pronounced.[3] As a small child, he had heard stories about things that were obedient to words that way.

All at once, Raoul remembers "a barred gate opening onto the Rue Scribe. An underground passage leading directly from the lake to the Rue Scribe." Yes, Christine had told him about it. After he has confirmed that, alas, the heavy key is not in the box, he runs nevertheless to the Rue Scribe.

Now he is outdoors; he passes his trembling hands over the enormous stones, searching for gaps, and encounters bars. Are these the ones, or these? Or is it, perhaps, this air vent? He casts his helpless gaze through the bars. How profoundly dark it is in there. He listens. How still it is. He circles the building. Ah, here are huge bars. Enormous gates. It's the door to the courtyard of the administrative offices.

Raoul runs to the gatekeeper. "Pardon me, madame. Can you show me where the gate is? Yes. A gate made of iron bars. A gate that faces the Rue Scribe and that leads to the lake. You know! The lake. Yes, the lake. The underground lake. Under the Opera."

---

[2]   "Radiant angels . . . its heavenly rest"
       Gounod's *Faust,* Act V, Scene 2.
[3]   "Perhaps certain words needed to be pronounced"
       Of course, the words are "open sesame" and it is Ali Baba who learns them and uses them. The relevant moment in Richard Burton's *Supplemental Nights to the Book of the Thousand and One Nights* (Vol. IV) reads as follows:

". . . Ali Baba saw the robbers, as soon as they came under the tree, each unbridle his horse and unhobble it; then all took off their saddle-bags which proved to be full of gold and silver. The man who seemed to be the captain presently pushed forwards, load on shoulder, through thorns and thickets, till he came up to a certain spot where he uttered these strange words, 'Open, O Simsim [Open Sesame]!' and forthwith appeared a wide doorway in the rock." (Sir Richard Burton, *Supplemental Nights* . . . Volume IV. The Burton Club ltd. ed., pp. 370–371.)

"Yes, sir. I know very well that there's a lake under the Opera, but I don't know which door leads to it. I've never gone there."

"And the Rue Scribe, madame. The Rue Scribe. Have you ever been to the Rue Scribe?"

She laughs out loud. Raoul runs off, groaning. He runs, climbs some stairs, runs down others, moves entirely around the courtyard of the administrative offices, and finds himself at last back under the light from the stage.

He stops. His heart beats wildly enough to break out of his panting chest. If only Christine Daaé had been found. Here's a group of people. He asks, "Excuse me, gentlemen. Have you seen Christine Daaé?"

And they laugh.

At the same moment, there is a new commotion on the stage. In the midst of a crowd of gesticulating men in evening dress there appears a very calm, well-fleshed man whose pleasant rubicund face is framed by wavy hair and whose blue eyes have a marvelous serenity. Mercier, the administrator, points out the new arrival to the Viscount de Chagny, telling him, "Sir, this is the man to whom you should address your questions from now on. Let me introduce you to M. Mifroid, the commissioner of police."[4]

"Ah, M. Viscount de Chagny. Glad to see you," says the commissioner. "If you'll be good enough to follow me. And now, where are the managers? Where are the managers?"

Since the administrator does not answer, Rémy, the secretary, takes it upon himself to inform the commissioner that the directors have locked themselves inside their office and that as yet they know nothing of what has happened.

"Can that be? Let's go to their office."

And M. Mifroid, followed by an ever increasing crowd, headed toward the administrative office. Mercier takes advantage of the confusion to slip a key into Gabriel's hand. "It's all turning out badly," he murmured. "Go on, then. Turn Mme. Giry loose."

Gabriel leaves.

Shortly thereafter, they arrive at the administrators' door. Mercier blustered in vain. The door stays closed.

"Open in the name of the law," commands Mifroid in a clear but slightly anxious voice. Finally the door opens. They rush into the office, following in the wake of the commissioner.

Raoul is the last one to go in. As he is about to follow the others, a

---

⁴ "Mifroid, the commissioner of police"
See Chapter XV, Note 2, page 198.

hand touches his shoulder and he hears these words in his ear, "Erik's secrets are nobody's business."

He turns, stifling a cry. The hand that was on his shoulder is now at the lips of the dark man whose eyes were the color of jade and who was wearing an astrakhan hat. The Persian.

The stranger continues his gestures urging discretion and, at the moment when the viscount, stupefied, is about to ask for an explanation for his mysterious intervention, the Persian bows and is gone.

Chapter XVII

❦

ASTONISHING REVELATIONS OF MME. GIRY REGARDING PERSONAL
RELATIONS WITH THE PHANTOM OF THE OPERA.

Before following the superintendent of police, Mifroid, into the
offices of the directors, the reader will permit me to inform him of certain
extraordinary events that had taken place in the office where secretary
Rémy and the administrator Mercier had tried in vain to enter, and where
Messrs. Moncharmin and Richard had hermetically sealed themselves off for
a purpose as yet undisclosed to the reader but which it is my historic
duty—that is, my duty as a historian—not to conceal any longer.

I have had occasion recently to note how much the mood of the two
directors had been disagreeably changed, and I have pointed out that the
change was not caused only by the fall of the chandelier in the circumstances
the reader already knows.

Let us now inform the reader, then, despite the desire the directors
might have to conceal such an event forever, that the Phantom had succeeded in being paid his first twenty thousand francs. Oh, there had been
a wailing and a gnashing of teeth. Just the same, it had happened in the
easiest way in the world.

One morning the directors had found an envelope in their office with
the inscription "To the Phantom of the Opera (Personal)." The envelope

contained a few words written by the Phantom, as follows: "The time to fulfill the conditions of the rule book has arrived. You will put twenty thousand franc bills into this envelope and you will seal it with your own seal, after which you will give it to Mme, Giry, who will do what is required."

The directors did not wait to be told twice. Without wasting time to wonder how these diabolical messages found their way into an office which they had taken particular care to keep under lock and key, they seized upon this opportunity to get their hands on the mysterious blackmailer. Then, after enjoining them to great secrecy, they told the whole story to Gabriel and Mercier and put the twenty thousand francs into the envelope and, without asking for any explanations, gave it to Mme. Giry, who had been restored to duty. The box attendant showed no surprise. I don't need to tell you that she was well watched. To conclude, then: she went at once to the Phantom's box, where she put the precious envelope in the armrest tray. The two directors, as well as Gabriel and Mercier, were hidden in such a way that the envelope was never out of their sight for a second throughout the evening's performance and even afterward because, since it never moved, those watching it did not move either even after the theater emptied out. Even after Mme. Giry left, the directors, Gabriel, and Mercier were still there. Finally they tired of waiting and opened the envelope, having first confirmed that the seals were not broken.

At first glance, Richard and Moncharmin concluded that the bills were still there, but at a second look, they saw that they were not the same bills. The authentic bills were gone and had been replaced by twenty "play money" bills. First, the directors were enraged, then, afraid.

"This is better than anything Robert Houdin[1] could do," Gabriel cried.

"And more expensive, too," said Richard.

Moncharmin wanted to send for the police superintendant at once, but Richard was against it. No doubt he had some plan in mind. He said, "Let's not be ridiculous. We'd be the laughingstock of Paris. The Phantom of the Opera has won the first round. We'll win the second." He was evidently thinking of the next monthly payment to come.

Just the same, they had been so thoroughly fooled that for the next few weeks they were unable to overcome a certain distress. And I must

---

[1] "Robert Houdin"

Robert Houdin (1805–1871), a famous French magician whose name the American illusionist and escape artist appropriated. He began his career as a maker of automata. He opened his internationally famous magic theater in the Palais Royale in 1845. In 1856, the French government sent Houdin to Algeria with a mission to cow Arab chieftains by a display of French magical powers.

say that was thoroughly understandable. If the superintendent was not called at that time, it is, one ought to remember, because the directors clung to the notion that the entire bizarre adventure could be nothing other than a hateful joke perpetrated on them by their predecessors, and that it would be better to say nothing about it until they had gotten "to the bottom of it." That idea, however was, occasionally displaced in Moncharmin's mind by the notion that it was Richard, who was given to such pranks, who might be at the bottom of this one.

And so, ready for any eventuality, they awaited events while they kept watch and arranged for Mme. Giry to be watched. Richard urged that she not be told anything. "If she's an accomplice, the money is long gone. But in my judgment, she's nothing but an imbecile."

"There are many imbeciles in this affair," replied Moncharmin thoughtfully.

"Could anyone have suspected it?" groaned Richard. "Next time I'll have taken my precautions."

And this is how the next time arrived—it happened on the same day that would see the disappearance of Christine Daaé. In the morning, a letter from the Phantom reminded them of their failure. "Do what you did the last time," the Ph. of the O. amiably informed them. "*It worked very well*. Give the envelope into which you will have put the twenty thousand francs to the same excellent Mme. Giry."

The note was accompanied by the usual envelope. They had only to fill it. This operation was to have been accomplished on the very same evening, half an hour before the performance. It is then, half an hour before the curtain goes up on that famous presentation of *Faust* that we penetrate into the directors' lair.

Richard shows the letter to Moncharmin. Then he counts out twenty thousand francs before him and slips them into the envelope, but does not close it. "And now," he says, "call Mme. Giry." Someone was sent to fetch the old woman. She came in and made a pretty curtsy. She still wore her usual black taffeta dress, which had faded to a rust and lilac color, and her soot-colored hat with its plumes. She seemed to be in a good mood. "Good evening, Messieurs," she said. "No doubt you wanted me to take another envelope."

"Yes, madame, the envelope," Richard said. "And for something else, as well."

"Something else?"

"First, Mme. Giry, I have a little question to put to you."

"By all means, M. Director. Mme. Giry is here to answer."

"Are you still on good terms with the Phantom?"

"Couldn't be better, M. Director. They couldn't be better."

"Ah. As you see, we're enchanted," Richard said in the tone of a man confiding something important. "Between us, we may as well tell you, you're nobody's fool."

"But, M. Director," said the box attendant as she halted the pleasing motion of the two black feathers in her soot-colored hat. "I beg you to understand, no one has ever doubted that."

"Well then, we agree and we can understand each other. This whole story of the Phantom—it's a joke, isn't it? But—just between ourselves—it's gone on long enough."

Mme. Giry looked at the directors as if they were speaking Chinese. Approaching Richard's desk, she said a bit uncertainly, "What are you trying to say? I don't understand you at all."

"Ah, you understand us very well. In any case, you'd better understand. First of all, you're going to tell us his name?"

"Whose?"

"The one who is your accomplice, Mme. Giry?"

"I'm the accomplice of the Phantom? Me. Someone's accomplice?"

"You do everything he asks."

"He doesn't ask for much, you know."

"And he always gives you tips."

"I'm not complaining."

"How much does he give you for bringing him the envelope?"

"Ten francs."

"That's not much."

"What do you mean?"

"I'll explain it to you in a little while. For the moment, we would like to know why it is that you've given yourself over, body and soul, to the Phantom. It's certainly not for a hundred sous, or for ten francs, that one has Mme. Giry's devotion."

"That's true. The reason, MM. Directors—and there's no dishonor in this. On the contrary . . ."

"We don't doubt that for a moment, Mme. Giry."

"Well . . . but you know, the Phantom doesn't like me to tell stories."

"Ah, ah," laughed Richard.

"But this is something that concerns only me," the old woman resumed. "It was in Box Number Five. I found a letter addressed to myself.

Sort of a note, written in red ink. That note—there's no reason for me to read you that note. I know it by heart. If I live to be a hundred, I'll always remember that note." And Mme. Giry promptly recites the note with a touching eloquence:[2]

"1825—Mlle. Ménétrier, leader of the ballet, becomes the Marquise de Cussy.

1832—Mlle. Marie Taglioni, dancer, is made the Countess Gilbert des Voisins.

1846—La Sota, dancer, marries a brother of the king of Spain.

1847—Lola Montes, dancer, marries morganatically King Louis of Bavaria and is created Countess of Landsfeld.

1848—Mlle. Maria, dancer, becomes the Baroness Hermeville.

1870—Therese Hessler, dancer, marries Don Fernando, brother of the king of Portugal . . ."

Richard and Moncharmin listen to the old woman who, as she advances farther into her strange enumeration of these glorious marriages, straightens up and progressively becomes more animated, until, as inspired as a sibyl over her tripod, and in a voice bursting with pride, she utters the final phrase of the prophetic letter, "1885, Meg Giry, Empress."[3]

Exhausted by this supreme effort, the box attendant falls back into her chair, saying, "Monsieur, the letter was signed, 'The Phantom of the Opera.' I had heard of the Phantom of the Opera, but I only believed half of what I heard. From the day that he announced that my little Meg, flesh of my flesh and fruit of my loins, would become an empress, I believed entirely in him."

---

[2] "recites the note with a touching eloquence"

Only two of the names on the note Mme. Giry is reading appear in the list of principal female dancers given in J. G. Prud'homme's *L'Opéra (1669–1925)*, pp. 145–146. They are: Amelie Taglioni (not Marie), who danced at the opera 1827–40 and again in 1844; and Lola Montes, who danced there in 1844.

Lola Montes, an Irish born "Spanish dancer," is famous for being an adventuress of uncommon beauty. She seduced Louis I of Bavaria, who made her first Baroness de Rosenthal and then Countess of Landsfeld (1847). Her influence produced a revolt in 1848, which resulted in the abdication of the king.

[3] "1885, Meg Giry, Empress"

Clearly, then, the "real time" of the *Phantom* is before that date.

Really and truly there was no need to study Mme. Giry's exalted physiognomy for any length of time to know just how much could be obtained from that fine intellect with those two words, "Phantom" and "Empress."

But who was manipulating the strings of this remarkable mannequin? Who?

"You've never seen him. He speaks to you, and you believe everything he says," Moncharmin asked.

"Yes. First of all because my Meg became a principal dancer because of him. I told the Phantom, 'If she's to be an empress by 1885, you don't have much time to lose.' He replied, 'You're right.' Then, with a word in M. Poligny's ear, it was done."

"Then M. Poligny has seen him?"

"No more than I have. But he has heard him. As I say, he put a word in his ear on the evening when he left Box Number Five. You know, the evening that he looked so pale."

Moncharmin heaves a sigh. "What a story," he groans.

"Ah," replies Mme. Giry, "I always thought that there were secrets between M. Poligny and the Phantom. He has always given the Phantom everything for which he asked. He has never refused him a thing."

"You hear, Richard? Poligny never refused the Phantom anything."

"Yes, yes. I hear it very well," Richard declared. "M. Poligny is a friend of the Phantom's. And, since Mme. Giry is a friend of M. Poligny," he added rather rudely, "so there we are. But it's not Poligny I'm thinking about. To tell the truth, the only person who really interests me—is Mme. Giry. Mme. Giry, do you know what is in this envelope?"

"Good heavens, no," she said.

"Very well. Take a look."

Mme. Giry looks nervously into the envelope, but brightens almost at once. "Thousand franc notes," she cries.

"Yes, thousand franc notes. And you knew that perfectly well."

"Me, M. Director Me? I swear to you . . ."

"Don't swear, Mme. Giry. And now I'll tell you the other reason I sent for you. Mme. Giry, I'm going to have you arrested."

The two black feathers, which normally took the shape of a pair of question marks on her soot-colored hat, now assumed the form of exclamation points; as for the hat itself, it shook threateningly above her chignon. For Mme. Giry, the mother of little Meg, surprise, indignation, protest, and fear were now transformed into a sort of extravagant pirouette—a *jeté glissade*[4]—of offended virtue, which carried her so closely under the director's nose that he was forced to push back his chair. "To have me arrested!"

The mouth with which she uttered these words seemed about to spit her three remaining teeth into the director's face.

M. Richard was heroic. He did not move back any further. He menaced the attendant of Box Number Five with a wagging forefinger to indicate the absent magistrates. "I'm going to have you arrested, Mme. Giry, as a thief."

"Say that again." And before Moncharmin could intervene, Mme. Giry delivered a vengeful slap against Richard's face. It was not the withered hand of the irritable old woman that struck the director's cheek, but the envelope itself, the cause of all the trouble. The magic envelope, which, under the impact of the blow, opened, allowing the bills to escape and to flutter away in a whirl of giant butterflies.

The two directors cried out, and seized by the same thought, they dropped to their knees to gather up and examine with feverish haste the precious bits of paper.

"Are they still real?" Moncharmin cried.

"Are they still real?" cried Richard.

"They're still real."

Above them, Mme. Giry's three teeth were clashing in a noisy melee mingled with hideous interjections within which one could discern a single theme: "Me. A thief? A thief? Me." She chokes. She cries out. "I'm horrified." Suddenly she leaps back and confronts Richard face to face. "In any case," she yelps, "you, M. Richard, you should know better than I where the twenty thousand francs are."

"I?" Richard asks, stupefied. "How is that?"

Moncharmin, looking severe and anxious, asks the good woman to explain herself. "What does this mean?" he asks. "And why, Mme. Giry, do you say that M. Richard should know better than you where the twenty thousand francs are?"

As for Richard, who feels himself blushing under Moncharmin's gaze, he takes Mme. Giry's hand and shakes it violently. His voice mimics thunder, it growls and roars and rolls. "Why should I know better than you where the twenty thousand francs are? Why?"

---

[4] *"jeté glissade"*

In ballet, a thrusting glide, transferring weight from one leg to the other (the combination of two steps: a *jeté*, a jump, and a *glissade*, a sideways step).

217

"Because," gasps the old woman, looking at him as if she had seen the devil, "they were put into your pocket."

It's M. Richard's turn to be thunderstruck, first because of this unexpected reply, then by M. Montcharmin's increasingly suspicious look. Suddenly, he loses the strength he should have to repel such a heinous accusation.

It is thus that innocent people, surprised in the peace of their hearts by the blow that strikes them, can suddenly appear to be guilty because they turn pale, or redden, or tremble, or recoil, or straighten up, or slump, or protest, or talk when they should be silent, or are silent when they ought to talk, or stay dry when they ought to sweat, or sweat when they ought to be dry.

Moncharmin, quelling the vengeful fury with which Richard, who was innocent, was going to fling himself upon Mme. Giry, took it upon himself to question her gently, encouragingly. "How could you have suspected my colleague Richard of putting twenty thousand francs into his pocket?"

"I never said that," declares Mme. Giry, "since it was I myself who put the twenty thousand francs in M. Richard's pocket." Then, under her breath she added, "Too bad. That's how it is. May the Phantom forgive me."

Richard would have shouted again, but Moncharmin, in a voice of authority, orders him to be silent. "Excuse me, please. Enough. Let the woman explain herself. Let me question her."

And he adds, "It's quite strange that you should take such a tone. We're approaching a point where the entire mystery might be cleared up. You're furious. You're wrong. As for me, I'm very amused."

Mme Giry, a martyr, lifts her head from which there radiated faith in her own innocence. "You tell me that there were twenty thousand francs in the envelope that I put into M. Richard's pocket, but I—I say it again— I knew nothing about that. Nor, for that matter, did M. Richard."

"Ah! Ah!" said Richard, suddenly affecting a bravado that displeased Moncharmin. "I knew nothing about it, either. You put twenty thousand francs into my pocket, but I knew nothing about that. That's good to hear, Mme. Giry."

"Yes," agreed the dreadful woman, "it's true. Neither of us knew anything about it, neither you nor I . . . but you, you ought finally to have noticed it."

Richard would certainly have torn the old woman to bits had Moncharmin not been there. But Moncharmin protects her. He resumes questioning her.

"What sort of envelope did you put into M. Richard's pocket? It was not the one we gave you, the one that we watched you carry to Box Number Five, and yet it was that one that contained the twenty thousand francs."

"Excuse me. It certainly was the one that M. the director gave me that I slipped into M. the director's pocket," Mme. Giry explains. "As for the one that I put into the Phantom's box, that was another envelope, exactly like it and which I had in my sleeve and which had been given me by the Phantom." Having said this, Mme. Giry takes an envelope out of her sleeve exactly like the one that was addressed and had contained the twenty thousand francs. The directors seize it, examine it, see that it is closed and sealed with their very own directors' seal. They open it. It contains twenty play money bills like those which had astonished them a month earlier.

"How simple it is," says Richard.

"How simple," repeats Moncharmin, more solemn than ever.

"The best tricks have always been the simplest. All it takes is an accomplice."

"Ah, an accomplice," says Moncharmin in a monotone voice. His eyes fixed on Mme. Giry as if he meant to hypnotize her, he goes on, "So it was the Phantom who gave you this envelope, and it was he who told you to substitute it for the one we gave you? It was he who told you to put that one into M. Richard's pocket?"

"Yes, it was he."

"Well, madame, would you give us an example of your little talents? Here's the envelope. Pretend that we know nothing about it."

"As you like, sirs."

Mme. Giry took the envelope containing the twenty notes and started toward the door. She started to go through it.

"Ah, no. Ah, no. Not that. We've had enough. We're not going to be tricked again."

"Excuse me, sirs," the old woman says apologetically, "you tell me to pretend that you knew nothing about it. Well then, if you didn't know anything, then I'd walk away with the envelope."

"All right, then. How would you slip it into my pocket?" queries Richard, while Moncharmin, intent on getting at the truth, keeps one eye on Richard and the other eye, hard though it was to accomplish, fixed on Mme. Giry.

"I'm supposed to slip it into your pocket at a moment when you least expect it, Monsieur director. You know that in the course of the evening I always made a little trip backstage, where I often accompany my daughter to the dancers' lounge—it's a mother's privilege. I bring her her shoes at the divertissement, and even her little watering can. In short, I come and go as I like. The male subscribers come backstage, too.[5] So do you, M. Richard. Everyone's there. I pass behind you and I slip the envelope into the back pocket of your suit. It's not magic."

"It's not magic," growls Richard, whose eyes rolled like those of the thundering Jove. "It's not magic. But I've caught you flagrantly lying, you old witch."

The insult offends the respectable woman less than the imputation that she could be dishonest. She straightens up, bristling and baring her three teeth.

"How is that?"

"Because I spent that evening in the theater watching Box Number Five and the false envelope that you had put there. I did not come into the foyer, not even for a second."

"But, M. director, that wasn't the evening when I put the envelope into your pocket. It was at the next performance. It was the evening when the undersecretary for the School of Fine Arts—"

Here, M. Richard interrupts Mme Giry abruptly. "It's true," he says thoughtfully. "I remember . . . I remember now. The undersecretary came backstage. He sent for me. I came down for a moment into the dancers' dressing room. I was on the steps. The undersecretary and his office director were in the lounge itself. All at once, I turned around. You had passed behind me, Mme. Giry. It seemed to me that you brushed against me. There was nobody behind me but you. Oh, I can still see you . . . I can still see you."

"Yes, that's it, M. director. That's exactly it. I had just finished doing my little business with your pocket. That pocket, M. director, is very

[5] "The male subscribers come backstage, too"

On page 64 of his L'Opéra de Paris, Alain Duault writes, "At the Opera, in fact, the subscribers had acquired the right to go through the wings to the Dancers' Lounge. This custom dated back to the end of the XVIII century with the construction of the second auditorium of the Palais Royale in 1770. Thus we read in the Mémoires Secretes of Bachaumont, that 'After the performance it was there [in the lounge] that the actresses were to be found, where they put themselves on display on benches arranged in a semi-circle. There they received the homage of the spectators, who showed up there in throngs, each of whom was free to approach the divinities.' "

convenient." And once again, Mme. Giry suited her action to her word. She went behind M. Richard and, so quickly that she impressed Moncharmin himself, who was watching intently, she put the envelope into one of Richard's tailcoat pockets.

"Evidently," exclaims a pale Richard. "It's very clever of the Phantom of the Opera. The problem for him can be put this way: He has to eliminate any dangerous intermediary between the one who gives the twenty thousand francs and the one who gets them. He could do no better than to get them out of my pocket without my knowing it, since I had no idea they were there."

"Oh, admirable, no doubt," adds Moncharmin. "But you're forgetting, Richard, that ten thousand of that twenty thousand francs are mine, and that no one has put anything into my pocket!"

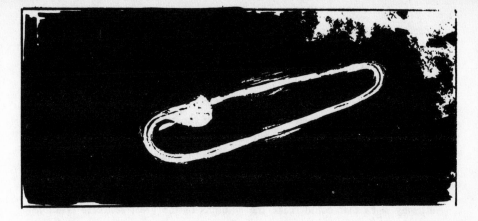

Chapter XVIII

※€

MORE ABOUT THE REMARKABLE BEHAVIOR OF A SAFETY PIN

Moncharmin's last sentence expressed so clearly his suspicion of his colleague that there had to be an immediate and stormy explanation at whose end it was agreed Richard would comply with anything Moncharmin asked him to do in order to discover the scoundrel who was toying with them.

Thus we arrive at "the garden intermission"[1] during which Mr. Rémy, the secretary whom nothing could escape, made the curious observation about the strange conduct of the directors. Consequently, it will be easy to find an explanation for behavior so uniquely bizarre and so little resembling that which one associates with directorial dignity.

Richard and Moncharmin's conduct can be traced to the following arrangement that they had just made: 1. That that evening Richard would repeat exactly the movements he had made at the time of the disappearance of the first twenty thousand francs; 2. Moncharmin was not to lose sight, even for a second, of Richard's tailcoat pocket into which Mme. Giry was to slip the second twenty thousand.

Richard, then, stood in the exact place where he had stood when he

---

[1] "the garden intermission"
  That is, the intermission that followed on Act III of Gounod's *Faust*.

greeted the undersecretary for the School of Fine Arts, while M. Moncharmin stood a few steps behind him.

Madame Giry passed by, brushed against Mr. Richard, put the twenty thousand francs into the director's pocket, and disappeared.

Or, better, she was made to disappear. Obedient to the order he had been given a few moments earlier, before the reenactment of the scene, Mercier shut the good woman into the directors' office. That way it would be impossible for her to communicate with the Phantom. And she allowed it to happen because Mme. Giry was no more now than a poor, scared, feather-ruffled fowl, with wide, stunned eyes under her disordered crest, uttering sighs that could make the columns of the great staircase crumble and imagining that she could already hear the loud tread in the hallway of the police chief with whom she had been threatened.

In the meantime, M. Richard bowed, making a respectful greeting, and walked backward as if he had before him the all-powerful bureaucrat who was the undersecretary of state at the Fine Arts.

Such a show of politeness would have caused no surprise had the undersecretary of state been standing before the director, but since there was nobody standing in front of the director, the bystanders who witnessed this natural but inexplicable scene were understandably struck dumb.

M. Richard greeted the empty air . . . bowed before nothing . . . and walked backward, walked backward, away from no one.

And, a few paces away, M. Moncharmin was doing the same thing. And, as he thrust M. Remy out of the way, he was begging the Ambassador de la Borderie and the director of the Crédit Central not "to touch M. Richard, the director."

Moncharmin, who had his own notions, did not want Richard to come to him later, when the twenty thousand francs had disappeared, and say, "Maybe it's the ambassador, or the director of Crédit Central, or perhaps even M. Remy who took them."

This was particularly so because, according to Richard's account of the first scene, Richard, after Mme. Giry brushed against him, had not encountered anyone in that part of the theater. Then let me ask you, why is it, since they were supposed to repeat everything they had done before, should Richard meet anyone today?

Having first walked backward by way of greeting, Richard continued to walk that way out of prudence, all the way to the administration hallway, being watched all the while from behind by Moncharmin, while he himself kept a sharp eye on "the approaches before him."

Obviously, this new way of walking backstage, which the directors of the National Academy of Music had adopted, could not pass unnoticed. It was noticed.

Happily for Messers Richard and Moncharmin, at the time of this strange scene, the "rats" were almost all in their garret. Otherwise, the directors would have caused a sensation among them.

But all the directors could think of was their twenty thousand francs.

When they reached the half-dark administration hallway, Richard whispered to Moncharmin, "I'm sure nobody touched me. Now, keep your distance and watch me as I go through the shadows until I get to the door of my office. Let's not rouse anyone's suspicions, and we'll soon see what will happen."

But Moncharmin replied, "No, Richard, no. Walk straight ahead. I'll walk *right* behind you! I won't lag by so much as a step."

"But," cried Richard, "then no one will be able to steal the twenty thousand francs from us."

"I sincerely hope not," Moncharmin declared.

"Come on. What we're doing is absurd."

"We're doing exactly what we did the last time. The last time, I joined you at the stage exit at the hallway corner, and I followed *close behind you*."

"You're certainly right," sighed Richard, shaking his head as he obeyed Moncharmin. Two minutes later, the two directors locked themselves into their office. It was Moncharmin himself who put the key into his pocket.

"We were both of us locked in like this the last time," he said, "until the moment that you left the Opera to go home."

"That's true, and no one came to disturb us."

"No one."

"Then," asked Richard, who was trying to get his memories in order, "then I must have been robbed on my way home?"

"No," said Moncharmin, his tone dryer than ever. "No, that's not possible. I took you home in my carriage. I haven't the faintest shadow of a doubt that the twenty thousand francs *disappeared in your house*."

That was Moncharmin's present notion.

"That's incredible," protested Richard. "I trust my servants absolutely, and if one of them had done it, he would have disappeared long ago." Moncharmin shrugged his shoulders as if to say that he was not about to go into detail.

At this, Richard began to think that Moncharmin's tone toward him was becoming unbearable. "Moncharmin," he said, "that'll be enough."

"More than enough, Richard."

"You dare to suspect me?"

"Yes, of a deplorable practical joke."

"There's no joking about twenty thousand francs."

"That's what I think," declared Moncharmin as he opened a newspaper and ostentatiously settled down to read it.

"What are you going to do?" asked Richard. "You're going to read the paper now?"

"Yes, Richard. Until it's time to take you home."

"Like the last time."

"Like the last time."

Richard grabbed the newspaper out of Moncharmin's hands. Moncharmin stood, more irritated than ever. Before him stood an exasperated Richard who, folding his arms over his chest—a sign of insolent defiance since the world began—said, "All right. This is what I think. *I think what I might be thinking* if, like the last time, after having passed the evening talking with you, you were to bring me home and if, after we had parted, I happened to notice that twenty thousand francs had disappeared from my tailcoat pocket . . . like the last time."

"And what would you be thinking?" Moncharmin asked, his face flushed.

"I would be thinking that, since you had never been farther away from me than an inch, and since, by your own wish, you were the only one to come near me—like the last time—I might be thinking that if the twenty thousand francs were not in my pocket, then there was a very good chance that they were in yours."

Moncharmin started back at this suggestion. "*Oh*," he cried, "*a safety pin.*"

"What do you want to do with a safety pin?"

"To pin you up. *A safety pin. A safety pin.*"

"You want to pin me up with a safety pin?"

"Yes, to attach you to the twenty thousand francs. That way, whether it happens here or on the way to your house, you'll be able to feel the hand pulling at your pocket. And you'll see whether it's mine, Richard. Ah, now it's you who suspects me. A safety pin!"

And it was at that moment that Moncharmin opened the hallway door crying, "A safety pin. Will someone get me a safety pin?" And we also know how, at that moment, Rémy, the secretary, who didn't have a safety pin, was received by the director, Moncharmin, even as an office boy brought him the much desired pin.

Women's costumes from the Museum of the Opéra Garnier

Here's what happened then. Moncharmin, after he had shut the door, knelt down behind Richard. "I hope," he said, "that the twenty thousand francs are still here."

"So do I," said Richard.

"Are they the real ones?" asked Moncharmin, who had decided this time not to let himself be fooled.

"You look! I don't want to touch them," said Richard.

Moncharmin pulled the envelope from Richard's pocket and removed the bills. He was trembling, because this time, in order to be able to check the presence of the bills frequently, they had not closed the envelope or sealed it shut. He looked at the bills to reassure himself they were all there and all genuine, and returned them to the back pocket, which he then pinned up with great care. Then he sat back down behind the coattail pocket, which he never stopped watching while Richard, seated at his desk, sat perfectly still.

"A little patience, Richard," Moncharmin urged, "it'll only be for a few minutes. The clock's going to strike twelve midnight soon. It was at twelve midnight that we left the last time."

"Oh, I'll have all the patience I'll need."

It was a stifling, heavy, slow, mysterious passage of an hour. Richard tried to laugh. "I'm going to end up believing in the Phantom's omnipotence. And then, don't you find that there's something in the atmosphere of this room . . . something unsettling, something frightening and disturbing?"

"That's true," admitted Moncharmin, who was really quite upset.

"The Phantom," Richard resumed in a low voice as if he feared to be overheard by invisible ears. "The Phantom! If indeed that was the Phantom who, as we clearly heard, knocked three times on this table . . . who deposited the magic envelopes, who made the chandelier fall, and who has robbed us. Because finally . . . because finally . . . finally, after all, there was no one here but you and me, and if the bills disappeared without either of us seeing anything . . . then one has to believe in the Phantom . . . the Phantom."[2]

At that moment the clock on the mantelpiece gave a warning whir, then it sounded the first stroke of midnight.

The two directors shuddered, seized by an anxiety whose origin they could not explain and which they were unable to combat. The twelfth stroke of midnight sounded strangely in their ears.

When the sound of the clock striking subsided, they heaved a sigh and got up. "I think we can go now," said Moncharmin.

"I think so," Richard agreed.

"Before we leave, will you let me inspect your pocket?"

"But of course, Moncharmin. You must. Well, then?" Richard inquired of Moncharmin, who was patting the pocket.

"Well, I keep feeling the pin."

"Of course you do. As you so well put it, nothing can be stolen without my noticing it."

But Moncharmin, whose hands were still busy at the pocket, cried, "*I still feel the pin, but I can't feel the bills.*"

"No? Stop joking, Moncharmin. This isn't the right time for it."

"But feel for yourself."

Richard shrugged off his coat. The two directors clutched at the pocket. *The pocket was empty.* What was the strangest of all was that the pin was still in the same place.

Richard and Moncharmin paled. There was no doubting any longer that it was something unnatural.

---

[2] "one has to believe in the Phantom . . . the Phantom"

If we remember that the first words of the novel are "The Phantom of the Opera existed," then we can see that these words are Leroux's way of reminding us that his first person narrator is making good on his promise to prove that the Phantom is real. Especially since they are spoken by Firmin Richard, one of the two who have been the most skeptical about his existence.

"The Phantom," whispered Moncharmin.

But Richard leaped toward his colleague. "There was no one but you who touched my pocket. Give me back my twenty thousand francs. Give me back my twenty thousand francs."

"I swear by my immortal soul," sighed Moncharmin, who seemed about to faint, "I swear that I don't have them."

And then, since someone was knocking again at the door, he went to open it, walking almost mechanically, hardly able to recognize Mercier, his business manager, with whom he exchanged a few words without knowing anything that Mercier said, as with an unconscious gesture he put into the hand of his faithful employee the safety pin which could no longer do him any good.

Chapter XIX

The Superintendent of Police, the Viscount, and the Persian

The police superintendent's first words as he entered the directors' office were, "Isn't Christine Daaé here?" He was followed, as I have said, by a dense crowd.

"Christine Daaé? No," replied Richard.

As for Moncharmin, he had no strength left to say a word. His state of mind was much worse than Richard's, because Richard was still able to suspect Moncharmin, while Moncharmin found himself faced with a great mystery . . . the one that has caused all of humanity to shudder from birth—that of the Unknown.

Because the crowd surrounding the directors and the police superintendent maintained an impressive silence, Richard resumed speaking. "Why do you ask whether Christine Daaé is here?"

"Because she must be found," the police superintendent said solemnly.

"What? She must be found? Why then, has she disappeared?"

"In the middle of the performance."

"In the middle of the performance? That's extraordinary."

"It certainly is. And what's even more extraordinary is that I'm the one who is telling you about it."

"Indeed," Richard said, holding his head in his hands as he murmured,

"Now what else is happening? Oh, it's enough to make a man resign."
And, without being aware of it, he plucked a few hairs from his mustache.
"So," he said, as in a dream, "she's disappeared in the middle of the
performance?"

"Yes. She was abducted during the prison scene, just as she was invok-
ing the help of heaven, but I doubt that she was kidnapped by angels."

"And I'm sure she was."

Everyone turned. A young man, pale and trembling with emotion,
repeated, "I'm sure she was."

"What are you sure of?" asked Mifroid.

"That Christine Daaé was abducted by an angel, sir, and I can tell you
his name."

"Ah, M. Viscount de Chagny. You claim then that Mademoiselle Christine Daaé has been abducted by an angel? By an Opera angel, no doubt?"

Raoul looked around him, evidently searching for someone. At that
moment when he felt it necessary to ask the police for help for his fiancée,
he would not have been displeased to see the mysterious unknown[1] who,
a while earlier, had urged him to be discreet. But he did not see him
anywhere. Well, Raoul would have to speak, but he did not see how he
could talk before this crowd, which was staring at him with unabashed
curiosity.

"Yes, sir, by an Opera angel," he said to Mifroid, "and I'll tell you
where he lives when we're alone."

"You're right, sir." And the police chief, having seated Raoul near
him, sent everyone else away except, naturally, the directors, though, since
they appeared to be unconnected with what was happening, they might not
have protested had they been sent away.

Raoul made up his mind. "Sir, this angel is named Erik. He lives in
the Opera and he is *The Angel of Music.*"

"*The Angel of Music!* Really! That's very strange. *The Angel of Music.*"

Turning toward the directors, the police superintendent asked, "Sir,
do you have an angel of music here?"

Moncharmin and Richard shook their heads without so much as a
smiled.

"Oh," said the viscount, "these gentlemen have certainly heard about
the Phantom of the Opera. And I can tell them that the Phantom of the

---

[1] "the mysterious unknown"
Who is, of course, the Persian.

232

Opera and the Angel of Music are one and the same. And that his real name is Erik."

M. Mifroid had stood and was looking carefully at Raoul. "Excuse me, sir, but are you mocking the police?"

"Me?" protested Raoul, who thought sadly, "Again someone who doesn't want to listen to me."

"Well then, what is all this about the Phantom of the Opera?"

"I say that these gentlemen have heard him speak."

"Sirs, it would appear that you know the Phantom of the Opera."

Richard rose, the last of his mustache hair in his hand. "No, officer, but we would very much like to know him, because only just this evening he stole twenty thousand francs from us."

And Richard gave Moncharmin a terrible look that seemed to say, "Give me back the twenty thousand francs or I'll tell all." Moncharmin understood it so well that he replied with a distraught look that said, "Oh, tell all. Tell all."

As for Mifroid, he passed a hand through his hair and looked at each of the directors in turn, wondering if he had not stumbled into a lunatic asylum. "A phantom," he said, "who, on the same evening, kidnaps a singer and steals twenty thousand francs, is a busy phantom. If you wish, we can organize your questions. First, the kidnapping of the younger singer. And then the disappearance of the twenty thousand francs. Well, now, M. de Chagny, let's try to speak seriously. You believe that Mademoiselle Daaé has been kidnapped by an individual named Erik. Do you know that individual? Have you seen him?"

"Yes, officer."

"Where was that?"

"In a cemetery."

M. Mifroid made a startled move, then as he resumed his contemplation of Raoul, he said, "Obviously. That's generally where one meets phantoms.[2] And what were you doing in a cemetery?"

"Sir," said Raoul, "I realize how strange my answers are and the effect they are having on you. But I beg you to believe that I am not out of my mind. The well-being of the person who is dearest in the world to me, as well as that of my beloved brother Philippe, depends on it. I'd like

---

[2] "where one meets phantoms"
The French word, *fantôme*, as I have pointed out in the Introduction, has the meaning of "ghost," which explains Mifroid's feeble joke.

to convince you in a few words, because time is short and every moment is precious. Unfortunately, if I do not tell you the strangest of stories from the very beginning, you will not believe me. I'm going to tell you, sir, everything I know about the Phantom of the Opera. Alas, I do not know much.''

Immediately interested, Richard and Moncharmin exclaimed, ''Tell it anyway, tell it anyway.''

Unfortunately for them, the hope they had felt a moment ago, that they were going to learn something that would set them on the trail of their mysterious antagonist, had to give way very soon to the sad conclusion that M. Raoul de Chagny was completely out of his mind. All those stories of Perros Guirec, of the death's-head, of the enchanted violin, could only have sprung from the unhinged mind of a man in love.

In any case, It was perfectly clear that police officer Mifroid increasingly shared that point of view. Certainly the officer would have put an end to this disordered tale, a glimpse of which we have given in the earlier part of this narrative, if events themselves had not interrupted it. Because just then the door opened and a person came in who was singularly garbed in a long topcoat and a threadbare and shiny top hat that covered his head down to his ears. Hurrying to the police superintendent, he whispered something to him. He was, evidently, a police agent reporting on some urgent business. Throughout the exchange, Mifroid never took his eyes off Raoul.

Finally, addressing him, he said, ''Sir, that'll be enough talk about the Phantom. Let's talk a little about yourself, if you don't mind. You were planning to elope with Mademoiselle Daaé this evening?''

''Yes, sir.''

''At the exit to the theater?''

''Yes, sir.''

''You had made arrangements to that end?''

''Yes, sir.''

''The coach that brought you was to have drive you both away? The coachman had been instructed, his route planned in advance. Better yet, he was to be provided with fresh horses at each stage of the journey?''

''That's true, sir.''

''And yet your coach is still there, beside the rotunda, awaiting your orders, is that right?''

''Yes, sir.''

''Did you know that there were three other coaches in addition to yours?''

''I paid not the slightest attention to that.''

"The coaches belonged to Mademoiselle Sorelli, who had not found a place in the administration courtyard; to Carlotta; and finally to your brother, the Count de Chagny."

"It's possible."

"On the other hand, what is definite is that your own carriage, Mademoiselle Corelli's, and Carlotta's are still standing beside the rotunda sidewalk, but that of the Count de Chagny is no longer there."

"Sir, that has nothing to do with—"

"Pardon me. Was not the count opposed to your marriage with Mademoiselle Daaé?"

"That's a family matter."

"Then your answer is he was opposed to it, and that's why you were going to take Christine Daaé out of reach of any actions the count might take. Well, M. de Chagny, permit me to inform you that your brother was quicker than you. He is the one who has taken Christine Daaé away."

"Oh," groaned Raoul, his hand on his heart, "it's not possible. Are you sure?"

"Immediately after the singer's disappearance, which was organized by means that we have yet to establish, he leaped into his coach and drove furiously across Paris."

"Across Paris," said poor Raoul, his voice like a death rattle. "What does that mean?"

"And beyond Paris."

"Beyond Paris? Which road?"

"The road to Brussels."

The unhappy young man uttered a hoarse cry. "Oh," he exclaimed, "I swear I'll catch up with them." And in two quick strides, he was gone from the office.

"And bring her back to us," the police superintendent called cheerfully. "Ah, now there's a tip worth more than the Angel of Music." At this, the police superintendent turned to his stupefied auditors and gave them this honest but by no means childish little lecture on police work. "I'm by no means certain that the Count de Chagny actually kidnapped Mademoiselle Daaé. But I need to know it, and I don't believe that, at this moment, there is anyone more eager to inform me than his brother, the viscount. Right now he is running, flying. He's my chief helper. That, gentlemen, is the art of police work which is believed to be so complicated and which is, nevertheless, so simple when one learns that it consists above all of getting the police work done by people who aren't police."

But Mifroid might not have been so pleased with himself had he known that the flight of his hurrying messenger had come to a dead halt as soon as he came to the first corridor, even though it was now empty because the crowd of curious onlookers had dispersed.

Though it appeared to be deserted, Raoul found his way barred by a looming shadow. "Where are you off to in such a hurry, M. de Chagny?" inquired the shadow.

Raoul looked up impatiently and recognized the astrakhan hat he had seen earlier. He stopped. "It's you again," he cried, his voice feverish. "You, the man who knows Erik's secrets and won't let me talk about them. And who are you?"

"You know that very well. I'm the Persian," replied the shadow.

Chapter XX

⊰⊱

The Viscount and the Persian

It was then Raoul remembered that his brother, at a performance one evening, had pointed out this mysterious character about whom, once he was identified as "the Persian," nothing else was known beyond the fact that he lived in a small, old apartment on the Rue de Rivoli.

The dark-skinned man with the jade green eyes, who was wearing an astrakhan hat, leaned over Raoul. "I hope, M. de Chagny, that you have not betrayed Erik's secret?"

"And why should I hesitate to betray that monster, sir?" Raoul replied haughtily, meaning to free himself of this irksome individual. "Is he, then, a friend of yours?"

"I hope you've said nothing about Erik, because Erik's secret is also Christine Daaé's. If you speak of one, you speak of the other."

"Oh, sir," said Raoul more and more impatiently, "you seem to know about many things that interest me, and yet I haven't time to listen to you."

"Let me ask you again, M. de Chagny. Where are you off to in such a hurry?"

"Can't you guess? To save Christine Daaé."

"Then, sir, stay where you are. Christine Daaé is right here."

"With Erik?"

"With Erik."

"How do you know?"

"I was at the performance, and there is no one in the world but Erik who could have pulled off an abduction like that. Oh," he said with a deep sigh, "I could see that the monster had a hand in it."

"Then you know him."

The Persian made no reply, but Raoul heard another sigh.

"Sir," said Raoul," I don't know what you intend but . . . can you do anything for me? I mean for Christine Daaé?"

"I think so, M. de Chagny. That's why I approached you."

"What is it you can do?"

"Try to bring you to her . . . and to him!"

"Sir, that's something I've already tried to do tonight, but if you can do that for me, if you can do that service for me, my life belongs to you. One more word, the police superintendent has just told me that Christine Daaé was abducted by Count Philippe, my brother."

"Oh, M. de Chagny, I don't believe that."

"It's not possible, isn't that so?"

"I don't know whether it's possible, but there are various techniques of abduction, and Count Philippe, so far as I know, *has never worked at witchcraft.*"

"You make a convincing argument, sir, and I'm nothing but a fool. Oh, let's go quickly, sir, quickly. I put myself entirely in your hands. Why shouldn't I believe you when nobody else but you will believe me? When you are the only one who doesn't smile when I pronounce Erik's name?"

With that, the young man put out his feverish hands and, in a spontaneous gesture, seized the Persian's. They were as cold as ice.

"Hush," said the Persian as he stopped and listened to the distant sounds from the theater and the faint creaking noises that could be heard in the nearby walls and hallways. "Let's not say that word here. Let's say *he.* It cuts our chances of attracting his attention."

"You think, then, that he's nearby?"

"Sir, anything's possible. Unless he happens to be with his victim *at his home beside the lake.*"

"Ah, so you also know where he lives?"

"Oh, you also know about that home?"

"If he's not there, he could be in this wall, in this floor, in this ceiling. How do I know? His eye is in this lock, his ear in that beam." And the Persian, begging him to muffle the sound of his footsteps, led Raoul down corridors the young man had never seen even when Christine had shown him around the labyrinth.

"Let's hope," said the Persian, "that Darius has returned."

"Who is Darius?" the young man asked as he ran.

"He's my servant."

At that moment they were at the center of a veritable public square, an enormous room poorly illuminated by a single candle stub. The Persian stopped Raoul and, speaking softly, so very softly that Raoul had trouble hearing him, said, "What did you say to the police superintendent?"

"I told him that Christine Daaé's kidnapper was the Angel of Music, known as the Phantom of the Opera, and that his real name was . . ."

"Hush. . . . And the superintendent believed you?"

"No."

"He attached no importance to what you said?"

"None."

"He took you for a madman?"

"Yes."

"That's good," sighed the Persian, and they were off again.

After having descended several staircases unknown to Raoul, the two men came to a door which the Persian opened with a small passkey that he took from a pocket in his waistcoat. Naturally, the Persian, like Raoul, was wearing formal dress, but whereas Raoul was wearing a top hat, the Persian, as I have already pointed out, was wearing an astrakhan hat. It was a violation of the code of elegance governing backstage, where a top hat was required, but it is well known that in France everything is permitted to foreigners: the traveler's cap to the English; the astrakhan hat to the Persians.

"Sir," said the Persian, "your top hat is going to be a problem on the expedition we are about to make. You'd do better to leave it in a dressing room."

"Which dressing room?"

"Why, Christine Daaé's." And, passing Raoul through the door he had just opened, the Persian showed him Christine's dressing room right before them. Raoul had not known that one could come into Christine's dressing room by any other route than the one he customarily took. He was now at the end of the passage he usually traversed before knocking at her dressing room door.

"Oh, sir. How well you know the Opera!"

"Not as well as *he* knows it," the Persian said modestly as he pushed

239

Raoul into Christine's room. It was just as Raoul had left it a few minutes ago.

The Persian, after he had again closed the door, made his way toward the very thin panel that separated the dressing room from a large storeroom next to it. He listened, then coughed loudly.

At once, there were sounds of movement heard from inside the storeroom. A few seconds later, there was a knock at the dressing room door. "Come in," said the Persian.

A man wearing an astrakhan hat and a long, loose-fitting overcoat came in. He bowed and took a richly carved box from under his coat. He put the box on the dressing table, bowed again, and started toward the door.

"No one saw you come in, Darius?"

"No, master."

"Let no one see you leave." The servant risked a quick glance into the corridor, then disappeared quickly.

"Sir," said Raoul, "I've been thinking that someone could find us here, and that, of course, could prove embarrassing. The police superintendent won't put off searching this room for long."

"But he's not the one we have to fear."

The Persian opened the box. There was a pair of magnificently designed and decorated pistols in it. "A little while after Christine Daaé was abducted, I sent a message to my servant to have him bring these weapons to me. I've had them for a very long time and there can be none more reliable."

"You mean to fight a duel?" asked the young man, surprised by the arrival of such an arsenal.

"We are indeed going to a duel, sir," the Persian replied as he examined the percussion caps of his pistols. "And what a duel! In this one, we will be two against one, but you must be prepared for everything, sir, because I'll not hide from you the fact that we're facing the most dreadful adversary imaginable. But you love Christine Daaé, isn't that so?"

"Do I love her? But you, you do not love her. Tell me why you are ready to risk your life for her. You must hate Erik."

"No, I don't hate him," said the Persian sadly. "If I did, he would have stopped doing harm long ago."

"He has harmed you?"

"I forgave him for it."

"It's very extraordinary," the young man said, "to hear you speak of this man! You call him a monster, you speak of his crimes; you say he has harmed you, and yet I find that you have the same incredible pity[1] for him that, when I found it in Christine, drove me to despair.''

The Persian made no reply. He went to get a stool and placed it against the wall before the large mirror that entirely covered it. Then he stood on the stool, and with his nose against the wallpaper, he seemed to be searching for something.

''Well, sir,'' said Raoul, who was seething with impatience. ''I'm waiting for you. Let's go.''

''Go where?'' the Persian asked without turning his head.

''Why, forward, to the monster. Let's go down. Haven't you told me that you know how?''

''That's what I'm looking for.'' And again his nose seemed to wander across the wall. ''Ah,'' said the man in the astrakhan hat, ''it's here.'' And he raised his hand to press with his finger at a corner of the wallpaper design above his head. Then he turned and jumped down from the stool.

''In half a moment,'' he said, ''we'll be *on his trail*.''

And, crossing the entire dressing room, he began to tap along the entire surface of the mirror.

''No,'' he said. ''It hasn't yielded yet,'' he murmured.

''Oh! Are we going to go through the mirror, like Christine?''

''So you know that Christine went through the mirror?''

''Right in front of me, sir. I was hiding there, under the boudoir curtain, and I saw her disappear, not through the mirror, but into it!''

''And what did you do?''

''I thought, sir, that I was seeing things. That my mind was playing tricks on me. That I was mad, or dreaming.''

''That it was some new trick of the Phantom's,'' said the Persian with a laugh. ''Ah, M. de Chagny,'' he went on, his hand still against the mirror, ''would to God that we were dealing with a phantom. We could leave our pair of pistols in the box. Put your hat down, please. Here. . . . And now, close your coat as tightly as you can over your shirt . . . like me . . . pull the lapels forward . . . pull up the collar . . . we need to make ourselves as invisible as possible.''

Still pressing against the mirror, he added, after a short silence, ''When you put pressure on the spring from inside the dressing room, the counter-

---

[1] ''incredible pity''

The reader, too, may find it hard to believe that the Persian is willing to risk his life combating the Phantom for no better reason than that he has compassion for him. And yet it will be the Persian who will put into words the last terrifying—and compassionate—question with which the book draws to its end.

weight produces its effect a bit more slowly. It's different when you're behind the wall and you can press against the counterweight directly. Then the mirror turns at once and moves with incredible speed.''

"Which counterweight" asked Raoul.

"Why, the one that makes this entire wall panel turn on its pivot. Surely you know that it isn't moved by magic.'' And the Persian, drawing Raoul toward him with one hand, pressed his other hand (the one holding the pistol) against the mirror "If you pay attention, you'll soon see the mirror rise a few millimeters, and then move a few millimeters to the right and left. It will then be on its pivot and it will turn. There's no end of things one can do with a counterweight. A child can move a house with its little finger. . . . When one of the wall panels, no matter who heavy it is, is balanced on its pivot by the counterweight, it weighs less than a top spinning on its point.''

"It's not turning," Raoul said impatiently.

"Oh, just wait a moment. You can be impatient later. Evidently the mechanism is rusty, or else the spring doesn't work anymore.'' A worried wrinkle appeared on the Persian's brow. "Or something else may be wrong.''

"What else?''

"He may simply have cut the cord to the counterweight and immobilized the entire system.''

"Why? He doesn't know we're going down this way.''

"It may have occurred to him, because he's aware that I know how the system works.''

"He showed you how it works?''

"No. I analyzed him and his mysterious disappearances, and I found it. Oh, it's the simplest of secret door systems. It's a mechanism as old as the sacred palaces of Thebes[2] with their hundred doors, or the throne room of Ecbatane,[3] or the hall of the tripod at Delphi.''[4]

---

[2] "the sacred palaces of Thebes"

Thebes was the Egyptian city known as Thebais. Situated on the left bank of the Nile, it is distinguished for several reasons. The poet Pindar (518–439 B.C.) was born here, and it is the site of the temple of Karnak. Thebes was known to Homer as the "Hundred-Gated" city. According to Homer, two hundred war chariots could issue from each gate.

[3] "Ecbatane"

The modern Iranian city of Hamadan occupies the site of ancient Ecbatane. It was said, by Herodotus, to have been surrounded by seven walls.

Ecbatane was the capital of Media and the summer residence of the Achaemenian kings. Taken in 550 BC. from the Median ruler by the Persian, Cyrus the Great, it was in turn captured by Alexander the Great in 330 B.C.

The biblical Queen Esther and her uncle Mordecia are said to have their tomb here.

"It isn't turning. And Christine . . . what about Christine?"

Coldly, the Persian said, "We'll do all that is humanly possible. But he may stop us right at the start."

"Then he's the master of these walls."

"He's the master of the walls, the doors, the trapdoors. In my country, they called him by a name that means 'the trapdoor lover.' "

"That's how Christine spoke to me about him, with the same mystery, and ascribing to him the same formidable power. But it all seems very remarkable to me. Why do the walls obey only him? He hasn't built them."

"Yes, he has."

And since Raoul looked nonplussed, the Persian signaled to him to be quiet, then he gestured toward the mirror. It was like a trembling reflection. Their double image trembled as in a rippling sheet of water, then became still again.

"You see, sir, it's not turning. Let's take another route."

"Tonight there are no others," the Persian declared, his voice singularly lugubrious. "And now, be careful. And be ready to shoot."

As for him, he raised his pistol before the mirror. Raoul imitated the movement. With his free hand, he drew the young man near to his chest, and suddenly the mirror turned in a dazzle, like an intersection of blinding fires, like one of those revolving doors with compartments that now open public buildings. It turned, carrying Raoul and the Persian in its irresistible movement until it flung them brusquely out of the bright light into the most profound darkness.

---

⁴ "Delphi"

Delphi was considered by the ancient Greeks to be the center or the navel of the world. From about 600 B.C. Delphi was the site of the temple of Apollo, presided over by the Delphic oracle. The oracle was consulted on both public and private matters. The importance of the temple at Delphi began to decline as Christianity spread throughout the Greek-speaking world.

Chapter XXI

IN THE OPERA'S CELLARS

"Keep your hand high, ready to shoot," the Persian said again hurriedly. Behind them, the wall, having made a complete circle on its pivot, closed. The two men stood still for a few moments, holding their breath.

In the shadedness an uninterrupted silence reigned. Finally, the Persian chose to make a movement, and Raoul heard him sliding about on his knees and feeling for something with his hands.

Suddenly, the darkness before Raoul was illuminated carefully by the light of a shaded lantern, and Raoul recoiled instinctively as if to escape the scrutiny of a secret enemy. But he soon understood that the light was the Persian's, whose every gesture he followed. The small red disk was meticulously turned on the walls, above, below, all around them.

These partitions were formed on the right by a wall, on the left by a panel of boards both above and below the floor. Raoul said to himself that Christine had passed this way on the day she had followed the voice of *the Angel of Music*. This must be Erik's usual route when he came through the walls to impose on Christine's good faith and to intrigue her innocence. And Raoul, who remembered the Persian's words, thought that this route had been mysteriously established by the efforts of the Phantom himself. Later, he would learn that Erik had found the secret corridor there, all ready for him, and for a long time, no one but he knew anything about its existence. This corridor had been constructed at the time of the Paris Commune to permit the jailers to conduct their prisoners directly to their cells in the basement. The Communards had occupied the building soon after March 18. At the bottom of the building they had constructed a state prison[1] and at its top a launching pad for the balloons that were charged with carrying their incendiary proclamations to the surrounding areas.

The Persian was on his knees and had put the lantern down on the ground. He seemed occupied with some hurried task on the floor. Suddenly, he put out his light.

Then Raoul heard a light click and noticed a very pale square of light on the floor of the corridor. It was as if a window had just been opened onto the still illuminated lower levels of the Opera. Raoul no longer saw the Persian, but he felt him suddenly at his side and heard his breathing. "Follow me, and do everything that I do."

Raoul was led toward the square of light. Then he saw the Persian again. He was kneeling once more and gripping the edge of an opening in the floor. For a while he hung there by his hands, his pistol between his teeth, then he lowered himself into the cellar below.

Curiously enough, the viscount had complete confidence in the Persian. Though he knew nothing about him, and though most of the things he had said had served only to add to the mystery of this adventure, he had no hesitation in believing that at this decisive hour the Persian was with him against Erik. He had seemed to be sincere when he spoke to Raoul of the monster, and the interest he had shown in Raoul did not seem suspect. Finally, if the Persian had nourished some sinister plot against him, he would not have armed him. And then, when all was said and done, didn't he have to find Christine at any cost? Raoul had no choice. If he had hesitated, given some of the doubts he had about the Persian's intentions, the young man would have considered himself the basest of cowards.

So Raoul, in his turn, knelt and held onto the trap with both hands. He heard the words, "Let go," and he fell into the arms of the Persian, who immediately commanded him to fall flat on his belly and, though Raoul

---

[1] "state prison"

In the brief time that the commune was in power, says Edward S. Mason, author of *The Paris Commune*, "The number of arrests was far above the normal. From the 29th of March to the 23d of May, 3,201 were incarcerated . . ." (p. 26). However, in a footnote on that page, he cites Edmond de Pressensé, who says that ". . . during this time of social anarchy, the streets have been as safe at night as by day . . . theft has been rare . . ." (Edward S. Mason, *The Paris Commune: An Episode in the History of the Socialist Movement*. New York: Macmillan, 1930.)

could not see how it was done, closed the trapdoor over their heads. Then the Persian came to lie down beside him. Raoul wanted to ask him something, but the Persian put a hand to his mouth and Raoul heard a voice he recognized as that of Mifroid,[2] the police superintendent who had questioned him a while ago.

Raoul and the Persian were behind a partition that concealed them perfectly. Nearby, a narrow staircase led up to a small room in which the police superintendent was evidently walking about asking questions, because one could hear his footsteps and the sound of his voice.

The light around them was weak, but now that they were out of the thick darkness of the secret hallway above them, Raoul had no trouble distinguishing the shapes of things. He could not repress a muffled cry at the sight of three bodies. One of them was lying on the landing of the small stairway that led to the door behind which the police superintendent was heard. The other two, their arms crossed, had rolled to the bottom of the stairway. Had Raoul been able to pass his hand through the panel that was hiding him, he could have touched one of the poor creatures.

"Quiet," the Persian whispered again. He, too, had seen the outstretched bodies and he had one word to explain everything: "*Him.*"

The police superintendent's voice could be heard, louder now. He asked for an explanation of the lighting system and the stage manager gave it to himt. The superintendent must then have been in the alcove of the pipe organ or in a nearby room.

Contrary to what one might think, especially when one is talking about an opera house, the pipe organ is in no way meant to be a musical instrument. At that epoch, electricity was not used except for certain specialized stage effects and for the bells. The huge building and the stage itself were still lit by gas. Hydrogen gas was used to modify the lighting on any given scene, and this was achieved by means of a special apparatus whose many pipes earned it the name "pipe organ."[3]

There was a niche near the prompter's box that was reserved for the chief of the lighting crew. From there he gave his orders to his crew and supervised their work. It was in this niche that Mauclair stayed during every performance.

---

[2] "Mifroid"

My guess is that Leroux planned to give Mifroid a fairly large role in the novel, but as we will see, Mifroid became one of the book's throwaway characters.

[3] "whose many pipes earned it the name 'pipe organ' "

This is an accurate description of the bank of jets and the space within which they were housed in the days when the opera's lighting system used hydrogen gas as its fuel.

Now, however, neither Mauclair nor his employees were in their place. "Mauclair! Mauclair!" The stage manager's voice resounded through the subcellars like a drum. But there was no reply from Mauclair.

We have said there was a door that opened onto the small staircase that led up from the second subcellar. The police superintendent pushed against it, but it resisted. "Hm, hm," he said. "Let's see! I can't open this door. Is it always so difficult?" he asked the stage manager.

The stage manager thrust at the door vigorously with his shoulder. He realized that he was pushing a human body at the same time and, recognizing the body at once, he cried, "Mauclair."

Everyone who had followed the police superintendent to the organ alcove moved forward anxiously. "The poor fellow's dead," the stage manager moaned.

But Mifroid, the police superintendent, whom nothing could surprise, was already bent over the body. "No," he said, "he's dead drunk. It's not the same thing."

"Then it's the first time," the stage manager said.

"It may be he's been given a narcotic. It's very possible."

Mifroid rose, walked down a few steps, and cried, "Look!"

By the light of a small red lantern at the foot of the staircase they saw two other bodies sprawled. The stage director recognized Mauclair's crew. Mifroid went down and put his ear to their chests. "They are sleeping soundly," he said. "A strange business. There can be no doubt that some unknown person interfered with the lighting crew. And he was working for the abductor. But what a strange idea. To abduct a performer from the stage. That's doing it the hard way, if I'm any judge. Will someone send for the theater's doctor?" And Mifroid repeated, "Strange. A very strange business."

Then he turned toward the interior of the little room and spoke to some people whom neither Raoul not the Persian could see from where they were. "What have you to say about all this, gentlemen?" he asked. "You're the only ones who haven't said what you think. But you must surely have an opinion of some sort."

Then, above the landing, Raoul and the Persian saw the faces of the two frightened directors—only their faces could be seen—and they heard Moncharmin's troubled voice. "Sir, things are happening here that we can't explain." And the two faces disappeared

"Gentlemen, thanks for the information," said Mifroid sarcastically.

The stage manager, whose chin was resting in the palm of his hand, a gesture indicating profound thought, said, "It's not the first time that Mauclair has fallen asleep in the theater. I remember finding him one evening snoring in his niche with his snuffbox beside him."

"Was that long ago?" Mifroid asked as he wiped the lenses of his pince-nez meticulously—because the police superintendent was nearsighted, something that can happen even to the most beautiful eyes in the world.

"No, my God," said the stage manager, "it was not long ago. Listen. It was the evening when . . . Good Lord, yes . . . it was the night that Carlotta, you remember . . . when Carlotta emitted her famous 'croak.' "

"Really, the night when Carlotta emitted her famous 'croak.' " And Mifroid, having affixed his pince-nez with its clear lenses to his nose, fixed his eyes on the stage director as if he meant to penetrate his mind.

"Mauclair used snuff, then?" he asked casually.

"But of course. His snuffbox is here, right over here on this shelf. Oh, he's a real snuff user."

"I am, too," said Mifroid as he put the snuffbox into his pocket.

Raoul and the Persian, without anyone suspecting their presence, watched the stagehands removing the three bodies. The police superintendent followed them and everyone else followed him as he went back up. A few moments later, their footsteps could be heard resounding on the stage.

When they were alone, the Persian signed to Raoul to get up. He did so, but he failed to raise his hand to the level of his eyes in a position ready to shoot as the Persian very carefully did. The Persian advised him again to remember to assume that position and not to vary it under any circumstances.

"But it tires my arm unnecessarily," Raoul murmured. "And if I shoot, I'll no longer be sure of myself."

"Switch your shooting hand, then," the Persian assented.

"I don't know how to shoot with me left hand."

At which the Persian made the following strange declaration not intended, evidently, to clarify the situation for the young man's troubled mind:

"*It has nothing to do with shooting either with the right or the left hand; the point is to have one of your hands placed as if you were going to pull the trigger of a pistol and your arm partly bent. As for the pistol, you might just as well leave it in your pocket.*" He added, "Let that be understood, or I can't be responsible for anything. It's a matter of life or death. Now, silence! And follow me."

They were then in the second subcellar. What Raoul could see by the dim glow of a few candle stubs fixed here and there in their glass prisons was the smallest part of that extravagant, sublime, and childlike abyss, as amusing as a puppet show, as frightening as a chasm, which is the cellar world of the Opera.

There are five cellars and they are tremendous. They reproduce the plan of the stage with its trapdoors, its hatches. The slots in the floor, however, are replaced by rails. Transverse beams support the traps and the hatches. Posts leaning on iron or stone or concrete supports form a series of flats that are used in performances for special effects. These devices are given an added stability by linking them with iron hooks according to the needs of the moment. Winches, revolving doors, and counterweights are generously distributed in the cellars. They serve to shift the huge sets, change the scenes, stage the sudden disappearances of performers in scenes requiring special effects. It is in these cellars, say Messrs. X, Y, and Z, in an interesting study of Garnier's work, that doddering old men are transformed into handsome knights, hideous witches into radiantly youthful fairies. Satan comes out of these cellars, just as he disappears into them. The flames of hell escape from them and there the chorus of demons gathers.

And phantoms walk about there, as if at home.

Raoul followed the Persian, obedient to the letter of his instructions, without understanding the gestures he was ordered to make. He told himself that he could hope for help from no one but the Persian. What could he have done without him in this dreadful labyrinth?

Wouldn't he have been stopped at every step by the vast tangle of beams and ropes? Or have been caught unable to free himself in this gigantic spiderweb?

And even if he had been able to make his way through the network of wires and counterweights endlessly rising before him, would he not have risked falling into one of those holes that kept opening at his feet and into whose shadowy depths his eye could not penetrate?

Down they went, and down again.

Now they were at the third subbasement. And their way continued to be lit by a few distant lamps. The Persian seemed to take more precautions the lower they went. He kept turning back to Raoul to urge him to hold his hand up properly, showing him how he himself was holding his hand, as if steady to shoot, though he had no pistol in it.

Suddenly, a loud voice rooted them to the spot. Someone above them was shouting, "Door-closers, all door-closers on stage. Superintendent Mifroid wants them."

Steps were heard, shadows glided past in the dark. The Persian drew Raoul behind a stage set. They watched as old men, bent by years and the weight of opera scenery, went by near them and above them. Some of them could scarcely drag themselves along; others, their spines bent, their hands outstretched, sought for doors to close out of old habit.

Because these were the door-closers. Worn out old stagehands on whom the Opera's administration had taken pity. It had made aboveground and underground door-closers of them.*[4] They went constantly back and forth, above and below the stage, closing doors. I think by now they must all be dead, but in those days they were also called "draft chasers." Because drafts, no matter where they come from, are very bad for the voices of singers.

In an aside, the Persian and Raoul congratulated themselves on this incident, which rid them of annoying witnesses, because some of the door closers, having nothing to do and, for many, no place to sleep, stayed in the Opera overnight out of laziness or need. Raoul and the Persian might have run into them, woken them, or provoked demands for an explanation. For the moment, M. Mifroid's inquiry saved our two friends from such unpleasant encounters.

But they were not to enjoy their solitude for long. Now other shadows came down the same route by which the door-closers had gone up. Each of these shadows carried a small lantern before him which he swung back and forth, raising it up or down, examining everything around them and, apparently, searching for something or someone.

"Damn," muttered the Persian, "I don't know what they're looking for, but they just might find us. Let's get out of here, at once. Your hand up, sir, always ready to shoot. Bend your arm. Hands at eye level as if you were in a duel waiting for the command to fire. Leave your pistol in your pocket. Quickly, down. . . ." He led Raoul into the fourth basement. "At eye level . . . it's a matter of life and death . . . here, this way, this staircase!" They had arrived at the fifth basement. "Oh, what a duel. What a duel!"

Having reached the fifth basement, the Persian caught his breath. He seemed to feel more secure than he had been when he and Raoul had stopped at the third level; just the same, he kept his hand in the pistol position.

---

* M. Pedro Gailhard has told me that he created more door-closer jobs for old stagehands whom he did not himself want to dismiss.

[4] "door-closers*", "firemen making their rounds**", "without further explanation***", "rat-killer****", "Shoes*****"

Note that these asterisked footnotes, which are to be found at the end of this chapter, are *not* those of the annotator of this edition. They purport to be inserted by Leroux's fictional first-person narrator.

Again, Raoul had occasion to be surprised—not that he had any new observations to make—he had none—because in fact, this was no time to be astonished by this strange mode of personal defense that consisted of keeping one's pistol in one's pocket while your hand was held at eye level in the position of a pistol ready to be used. In those days that was the position in a duel when one waited for the command to fire. And in this connection, Raoul remembered very clearly what the Persian had said, "These are pistols in which I have every confidence." Consequently it seemed logical to ask, "What does it mean to have confidence in a pistol which he finds it futile to use?"

But the Persian interrupted him in the midst of these vague cogitations. Signaling to him to stay put, he went back up a short way on the staircase they had just left. Then he came back rapidly to Raoul. "How stupid of us," he whispered. "We'll soon be quit of these shadows with their lanterns. They're firemen making their rounds."**

The two men stayed on the defensive for at least another five long minutes, then the Persian led Raoul back to the stairway down which they had come. Suddenly, he made a signal to stand still again. Before them, there was movement in the dark.

"Get down, flat on your belly," the Persian whispered. The two men lay on the ground. And just in time. A shadow not carrying a lantern, simply a shadow moving in the dark, passed by. It passed so near it almost touched them. They felt the warm breath from its cloak on their faces.

They could just make out that the shadow was enveloped in a cloak from head to foot, that it wore a soft felt hat. It moved away brushing against the wall with its foot and kicking it at intersections.

"Whew," said the Persian, "that was close. That shadow knows me and has taken me twice to the directors' office."

"Is he an Opera policeman?" asked Raoul.

"Someone much worse," the Persian replied without further explanation.***

** At that time, the firemen still had a duty, even when there was no performance going on, to watch over the Opera's security; but this service has since then been done away with. When I asked M. Pedro Gailhard the reason for this, he replied that: "It was because they feared that the firemen, in their complete inexperience of the theater's basements, *would set them on fire*."

*** The author, like the Persian, will give no further explanation of the appearance of this shadow. Since everything in this historical account is normally explained though sometimes it may appear abnormal, the author cannot explain to the reader precisely what the Persian meant when he said, "Someone much worse" (than an Opera policeman). The reader will have to guess, because the author has promised M. Pedro Gailhard, the former director of the Opera, not to disclose the identity of the extremely interesting and useful shadowy person in a cloak who, condemned to live in the depths of the theater, rendered such prodigious service to those who, on gala evenings, risked going into the cellars. I'm speaking here of service to the state, and on my word, I can say no more.

"It isn't *he?*"

"*He?* Unless he comes from behind us, we'll always see his golden eyes. It's the small advantage we have in the dark. But he can come from behind, silently. And if we don't keep our hands in front of us and at eye level as if they are about to shoot, then we're dead."

The Persian had hardly finished formulating a new this line of conduct when a fantastic face appeared before the two men.

A face, an entire visage, not just two golden eyes.

A complete, luminous face. An entire face of fire. Yes, *a disembodied face* advancing toward them at the height of a man's body.

The face emanated fire. In the dark, it appeared like a human face made of fire.

"Oh," said the Persian through gritted teeth, "it's the first time I've seen that. The fire lieutenant wasn't crazy. He had surely seen it. What is there about this flame? It's not *he.* But it may be that he's sending it to us. Careful. Careful. Your hand at eye level, in Heaven's name . . . at eye level."

The disembodied face of fire appeared to be a physiognomy out of hell—of a demon ablaze—and it continued to move forward at a man's height toward the two frightened men.

"Maybe *he's* sent this face in front of us the better to take us by surprise from behind. With him, you never know. I know many of his tricks, but this one . . . not yet this one. Let's get out of here . . . for safety's sake . . . right? . . . for safety's sake . . . keep your hand at eye level." And they fled together down the entire length of the long underground corridor that opened out before them.

After running that way for a few seconds which appeared like long, long minutes to them, they stopped. "Still," said the Persian, "*he* rarely comes this way. This side is of no interest to him. It doesn't lead to the lake, or to his home by the lake. But maybe he knows that *we're on his trail.* Even though I've promised to leave him alone and not to meddle again in his business." Saying this, he turned his head and so did Raoul. What they saw was the fiery head still behind them, still following them. It had, evidently, also run, and perhaps more quickly than they had because it appeared now to be closer.

At the same time, they were beginning to hear a sound whose nature they could not guess, though it was easy enough for them to tell that it seemed to keep pace with the approach of the flaming head. The sound was like squeaking—or, rather, the screeching of thousands of fingernails being dragged across a blackboard—a frighteningly unbearable sound that is still occasionally produced when a bit of stone is lodged in a stick of chalk being drawn across a blackboard.

They moved back again, but the flaming face advanced, kept advancing, gained on them. One could see its features very clearly now. Its eyes were round and fixed, its nose a bit slanted, it mouth huge with a semicircular, pendulous lower lip. Eyes, nose, and mouth resembled, in their entirety, the face of the moon when it is all red, the color of blood.

How that red moon could glide through the dark at the height of a man without support of any kind, or so far as one could tell, without a body to sustain it, was not so clear. Nor how it could move so swiftly, straight as an arrow, and with its eyes so fixed, so fixed. And where did all that grinding, scraping, squealing sound that followed in its wake come from?

At that point, the Persian and Raoul were no longer able to retreat. They flattened themselves against the wall, not knowing what was to become of them because of the mysterious flaming face and the sounds, louder now than before, more swarming, more vibrant, more "numerous," because certainly this sound was the sum of hundreds of little sounds moving beneath the face of flame in the dark.

The fiery head advanced. It was here. With its noises. Here, and at their level.

And the two men, flattened against the wall, felt their hair standing on end with horror because they now knew where the myriad sounds were coming from. They came in droves thrust through the darkness, moving more quickly than the innumerable small wavelets that wash up on the sand with the incoming tide, the little white-capped night-waves under the moon, under the flame-headed moon.

And the little waves passed under this legs, climbed irresistibly up their legs, and Raoul and the Persian could no longer hold back their screams of horror, of fear and pain. Nor could they any longer continue to hold their hands up at eye level in the position of duelists waiting for the order to "fire." They brought their hands down to their legs to brush away the gleaming wavelets that were thronging with sharp little paws and claws and nails and teeth.

Yes, yes. Like the fire lieutenant, Papin, Raoul, and the Persian were on the verge of fainting. But at their cry, the fiery head turned toward them and spoke, "Don't move. Don't move. And above all, don't follow me. I'm the rat-killer.****[5] Let me pass with my rats!!!''

And suddenly, the fiery head disappeared, vanishing in the dark while the corridor before them brightened simply because of the maneuver the rat-killer had made with his dark lantern. What he had done to keep the rats in front of him from being frightened off was to point his lantern at himself, at his head, lighting it up. Now, to speed his flight, he pointed his lantern into the dark ahead of him. Hurrying forward, he drew the waves of rats with their myriad scraping, scratching, squeaking sounds after him.

The Persian and Raoul, still trembling but relieved, breathed again. "I should have remembered that Erik told me about the rat-killer," said the Persian. "But he didn't describe his appearance to me. And it's strange that I haven't met him before.

"Oh, I really believed that that was another of the monster's tricks." He sighed, "But no. He never comes to this part of the Opera."

"Are we then far from the lake?" asked Raoul. "When will we get there? Let's go to the lake. To the lake. When we get to the lake, we'll call for Christine; we'll shake the walls, we'll shout. Christine will hear us. And he will hear us. And since you know him, he'll talk to us."

**** The former director of the Opera, M. Pedro Gailhard, described to me one day at the home of Mme. Pierre Wolff the immense depredations committed underground by rats until the day that the administration made a deal—for a considerable price—with an individual who claimed he could end the plague by walking through the cellars every two weeks.

Since then, there have been no rats in the Opera except for those that are admitted to the dancers' lounge. M. Gailhard thought that this man had discovered a secret scent that attracted the rats to him, like the "bait" certain fishermen put on their legs to attract fish. The rat-killer then would lead the rats to some cavern where the intoxicated rats would permit themselves to be drowned. We have seen the horror that the appearance of this face caused the fire lieutenant—a horror that, according to a conversation with M. Gailhard, was so intense that the fireman fainted. As for myself, I have not the slightest doubt that the flaming head encountered by the fireman was the same head that so terrified the Persian and the Viscount de Chagny (*The Persian's Papers*).

[5] "I'm the rat-killer"

This creepy rat-filled scene necessarily reminds us of two British works that I am by no means sure Gaston Leroux had read. First, there is Robert Browning's "The Piped Piper of Hamelin" (1843) and then there is Bram Stoker's *Dracula* (1897). Browning's poem also has a sea of rats, but the tone in which he describes them is whimsical:

> "Great rats, small rats, lean rats, brawny rats,
> Brown rats, black rats, gray rats, tawny rats . . ."

(Horace E. Scudder, ed., *The Complete Poetic and Dramatic Works of Robert Browning*. Cambridge: Houghton Mifflin, 1895, p. 269.)

The tone describing the rats in Stoker's *Dracula* is altogether grim. ". . . we saw a whole mass of phosphorescence, which twinkled like stars. We all instinctively drew back. The whole place was becoming alive with rats . . . They seemed to swarm over the place all at once, till the lamplight, shining on their moving dark bodies and glittering, baleful eyes, made the place look like a bank of earth set with fireflies." (Leonard Wolf, ed., *The Essential Dracula*. New York: Plume, 1993, pp. 303–304.)

The boxes at the Opéra Garnier

"Don't be a child," said the Persian. "We'll never get into the house by the lake."

"Why is that?"

"Because that's where he's concentrated his entire defense. Even I have never been able to get to the other shore. The shore where the house is. First you have to get across the lake, and it's well guarded. I'm afraid that more than one of the old stagehands and door-closers, who have never been seen again, tried to get across that lake. It's dreadful. I, too, nearly died there, but the monster recognized me in time. A piece of advice, sir. Never go near the lake. And above all, stop your ears if you hear the singing of *the voice under water*, the voice of the siren."[6]

"But then," asked Raoul in a transport of feverish impatience and rage, "what are we doing here? If you can't do anything for Christine, at least let me die for her."

The Persian tried to calm the young man.

---

[6] "the voice of the siren"

In Greek mythology, the sirens were a pair of maidens who lived on an island in the ocean. Sitting in a meadow near the sea, they sang so captivatingly that passing mariners forgot everything but their music and thus perished. Ulysses and his companions on their homeward voyage escaped the usual fate because, guided by the advice of Circe, Ulysses stopped the ears of his men with wax and then tied himself to the mast.

"There's only one way to save Christine Daaé, believe me. And that is to get into his house without the monster seeing us."

"Can we hope to do that?"

"If I hadn't had that hope, I wouldn't have sought you out."

"And how can we get into the house by the lake without crossing the lake itself?"

"By the way of the third subcellar from which we have been so unfortunately chased and to which we will return at once. I'm going to tell you the precise place," he said, his voice faltering. "It's between a flat and an abandoned canvas from *Le Roi de Lahore*, precisely at the spot where Joseph Buquet died."

"Ah, the chief stagehand whom they found hanged."

"Yes, sir," the Persian added in a singular tone. "And the rope was never found. Let's go. Buck up and let's get going. And put your hand back in place, sir. But . . . where are we?"

The Persian had to light his dark lantern again. He sent its bright beam into the two vast corridors that intersected at a right angle and whose archways seemed to disappear into infinity. He said, "We must be in the part reserved especially for the waterworks. I don't see any flames coming from the furnaces."

He walked ahead of Raoul, feeling his way, stopping abruptly when he felt that a hydraulic engineer might be passing by; then they had to steer clear of a sort of underground forge whose fires were being put out and in front of which Raoul recognized the demons Christine had glimpsed on the first day of her captivity.

Thus it was that, little by little, they found their way back tot he enormous subcellar beneath the stage.

Probably, they were then at the bottom of the cistern whose depth must have been prodigious,[7] if one considers that fifteen meters of earth below the level of the water that existed in that part of the capital had been removed, and that they had had to pump out all of the water. Such a huge amount that, to have any idea of the mass of water expelled by the pumps, one has to imagine a lake with a surface area equal to the courtyard of the Louvre and a height that is one and half times the height of Notre Dame. Even so, they had to keep a lake.

---

[7] "whose depth must have been prodigious"

The work of excavation *was* prodigious (see Chapter XIII, Note 10, page 170). Leroux's language here echoes the historian Charles Nuitter (*Le Nouvel Opéra de Paris*. Paris: Hachette, 1875), cited by Alain Duault in *L'Opéra de Paris* (p. 32), who writes, "To get an idea of the amount of water pumped out, one has to think of a surface the size of the courtyard of the Louvre, and a height one and a half times the height of the towers of Notre Dame."

At that moment, the Persian touched a wall and said, "If I'm not mistaken, here's a wall that belongs to the lake house." He then knocked against the wall of the cistern.

It may be useful to explain to the reader how the foundation and the walls of the cistern had been built. In order to keep the waters surrounding the construction from coming in direct contact with the walls supporting the whole complex of theatrical apparatus that included frameworks, wood, and metal artifacts and painted canvas—all of which needed to be particularly protected against dampness—the *architect had found it necessary to surround the whole thing with a double caisson* that took an entire year to build.

It was against the inner first wall that the Persian knocked when he spoke to Raoul about the lake house. For anyone who might have known about the architecture of the structure, the Persian's gesture would have seemed to indicate that *Erik's mysterious house had been built inside the double caisson*, with one thick wall built as a cofferdam, then a brick wall, then an enormous layer of cement and another wall that was several meters thick.

At the Persian's words, Raoul threw himself against the wall and listened eagerly. But he heard nothing. Nothing but the distant footsteps that resounded on the floor in the upper levels of the theater.

The Persian extinguished his lamp once more. "Attention," he said, "keep your hand up. And now, silence. Because now we're going to try to get inside his house." And he led Raoul to the little staircase down which they had come a while ago. They went up, stopping on each stair, peering into the silent darkness. Then they came to the third basement. The Persian made a sign for Raoul to kneel. Then, dragging themselves forward using their knees and one hand—the other hand always held up in the prescribed manner—they came to the back wall. Here there was a large abandoned canvas from *Le Roi de Lahore*. And right beside it a flat. Between the canvas and the flat there was just enough space for a body.

A body that, one day, had been found hanged . . . the body of Joseph Buquet.

The Persian, still on his knees, had stopped. He was listening. For a moment he seemed to hesitate and looked at Raoul, then he lifted his gaze upward toward the second basement where, through a crack in the floorboards, the feeble light of a lantern could be seen. Clearly, this light was troubling the Persian. Finally, he nodded his head, his mind made up.

He slipped between the flat and the canvas from *Le Roi de Lahore*. Raoul was right behind him.

The Persian's free hand tapped against the wall. Raoul saw him push hard against the wall for a moment, as he had pushed against the wall in Christine's dressing room. And a stone toppled over. Now, there was a hole in the wall.

The Persian took his pistol from his pocket and indicated for Raoul to do the same. He loaded his pistol. Then, resolutely and still on his knees, he went through the hole made by the falling stone. Raoul, who had wanted to be the first to go through, had to be content with following him.

The passage was very narrow. Almost at once, the Persian came to a stop. Raoul heard him whispering, "We're going to have to let ourselves fall a few meters without making any sound. Take off your shoes."*****

The Persian was already performing that operation. He passed his shoes to Raoul. "Leave them beside the wall," he said. "We'll find them on our way out."

With that, the Persian moved forward a little. Then he came back, still on his knees, until he was head to head with Raoul, to whom he said, "I'm going to hang by my hands to the edge of the stone, then I'll let myself fall into *his house*. Then you do exactly the same thing. Don't be afraid. I'll catch you."

The Persian suited his action to his words. And Raoul heard a muffled sound beneath him, produced, evidently, by the Persian's fall. The young man trembled, fearing that the sound might reveal their presence.

Yet, what was even more agonizing to Raoul beyond that noise was the absolute absence of any other sound. How could it be? If, as according to the Persian, they had penetrated the very walls of the lake house, then why didn't they hear Christine? Not a cry. Not a call. Not a groan. Good God! Had they arrived too late?

Scraping the wall with his knees, clinging to the stone with his wiry fingers, Raoul let himself fall. And felt himself being firmly held. "It's me," the Persian said. "Quiet!" They stood without moving, listening. The darkness around them had never been so dense, the silence heavier or more dreadful. Raoul dug his fingernails against his lips to keep from screaming, "Christine! It's me. If you're not dead, answer me, Christine."

Finally, the game with the dark lantern began again. The Persian directed its rays above them, against the wall, searching for the hole through which they had come and no longer finding it. "Oh," he said, "the stone

_____

***** The two pairs of shoes, which, according to the Persian's papers, were put down beside the canvas from *Le Roi de Lahore* and the flat at the place where Joseph Buquet was found hanged, were never found. They must have been taken by some stagehand or door-closer.

fell back into place by itself." And the lantern's bright ray descended the length of the wall to the floor.

The Persian knelt and picked something up. A sort of wire that he examined for a second and then threw away in horror. "The Punjab lasso,"[8] he murmured.

"What's that?" Raoul asked.

"That," said the Persian, trembling, "that could very well be the hanged man's rope they searched so hard for."

Then, seized by a new anxiety, he swept the red disk of his lantern over the wall, illuminating, strangely enough, the trunk of a tree that seemed still to be alive with its leaves. The tree's branches spread upward beside the wall until they disappeared into the ceiling.

Because the bright disk of light was so small it was hard at first to take everything in . . . they saw a cluster of branches, and then a leaf . . . and another leaf . . . and then, beside it, nothing at all. Nothing but the bright light that seemed to be a reflection of itself. Raoul passed his hand over that nothing, over that reflection.

"Look here," he said. "The wall is a mirror."

"Yes, a mirror," said the Persian in a tone of the most profound emotion. "And," he added, passing the hand that held the pistol over his sweating brow, "we have fallen into the torture chamber."

---

[8] "Punjab lasso"

I have been unable to find any reference to a "Punjab lasso" as such. However, in Eugène Sue's *The Wandering Jew*, a work that Leroux undoubtedly knew, there is a scene in which a member of an Indian cult of stranglers called Lughardars (also known as Thugs or Thuggees) stalks and kills his victim:

. . . an Indian, passing through an open space in the jungle, approached the spot where the Thug lay concealed.

The latter unwound from his waist a long thin cord, to one of the ends of which was attached a leaden ball, of the form and size of an egg; having fastened the other end of this cord to his right wrist, the Strangler again listened, and then disappeared, crawling through the tall grass in the direction of the Indian. . . .

[The Indian] sees a dark figure rise before him: he hears a whizzing noise like that of a sling; he feels a cord, thrown with as much rapidity as force, encircle his neck with a triple band, and, almost in the same instant, the leaden ball strikes violently against the back of his head . . . he tottered—the Strangler gave a vigorous pull at the cord—the bronzed countenance of the slave became purple, and he fell upon his knees, convulsively moving his arms. Then the Strangler threw him quite down, and pulled the cord so violently, that the blood spurted from the skin. The victim struggled for a moment—and all was over (Eugène Sue, *The Wandering Jew*, Book I. New York: Modern Library, 1968, pp. 141–142.)

Chapter XXII

INTERESTING AND INSTRUCTIVE TRIBULATIONS OF A PERSIAN IN THE
OPERA'S CELLARS

The Persian himself has recounted how, until that night, he had tried in vain to get into the lakeside house via the lake; how he had discovered the entrance in the third subbasement and how, finally, he and the Viscount de Chagny confronted the Phantom's infernal imagination in *the torture chamber*.

Here is the written account that he left us (under conditions that will be specified later). I have not altered a word of it. I give it just as it is, because I have not thought it right to pass over in silence the personal adventures of the daroga in the house by the lake before he fell into it with Raoul. If for a little while this very interesting beginning would seem to distance us a bit from the torture chamber, it is only so that we may soon return to it after you have had some important things, as well as certain of the Persian's quite extraordinary attitudes and behavior, explained to you.

The Persian wrote,[1] "It was the first time that I got into the lake

---

[1] "The Persian wrote . . ."

From this point on up to and including Chapter XXVI, the novel's first-person narrator steps back and we get a separate narrative unit in which the Persian's voice carries the story forward.

house. In vain had I begged the *trapdoor lover* [that's what he was called among us in Persia] to open his mysterious doors. He had always refused. I, who was paid to know many of his secrets and his tricks, had tried in vain to get into the house by guile. Ever since I had found Erik at the Opera, where he seemed to have chosen to live, I had spied on him sometimes in the corridors of the upper levels, sometimes in those of the basements, sometimes on the very banks of the lake when, thinking he was alone, he got into his little boat and reached the opposite shore. But the darkness that always surrounded him was always too dense to allow me to see exactly where in the wall it was that he opened his door. Curiosity, and also a formidable idea that had come to me while thinking about some of the things the monster had told me, prompted me one day when I thought myself to be alone to leap into his little boat and send it toward that part of the wall where I had seen him disappear. It was then that I had to deal with the siren who guards the banks of the lake, and whose charm, under the following conditions, nearly proved fatal to me. Here's what happened:

"I had no sooner left the shore when the silence through which I was navigating was imperceptibly troubled by a sort of whispered song which surrounded me. It was both breath and music at the same time. It rose softly from the waters of the lake and, by some contrivance I could not discover, enveloped me. The music followed me, moved with me, and was so sweet that I had no fear of it. On the contrary, in my desire to get nearer to that sweet and captivating harmony, I leaned over the little boat toward the water, because I had no doubt at all that's where the song came from. I was already in the middle of the lake and there was no one there but myself; the voice—because it was now clearly a voice—was beside me on the water. I leaned over . . . I leaned still farther. The lake was perfectly calm and the moon's ray which, after having passed by the barred window of the Rue Scribe, shone on the lake, showed me absolutely nothing on its surface, which was as smooth and black as ink. I shook my head, hoping to rid myself of what might possibly be a ringing in my ears, but it was soon very clear to me that there could be no ringing in my ears as melodic as that singing whisper that followed me and which, now, was drawing me.

"If I had been a superstitious man or easily susceptible to weakness, I could not have failed to think that I had to do with a siren of some sort whose task was to trouble the voyager bold enough to travel on the waters of the lakeside house; but, thank God, I come from a country where the fantastic is so cherished that we know it to its depths and in times past I myself have studied it extensively. Anyone who knows the magician's trade can excite the human imagination with a few simple tricks.

"I had, then, no doubt at all that I was confronting one of Erik's new inventions, but again, this invention was so perfect that, as I leaned over the little boat, I was less pushed by the desire to discover the hoax than by the wish to enjoy its charm.

"And I leaned over . . . leaned over . . . and almost capsized.

"All of a sudden, two monstrous arms emerged from the water and grasped my throat and dragged me irresistibly down into the gulf. Certainly I would have been done for had I not had time to utter a cry that allowed Erik to recognize me.

"Because it was he, and instead of drowning me as had certainly been his intention, he swam to the shore, where he put me down gently. 'See how careless you are,' he said as she stood before me, with that hellish water streaming from him. 'Why are you trying to get into my house? I haven't invited you. I don't want you there, or anyone else in the world. Have you saved my life only to make it unbearable? No matter how great the service was that you did him, Erik may end by forgetting it, and you know that nothing can restrain Erik, not even Erik himself.'

"He talked on, but now I had no other desire except to know about what I have called *the trick of the siren*. He was happy to satisfy my curiosity, because Erik, veritable monster though he is—and that is my judgment of him having, alas, had occasion to see his work in Persia—is in certain ways a presumptuous and vain child[2] who, after he has astonished the world, likes nothing better than to prove the truly miraculous ingenuities of his mind.

"He laughed and showed me the long stem of a reed. 'Nothing could be simpler. It's quite convenient for breathing and for singing under water. It's a trick I learned from the Tonkin pirates* who can stay at the bottom of their rivers for hours.'[3]

" 'It's a trick,' I said severely, 'that almost killed me, and that has perhaps been fatal to others.'

---

[2] "vain child"

Since I have emphasized how frequently Leroux describes Raoul as childlike, it is only fair to note here this characterization of Erik by the Persian. Raoul's childlike nature renders him incompetent to death with the crisis in which he is involved. Erik's is a boyish pride in his own ingenious accomplishments.

* An administrative report from Tonkin which arrived in Paris at the end of July 1900 tells how the famous head of the De Tham group of pirates was tracked down by our soldiers and escaped them, along with all his men, thanks to the use of reeds.

[3] "Tonkin pirates . . . for hours"

Formerly the name of the northern part of Vietnam, and, until the Vietnam War, a part of French Indochina. It is bounded on the north by China, on the east by the Gulf of Tonkin, on the south by northern Annam, and Laos on the south and southwest. The river pirates probably practiced their trade on the Croi River, preying on the commerce that flows between Vietnam and China.

The trick of breathing through a tube while hiding under water is featured in the *Fantomas* film serial produced in 1914. There, the master criminal, Fantomas, hides inside a vat filled with water and breathes though a bottle that appears to be floating on the surface of the water.

"He did not answer, but stood before me in an attitude of childish menace that I knew well.

" 'I would not "let myself be impressed," ' I said clearly. 'Erik, you know what you promised me. No more murders.'

" 'Is it true,' he said amiably, 'that I have committed murders?'

" 'Wretch,' I cried. 'Have you forgotten *the rosy hours of Mazendaran?*'[4]

" 'Yes,'' he replied, suddenly mournful. 'I'd prefer to forget them. But I certainly made the little sultana laugh.'

" 'All that,' I declared, 'is in the past. But this is now. And you have to account to me for the present, since, had I wished it, there would be none of it for you. Remember that, Erik. I saved your life.'

"And I profited from the turn the conversation had taken to speak to him of something that for some time had been much on my mind. 'Erik,' I said, 'Erik, swear that . . .'

" 'What?' he said. 'You know very well that I don't keep my oaths. Oaths are made for entrapping fools.'

" 'Tell me . . . you know you can tell me . . .'

" 'Well?'

" 'The chandelier, Erik. The chandelier . . .'

" 'What about the chandelier?'

" 'You know very well what I mean.'

" 'Ah,' he said, laughing, 'the chandelier. I'll tell you gladly. *I had nothing to do with the chandelier. The chandelier was very worn.*'

"Erik was even more frightening when he laughed. He leaped into his boat with a laugh so sinister I could not help trembling. 'Very worn, dear daroga.** A very worn chandelier. It fell by itself. It went boom! And now, a word of advice, daroga. Go dry yourself if you don't want to catch cold. And don't ever get into my boat again. And above all, don't try to get into my house. I'm not always there, and I would be very sorry to have to dedicate *my requiem mass* to you.'

"He laughed as he said this, standing in the stern of his boat, swaying back and forth like a monkey as he sculled it. He had the look of a deadly rock topped by his golden eyes. It was not long before I saw only his eyes, and finally he disappeared into the darkness of the lake.

** Daroga, in Persian, means the chief of the National Police.
4 *"Mazendaran"*

A northeastern province of Persia with a single port city, Meched-i-Ser, on the Caspian Sea. At the time Leroux was writing *The Phantom*, it was a fertile province in which lemon, orange, and almond orchards were cultivated, as well as rice and wheat. Mazendaran had an active trading relationship with Russia, exporting silk and caviar.

"From that day on, I gave up trying to get into his house by the lake. Clearly, the entrance there was too well guarded, particularly now that he knew that I knew about it. But I was fairly sure that there must be another entrance, because when I had followed him, I had seen him disappear more than once in the third basement without being able to figure out how he did it.

"I can't say often enough that, from the time I first learned that Erik had established himself in the Opera, I lived in constant fear of his dreadful fantasies, not only in regard to myself, but I was afraid also for others.***

"And when there was some accident or fatal event, I couldn't help saying to myself, 'Maybe it was Erik!' while others around me were saying, 'It's the Phantom.' How often did I hear that sentence spoken by people who were smiling? Poor fools! Had they known that there was a flesh and bones phantom and that he was many times more dreadful than the shade they invoked, I swear that they would have stopped their joking. Had they only known what Erik was capable of, especially in a field of action like the Opera . . . and if they had known the full range of my own fearful thoughts . . .

"As for me, my life was no longer my own. Though Erik had announced solemnly that he had changed, and that he had become the most virtuous of men *since he was loved for himself,* a phrase that, when I thought of the monster, left me so terribly perplexed I could not keep from shuddering when I heard it. His unique, horrible, and repulsive ugliness put him beyond the pale of mankind, and it had often seemed to me that, for that reason alone, he no longer felt he owed anything to the human species. When he spoke to me of his love affair, my fears only increased, because I could foresee, from that boasting tone of his with which I was familiar, a cause of new tragedies more terrible than all the rest. I knew the sublime and disastrous degree of despair Erik's sorrow could attain—and the words he had spoken to me, hinting vaguely at the most horrible catastrophe, were never out of my anxious mind.

"On the other hand, I had discovered the strange relationship that the monster and Christine Daaé had established. Hidden in the storage room adjoining the young diva's dressing room, I had seen admirable music sessions, which apparently plunged Christine into an amazing ecstasy, but just the same I could not possibly think that Erik's voice, which, when he

*** Here, the Persian might have acknowledged that Erik's fate interested him for reasons of his own, as well. He was not unaware that if the government in Teheran were to learn that Erik was still alive, it would mean the end of the former daroga's modest pension. It is fair, besides, to add that the Persian had a noble and generous heart, and we do not doubt that the disasters he feared for others were a profound source of anxiety for him, as his praiseworthy behavior in this entire affair sufficiently proves.

wished, could be as loud as thunder or as gentle as the voices of angels, could make her forget his ugliness. I understood everything when I discovered that Christine had not yet seen him.

"I had occasion to go into her dressing room, and remembering the lessons he had give me on other occasions, I had no trouble discovering the trick that made the wall supporting the mirror turn on its pivot, and I discovered how, by means of hollow bricks that were made to act as speaking tubes, he was able to make Christine hear him as if he were at her side. In that way, too, I discovered the path that leads to the fountain and to the prison cells—the Communards' prison cells—and also the trap-door that must have given Erik direct access to the basements under the stage.

"How astounded I was, a few days later, to learn with my own eyes and ears that Erik and Christine were seeing each other, and to surprise the monster leaning over the little weeping fountain in the Communards' passage (underground and all the way in the back) and sprinkling water on the unconscious Christine Daaé's forehead. A white horse, the horse from *The Prophet*, which had disappeared from the Opera's stables, was standing calmly beside them. I showed myself. It was dreadful. I saw sparks darting from the golden eyes and, before I could say a word, I was struck full on the forehead by a blow that knocked me out. When I came to, Erik, Christine, and the white horse was gone. I had no doubt that the poor young woman was a prisoner in the house by the lake.

"Without hesitation, I resolved, despite the certain danger of such an undertaking, to return to the shore. For twenty-four hours, hidden near the dark riverbank, I waited for the monster to reappear, because I thought that he would be forced to go out for provisions. On that score, I ought to say that in the city, or when he risked going out in public, he would cover his horrible nose-hole with a papier-mâché nose complete with a mustache, which did not at all keep him from looking macabre since, as he went by, people behind him would say, 'There goes the grim reaper.'[5] Still, the nose made him almost—I stress almost—bearable to look at.

"I was, then, watching for him on the shore of the lake—'Lake Avernus,' as he had many times laughingly called his lake in my presence. Tired of my long patience, I said to myself once more, 'He's gone through another door, the one at the "third subbasement."' Just then I heard a little splashing sound

---

[5] "There goes the grim reaper"
   The French reads, " . . . *voilà le pére Trompe-la-Mort*," literally, "There he is, Father Death-Fooler."

266

in the dark. I saw the two golden eyes shining like lanterns, and soon the boat was beached. Erik leaped to shore and came toward me.

"'It's been twenty-four hours since you've been here,' he said. 'You're annoying me. I warn you, this is going to end badly. And you'll have brought it on yourself. Because I've been remarkably patient with you. You stupid fool, you think you're following me. It's I who am following you. And I know all that you know about me here. I spared you yesterday, on the *Communards' path*. But let me tell you, once and for all, I don't want to see you again. This is all very careless of you. I'm beginning to wonder whether you still know how to take a hint?'

"He was so angry that I was careful not to interrupt him just then. After snorting like a seal, he let me know his dreadful thoughts whose details corresponded to my fearful imaginings.

"'Yes, once and for all, you ought to know—do you understand, once and for all—what it means to take a hint. I tell you that your carelessness—because you've been stopped twice already by the shadow in the felt hat,[6] who had no idea what you were doing in the basements and who took you to the directors, who supposed you were an eccentric Persian who loves backstage special effects. (I was there. Yes, I was in the office; you know very well that I'm everywhere.) I tell you, then, that given your carelessness, they're going to ask themselves what it is you're looking for— and they'll end by knowing that it's Erik you're seeking. Then they'll seek Erik, too. And they'll find the house by the lake. Then—too bad for you, my friend. Too bad. I won't answer for anything.'

"Again, he snorted like a seal. 'For anything. If Erik's secrets don't stay secret, then too bad for a great many members of the human race. That's all I have to say to you. And unless you are a stupid ninny, that ought to be enough for you, unless you *don't* know how to take a hint.'

"He sat down at the stern of his boat and tapped the boards with his heels, waiting for me to reply. I said simply, 'I haven't come here looking for Erik.'

"'Who then?'

"'You know very well. It's Christine Daaé.'

"He replied, 'I have a right to meet her in my house. I am loved for myself.'

---

[6] "the felt hat"

This is the mysterious personage, presumed to be an employee of the opera's management, but whose identity we will never learn. See Chapter XXI, third note, page 252.

" 'That's not true,' I said. 'You've kidnapped her and you're keeping her prisoner.'

" 'Listen,' he said, 'if I prove to you that I am loved for myself, will you promise never to meddle in my affairs again?'

" 'Yes, I promise,' I said without hesitation, thinking that for such a monster no such proof could be possible.

" 'All right, then. It's very simple. Christine Daaé can leave here whenever she wants. Yes, and she'll come back, because it pleases her, because she loves me for myself.'

" 'Oh, I doubt that she'll come back. But it's your duty to let her go.'

" 'My duty, you stupid ninny. It's what I want. I want to let her go—and she'll come back . . . because she loves me . . . I tell you that this will all end in a marriage. A marriage in the Madeleine, you stupid ninny. Do you believe me, finally? When I tell you that the marriage mass has already been written. You'll see the *Kyrie* . . .'

"Again he tapped his heels on the floorboards of the boat in a sort of rhythm that he accompanied by singing softly, '*Kyrie* . . . *Kyrie* . . . *Kyrie Eleison*. . . .[7] You'll see. You'll see the mass.'

" 'Listen,' I said finally, "I'll believe you when I see Christine Daaé leaving the lake house and coming back to it of her own free will.'

" 'And you won't meddle in my affairs again? All right, you'll see it tonight. Come to the masked ball. Christine and I are going to be there for a while. You can go hide in the storage room, and you'll see that Christine, who will have returned to her dressing room, will ask for nothing more than to go back to the path of the Communards.'

" 'Agreed.'

"If I were to see that then, I would have to yield, because someone beautiful has every right to love the most horrible of monsters, especially when, as with him, he has the seductiveness of music in his favor and when, as with her, she is a very distinguished singer.

" 'And now, go away. Because I have to do my shopping.'

"I went, then, still worrying about Christine Daaé, but also mulling over the terrifying thought he had awakened in me regarding my imprudence.

"I said to myself, 'How is this all going to end?' And though I was

---

[7] "*Kyrie Eleison*"
   "Lord have mercy." The *Kyrie eleison* is the first of three petitions made in the Roman Catholic mass. They are "*Kyrie eleison*, Lord have mercy," "*Christe eleison*, Christ have mercy," and "*Kyrie eleison*, Lord have mercy."

something of a fatalist by temperament, I could not rid myself of an indefinable anguish because of the incredible responsibility I had assumed on the day that I had spared the life of this monster who today menaced *a great many members of the human race.*

"I was enormously astonished when things turned out the way he had said they would. Christine Daaé left the house by the lake and came back several times without any apparent duress. I tried not to think about this mysterious love affair, but it was very hard, especially for me with my anxieties, not to think about Erik. Still, having decided to be very prudent, I did not make the mistake of going back to the shore of the lake or to go there via the Communards' path. But being obsessed by the secret door in the third subbasement, and knowing that it was usually deserted during the day, I went there several times, staking out the place for hours on end, twiddling my thumbs beside a painting from *Le Roi de Lahore* that had been left there, I don't know why, since *Le Roi de Lahore* was seldom played. So much patience ought to have been rewarded. One day, I saw the monster coming toward me on his knees. I was certain he did not see me. He passed between the painting that was there and a flat, and went all the way to the wall to a point I made note of, and pressed against a spring that made a stone topple, which thereby opened a space through which he could pass. He disappeared through this space and the stone fell back into place behind him. I had the monster's secret which, when I was ready, would give me access to his house on the lake.

"To make sure of it, I waited at least half an hour, then I pressed the spring. Everything happened as it had for Erik. But knowing he was at home, I was not about to go through the hole. Besides, the thought that Erik might find me here put me suddenly in mind of Joseph Buquet's death. Then, not wishing to jeopardize the important discovery I had made, a discovery that might prove helpful to 'many members of the human race,' I put the stone carefully back into place following an old Persian system, and left the theater basements.

"You are right if you're thinking that I was still very interested in the love affair between Christine Daaé and Erik, not from any morbid curiosity, but for the reason I've already given—the terrifying thoughts about Erik that would not leave me. 'If,' I thought, 'Erik learns that he is not loved for himself, anything can be expected.' And, since I never stopped moving about the Opera—very carefully—I soon learned the truth about the monster's sad love affair. He occupied Christine's mind by terror, but the sweet child's heart belonged entirely to the Viscount Raoul de Chagny. While these two played like an innocent engaged couple in the upper reaches of the Opera—fleeing the monster—they did not suspect that someone was watching them. I had decided to do anything I could: to kill the monster if necessary, and then explain to the police. But Erik was not to be found, and that did not reassure me.

"I need to explain my entire plan. I thought that the monster, driven from his home by jealousy, would therefore give me the chance, via the third subbasement, to get into the lake house without danger. It was important, for everyone's sake, to know exactly what there might be in it. One day, tired of waiting for an opportunity, I set the stone in motion and I immediately heard remarkable music; with all the doors of his home open, the monster was at work on his *Don Juan Triumphant*. I knew that it was his life's work. I didn't dare move and stayed carefully in my dark hole. He stopped playing for a moment and began walking around his house like a madman. In a ringing voice, he said, 'This has to be finished *before*. Absolutely done.' There was nothing in the words to reassure me, and since the music began again, I replaced the stone very gently. Yet, despite the stone's being in place, I still heard a vague voice rising far, far away from the depths of the earth, as I had heard the siren's song rising from the bottom of the lake. And I recalled that at the time of Joseph Buquet's death some stagehands had said—and been laughed at for saying—they 'heard a sound like the singing of the dead hovering over the hanged man's body.'

"The day on which Christine Daaé was kidnapped, I arrived at the theater fairly late in the evening, afraid that I would hear bad news. I had spent an awful day. Ever since reading the announcement in the morning newspaper of Christine Daaé's engagement to the Viscount de Chagny, I had been continually wondering *whether I ought not denounce the monster after all*. But my reason prevailed, and I was persuaded that such behavior would simply hasten any possible disaster.

"When my coach left me off in front of the Opera, I looked at the building as if, in truth, I was astonished *to see it still standing*.

"But, like all orientals, I am a bit of a fatalist and I went in, ready for anything.

"The abduction of Christine Daaé during the prison act, which naturally surprised everyone, found me prepared. It was certain that Erik had conjured her away, like the king of magicians that in truth he was. And I thought that for sure this time it was the end of Christine *and perhaps of everyone*.

"I was so convinced of this that at one point I wondered whether I ought not to warn latecomers to the theater to run away. But again, I was kept from making a denunciation by the certainty that I would be thought mad. Finally, I was not unaware that if, for example, I cried 'Fire!' to make people leave, I might be the cause of a disaster—people smothered in flight, savage battles—that could be even worse than the catastrophe itself.

"Just the same, I resolved personally to act without delay. The timing for it seemed propitious. I had plenty of opportunity since, at the moment, Erik would be thinking only of his captive. It was necessary to take advantage of this fact and get inside his house via the route of the Communards and through the trapdoor.

"The young viscount, when he saw the pistols, asked me whether we were going to be dueling. 'Yes. And what a duel,' I said. But of course I didn't have time to explain anything to him. The young viscount is brave, but after all, he knew hardly anything about his adversary, which was all to the good.

"What was a duel with the fiercest of duelers compared with a battle against the most accomplished of magicians? I myself had difficulty accepting the notion that I was about to begin a struggle with a man who was only visible when he wanted to be and who, on the other hand, could see everything around him while you could see nothing but darkness. With a man whose strange science, subtlety, and skill allowed him to make use of a combination of his natural forces to create in your eyes and ears the illusion that you were doomed. And all of that in the subbasements of the Opera, which is to say, in the very heart of fantasyland. Can one imagine that without trembling? Can one have any idea of what could happen to the eyes and ears of an inhabitant of the Opera with a ferocious and whimsical Robert Houdin, who sometimes joked with and sometimes hated you, who picked your pockets, or killed you when you were locked into the building with its five basements and twenty-five upper levels? Can you imagine fighting the trapdoor lover? My God, he built some of those trapdoors in all the palaces of my country; those astonishing pivoting trapdoors which are the best ever made. Think of fighting the trapdoor lover in trapdoor country!

"If my hope was that he was still with Christine Daaé in the lake house where he had taken her when she fainted, my fear was that he was somewhere near us, preparing the Punjab lasso.

"No one knew better than the how to throw the Punjab lasso, and he was the prince of stranglers, just as he was the prince of magicians. When he had finished making the little sultana laugh, in the epoch of *the rosy hours of Mazendaran*, she would herself ask him to please her by making her shudder. And he found that nothing succeeded better than the game of the Punjab lasso. Erik had traveled in India and had come back with an incredible skill at strangling. He would have himself locked in a courtyard into which they would lead a warrior armed with a long pike and a broadsword—most often a man condemned to death. Erik himself had only his lasso, and it was always at the point when the warrior thought he had beaten Erik with a formidable blow that the hiss of the lasso was heard. With a twist of his wrist, Erik tightened the thin lasso around his enemy's neck and dragged him at once before the little sultana and her women who were watching from a window and applauding. The little sultana herself learned how to throw the Punjab lasso and killed several of her women, including some visiting friends of hers. But I prefer to leave the dreadful subject of *the rosy hours of Mazendaran*. If I have talked about it it is only because, having arrived in the subbasements of the Opera with the Viscount de Chagny, I had to put my companion on guard against the constant possibility that we might be strangled. Of course, once we were in the subbasements, my pistols would have been useless, because I was certain that though Erik had not opposed us at the moment of our entrance onto the path of the Communards, he would not then allow himself to be seen. But he could still strangle us. I didn't have the time to explain all that to the viscount, and I don't know whether, if I had had time, I would have used it to tell him that somewhere in the dark there was a Punjab lasso ready to hiss. It would have been useless to complicate the situation, and I limited myself to advising M. de Chagny always to keep his hand at eye level, arm bent in the position of a marksman waiting to hear the command to 'fire.' In that position, it was impossible, even for the most adept strangler, to throw the Punjab lasso effectively. It loops around an arm or a hand just as it would around a neck, and thus the lasso could be easily untied and rendered harmless.

"After having evaded the superintendent of police, some door-closers, the firemen, and then meeting the rat-killer for the first time, as well as passing by the man with the felt hat without attracting his attention, the viscount and I arrived without mishap in the third basement between the flat and the painted canvas from *Le Roi de Lahore*. I moved the stone, and we jumped down into the home Erik had made for himself inside the double caisson walls of the Opera's foundation (which he had no difficulty at all in doing, since he was one of the foremost masonry contractors[8] of

---

[8] "masonry contractors"

This detail will acquire even more interest later. See Epilogue, Note 8, page 326.

Philippe Garnier, the Opera's architect, and he had continued to work, mysteriously and all alone, when the work was officially suspended during the war and the siege of Paris at the time of the Commune).

"I knew Erik well enough to cherish the notion that I would be able to discover all the tricks he had contrived for himself during all this time. But I was by no means reassured as I dropped into his home, because I knew what he had done in certain palaces in Mazendaran. He had turned the most honest construction in the world into a demonic house where one could not speak a word without being watched or betrayed by an echo. How many family quarrels, how many bloody tragedies had the monster left in his wake with his trapdoors? Not to mention the fact that one could never be sure where one was in the palaces he had rigged. He had astonishing inventions. Certainly, the strangest and the most horrible as well as the most dangerous of all was the *torture chamber*. In all but a few exceptional cases, when the little sultana would amuse herself by making some middle-class citizen suffer, no one was allowed into it except prisoners condemned to death. In my opinion, that chamber was the most atrocious of the imaginative creations of *the rosy hours of Mazendaran*. And, when a visitor who had entered the *torture chamber* had 'had enough,' he was always allowed to finish himself off by using the Punjab lasso, which was left for his use at the foot of the iron tree.

"Then you can imagine how I felt when, soon after I entered the monster's home, I saw that the room into which the Viscount de Chagny and I had leaped was an exact replica of the chamber of horrors from *the rosy hours of Mazendaran*.

"At our feet, I found the Punjab lasso which, all that evening, I had feared. I was convinced that it had been used already for Joseph Buquet. The chief stagehand had, evidently, like myself, come upon Erik one evening when he was moving the stone in the third subbasement. Curious, he had, in his turn, tried the passage before the stone dropped back into place and had fallen into the torture chamber and only left it after he had been hanged. I can easily imagine Erik dragging the body he wanted to be rid of as far as the painted canvas from *Le Roi de Lahore* and hanging it there as an example or to increase *the superstitious fear that helped him guard the approaches to his lair*.

"But, after thinking about it, Erik returned to get the Punjab lasso, which is very uniquely made of catgut and which might have incited the curiosity of a magistrate. That would explain the disappearance of the rope from the hanged man's body.

"And now, in the torture chamber, I found the lasso at our feet. I am not a coward, but a cold sweat broke out on my face. The lantern, whose red disk I was moving over the walls of the infamous room, trembled in my hand.

"M. De Chagny noticed it and asked, 'What's the matter, sir?'

"I made a violent sign for him to be still, because I continued to have the supreme hope that we were in the torture chamber without the monster's being aware of it. But even that hope was no comfort, because I could imagine that the torture chamber was designed to guard the lake house from the third subbasement, and it might do it automatically.

"Yes, the tortures might begin *automatically*. Who could say which of our movements might set them off?

"I urged my companion to keep absolutely still.

"A crushing silence pressed down upon us. And my red lantern continued to move around the torture chamber . . . I recognized it . . . I recognized it . . .

Chapter XXIII

IN THE TORTURE CHAMBER

The Persian's Narrative (Continued)

"We were at the center of a small perfectly hexagonal chamber. From top to bottom, the six panels of the walls had mirrors affixed to them. At the corners of the room one could clearly see where the mirrors were joined and how the small segments were designed to turn on their drums. Yes, yes, I recognized them, and I recognized the iron tree at the corner at the bottom of one of the segments—the tree of iron with its iron branch for those who were hanged. I had seized my companion's arm. The Viscount de Chagny was all atremble, ready to shout to his beloved that help was on its way. I was afraid he would be unable to contain himself.

"All at once we heard a sound at our left. It was, at first, as if a door had opened and then closed in the room next to us. Then there was a muffled groan. I held Monsieur de Chagny's arm more tightly. Then we distinctly heard these words, 'Take it or leave it. The requiem mass or the wedding mass.'

"I recognized the monster's voice. There was another groan, after which there was a long silence. I was persuaded now that the monster did not know we were in his home, because if it had been otherwise, he would have arranged it so that we could not hear him at all. All he would have

275

had to do was to seal the small invisible window through which torture aficionados could look into the chamber. Beyond that, I was sure that if *he* had known of our presence, the tortures would have begun at once.

"We had, then, a great advantage over Erik. We were near him and he did not know it. What was important was to keep him from knowing it, and I feared nothing so much as the Viscount de Chagny's impetuousity, which would impel him to break through the walls to join Christine Daaé, whose groans we thought we could hear at intervals.

" 'The requiem mass it not a happy one,' Erik's voice went on, 'while the marriage mass—now that's something—is magnificent. You need to choose the one you want. As for me, I can't go on living like this . . . like a mole deep underground. *Don Juan Triumphant* is finished. Now I want to live like the rest of the world. I want to have a wife like everyone else. With whom I can take a Sunday walk, like everyone else. I have devised a mask that allows me to have a normal face. No one will ever turn around to look. You'll be the happiest of women. We will sing ecstatically to each other.

" 'You're crying. You're afraid of me. And yet, at heart I'm not so wicked. Love me and you'll see. *To be good, I needed only to be loved.*[1] If you loved me, I'd be as gentle as a lamb, and you could make of me whatever you wanted.'

"Soon, the groans that accompanied this love litany grew louder. I've never heard anything so desperate, and M. de Chagny and I recognized that this frightful lamentation belonged to Erik himself. As for Christine, she was perhaps somewhere on the other side of the wall before us, with the monster at her knees. She must have been mute with horror, without the strength to cry out.

"The lamentation was resonant, menacing, and as hoarse as the grief of an ocean. Three times, Erik's accusation left the rocky cavern of his throat, 'You don't love me; you don't love me; you don't love me.'

"Then, more gently, 'Why are you crying? You know very well that that hurts me.'

"Silence.

"Each silence gave us hope. We said to each other, 'Perhaps he has left her there behind the wall.' We thought of nothing except how to let Christine know that we were there without alerting the monster to our

---

[1]   *"To be good, I needed only to be loved."*

It's hard not to hear in Erik's words an echo of the Creature's complaint in Mary Shelley's *Frankenstein*. There, in their confrontation on the glacier, the Creature says to Victor, his creator, "Everywhere I see bliss, from which I alone am irrevocably excluded. I was benevolent and good; misery made me a friend. Make me happy, and I shall again be virtuous." (Leonard Wolf, ed., *The Essential Frankenstein*. New York: Plume, 1993, p. 140.)

presence. We could not leave the torture chamber unless Christine opened its door for us. That was the necessary condition we needed if we were to help Christine, because we had no idea where the nearby door might be.

"All of a sudden, the silence in the next room was shattered by the sound of an electric bell. There was a movement on the other side of the wall, then Erik's voice thundered, 'The bell! By all means, come in.' Then there was a melancholy laugh. 'Who's coming to bother us now? Wait a bit for me . . . *I'm going to tell the siren to open up.*'

"The sound of his steps grew fainter, and a door closed. I had no time to think of the new horror that was being prepared. I forgot that the monster might be leaving only in order to commit a new crime. I thought of one thing only: Christine was alone behind that wall.

"The Viscount de Chagny was already calling to her, 'Christine, Christine.' Once it was clear that we were able to hear what was being said on the other side of the wall, there was no further reason why my companion should not be heard in his turn. Even so, the viscount had to call several times. Finally, a feeble voice succeeded in reaching us.

" 'I'm dreaming,' she said.

" 'Christine! Christine! It's me, Raoul.'

"Silence.

" 'Answer me, Christine. In the name of Heaven, answer me.'

"Then Christine's voice murmured Raoul's name.

" 'Yes, yes. It's me. It's not a dream. Christine, trust me. We are here to save you. But be careful. When you hear the monster, warn us.'

" 'Raoul, Raoul.'

"She made us repeat several times that she was not dreaming and that Raoul de Chagny had reached her, conducted by a devoted companion who knew the secret of Erik's domain. Then, all at once, the too rapid joy we had brought her was followed by an even greater terror. She wanted Raoul to leave at once. She trembled lest Erik discover his hiding place, because in that case he would not hesitate to kill him.

"In a few hasty words, she let us know that Erik had gone completely mad for love of her and that *he had decided to kill everyone, and himself along with them* if she did not agree to become his wife in the presence of the mayor and the priest . . . the priest of the Madeleine.[2] He had given her

---

[2] "the priest of the Madeleine"

The Church of the Madeleine on the Place de la Madeleine in Paris. Work on the church was begun in 1764. The revolution brought construction to a halt. Work was resumed again in 1807 and it was not completed until 1842.

until eleven o'clock the next evening to think things over. It was the last delay. She would then need to choose, as he said, between the marriage mass or the funeral mass.

"And Erik had spoken this phrase which Christine had not fully understood: 'Yes or no. If no, then the world is dead and *buried.*'

"I understood that phrase because it corresponded in a terrible fashion with an anxious thought of my own.

" 'Can you tell us where Erik is?' I asked.

"She replied that he must have left the place.

" 'Can you make sure of that?'

" 'No. I'm tied up. I can't make a move.'

"Hearing that, neither M. de Chagny nor I were able to repress a cry of rage. Our safety, the safety of all three of us, depended on her ability to move about freely.

" 'Oh . . . to save her. To get to her!'

" 'But where are you?' Christine asked again. 'There are only two doors in my room: the Louis Philippe door, about which I've told you, Raoul! The door by which Erik comes and goes. And another door that he has never opened before me and which he has forbidden me ever to go through because, he says, it is the most dangerous of doors. The door of the torture chamber.'

" 'Christine, we're behind that door.'

" 'You're in the torture chamber.'

" 'Yes, but we can't see a door.'

" 'Ah, if I could only drag myself to it. I would knock on the door and you'd be able to tell where it is.

" 'Is it a door with a lock?'

"I thought: 'On the other side, it opens with a key, like any door, but on this side it opens with a spring and counterweights which won't be easy to find.

" 'Madmoiselle,' I said, 'it's absolutely essential for you to open the door for us.'

" 'But how?' replied the unhappy woman tearfully. We heard a rubbing sound as of a body trying to free itself from its bonds.

" 'We're not going to get out of here without a ruse of some kind,' I said. 'We need the key to the door.'

" 'I know where it is,' said Christine, who seemed worn out by the effort she had just made. 'But I'm too well tied. Oh, the wretch.' There was a sob.

" 'Where is the key?' I asked, making a sign to M. de Chagny to keep still and let me handle things, since we had not a moment to lose.

" 'In the room beside the organ, with another little bronze key which he has also forbidden me to touch. Both keys are in a little leather sack which he calls "the little sack of life and death." Raoul, Raoul. Get away. Everything here is mysterious and terrible. Erik is going to go completely mad. And you're in the torture chamber. There must be a reason that it's called that. Go back where you came from.'

" 'Christine,' the young man said, 'we'll leave here together or we'll die together.'

" 'It's up to us to get out of here safe and sound,' I whispered, 'but we have to keep our wits about us. Why, Mademoiselle, has he tied you up? You couldn't escape in any case. He knows that well.'

" 'I wanted to kill myself. After he brought me here, unconscious, half-chloroformed, he went away—*to his banker*, according to him. When he came back, he found me with my face all bloodied. I had tried to kill myself by banging my head against the walls.'

" 'Christine,' Raoul groaned, and began to sob.

" 'Then, he tied me up. I don't have the right to die until tomorrow night at eleven o'clock.'

"This entire conversation through the wall was considerably more fragmentary and more wary than I can indicate here in writing. Often we would stop in the middle of a sentence because we thought we heard something scrape, or the sound of a step, or some unaccustomed movement. And Christine would say, 'No, no. It's not he. He's gone out. He has certainly gone out. I recognized the sound the wall makes as it closes on the lake.'

" 'Mademoiselle,' I said, 'it's the monster himself who tied you; and it's he who will untie you. All it will take is for you to play your role properly. Remember that he loves you.'

" 'Woe's me,' we heard her say. 'Will I ever forget it?'

" 'Remember to smile at him. Beg him . . . tell him your bonds are hurting you.'

"Christine Daaé said, 'Hush. I hear something at the lake wall. It's he. Run. Get away. Run.'

" 'We couldn't go, even if we wanted to,' I said as urgently as I could. 'We can't leave. And we're in the torture chamber.'

" 'Hush,' Christine whispered again.

"The three of us were silent.

"Heavy steps sounded slowly behind the wall, then stopped, then they made the floor creak once more.

"There was a heavy sigh followed by a cry of horror from Christine. Then we heard Erik's voice speaking to Christine in the personal form of address. 'I beg your pardon for showing you a face like mine. What a state I'm in. It's the *other one's* fault. Why did he ring the bell? Do I ask passersby what time it is? He won't ask that of anyone anymore. It's the siren's fault.'[3]

"Again there was a sigh, more profound, more awful, coming from the very depth of an abyss in the soul.

" 'Christine, why did you cry out?'

" 'Because I'm in pain, Erik.'

" 'I thought I had frightened you.'

" 'Erik, untie my hands. Am I not your prisoner?'

" 'Do you still want to die?'

" 'You've given me until tomorrow night at eleven, Erik.'

"Steps were heard crossing the floor again.

" 'Since we are going to die together, and I'm as eager as you are . . . yes, I, too, have had enough of this life. Wait. Don't move. I'm going to untie you. You have only to say one word, *no,* and it will be finished at once, *for the whole world.* You're right. You're right. Why wait until tomorrow night at eleven? Oh, yes, because it will be more beautiful. I've always been afflicted by decorum. By grandiosity. It's childish. In this life, one must think only of oneself . . . of one's own death . . everything else is superfluous. *Just see how drenched I am.* Ah, my dear, I was wrong to go out. One shouldn't let a dog out on a night like this. Besides that, Christine, I really believe I've been hallucinating. . . .[4] Do you know whoever it was that rang the siren's bell a while ago . . . if you want to see whether he's still ringing it, you'll have to go to the bottom of the lake. There, turn this way. Is that all right? There you are, freed. My God, your wrists, Christine. Tell me, have I hurt you? That merits death. Speaking of death, *I need to sing him the funeral requiem.'*

"Hearing these dreadful words, I could not help having a terrible presentiment. I, too, had rung the monster's doorbell without being aware of it. I must have turned on a warning current. And I recalled the two

---

[3]   "The siren's fault"
      First Erik blames the *other one,* then the siren. Since Erik is the siren, we are left in some perplexity. Whom is Erik blaming?

[4]   "I've been hallucinating"
      Certainly his speech, for the last couple of pages, has seemed disordered.

arms that emerged from the inky black waters. Who might the unhappy person be who had wandered to those shores?

"The thought of that unfortunate man kept me from rejoicing at Christine's stratagem; meanwhile, the Viscount de Chagy murmured the magic word 'freed' into my ear. Who, then . . . who then was that other person? The one whose requiem mass we were hearing sung at this moment?

"Ah, that sublime and frenzied song. The entire house beside the lake trembled. The very bowels of the earth shivered. We had pressed our ears to the mirror the better to hear Christine Daaé's ruse, the ruse that would free us, but we heard nothing but the sound of the requiem mass. It was, moreover, a requiem for the damned, as if made at the bottom of the world by a circle of demons.

"I remember that the *Dies Irae* that he sang enclosed us as by a storm. Yes, there was thunder around us, and lightning. Of course, I had heard him sing at other times. *He* had been able to make the stone throats of my human-headed bulls[5] sing on the walls of the palace of Mazendaran. But to sing like this! Never. Never. He sang like the god of thunder.[6]

"All at once, the organ music stopped so suddenly that M. de Chagny and I started back from the wall. The voice quickly changed, transformed, harshly enunciating these metallic syllables: *'What have you done with my pouch?'* "

---

[5] "human-headed bulls"

A familiar decorative motif in ancient Persian structures. The approach to the audience hall at Persepolis has a parallel row of sculptures depicting man-headed bulls.

It is an easy leap from this poignant image of Erik ecstatically bellowing the *dies irae* in his underground retreat to thoughts of the Minoan minotaur, a bull-headed man who was so frightful to see that he was hidden away at the center of a maze.

[6] "god of thunder"

Jupiter, who was described as sitting on his throne holding a scepter in his left hand and thunderbolts in his right.

Chapter XXIV

❊

The Tortures Begin

The Persian's Narrative (Continued)

"Furiously, the voice repeated, 'What have you done with my pouch?'

"Christine Daaé could not have been trembling more than we were.

" 'You wanted me to untie you so you could take my pouch, isn't that so?'

"We heard hasty footsteps as Christine ran back to the Louis Philippe room as if to find refuge against our wall.

" 'Why are you running away?' said the furious voice that had followed her. 'Will you give me back my pouch? Don't you know that it's the pouch of life and death?'

" 'Listen, Erik,' sighed Christine, 'since it's understood that from now on we're going to be living together . . . what does it matter? What belongs to you belongs to me.'

"This was said in a manner so fearful, it could rouse pity. The unhappy young woman had to summon what remained of her energy to master her terror. But the monster could not be fooled by such childish deceptions, spoken through chattering teeth.

" 'You know very well that there are only two keys in it. What is it you want to do?' he asked.

"She said, 'I wanted to go into the room I haven't seen and that you've always hidden from me. It's a woman's curiosity,' she added in a tone meant to be playful but which sounded so false that it succeeded only in heightening Erik's suspicions.

" 'I don't like curious women,' Erik replied. 'You'd better remember the Bluebeard story and be careful.[1] Come now, give me my pouch. Give me my pouch. Leave that key alone, inquisitive girl.' And he laughed as Christine uttered a cry of pain. Erik had taken the pouch from her.

"It was at this moment that the viscount, unable to restrain himself, uttered a helpless cry, which I was able to stifle only with difficulty by putting my hand over his mouth.

" 'Ah . . . what was that?' said the monster. 'What's that? Haven't you heard it, Christine?'[2]

" 'No, no,' she replied. 'I haven't heard anything.'

" 'It seemed to me that somebody cried out.'

" 'A cry! Have you gone mad, Erik? Who do you suppose could be crying out in this house . . . It's me. I did, because you hurt me. But I . . . I haven't heard anything.'

" 'Look at how you say that! You tremble. You're upset. There was a cry. There was a cry. There's someone in the torture chamber. Ah, now I understand.'

" 'There's nobody there, Erik.'

" 'I understand.'

" 'Nobody.'

" 'Your fiancé, maybe?'

" 'Ah, I have no fiancé. You know that very well.'

"Again a wicked laugh.

---

[1] "remember the Bluebeard story and be careful"

The story of Bluebeard that most of us know comes to us from the seventeenth century rendering by Charles Perrault, who describes him as a wealthy man whose misfortune was that he had a blue beard which made him so frightfully ugly that all the women and girls ran away from him. Still, because of his wealth, a neighbor of his gave him his daughter in marriage.

Some time after the wedding, the wife, who had been told that Bluebeard would be gone for about six weeks, disobeyed his instructions *not* to enter "the closet at the end of the great gallery on the ground floor." There, she found a room splattered with clotted blood and the bodies of seven women.

Her husband returned that very same evening and, seeing bloodspots on his keys, discerned at once that his wife had disobeyed his instructions. The story has a cliff-hanger ending as Bluebeard is about to immolate his wife even as her brothers ride to the rescue.

The historical Bluebeard, the Frenchman Gilles de Rais (1404–1440), killed scores, perhaps hundreds, of children, not wives. (See Leonard Wolf, *Bluebeard: The Life and Crimes of Gilles de Rais.* New York: Clarkson N. Potter, 1980, pp. 218–22.)

[2] "Haven't you you heard it, Christine?"

From here until page 285 where Erik says, "Go to the little window," Erik speaks to Christine in the *tu*, or intimate, second-person form of address, after which he reverts to the *vous*, or formal, form.

284

" 'It's easy enough to find out, my little Christine, my love; there's no need to open the door to see what's happening in the torture chamber. Do you want to see? Do you want to see? Here. If there *is* someone . . . if there really is someone, you'll see light from the invisible window there, near the ceiling. I need only to pull the black curtain and then to put out the light here. There, it's done. We've put it out. You're not afraid of the dark when you're with your darling husband?'

"Christine's agonized voice was heard. 'No! Yes, I am afraid. I've told you, I'm scared of the dark. That room doesn't interest me anymore at all. It's you who were constantly scaring me like a child with that torture chamber. Earlier, I was curious, that's true. But it doesn't interest me anymore at all, at all.'

"And now what I had feared above all began, *automatically*: suddenly, we were flooded with light. Yes. Everything on our side of the wall seemed aflame. The Viscount de Chagny, who was not expecting it, staggered. In the adjacent room, the angry voice erupted. 'I told you there was someone. Do you see now? In the window? The illuminated window. At the very top. Whoever is behind the wall can't see it. But you, you're going to go up that double ladder. That's what it's there for. You've often asked what it's used for. Well, now you'll know. It's there, my curious one, so you can look through the window into the torture chamber.'

" 'What tortures? What tortures are in there? Erik, Erik, tell me that you're trying to scare me. If you love me, Erik, tell me. It's true, isn't it, that there are no tortures there? Those are stories for children.'

" 'Go to the little window and see, my dear.'

"I don't know whether the viscount beside me heard Christine's fading voice, because he was so occupied with the unheard-of sight that met his dazed eyes. As for me, who had only too often witnessed this spectacle through the small windows at the time of the rosy hours of Mazandaran, I paid no attention to anything but what was being said in the next room, trying to find there some hint of how to act, or some decision to make.

" 'Go look, go look through the little window. You'll tell me later what his nose is like.'

"We heard the sound of the ladder being rolled and then leaned against the wall.

" 'Climb on up. No! No. I'll go up. I will, my darling.'

" 'Ah, yes. I'll go up. Let me.'

" 'Ah, my little darling. My little darling. How sweet you are. How good of you to spare me this trouble at my age.[3] You'll tell me what condition his nose is in.[4] If only people understood how lucky they were to have a nose . . . a nose of their own . . . they would never wander about in a torture chamber.'

"At that moment, we distinctly heard Christine's words overhead, '*My friend, there's no one there.*'

" 'No one. You're sure there's no one?'

" 'Absolutely. No. There's no one.'

" 'Well, so much the better. What's wrong, Christine? What? You're not going to faint, are you . . . since there's no one there. But how do you like the landscape?''

" 'Oh, very much.'

" 'Well, so you're feeling better. Isn't that so? You're better. So much the better that you're better. No need to get excited. And what a funny house it is where one can see landscapes like this.'

" 'Yes, it's like being at the Grévin Museum.[5] But tell me, Erik. There are no tortures in there? You know, you've quite scared me.'

" 'Why, since there's no one there?'

" 'Did you create that room, Erik? You know, it's very beautiful. You're really a very great artist.'

" 'Yes, a great artist, "in my fashion." ' '

" 'But, Erik, tell me. Why have you called it a torture chamber?'

" 'Oh, that's very simple. But first, what have you seen?'

" 'A forest!'

" 'And what is there in the forest?'

" 'Trees.'

' 'And what's in a tree?'

" 'Birds.'

" 'Have you seen birds?'

" 'No, I haven't seen any birds.'

---

[3] "at my age"

We are not told how old Erik is, though from the number and variety of the things the Persian tells us he has done, we have to assume that he is clearly no longer a young man.

[4] "what condition his nose is in"

Since, in some cultures, the size of one's nose is said to indicate the size of a man's phallus, Erik's noselessness has prompted a certain amount of Freudian speculation (see Slavoj Zizek, "Grimaces of the Real, or When the Phallus Appears," in *October,* vol. 58, Fall, 1991, p. 46). For this annotator, the Phantom's near noselessness is simply one more detail in the sum of the revolting features that make him an exile from the human condition. That that exile necessarily brings with it sexual frustration almost goes without saying (see Introduction, p. 3).

[5] "the Grévin Museum"

From *The Phantom of the Opera* (1943)

" 'Well, what have you seen? Think. You've seen branches. And what is there on a branch?' said the dreadful voice. 'There is a *gallows*. And that's why I call my forest a torture chamber. You see that it's only a manner of speaking. It's all meant to be funny. I never express myself like anyone else. I don't do anything like anyone else. But I'm very tired of it. Very tired. You see, I've had enough of owning a forest in my house, and a torture chamber. And of living like a charlatan at the bottom of a double-bottomed box. I've had enough . . . enough. I want to have a quiet apart-ment, with ordinary doors and windows, and an honest wife, like the rest of the world. You should be able to understand that, Christine, and I shouldn't have to keep repeating it. A wife, like the rest of the world. A wife whom I would love, and with whom I could take Sunday walks, and whom I would amuse all week long. Ah, you would never be bored with me. I have more than one trick up my sleeve, not counting card tricks. Here, would you like m⸱ to do some card tricks? It'll help us to pass the

Alfred Grévin (1827–1892) was a designer and caricaturist famous, among other things, for his founding of an early version of a wax museum. In his lifetime, he published more than 40,000 drawings.

time until eleven o'clock tomorrow night. My little Christine . . . my dear little Christine. Do you hear me? You won't reject me away anymore. You love me. No. You don't love me. But, never mind. You will love me. Time was when you couldn't look at my mask, because you knew what was behind it. And now you don't mind looking and you forget what's behind it, and you won't reject me again. When one wants to, and is well-intentioned, one can get used to anything. Many young people who don't love each other before marriage adore each other afterward. Ah, I no longer know what I'm saying. But you'll have fun with me. There's no one like me.

" 'I take my oath on it, that we'll be married—if you are reasonable. When it comes to ventriloquism, there's no one like me. I'm the greatest ventriloquist in the world. You laugh. Maybe you don't believe me. Listen!'

"It was perfectly clear to me that the pitiful creature (who, in fact, really was the greatest ventriloquist in the world) was trying to stupefy the poor dear to distract her from looking into the torture chamber. It was a stupid strategy. Christine thought of nothing but us. Several times, and in the gentlest possible tone, she begged, 'Erik, put the light out in the little window.'

"Because she thought that there must be some dreadful reason that the monster had spoken so menacingly about the light that had suddenly appeared at the little window. One thing must have calmed her briefly and that is that she had seen the two of us standing safely behind the wall at the center of the magnificent blazing light. But certainly she would have been more reassured had the light gone out.

"Erik had already begun his ventriloquism. He said, 'Look, I'll raise my mask a little. Oh, just a little. You see my lips—such lips as I have. They don't move. My mouth is closed. Whatever, that is, that I have in the way of a mouth. And meanwhile, you hear my voice. I talk with my stomach. It's very natural. And it's called ventriloquism. It's well known. Listen to my voice. Where do you want it to go? Into your left ear? In your right ear? In the table? Into the ebony boxes on the mantelpiece? Ah! That astonishes you? My voice is in the little boxes on the mantelpiece. Do you want it farther away? Do you want it nearer? Loud? Sharp? Nasal? My voice can go anywhere. Anywhere. Darling, listen . . . to the little box on the right and hear what it says: "Shall I turn the scorpion?" And now— snap!—listen again to what it says in the little box on the left: "Shall I turn the grasshopper?" And now—snap—there you are, the voice is in the little leather pouch. What does it say? "I am *the little pouch of life and death.*" And now—snap—my word, now it's in Carlotta's throat; at the bottom of Carlotta's gilded, crystalline throat. What does it say? It says, "It's me, Mr. Toad, who sings. *I hear a solitary voice 'quack' that sings in my 'quack.'* " And now *snap,* the voice reaches the seat in the Phantom's box and it says, "Tonight, Madame Carlotta's singing will bring down the chandelier." And now, snap. Ah, ah. Where's Erik's voice now? Listen, my darling Christine. Listen. The voice is behind the door to the torture chamber. Listen to me. It's I who am in the torture chamber. And what do I say? I say, "Woe unto those who have the good luck to have a nose, a real nose, and who come strolling into the torture chamber. Ah! Ah. Ah." '

"The cursed voice of the formidable ventriloquist was everywhere, everywhere. It passed through the invisible little window, through the walls. It ran around us, between us. Erik was there. He spoke to us. We made a move as if to fling ourselves on him. But more quickly, more unseizably even than its echo, Erik's voice had leaped behind the wall.

"Soon, we were unable to hear anything more because this is what happened:

"Christine's voice: 'Erik, Erik, your voice is tiring me. Be still, Erik. Don't you think it's getting warm here?'

" 'Oh yes,' Erik's voice replied. 'The heat is becoming unbearable.'

"And again Christine's voice, made hoarse with anguish, 'What's happening? The wall is hot. The wall is burning.'

" 'I'll tell you, my dear Christine. It's because of the forest next door.'

" 'Well, then. What do you mean? The forest . . . ?'

" *'Don't you see that it's a forest in the Congo?'*

"And the laugh the monster uttered was so terrible that we could no longer hear Christine's supplicating cries. The Viscount de Chagny shouted and beat against the walls like a madman. I could not restrain him anymore. But all that one heard was the monster's laugh . . . and the monster himself could hear nothing but his own laughter. Then there was the sound of a quick struggle, of a body falling to the floor and being dragged . . . the sound of a door slamming shut . . . and then . . . nothing more . . . nothing more around us but a tropical midday silence at the heart of an African forest."

Chapter XXV

"Barrels! Barrels!
"Have You Any Barrels for Sale?"

The Persian's Narrative (Continued)

"I have said that the room in which the Viscount de Chagny and I found ourselves was a regular hexagon and that it was entirely covered with mirrors. Since then, especially at certain exhibition halls, one has seen rooms completely arranged that way that are called 'mirage houses' or 'palaces of illusion.' But their invention belongs entirely to Erik who, right before my eyes, constructed the first hall of this type during *the rosy hours of Mazendaran.* One needed only to put a decorative object like a column, for example, into a corner of one of those rooms to create the illusion of a palace with thousands of columns, because, by means of the mirrors, the real room grew into six hexagonal rooms each of which multiplied itself infinitely. In the past, to amuse the little sultana, he had thus decorated a room that became the 'unending temple'; but the little sultana quickly tired of such a childish illusion, so Erik turned his invention into a torture chamber. Instead of an architectural motif, he placed an iron tree in a corner.

"Why was this tree, which with its painted leaves perfectly imitated a real tree, made of iron? Because it had to be strong enough to resist any attacks by the 'patient' who was locked inside the torture chamber. We will see how the scene thus obtained was transformed instantaneously into two other successive scenes, thanks to the automatic rotation of the drums in the corners, drums that had been divided into thirds and were fitted into the angles of the mirrors. Each of them bore a decorative motif that followed one after the other.

"The walls of this strange room offered no handhold for the 'patient' because, except for the decorative motif which was strong enough to withstand any force, they were furnished only with mirrors; mirrors so thick that they were in no danger of damage from the miserable victim who had been thrown into the room, his hands and feet bare.

"No furniture. The ceiling glowed. An ingenious electric heating system, which has since been imitated, allowed the temperature of the walls—and, therefore, that of the room—to be raised at will.

"I give all of these details of a perfectly natural invention that by means of some painted branches gave the illusion of a supernatural equatorial forest set ablaze by the midday sun, so that no one may doubt the present tranquility of my mind; so that no one may be justified in saying, 'This man has gone mad,' or 'This man is lying,' or 'This man takes us for fools.'

"If I had simply recounted things as follows, 'Having descended to the bottom of a basement, we encountered an equatorial forest set ablaze by the midday sun,' I would have created an effect of baffled astonishment, but I am not interested in creating an effect. In writing these lines, my goal is to tell exactly what happened to us—to M. de Chagny and me—in the course of a dreadful adventure which, for a while, involved this country's legal system.

"I will now go on with the facts where I left them.

"When the ceiling lit up and the forest glowed around us, the viscount was astonished beyond measure. The appearance of the impenetrable forest whose countless trunks and branches intertwined *into infinity* threw him into a state of terrified consternation. He passed his hands across his forehead as if to chase away a dream vision and his eyes blinked as if he had just wakened and was having trouble adjusting to reality. For a moment, he forgot to *listen*.

"I have said that the appearance of the forest did not surprise me. And that's why I listened to what was going on in the next room. Finally, my attention, which was not particularly drawn to the scenery, focused instead on the mirrors producing it. And the mirrors *were scratched* here and there.

"Yes, they had scratches. Despite their solidity, someone had 'crazed' them, which proved to me that the torture chamber in which we found ourselves had *undoubtedly been used.*

"Yes, some poor fellow whose hands and feet were not as bare as those of the victims of *the rosy hours of Mazendaran* had surely fallen into this 'mortal illusion' and, driven mad with rage, had hurled himself against these mirrors which, despite their fine cracks, continued to reflect his agony. And the branch of the tree where he had ended his suffering was positioned in such a way that before he died, he could see—supreme consolation—a thousand hanged men twisting spasmodically around him.

"Yes! Yes! Joseph Buquet had undoubtedly been here.

"Were we going to die, like him?

"I didn't think so because I knew that we still had several hours before us, and that I could make better use of them than Joseph Buquet had been able to.

"Was it not true that I had a profound knowledge of most of Erik's tricks? Now or never was the time to use what I knew.

"First, I did not dream of going back by way of the passage that had brought us to this accursed chamber, or of activating the interior stone that closed that passage. The reason for that is very simple. I did not have the means. We had dropped into the torture chamber from too high a height and there was nothing we could use as a step stool to reach that passage: neither a piece of furniture, nor a branch of the iron tree. Not even if we climbed upon each other's shoulders.

"There was only one possible exit left, the one that opened onto the Louis Philippe room where Erik and Christine Daaé were. But if on Christine's side the door was an ordinary one, it was absolutely invisible to use. We then had to try opening it even though we didn't know where it was— no ordinary task.

"When I was sure that there was no other hope for us on Christine Daaé's side . . . when I heard the monster leading, or rather dragging, the unfortunate young woman out of the Louis Philippe room *to keep her from interfering with our torture,* I resolved to settle down at once to the task of finding the device that would open the door.

"But first of all, I had to calm M. de Chagny, who was already walking about in the clearing uttering incoherent cries like a man hallucinating. The snatches of conversation between Christine and the monster that he had been able to overhear despite his agitation had entirely disordered him. If you add to that the magic forest and the blazing heat that was causing sweat to stream down his temples, you will have no difficulty understanding that

M. de Chagny was becoming overexcited. Despite all my advice, my companion was no longer being prudent.

"Believing he was entering a passage that would lead him to the horizon, he walked back and forth aimlessly, hurrying toward a nonexistent space until, after a few steps, he banged his forehead[1] against the reflection of the illusive forest.

"Shouting, 'Christine! Christine!' he waved his pistol about, calling with all his might for the monster, challenging the Angel of Music to a duel to the death and reviling the illusory forest. I did all I could to 'modify his behavior,' reasoning with the poor viscount as calmly as I could, making him touch the mirrors and the iron tree, the branches on the revolving drums, and explaining to him the optical laws that produced the glowing imagery that surrounded us and to which we could not, like ordinary uneducated people, succumb. ' "We're in a room. A little room," that's what you have to repeat to yourself. "And we'll leave this room as soon a we can find the door." Well, then. Let's search.'

"And I promised that, if he would let me act without driving me dizzy with his screams and crazed wanderings, I would find the trick that controlled the door within the hour.

"At that, he lay down on the floor as one might in the woods and announced that, since he had nothing better to do, he would wait until I had found the door out of the forest. And he added that from where he was, 'the view was splendid.' (The torture, despite everything I had said, was at work.)

"As for me, *I put the forest out of my mind* and focused on one of the mirror panels which I began to tap on in every direction, *looking for the weak spot* that needed to be pressed to make the door turn according to Erik's system of pivoting doors and trapdoors. Sometimes that weak point might be a simple spot on the glass no larger than a pea beneath which the activating spring lay. I searched. I searched. I felt as high as I could reach. Erik was about my height, and I thought that he wouldn't have put the spring any higher than his own reach. That was no more than a hypothesis, but it was my only hope. I had decided to press this search without weakness, and meticulously, on all six of the mirrored panels, and then to examine the floor just as attentively.

---

[1] "he banged his forehead"
Here Leroux, who prided himself on having even his weirdest plot ideas rooted in reality, may have overreached himself. If, this early in the torture chamber, Raoul bumps his head on the glass mirror, how can he (and, even less believably, the Persian), fall prey to the illusion that they are in a jungle?

"At the same time as I was tapping on the panels with great care, I forced myself not to lose a minute, because the heat was affecting me with increasing intensity and we were literally cooking in that blazing forest.

"After half an hour of working that way, I had already done three panels when, as ill luck would have it, I turned at the viscount's muffled exclamation. 'I'm suffocating,' he said. 'These mirrors are reflecting an infernal heat. How soon are you going to find that spring? If it takes any longer, we'll roast in here.'

"I was not unhappy to hear him talk like that. He had said not a word about the forest, and I hoped that my companion's reason would hold out for a while longer against the torture. But he added, 'What consoles me is that the monster has given Christine until eleven o'clock tomorrow night. If we can't get out of here to save her, at least we'll be dead before she is. Erik's requiem mass will do for us all.' And he inhaled a blast of hot air that almost made him faint.

"Since I did not have the Viscount de Chagny's desperate reasons for accepting death, I turned back to my panel after a few words of encouragement, but as I spoke, I made the mistake of taking a few steps so that, in the unutterable confusion of the illusory forest, I could not be sure I was back at the right panel. I was obliged, therefore, to begin the task anew— at random. I could not help showing my disappointment, and the viscount understood that everything would have to be done again. It was one more blow. 'We'll never get out of this forest,' he groaned.

"As his despair mounted, he forgot that he was dealing only with mirrors and he increasingly believed that he was in the grip of a real forest.

"As for myself, I began searching again. It was my turn to grow feverish. Because I was finding nothing. Absolutely nothing. In the room next to us, the same silence prevailed. We were well and truly lost in that forest, without an exit, without a compass, without a guide, without anything. Oh, I knew what awaited us if no one came to our aid. Or if I couldn't find the activating spring. I had searched in vain for it, only to find branches. Admirable, beautiful branches, which stood straight up in front of me, or spread gracefully over my head but gave no shade. It was natural enough, since we were in an equatorial forest with the sun just above our heads. A forest in the Congo.

"Several times, M. De Chagny and I had taken off our coats and put them back on, sometimes finding that they made us hotter and sometimes, on the contrary, that they protected us from the heat.

"My morale was still high, but M. de Chagny's seemed to be altogether 'gone.' He now claimed that he had been ceaselessly walking in this forest for three days and three nights searching for Christine Daaé. From time to time he thought he saw her behind a tree, gliding among the branches, and he called so beseechingly to her that his words brought tears to my eyes. 'Christine! Christine!' he begged. 'Why do you run away from me? Don't you love me? Aren't we engaged? Stop, Christine. You can see that I'm worn out. Christine, have pity. I'll die in the forest, so far away from you.'

" 'Oh, I'm thirsty,' he said, delirious at last.

"I was thirsty, too. My throat was on fire, but that did not stop me from crouching down on the floor, searching, searching for the spring that would move the invisible door. Especially since, with the oncoming night, staying in the forest was becoming dangerous. Already, we were being enveloped by the shadow of night. It had come on very quickly, the way it does in equatorial countries, abruptly, with almost no twilight.

"Indeed, night in an equatorial forest is always dangerous, especially when, as with us, one has nothing to light a fire with to keep wild animals away. When I wearied for a moment from my search for the spring, I was tempted to break off some branches which I would have lighted with my dark lantern, but when I bumped into the infamous mirrors, I was reminded in time that they were only the images of branches.

"The heat did not dissipate with the declining day. On the contrary, it was now even hotter under the blue glow of the moon. I urged the viscount to keep our weapons ready to fire and not to stray from our campsite while I continued my search for the spring.

"Suddenly, from only a few steps away, the ear-splitting roar of a lion was heard.

" 'Oh,' said the viscount, in a low voice, 'he's not far off. Don't you see him? There, through the trees. In that thicket. If he roars again, I'll shoot.'

"And the roaring began again, more dreadful than before. The viscount fired, but I don't think he hit the lion. All he did was break a mirror, as I could see the next morning at dawn. We must have traveled far during the night, because all at once we found ourselves at the edge of a desert.[2] An immense desert of sand, stones, and rocks. But what was the point in leaving the forest only to enter a desert?

"At last, I tired of fighting and, utterly weary of looking for a release

---

[2] "edge of a desert"

Leroux's mirror illusions at least seem to have an origin in the real world, but there is no explanation of how Erik has created the illusion of a desert by means of mirrors.

button that I could not find, I lay down beside the viscount. I was very surprised (as I said to the viscount) that we hadn't had other encounters with animals during the night. Ordinarily, a leopard would have followed on the lion, and sometimes, the buzzing of a tsetse fly.[3] As I explained to the viscount as we rested before crossing the desert, these effects were all easy to achieve. Erik simulated the roaring of a lion by means of a long narrow drum with a donkey's hide stretched across one end. A length of catgut was tied to the center of the hide and attached to another piece of gut that ran from one end of the drum to the other. Erik had only to rub the string with a rosin-coated glove and, depending on how he rubbed it, he could imitate unerringly the voice of a lion, or a leopard, or, even, the buzzing of the tsetse fly.

"All at once, the thought that Erik, with all his tricks, might be in the adjacent room, prompted me to call to him because, obviously, it was necessary to renounce the idea that we might surprise him. By now, he must surely know who were the occupants of the torture chamber. I called as loudly as I could across the desert, 'Erik, Erik,' but there was no reply. All around us lay the vast, barren expanse of the rocky desert. What was to become of us in the midst of this frightful solitude?

"We were literally beginning to die of heat, of hunger and thirst. Of thirst above all. . . . Finally, I saw M. de Chagny raise himself on an elbow and point to something on the horizon. He had discovered an oasis.

"Yes, over there, all the way out there, the desert gave way to an oasis . . . an oasis with water . . . water as clear as ice . . . water that reflected the iron tree.

"Ah, but that was a mirage. I recognized it at once. It was more dreadful than anything. No one could have resisted it. No one. I forced myself to hold fast to my reason. *And not to hope for water.* Because I knew that if one did hope for it, and then collided with the mirror, there would be nothing left to do but to hang oneself on the iron tree.

"And so I called to M. de Chagny, 'It's a mirage. It's a mirage. Don't believe in that water; it's another trick of the mirror.' But he sent me packing, as they say, me along with my mirror tricks, my springs, my revolving doors, and my palace of mirages. Angrily, he said that I was mad or blind to suppose that all that water flowing over there between the innumerable lovely trees was not real. The desert was real. And the forest,

---

[3] "tsetse fly"
    A fly that is to be found in sub-Saharan Africa and which is the host to the parasitic protozoa that cause sleeping sickness.

too. It was not right to deceive him . . . he had traveled widely . . . in many lands . . .

"He dragged himself along, saying, 'Water! Water!' And his mouth was open as if he were drinking. And I, too, had my mouth open, as if I were drinking.

"Because we not only saw the water, but now *we heard it*. We heard it flowing, splashing. Do you understand? *Splashing. That's a word that one understands with one's tongue.* The tongue protrudes from one's mouth in order to hear it better.

"Finally, there was the most intolerable torture of all. We heard rain and it was not raining! That was a diabolical invention. Oh, I knew very well how Erik did it! Taking a very long and narrow box that had been fitted with wood and metal vanes, he filled it with small stones. The falling stones, striking the vanes, bounced from one to the other making staccato sounds that were deceptively like those made by a rainstorm.

"Ah, you should have seen us, our tongues hanging out, dragging ourselves along toward that splashing shore . . . *our eyes and ears filled with water, but our tongues as dry as dust.*

"When we reached the mirror, M. de Chagny licked it. And I, too, licked it. It was hot. We writhed on the ground, groaning desperately. M. de Chagny put the still loaded pistol to his temple and I, looking down, saw the Punjab lasso at my feet. Now I knew why in that third scene the iron tree had returned. It was waiting for me.

"But as I looked at the Punjab lasso, I saw something that made me tremble so violently that M. de Chagny, who was already whispering, 'Good-bye Christine,' interrupted his suicidal gesture.

"I took his arm. I took the pistol away and then, on my knees, I dragged myself all the way to the thing I had seen. Right next to the Punjab lasso, in a groove in the floor, there was a black-headed nail.

"At last! I had found the spring. The spring that would activate the door. That would free us. That would deliver Erik into our power.

"I pressed the nail. My face glowing, I looked up at M. de Chagny. The black-headed nail yielded to my pressure.

"And then . . .

"And then . . . it was not a door that opened in the wall, but a trapdoor that gave way in the floor.

"All at once fresh air reached us from that black hole. We leaned over the square of darkness as over a clear fountain. Our chins deep in the shade, we drank the coolness in.

"And we leaned farther and farther over the trapdoor. What could there be in this hole, in this basement that had so mysteriously opened for us in the floor? Perhaps there was water there.

"Water to drink!

"I reached my arm into the darkness and touched a stone, and then another. A staircase. A black staircase that went down into a basement.

"The viscount was ready to fling himself into the hole. Down there, even if we found no water, we would escape from the radiant embrace of the abominable mirrors.

"I kept the viscount from jumping because I feared another of the monster's tricks. With my lantern lighted, I went down first.

"The profoundly dark staircase wound round and round. Ah, the marvelous coolness of the staircase and the dark! This coolness did not come from the ventilation system established by Erik, but rather, it came from the earth itself, which, at the level where we were, must have been saturated with water. The lake, then, could not have been far away.

"Soon, we were at the bottom of the staircase. Our eyes, growing accustomed to the dark, began to make out shapes . . . round shapes onto which I directed my lantern's beam.

"Barrels. Evidently we were in Erik's wine cellar. It was here that he stored his wine, and perhaps his drinking water.

"I knew that Erik was a lover of fine wine.[4] Ah, there was plenty to drink here.

"M. de Chagny caressed the round shapes, repeating endlessly, 'Barrels! Barrels! Barrels aplenty.'

"And indeed there were a great many of them, lined up in two very symmetrical rows between which we found ourselves.

"They were small barrels, and I supposed that Erik had chosen that size to make it easier to carry them down to the lake house.

"We examined them one after the other to see if any of them had a spigot attached that would indicate it had been tapped from time to time. But all the barrels were hermetically sealed.

"Then, after having lifted one of them partway to see whether it was full, we got down on our knees, and with the blade of a little knife that I had, I tried to remove the 'bung.'

---

4 "Erik was a lover of fine wine"
   An interesting detail we have not been given before, and which Leroux never elaborates. If we look at the three great monsters of popular culture, we note the Creature in Mary Shelley's *Frankenstein* drank water; Dracula did not drink—wine; Hyde, in *The Strange Case of Dr. Jekyll and Mr. Hyde*, however, had a taste for fine wine.

"At that moment, it seemed to me that I heard, coming from after, a sort of monotonous song whose rhythm I knew, because I had heard it often in the streets of Paris. 'Barrels! Barrels! Have you barrels to sell?'

"My hand froze on the bung. M. de Chagny heard the song, too. He said, 'That's strange. It's as if the barrel were singing.' The song began again, even farther away, 'Barrels! Barrels! Have you barrels to sell?'

"The viscount said, 'Oh, no. I swear that the song is *in* the barrel.'

"We got up and went to look behind the barrel. 'It's inside!' said M. de Chagny. 'It's inside.'

"But we heard nothing more. And we were reduced to blaming the poor state of our senses.

"We went back to the bung. M. de Chagny put both his hands under it, and with a final effort, I pulled it off.

" 'What's this?' cried the viscount. 'It's not water.'

"The viscount held his full hands under my lantern. I leaned over them and then threw the lantern away so abruptly and so far that it broke and was lost to us with its light out.

"What I had seen in M. De Chagny's hands . . . was gunpowder."

Chapter XXVI

To Turn the Scorpion?
Or
To Turn the Grasshopper?

The Conclusion of the Persian's Narrative

"So it was that on descending to the bottom of the cellar I touched the nadir of my terrifying thoughts. The wretch had not been fooling with his threats to harm a great many members of the human race.[1] Excluded from humanity himself, he had built himself an underground lair far from mankind, determined to blow everything up with him in a devastating disaster if those from above tracked him down to his den where he had concealed his monstrous ugliness.

"The discovery we had just made threw us into a turmoil that made us forget all of our present sufferings. Though our exceptional situation had nearly driven us to suicide, it had not yet appeared to us in its fully detailed horror. We understood now all that the monster meant when he used the

---

[1] "the human race"

This phrase will be repeated here. It is used with similar intent in Leroux's novel *Balaoo*. There, Noël, who belongs to a race which, in evolutionary terms, is one level higher than the apes and lower than mankind, hates "the human race" and wreaks havoc on it, because it does not accept *his* humanity. (*Balaoo*, in Francis Lacassin, ed., *Les Aventures Extraordinaires de Joseph Rouletabille, Reporter*, Paris: Robert Laffont, 1988, p. 374.)

atrocious words to Christine Daaé: 'Yes or no. If it's no, everyone is dead and buried.'

"Yes, buried under the debris that had been the Paris Opera. Could anyone have imagined a more appalling crime, a greater apotheosis of horror with which to leave the world? The disaster being prepared in the quiet of his lair would serve to avenge the love misfortunes of the most horrible monster still walking the earth.

"Tomorrow night. Eleven o'clock. The final deadline. Ah, he had chosen his time well! There would be a great many people at the party. A great many of the human race would be up there. There, in the flamboyant upper reaches of the House of Music. What more beautiful in the way of a funeral procession could he have dreamed? He would descend into the grave along with the most beautiful jewel-bedecked shoulders in the world. Tomorrow night. Eleven o'clock. We were to be blown up in the middle of the performance . . . if Christine Daaé said 'No.' Tomorrow night. Eleven o'clock. And how could Christine Daaé say anything but 'No'? Wouldn't she prefer to be married to death itself rather than to this living cadaver? And how could she know that the terrifying fate of 'many of the human race' was linked to her refusal? Tomorrow night. Eleven o'clock.

"As we dragged ourselves about in the dark, fleeing the gunpowder, trying to find the stone stairway, because above us the trapdoor that led to the mirrored room had also disappeared in the dark, we repeated, 'Tomorrow night. Eleven o'clock.'

"Finally, I found the stairway. But suddenly I was brought up short on the first stair because of a searing thought that occurred to me. *What time was it?*'

"Ah, what time is it? What time! Because tomorrow night, eleven o'clock might be today, and any minute now. Who could tell us the time? It seemed to me that we had been locked in this hell for days and days . . . for years . . . since the beginning of time. The whole place might blow up at any minute.

" 'A noise. A clicking mechanical noise. Did you hear it, sir? There, there, in the corner. God, God. The sound of a device. Again! Ah, there's light. Maybe it's the device that's going to blow everything up. A clicking sound, I say. Have you gone deaf?'

"M. de Chagny and I shouted like madmen. Dogged by fear, we scrambled hurriedly up the staircase. The trapdoor above us might be closed. Maybe it's the closed door that's making everything so dark. Oh, let's get away from the dark. Away from the dark. Find the deadly brightness of the Mirrored Room.

"We were already at the top of the stairway. No, the trapdoor was not shut. But, in the mirrored room it was as dark as the cellar we had just left. We were entirely out of the cellar. We dragged ourselves across the floor of the torture chamber. The floor that lay between us and the gunpowder. What time was it? We called, we shouted. M. de Chagny cried with all his resurgent might, 'Christine! Christine!' and I called Erik. I reminded him that I had saved his life! But there was no reply. Nothing but our own despair, our own madness.

"What time was it? Tomorrow night. Eleven o'clock. We argued. We forced ourselves to estimate the time we had passed here. But we were incapable of reason. If we could only see the face of a watch with its moving hands. My watch had stopped long ago, but M. de Chagny's was still working. He told me he had wound it when he put on his evening clothes to go to the opera. We tried to deduce something from this fact, which would keep us hoping that we had not yet arrived at the fatal moment.

"The slightest sound that reached us from the trapdoor that I had tried in vain to close reduced us once again to the most atrocious anguish. What time was it? We no longer had any matches. And yet, we had to know. M. de Chagny thought of breaking the lens of his watch and feeling its face with his fingers. The stem of the watch served as his point of reference. From the position of the watch hands, he deduced that it was precisely eleven o'clock.

"Wasn't it possible that the eleven o'clock that was making us tremble might have already gone by? Perhaps it was ten minutes after eleven. And we might still have twelve hours before us.

"Suddenly I cried, 'Silence.'

"I thought I heard footsteps in the adjoining room.

"I was not wrong. I heard the sound of doors, followed by quick footsteps. There was a knock on the wall. Christine Daaé's voice. 'Raoul! Raoul!'

"Ah, we shouted together from both sides of the wall. Christine sobbed. She had not known that she would ever see M. de Chagny alive. Evidently the monster had been dreadful. He had done nothing but rave while waiting for her to pronounce the 'yes' she had refused him. She had promised him that 'yes' if he would agree to bring her to the torture chamber! But, along with some atrocious threats against the human race, he had adamantly refused this. Finally, after hours of such hell, he had left her alone for a while, so she could think it through one final time.

" 'The hours. The hours. What time is it? What time is it, Christine?'

" 'It's eleven o'clock. Five minutes to eleven.'

" 'But which eleven o'clock?'

" 'The eleven o'clock that will decide between life and death. He repeated that as he was leaving,' Christine said, hoarsely. 'He's horrible. He's raving. He plucked off his mask. His eyes flashed fire. And he did nothing but laugh. Laughing like a drunken demon, he said, "Five minutes. I'm leaving you alone only because of your well-known modesty. I don't want you to blush before me when, like a shy bride, you say *Yes*. The devil take it. I know what's proper behavior." '

" 'I've told you he was a drunken demon.'

" 'He reached into his little bag of life and death and said, "Here, here is the little bronze key that opens the ebony boxes which are on the mantelpiece of the Louis Philippe room. In one of the boxes you'll find a scorpion and in the other a grasshopper,[2] creatures which have been beautifully imitated in Japanese bronze. These are the creatures that say 'yes' or 'no.' That is, you have only to turn the scorpion on its pivot in the direction opposite to the one it's in. That will mean 'yes' when I come back into the Louis Philippe room, the engagement room. If you turn the grasshopper, that will mean 'no' in the Louis Philippe room, the room of death." And he laughed like a drunken demon. I continued, on my knees, to beg him

---

[2] "In one . . . you'll find a scorpion and in the other a grasshopper"

In the zodiac, the sign of the scorpion represents the kidneys and the genitals. By extension it signifies the world of the desires. J. E. Cirlot, *A Dictionary of Symbols*, tr. by Jack Sage. London: Routledge and Kegan Paul, 1962, (pp. 280–281.) In Aesop's fable of the Ant and the Grasshopper, the Grasshopper is the improvident one of the pair, who sings and dances all summer long without care and makes no preparation for the winter.

This juxtaposition of a grasshopper with a scorpion might seem to be merely strange unless we follow this suggestive trail of Leroux's imagination: keeping in mind that the French word for "grasshopper" is *sauterelle*, and remembering that *grande sauterelle* (large grasshopper) is the French term for the "locust," we can see how Leroux, who was an omnivorous reader, might have recalled the biblical passages in the Revelation of St. John the Divine in which the locust and the scorpion are linked. The lines read:

"And the fifth angel sounded, and I saw a star fall from heaven unto the earth: and to him was given the key of the bottomless pit.

And he opened the bottomless pit; and there arose a smoke out of the pit, as the smoke of a great furnace; and the sun and the air were darkened by reason of the smoke of the pit.

And there came out of the smoke locusts upon the earth; and unto them was given power, as the scorpions of the earth have power."

(Revelation 9:1–3)

These lines are extraordinarily suggestive. It is not hard to see Erik as the fallen angel who has the key to the bottomless pit and who, by means of the threatened explosion that will follow if Christine turns the grasshopper, will cause a cloud of smoke, like the smoke of a great furnace.

for the key to the torture chamber, promising to be his wife for all time if he would give it to me. But he said that we would never again need that key and that he was going to throw it into the bottom of the lake. Then, laughing like a drunken demon, he left me, saying he would be back in five minutes because, as a gallant gentleman, he knew what was owed to female modesty.

" 'Ah. And again he cried, "The grasshopper. Beware of the grasshopper. It's not only the grasshopper that will hop, hop. *It hops quite well.*" '

"I've tried here to reproduce in these fragmentary words and exclamations the meaning of Christine's delirious speech. In those twenty-four hours, she too must have reached the depths of human suffering. And she may have endured more than we. At every moment, she would interrupt herself to cry, 'Raoul, are you suffering?' And, feeling the walls, which were now cold, she wanted to know why they had been hot. The five minutes were speeding by and the grasshopper and the scorpion in my brain were scratching away with their claws.

"I had, however, maintained enough lucidity to understand that if the grasshopper was turned, there would be an explosion that would take with it many 'members of the human race'! No doubt the grasshopper controlled an electric switch intended to make the gunpowder explode. M. de Chagny, having heard Christine's voice again, seemed to have recovered his moral fiber. Hurriedly he explained to her the terrible situation we were in. We and the entire Opera. *She had to turn the scorpion at once.*

"Turning the scorpion, which meant the 'yes' that Erik desired, might do something to avert the catastrophe.

" 'Go, Christine. Hurry, my adored wife,' Raoul urged.

"There was a silence.

" 'Christine,' I cried, 'where are you?'

" 'Beside the scorpion.'

" 'Don't touch it.' The thought had struck me—since I knew my Erik, that the monster had deceived the young woman once again. Maybe it was the scorpion that would set off the explosion. Because, finally, why wasn't he there? It had been a while since the five minutes had passed, and he had not come back. Certainly, he had taken cover. And perhaps he was waiting for the tremendous explosion. Was he waiting for more than that? He could not really believe that Christine would willingly agree to be his prey. Why hadn't he come back?

" 'Don't touch the scorpion.'

"Christine cried, 'I hear him. He's here!'

. . . .

"In fact, he was there. We heard his footsteps nearing the Louis Philippe room. Without saying a word, he rejoined Christine.

"I spoke up. 'Erik, it's me. Do you recognize my voice?'

"The tone of his reply was extraordinarily calm. 'So you're not dead in there. *Well, try to keep still.*'

"I would have interrupted him, but he spoke so coldly that I stood frozen behind my wall. 'Not another word, *daroga,* or I'll blow everything up.' And he added, 'That honor belongs to mademoiselle. Mademoiselle has not touched the scorpion [how calmly he spoke]. Mademoiselle has not touched the grasshopper [what frightful composure], but it's not too late to do the right thing.

" 'See, I'll open—the little ebony boxes—without a key, because I'm the trapdoor lover, and I open and close what and how I like—and I'll look into them, mademoiselle. The pretty little creatures. Aren't they well imitated? And how harmless they seem. But, as they say, the hood doesn't make the monk. [All of this was spoken in a toneless, equable voice]. If the grasshopper is turned, we'll all hop, mademoiselle. There's enough gunpowder beneath us to blow up a quarter of the city of Paris. If the scorpion is turned, all of that gunpowder will be soaked with water. Mademoiselle, on the occasion of our wedding you'll be giving a considerable present to some hundreds of Parisians who are at this moment applauding a rather weak Meyerbeer masterpiece. You'll give them the gift of life. Because you, mademoiselle, with your pretty hands, [how tired his voice sounded] will have turned the scorpion. And merrily, merrily we'll be wed.'

"There was silence, then, 'If, mademoiselle, you have not turned the scorpion within two minutes—I have a watch,' Erik added, 'a watch that's running perfectly well. I'll turn the grasshopper and the grasshopper *hops very well.*'

"The silence that followed was itself more frightful than any of the previous terrifying silences. I knew that Erik, taking this calm, peaceful, weary tone, was at the end of his rope and was capable of the most titanic infamy, or of the most ardent devotion, and that a single displeasing syllable more could unleash the whirlwind. M. de Chagny having understood that there was nothing left to do but pray was on his knees, praying. As for me, my blood pulsed so rapidly that I had to press my hands over my heart to keep it from bursting, because we sensed only too horribly what was passing through Christine Daaé's distracted mind in those supreme moments. We understood her hesitation to turn the scorpion—and once again we wondered if it was the scorpion that would blow everything up and whether Erik had decided to take us all down with him.

"Finally, there was Erik's voice, gentle now. Angelically gentle. 'The two minutes have passed. Farewell, mademoiselle. Hop, grasshopper.'

" 'Erik,' cried Christine, who must have flung herself upon the monster's hand. 'Monster, will you swear to me, will you swear on your infernal love that it's the scorpion that must be turned?

" 'Yes, to make us hop to our wedding.'

" 'Ah. You mean that we will hop?'

" 'At our wedding, innocent child. The scorpion opens the ball. But enough of that. You don't want the scorpion. Let me turn to the grasshopper.'

" 'Erik!'

" 'Enough!' I had joined my cry with Christine's. M. de Chagny, still on his knees, continued to pray.

" 'Erik, I've turned the scorpion.'

"Ah, what a long moment we lived through.

"Waiting.

"Waiting to be blown to bits amidst thunder and ruin. To feel the ground splitting beneath us, the abyss opening. There were things . . . things that were the beginning of an apotheosis of horror. Because, from the open trapdoor, from that black maw in a black night, there came a disquieting sound, like the beginning of a rocket's hiss. First, very softly, then louder, then louder still.

"But listen! Listen, and press both your hands to your heart which, along with a great number of the human race, is about to explode.

"It was not a hiss of fire. Can one speak of a water rocket? To the trapdoor. To the trapdoor.

"What coolness. To the cool water. To the cool water. All the thirst that had disappeared when we were overwhelmed by horror returned more strongly now, along with the sound of the water.

"Water! Water! Rising water.

"Rising in the cellar, over the barrels. All the barrels of gunpowder. (Barrels, barrels. Any barrels for sale?) The water toward which we descended with our throats on fire. The water that rose to our chins, our mouths.

"And we drank. At the bottom of the wine cellar, we drank. Even in the wine cellar.

"Step by step we climbed the staircase in the dark. The same staircase down which we had come to encounter the water, we now mounted moving away from it.

"What a deal of gunpowder was lost, soaked in all that water. No one was saving water there at the lake house. If this kept up, the whole lake would flow into the cellar. Because, to tell the truth, how could one know where the water would stop?

"Then we were out of the cellar and the water was still rising. The water rose out of the cellar and spread across the floor. If it continued, the whole lake house would be flooded by it. In the mirrored room the floor had become a little lake in which our feet splashed. There was water enough. Erik should have closed the faucet. 'Erik! Erik! The water's done for the gunpowder. Shut the faucet. Turn the scorpion.'

"But Erik did not reply. There was nothing to be heard but the sound of the rising water, which now reached to our calves.

" 'Christine! Christine! The water's rising. Rising to our knees,' cried M. de Chagny. But there was no reply from Christine. There was nothing to be heard but the sound of the mounting water.

"Nothing. Nothing in the adjacent room. Nobody. Nobody to turn the tap. No one to turn the scorpion.

"We were all alone in the dark with the black water that had seized us, that was rising, that was freezing us. 'Erik! Erik! Christine! Christine!'

"Now we have lost our footing and are turning in the water, carried by an irresistible whirling motion because the water is turning with us, and we bump into the black mirrors which push us back. Raising our mouths above the whirlpool we yell.

"Are we going to die here? Drowned in the torture chamber? I never saw anything like that. In the time of *the rosy hours of Mazendaran* Erik never showed me anything like this through the invisible window. 'Erik! Erik! I saved your life. Do you remember? You were condemned. You were going to die. I opened the gates of life for you. Erik!'

"Ah, we whirled about in the water like flotsam.

"Suddenly I seized the iron tree with my frantic hands. I called to M. de Chagny. And there we were, both of us suspended from a branch of the iron tree.

"And the water kept rising.

" 'Ah, ah. Remember! How much space is there between the branch of the iron tree and the domed roof of the mirrored chamber? Try to remember. After all, the water may stop. It will surely crest. Here! It

308

seems to be stopping. No! No! Horrors! Let's swim! Swim!' We swim with our arms entwined. We are choking. We thrash about in the black water. We are already having trouble breathing the black air above the black water. The air that we can hear is escaping from above us by means of some sort of ventillation apparatus. Ah, let us turn, turn, turn until we've found the air vent. We put our mouths to it, but my strength abandons me. I try to cling to the walls. Oh! The glass walls are slippery to my searching fingers. We are still turning. We are drowning . . . One final effort. A last cry! Erik . . . Christine . . . a gurgling . . . in our ears . . . gurgling, gurgling . . . from beneath the black water we hear it. And before completely losing consciousness, it seems to me that I hear between two 'gurglings,' the cry of 'Barrels! Barrels! Have you any barrels for sale?' "

Chapter XXVII

THE PHANTOM'S LOVE STORY CONCLUDED

Here ends the *written* account that the Persian left me.

Despite the horror of a situation that seemed to have absolutely doomed them to death, M. de Chagny and his companion were saved by Christine Daaé's sublime devotion. And I had the rest of the story from the *daroga*'s own mouth.

When I went to see him, he was still living in the little apartment on the Rue de Rivoli, facing the Tuileries. He was very ill, and it took all my ardor as a historian–journalist in search of the truth to make him agree to relive with me the incredible tragedy. It was his old and loyal servant, Darius,[1] who still looked after him, who led me to his side. The *daroga* received me where he sat in a huge armchair beside a window that looked out on the Tuileries garden. As he sat up, I could see that he must have been handsome once. Our Persian still had magnificent eyes, but his face

---

[1] "Darius"

A fairly common Persian name.

Three Persian kings have been called Darius, the most famous of them being Darius Hystaspes, who was the greatest and most powerful king who ever sat on the Persian throne. His rule lasted from 521 to 486 B.C. He has been called the true founder of the Persian nation. The two others were Darius II, who reigned for twenty years, 424–404 B.C., and Darius III, whose rule lasted five years, 335–330 B.C.

looked very weary. The astrakhan hat that he usually wore had grown bare. He was dressed in a loose-fitting greatcoat with very simple sleeves within which he continually and unconsciously amused himself by twiddling his thumbs. But his mind had remained lucid.

He could not bring to mind the old torments without being seized again by a certain feverishness, and it was only by fits and starts that I extracted from him the surprising end of this strange story. Sometimes he had to be coaxed for a long time before he would answer my questions. And sometimes, stimulated by his memories, he would spontaneously evoke, in stark relief, Erik's horrid features for me and the dreadful hours that he and M. de Chagny had lived through in the lake house.

It was something to see, the way he trembled as he described his awakening in the disturbing shadows of the Louis Philippe room—after the dramatic water episode.

Here, then, is the story's dreadful end as he told it to me by way of concluding the written account which he had been good enough to give me:

When he opened his eyes, the *daroga* found himself lying on a bed. M. de Chagny was asleep on a sofa beside the mirrored closet. An angel and a devil were watching over them.

After the images and the illusions of the torture chamber, the specific middle-class details of this small quiet room seemed once again to have been invented to disorder the mind[2] of any mortal who had the temerity to venture into this domain of living nightmares. The bedstead, the chairs of waxed mahogany, the chest of drawers with its brass trim, the care with which the little squares of crocheted lace were placed on the backs of the armchairs, the clock, and the apparently harmless little ebony boxes on either side of the mantelpiece . . . finally, the shelves ornamented with shells, red pincushions, mother-of-pearl boats, and an enormous ostrich egg . . . all of them discreetly illuminated by a shaded lamp on a pedestal table—it all had a touching homeliness, so peaceful, so reasonable *"at the*

---

[2] "to disorder the mind"

The contrast between the "touching homeliness" of the room and the bizarre, even macabre, climax getting ready to be played out here is very deliberate. The ordinariness of the decor, as Leroux points out here, makes a frame for, and validates, the bizarre.

A reader who is familiar with Henri Fuselli's painting "The Nightmare" will have seen this principle in action. The painting shows a woman lying on a bed in an attitude that can be seen either as post-orgasmic lassitude or the moment after a violent death. There is a simian-looking creature squatting on the woman's bosom. The head of a horse with pupilless eyes is thrusting its way into the room through draperies. Beside the bed, there is a nightstand on which there is a covered glass jar and a slim bud vase with water in it. The point is that the squatting creature and the horse with bulging eyeballs are mere assertions of horror. What is horrifying comes from the familiarity of the glass jar and the bud vase, which therefore casts an aura of believability over the unbelievable details.

bottom of the Opera's cellars" that the imagination was more disconcerted than it had been by all the previous phantasmagoria.

And the shadow cast by the masked man in this neat, clean, old-fashioned setting seemed even more formidable. It bent and whispered into the Persian's ear, "Are you feeling better, *daroga*? You're looking at my furniture? They're all that's left from my poor miserable mother."[3]

The masked man said other things the Persian could no longer remember. But, and this seemed strange to him, he remembered clearly that in the course of the time he spent in that out-of-fashion Louis Philippe room, it was only Erik who spoke. Christine Daaé did not say a word; she moved about noiselessly, like a nun who has taken a vow of silence. She sometimes brought in a cup of cordial—or steaming tea. The masked man took it from her and handed it to the Persian.

As for M. de Chagny, he slept.

As Erik poured a bit of rum into the *daroga*'s cup, he indicated the sprawled viscount, and said, "He came to well before we knew *whether you would live*. He's doing well. He's sleeping. He ought not to be wakened."

Erik left the room for a moment and the Persian, raising himself on an elbow, looked about. He saw the white silhouette of Christine seated in the corner by the fireplace. He spoke to her. Called to her. But he was still very weak and fell back onto the pillow. Christine went to him, put her hand to his forehead, then moved away. And the Persian remembered that, as she went, she did not even glance at M. de Chagny who, it is true, was peacefully asleep nearby. As quiet as a nun who has taken a vow of silence, she resumed her seat in the armchair at the corner of the fireplace.

Erik returned with some little bottles that he put down on the mantelpiece. And, still very quietly, so as not to wake M. de Chagny, he sat down at the Persian's bedside. Taking his pulse, he said softly, "Now you've both been saved. Soon, I'll take you aboveground, *to please my wife*."[4] Then he rose and, without further explanation, disappeared once more.

The Persian regarded Christine Daaé's calm profile under the lamp. She was reading from a small book with gold leaf such as one sees on

---

[3] "my poor miserable mother"

This compassion for the mother who gave him his first mask signals the beginning of the part of this narrative that we might call "the rehabilitation of Erik."

The entire chapter has a tone of pervasive, poignant calm. The calm *after* the storm. The Persian has told us a great deal about Erik's brilliance, his creativity, and his cruelty. Now, Leroux is martialing his narrative skills to win our sympathy for the devil.

[4] "to please my wife"

Indeed, in this bourgeois setting, Christine and Erik might almost be mistaken for a married couple ministering to a pair of sick friends.

religious books. *The Imitation of Christ*[5] appears in some editions like that. In the Persian's ears, there still resonated the natural tone in which Erik had said "to please my wife."

Again, and very softly, the Persian called, but Christine must have been rapt in her book *because she did not hear.*

Erik came back. Then, after advising the Persian not to speak to "his wife," or to anyone else *because it could prove dangerous to everyone's health,* he made the Persian drink a potion.

What the Persian remembered from that moment on was Erik's black shadow and Christine's white silhouette gliding silently across the room and bending over M. de Chagny. The Persian was still very weak, and the smallest sound—the squeaking of the mirrored door to the closet as it opened, for example—gave him a headache. Then, like M. de Chagny, he fell asleep.

This time, he did not waken until he found himself at home being cared for by his faithful Darius, who told him that, on the preceding night, he had been found lying against his door, to which he had been brought by some unknown person who had rung the doorbell before he left.

As soon as the *daroga* had recovered his strength and was able to think clearly, he sent for news of the viscount at Count Philippe's home. He was informed that the young man had not reappeared and that Count Philippe was dead. His body had been found on the shore of the Opera lake, on the Rue Scribe side. The Persian remembered the funeral mass he had heard behind the wall of the mirrored chamber and he had no doubts either about the murder or about the murderer. Knowing Erik, alas, he had no trouble reconstructing the tragedy. Philippe, believing that his brother had abducted Christine Daaé, had pursued him on the Brussels road, where he knew that everything for the elopement had been prepared. When he did not find the young people, he returned to the Opera. There, he remembered some of the strange things Raoul had confided to him about his fantastic rival and learned that the viscount had tried to go down into the cellars of the theater, and, finally, that he had disappeared, leaving his hat next to a pistol case in Christine's dressing room. The count, who no longer had any doubt that his brother was mad, flung himself, in his turn, into the infernal underground labyrinth.

From the Persian's point of view, nothing more was needed to explain

---

[5] *"The Imitation of Christ"*

Imitatio Christi. A devotional book written between 1390 and 1440 that gives its readers advice on how to lead devout Christian lives. Although its authorship is unknown, it is traditionally attributed to Thomas à Kempis.

how the count's body came to be found on the shore that was guarded by the siren's song—Erik's siren, gatekeeper of the Lake of the Dead.[6]

And so, the Persian did not hesitate. Horrified by this new crime, and unable to endure the uncertainty in which he found himself regarding the fate of the viscount and Christine, he decided to tell the police everything.

The investigation of the case had been turned over to Judge Faure, and it was at his door that the Persian knocked. One can imagine how the *daroga*'s deposition was received by a skeptical, superficial, commonplace (I say what I think) sort of person who was utterly unprepared for such information. He was treated like a madman.

The Persian, losing hope that he would ever make himself heard, then began to write. Since the police paid no attention to his deposition, perhaps the press would take it up, and there came an evening when, having finished writing the last line of the account that I have faithfully set down here, his servant, Darius, announced a visitor who had not given his name, and whose features it was impossible to see, and who declared simply that he would not leave the place until he had spoken with the *daroga*.

The Persian, who sensed at once who that singular visitor might be, ordered him to be admitted at once. The *daroga* was not mistaken.

It was the Phantom. It was Erik.

He seemed extremely weak and leaned against the wall as if he was afraid of falling. With his hat removed, his forehead appeared as pale as wax. The rest of his face was concealed by a mask.

The Persian stood before him. "Murderer! You've killed Count Philippe. What have you done with his brother and Christine Daaé?"[7]

At this brusque accusation Erik trembled and was silent for a moment, then, dragging himself to an armchair, he fell into it, heaving a deep sigh. Then, speaking in short sentences, in breathless snippets of words, he said, "*Daroga*, don't speak to me of Count Philippe. He was already dead when the siren sang. It was an accident. A regrettably sad accident. He had, quite simply, naturally and awkwardly, fallen into the lake."

"You're lying," cried the Persian.

Erik bowed his head and said, "I haven't come here to speak to you about Count Philippe. But to tell you . . . that I'm dying."

---

[6] "gatekeeper to the Lake of the Dead"

Here, Leroux speaks of the gatekeeper as if he was someone other than Erik. See Chapter XXIII, Note 2, page 277.

[7] "What have you done . . ."

Throughout this chapter, wherever, in the French text, the Persian and Erik talk to each other they use the *tu*, or intimate form of personal address.

"Where are Raoul de Chagny and Christine Daaé?"

"I'm dying."

"Raoul de Chagny and Christine Daaé?"

"Of love . . . *daroga*. I'm dying of love. That's how it is. I loved her so much . . . I'm telling you I still love her, *daroga,* because love is killing me. If you knew how beautiful she was when she let me kiss her, *alive*— as she had sworn on her eternal soul. It was the first time, *daroga,* the first time, do you hear, that I kissed a woman. Yes, alive. I kissed her alive, and she was as beautiful as a dead woman."[8]

Approaching Erik, the Persian dared to touch him. He shook his arm. "Will you finally tell me if she's alive or dead?"

"Why do you shake me like that?" replied Erik with an effort. "I tell you that it's I who am dying. . . . Yes, I kissed her, alive."

"And is she dead, now?"

"I tell you, I kissed her like that, on the forehead, and she did not draw her forehead back from my lips. Ah, she's an honorable young woman! As for being dead, I don't think so, though that no longer concerns me. No! No! She's not dead. And I'd better not hear that anyone has touched a hair of her head. She's a brave and honorable young woman who, on top of it all, saved your life, *daroga,* at a moment when I wouldn't have given two sous for your Persian hide. Actually, you were of no interest to anyone. Why were you there with that little fellow? You were going to die just for being there. My word, how she begged for her little fellow, but I told her that, since she had turned the scorpion of her own free will, I had become her fiancé and that she didn't need two fiancés. That was fair enough. As for you, you didn't exist. I tell you again, you no longer existed and you were going to die, along with the other fiancé.

"Only, pay attention, *daroga,* since the two of you were yelling like people possessed because of the water: Christine came to me, her beautiful blue eyes wide open, and swore to me by her eternal salvation that she consented *to be my living wife!* Until then, I had always seen my dead wife

---

[8] "as beautiful as a dead woman"

This startling hint of necrophilia has not been prepared for. The notion is repeated on subsequent pages but is never clarified.

Actually, the word "necrophilia," though suggestive, may be misleading. The function of the words "dead woman" may be to emphasize for us Erik's excitement. As if in his fantasies about kissing, he could not imagine a living woman could bear the touch of his lips, and therefore he comforted himself with dreams of kissing one who was dead.

Leroux's first-person narrator, too, has gone to great lengths, as for instance, in the masked ball sequence, to make us see Erik as a living dead man.

Christine, too, has on several occasions described Erik as "dead." See Chapter XIII, where she speaks of his "dead fingers" and of his "horrible dead flesh."

From *The Phantom of the Opera* (1925)

in the depths of her eyes; this was the first time that I saw *my living wife* there. She was sincere—she swore by her eternal salvation that she would not kill herself. The bargain was struck. Half a minute later, all the water returned to the lake and I was surprised to find you, daroga, because I certainly thought you would die there. Anyway! There it is! It was understood! I'd have to get you back home aboveground. Finally, when I had cleared you out of the Louis Philippe room, I came back, alone."

"What did you do with the Viscount de Chagny?" interrupted the Persian.

"Oh, him. You understand, *daroga.* I wasn't about to take him back aboveground like that. He was a hostage. But I couldn't keep him in the lake house, either, because of Christine. The perfume of Mazendaran had made him as limp as a rag, so I shut him up comfortably. I chained him

317

neatly in the Communards' cavern, which is the most deserted and distant part of the Opera, below the fifth basement, where nobody ever goes and where nobody can be heard. Reassured thus, I returned to Christine. She was waiting for me."

At this point in his narrative, it appeared that the Phantom got up so solemnly that the Persian, who had resumed his place in his armchair, felt that he had to get up as well, as if responding to the same impulse and feeling that it was impossible to remain seated at such a moment. Moreover, as the Persian himself told me, he removed his astrakhan hat, even though his head had been shaven.

"Yes, she was waiting for me," Erik resumed, trembling like a leaf, but trembling with real and solemn emotion. "She waited for me, standing straight, alive, like a true fiancée who had sworn by her eternal salvation. And when I approached, more timidly than a little child, she did not run away. No, no. She stayed. She waited for me. I actually believe, *daroga,* that she slightly, oh, not very much, but ever so slightly, like a living fiancée, presented her forehead to me. And . . . and . . . I kissed it . . . I, I, I. And she is not dead. And she stayed normally beside me after I had kissed her like that, on the forehead. Oh! it's so good, *daroga*, to kiss someone! You can't know. But I . . . I . . . My mother, daroga, my poor miserable mother never wanted me to kiss her. She would run away . . throwing me my mask. . . . No woman . . . never . . . never . . . Oh! oh! oh! And, given such happiness, isn't that why I wept? I fell at her feet and wept. You, too, daroga, are weeping; and she also wept. That angel wept."[9]

As he recounted all this, Erik was sobbing and the Persian, indeed, was unable to hold back his tears before this masked man who, with shaking shoulders and hands clasped to his chest, groaned alternately with pain and tenderness.

"Ah, daroga, I felt her tears coursing down my forehead. Mine. Mine. Mine. They were hot. They were sweet. Her tears flowed under my mask. They united with the tears in my own eyes, flowing all the way to my mouth. Oh, her tears on me. Listen, *daroga,* hear what I did. I tore away my mask so as not to lose a single tear. And she did not run away. And she did not die. She stayed. Alive and weeping. Over me. With me. We wept together. God in Heaven! You've given me all the happiness in the world."

---

[9] "That angel wept"

There is an interesting symmetry here. Now Erik refers to Christine as an angel. We will remember that Christine, at the beginning of her relationship to Erik, thought of him as the Angel of Music.

And, with a moan, Erik collapsed into his armchair.

"Ah, I'm not going to die just yet . . . soon . . . but let me weep," he said to the Persian.

After a moment, the masked man resumed. "Listen, *daroga,* and listen well. As I lay at her feet, I heard her say, *'Poor, unhappy Erik.' And she took my hand.* I tell you, *daroga,* that by then I was no more than a dog ready to die for her.

"I had a ring in my hand, a gold ring that I had given her and that she had lost and I had found. A wedding ring. I slipped it onto her finger and told her, 'Here, take this. It's for you . . . and for him. . . . It will be my wedding gift . . . the gift of "poor unhappy Erik." I know that you love the young man. Don't cry anymore.'

"In a very sweet voice she asked me what I meant; I made her understand and she understood, too, that I was no more than a poor dog ready to die for her. And that she could marry the young man when she liked because she had wept with me. Ah, *daroga,* you can imagine that when I said that to her, it was as if I was quietly cutting my heart into four pieces, but she had wept with me. And she had said, 'Poor unhappy Erik.' "

Erik was so agitated that he had to warn the Persian to look away, because he was suffocating and needed to remove his mask. The *daroga* told me that, at these words, he had gone to the window, where his heart had swelled with pity, but that he had taken care to fix his eyes on the treetops in the Tuileries gardens so as not to look into the monster's face.

Erik went on. "I went to free the young man and told him to follow me to Christine. They kissed each other before me in the Louis Philippe room. Christine had my ring. I made her swear that when I died she would come one night to the Rue Scribe side of the lake to bury me in great secret with the gold ring, which she would have worn until that moment. I told her how she would find my body and what it was she would have to do. Then Christine kissed me for the first time, here, on the forehead. On my forehead! (Don't look, *daroga.*) And they both left. Christine was no longer crying. I alone wept, *daroga, daroga.* If Christine keeps her oath, she will be back soon."

And Erik stopped talking. The Persian had no questions to ask him. He was completely reassured about Raoul de Chagny and Christine's fate. And no one human who heard Erik weeping that night could possibly doubt a word that he said.

The monster had resumed his mask and gathered his strength to leave the *daroga.* He told him that when he felt his end nearing, he would send him, in gratitude for the kindness the Persian had shown him in the past, his dearest worldly possession—the papers Christine Daaé had written that were intended for Raoul and that she had left with Erik; as well as a few of her personal effects: two handkerchiefs, a pair of gloves, and the bow from a slipper. In reply to a question from the Persian, Erik told him that as soon as the two young people saw that they were free, they resolved to find a priest in some secluded spot where they could hide their happiness, and to achieve that end they had gone to "the train station for the north of the world." Finally, Erik relied on the Persian to announce his death to the young people soon after he should have received the promised relics and papers. He would need to pay for a line in the obituary columns of the newspaper *L'Epoque*.

That was all.

The Persian conducted Erik to the door of his apartment, and Darius helped him down to the sidewalk. A coach was waiting. Erik got into it. The Persian, who had come back to his window, heard Erik say to the coachman, "To the Opera."

And then the coach disappeared into the night. It was the last the Persian saw of poor unhappy Erik.

Three weeks later, the newspaper *L'Epoque* published this obituary:

"Erik is dead."

Epilogue

That is the true story of the Phantom of the Opera. As I declared at the beginning of this work, there can be no doubt that Erik actually lived. Too many proofs of his existence are now within reach of everyone so that they can *logically* follow the facts and his actions throughout the entire de Chagny tragedy.

There is no point in repeating here just how much this story fascinated Paris. The kidnapped singer, the death of the Count de Chagny under very strange circumstances, the disappearance of his brother, the three members of the lighting crew found asleep .. what tragedies, what crimes had unfolded around the idyll of Raoul and the gentle and charming Christine.[1] What had become of the sublime and mysterious singer of whom the world would never hear again? She was said to be the victim of a rivalry between the two brothers and no one could imagine what actually happened; nobody could understand that, since Raoul and Christine had both vanished, the two had retired far from society to partake of a happiness they did not

---

[1] "the idyll of Raoul and the gentle and charming Christine"

As our story comes to its close, we note that Leroux himself separates it into two parts: the *idyll* of Raoul and Christine and the *tragedy* of Erik and Christine. Raoul and Christine, to the very end, belong to never-never land fiction. Their story takes its place with the gentler myths of childhood or pure romance. They take a train to the North of the World, to Hans Christian Andersen country.

The Erik–Christine story, in turn, has a two part ending: first, the transformation of Christine into the compassionate woman who can kiss Erik on the forehead; then the earthly, real death (the last we see of him is his skeleton) of Erik, who has also been transformed by a compassionate selflessness.

want to make public after the unexplained death of Count Philippe. They had taken a train one day at the station for the North of the World. One day, I too may take the train at that station and go searching around your lakes, oh Norway, oh silent Scandinavia, for the still living traces of Raoul and Christine, as well as Madame Valérius, who also disappeared at the same time. Perhaps one day I shall hear the solitary echoes of the North Country repeating the song of the woman who knew the Angel of Music.

Long after the case had been filed away because of the unintelligent labors of M. Faure, the examining magistrate, the press tried from time to time to penetrate the mystery and continued to wonder whose was the monstrous hand that had prepared and executed so many unspeakable catastrophes (murder and kidnapping). A boulevard newspaper[2] which was aware of all the backstage theater gossip was the only one to write:

"It was the hand of the Phantom of the Opera." And even that had been written with a trace of irony. Only the Persian, to whom no one would listen and who did not, after Erik's visit, try to approach the police again . . . only the Persian knew the truth. And he had in his possession the principal evidence that had come to him with the pious relics the Phantom had promised him.

It has fallen tome to complete these proofs, with the help of the *daroga* himself. From day to day, I kept him abreast of my researchers and he guided them. He had not gone back to the Opera for many years, but he had retained a precise memory of the building and there could have been no better guide to help me discover its most secret recesses. He also gave me sources to pursue and the names of people to interrogate. It was he who urged me to knock at M. de Poligny's door at a moment when the poor man was almost on his deathbed. I did not know he was in such bad shape, and I will never forget the effect my questions about the Phantom produced. He looked at me as if he were seeing the devil, and he replied only with incoherent phrases which nevertheless testified (and that was the point) just how much disarray the Phantom of the Opera had injected into his already much disturbed life. (Because M. de Poligny was said to be a man who liked to live it up.)

When I reported the meager results of my visit with M. Poligny to the Persian *he* smiled vaguely, and said, "Poligny never knew how much wool this blackguard had been able to pull over his eyes [sometimes the Persian spoke of Erik as if he were a god,[3] and at others, as if he were

---

2 "A boulevard newspaper."
Such as *The Echo*, a gossip-mongering paper on which Joseph Leroux, Gaston's brother, worked.

the vilest rascal]. Poligny was superstitious and Erik knew it. Erik also knew a great deal about the public and private business of the Opera.[4]

"When Poligny heard the mysterious voice in Box Number Five telling him what use he made of his time and about his associate's secrets, he did not ask for more. At first, he was struck, as by a heavenly voice, and believed himself to be damned; then when the voice asked for money, he could see that he had been tricked by a master swindler of whom Debienne was also a victim. The two of them, weary, for a variety of reasons, of their work as managers, quit, without trying to understand the personality of that strange Phantom of the Opera, who had presented them with such a peculiar book of rules. Heaving a huge sigh of relief, they left the mystery to the directors who would succeed them, glad to be rid of an affair that intrigued them a great deal without either of them being amused."

It was thus that the Persian expressed himself regarding Messrs. Debienne and Poligny. In that connection, I spoke with him about their successors and was astonished to learn that in *The Memoirs of a Director,* by M. Moncharmin, he gave such a detailed account of events and actions involving the Phantom in the first part of the book, but when he comes to the second part he says nothing—or very little—about him. About that, the Persian, who was as familiar with those *Memoirs* as if he had written them, observed that I would find the explanation of the whole business if I took the trouble to think about the few lines in the second part of the *Memoirs* that Moncharmin had devoted particularly to the Phantom. Here are the lines that are of interest to us, particularly since we find in them a very simple account of the way the famous story of the twenty thousand francs ends.

Regarding the Ph. of the O. [Here, it's Moncharmin who is writing], some of whose singular fantasies I have described earlier in this narrative, I want to say only one thing here, and that is that he redeemed by a beautiful action all the trouble he had caused my dear colleague and, I must admit, for me. No doubt he judged that there were limits to any joke, especially

---

[3] "as if he were a god"

I have noted, in the Introduction, the structural similarities of the plot of Leroux's *Balaoo* and that of *The Phantom* and the way that both novels come to a slow, lachrymose close. In *Balaoo,* the narrator has Balaoo make this judgment about humanity: "Humans are gods manqué *(Les hommes, c'est des dieux manqués)."* (Francis Lacassin, ed., *Les Aventures Extraordinaires de Jóseph Rouletabille, Reporter.* Paris: Lafont, 1988, p. 891.)

[4] "public and private business of the Opera"

This phrase, taken with the remark above that ". . . M. de Poligny was said to be a man who liked to live it up," suggests that Poligny, "in his already much disturbed life" feared Erik as a potential blackmailer because Erik was omniscient about the concerns of the opera.

when it cost so much money, and when it *involved* a police superintendent. Because, several days after the disappearance of Christine Daaé, and at the very moment we had arranged to meet M. Mifroid in our office to tell him the whole story, we found on Richard's desk a handsome envelope on which was written in red ink, "From the Ph. of the O." In the envelope there were the fairly large sums from the administration's treasury that he had succeeded in making disappear temporarily and playfully. Richard immediately expressed the view that we should stop right there and not push the matter any further. I shared Richard's opinion. And all was well that ended well. Isn't that so, my dear, Ph. of O?

It is clear that Moncharmin, especially after the money was returned, continued to believe that he had been for a while the butt of Richard's sense of humor. As for his part, Richard never stopped believing that Moncharmin, to avenge himself for some practical jokes, had amused himself by inventing the entire Ph. of the O. business.

It seemed the right time to ask the Persian to tell me what trick the Phantom had used to make the twenty thousand francs disappear from Richard's pocket in spite of the safety pin. He replied that he had not gone deeply into this minor matter, but that if I wanted to "study" the scene of the incident myself, I would be sure to find the key to the mystery in the administrative office as long as I remembered that it was not for nothing that Erik had been called *the trapdoor lover*. I promised the Persian that, as soon as I had the time, I would investigate the matter. I will tell the reader at once that the results of that investigation proved entirely satisfactory. To tell the truth, I had not thought to discover so many undeniable proofs of the authenticity of the feats attributed to the Phantom.

And one ought to know that the Persian's papers, those of Christine Daaé, the statements made to me by former colleagues of Messrs. Richard and Moncharmin, and by little Meg herself (the excellent Mme. Giry being, alas, deceased), and by Sorelli, who is retired now in Louveciennes[5]—one ought, I say, to know those documents which constitute the evidence of the Phantom's existence, evidence that I will put in the Opera's archives, are corroborated by several important discoveries in which I can rightly take some pride.

Though I could not find the lake house again because Erik had com-

---

[5] "Louvecinennes"

A small town in the Versailles arrondissement that, says *Le Petit Larousse,* boasts a medieval church and a chateau built for Mme. du Barry.

pletely blocked all the secret entrances (though I am sure it would be easy enough to get in if one were to drain the lake as I have many times pleaded with the Ministry of Fine Arts to do),*[6] still, I did find the secret corridor of the Communards, whose planking has fallen in some places; I also revealed the trapdoor by whose means Raoul and the Persian descended into the basements of the theater. In the Communards' dungeon, I also found a number of initials traced on the walls by the unfortunate people who had been shut in there. There was an R. and a C. among those initials. R. C. Isn't that significant? Raoul de Chagny. The letters are very visible to this day. I did not, of course, stop there. In the first and third basements, I activated two trapdoors that were moved by a rotating system completely unknown to the stagehands, who only use trapdoors that slide horizontally.

Finally, and with full awareness of my reason, I can say to the reader: "Visit the Opera one day, ask for permission to walk about in peace, without a stupid guide. Enter Box Number 5 and knock on the enormous column that separates that box from the proscenium. Knock with your cane or your knuckles and listen. At the level of your head, you'll hear that *the column sounds hollow*. After that, the possibility that it might have been inhabited by the Phantom's voice will not surprise you; there is room for two people inside the column. If you are surprised that, at the time of the phenomena in Box Number 5, nobody turned to this column, just remember that it looks like massive marble and that the voice inside it seemed to be coming from the opposite side (because the Phantom could make his ventriloquist's voice come from anywhere)." The column is carved, sculpted, and intricately worked by the sculptor's chisel. I have not given up the hope that one day I will find the bit of sculpture that, designed to rise and fall at will, gave the Phantom free and mysterious means of communication between himself and Mme. Giry, as well as for his generosities to her. Of course, all this that I have seen, heard, and touched is as nothing compared with the reality that a being as prodigious and fabulous as Erik could create in the mysterious ambience of a building like the Opera. But I would trade all of those discoveries for the one that it was given me to

---

* Forty-eight hours before this work was to appear, I spoke again with M. Dujardin-Beaumetz, our sympathetic Undersecretary of State for the Fine Arts, who left me feeling hopeful; and I told him that it was the duty of the state to put an end to the legend of the Phantom and to put Erik's strange story on an indisputably solid historical footing. For that, it will be necessary—and it would be the crown to my personal endeavors—to rediscover the lake house in which perhaps there are musical treasures still to be found. There can no longer be any doubt that Erik was an incomparable artist. Who is to say that we will not find *Don Juan Triumphant* in the famous panel in the lake house?

[6] "pleaded . . . to do*"
This is Leroux's footnote and not the present annotator's.

make before the administrator himself. In the director's office, a few centimeters from the armchair, there was a trapdoor the width of a floorboard and no longer than a forearm . . . a trapdoor that swings open like the lid of a box; a trapdoor through which I could imagine seeing a hand emerging and skillfully working on the pocket of a swallow-tailed coat.

That was how the forty thousand francs disappeared. It was also the way that, thanks to an intermediary, they were returned.

When, speaking with considerable feeling, I said to the Persian, "Then, since the forty thousand francs were returned, Erik was simply amusing himself with his rule book."

He replied, "Don't you believe it. Erik needed money. Believing himself to an an outcast from humanity, he was not encumbered by scruples, and to compensate for the atrocious ugliness he was endowed with, he used the extraordinary gifts of dexterity and imagination that nature had given him to exploit mankind in the most artistic way. Because, sometimes the trick netted him its weight in gold. If, of his own accord, he gave the forty thousand francs back to Messrs. Richard and Moncharmin, it is because, when he did so, *he no longer needed the money.* He had renounced his marriage with Christine Daaé. He had renounced all terrestrial things.

According to the Persian, Erik was originally from a little town near Rouen.[7] He was the son of a masonry contractor.[8] Very early in his life, he ran away from home, where his ugliness had made him an object of fear and loathing to his parents. He exhibited himself sometimes at fairs where his manager billed him as "the living dead man." He must have traversed Europe, going from fair to fair[9] and completing his strange education as a musical performer and magician.

There is an entire period in Erik's life that is fairly obscure. We find him again in all of his dreadful glory at the fair in Nizhni Novgorod.[10] By then, he was already singing as no one in the world had ever sung. He performed as a ventriloquist and displayed such remarkable juggler's tricks

---

[7] "Rouen"

A French manufacturing city on the right bank of the Seine River some seventy miles from Paris. Leroux's parents were married there after he was born.

[8] "masonry contractor"

Leroux's father was a public works contractor.

[9] "going from fair to fair"

As did Christine and her father. This summary of Erik's early life has to be seen as paralleling and in some ways imagining the one we had of Christine's early life with her father in Chapter VI.

[10] "Nizhni Novgorod"

A Russian town situated on both sides of the Volkhov River. From the eleventh to the fifteenth centuries, it was the capital of the Novgorod principality. Throughout its history it has been a trading center because of its accessibility to both the Orient and the West.

that people in the caravans returning to Asia spoke of them all along their route.

It was thus that his reputation reached the palace in Mazendaran[1] where the little sultana, the Shah-in-shah's favorite,[12] was bored to death. A fur merchant returning to Samarkand from Nizhni Novgorod spoke of the miracles he had seen in Erik's tent. The merchant was brought to the palace, and the *daroga* of Mazendaran questioned him. The *daroga* was instructed to find Erik. He brought him back to Persia, where for several months, as they say in Europe, his word was law.

He committed a number of horrors because he seemed not to know the difference between good and evil, and participated in several important political assassinations as calmly as when, with his diabolical inventions, he fought the emir[13] of Afghanistan, who was at war with the empire.[14] The Shah-in-shah became very fond of him. That was the time of *the rosy hours of Mazendaran,* about which we have learned something from the Persian's account.

When it came to architecture, Erik had entirely idiosyncratic notions. He conceived a palace on the principle of a trick box, the sort of palace a magician might imagine. The Shah-in-shah ordered him to build such a palace, and Erik built it so ingeniously that his majesty could walk about everywhere in it without being seen by anyone, and could disappear without anyone's knowing how the trick was done. When the Shah-in-shah found himself the owner of such a gem, he did as a certain tsar had done to the brilliant architect who built the church in Red Square.[15] He commanded that Erik's golden eyes be plucked out. But it occurred to him that Erik, even blind, could build another such incredible palace, and that a live Erik would always know the secret. He decided therefore to kill Erik, as well

---

[11] "the palace in Mazendaran"
 See Chapter XXII, Note 4, page 264.
[12] "the Shah-in-shah's favorite"
 The Shah of Shahs, or the Emperor of Emperors. A title used to designate the emperor of Persia.
[13] "emir"
 A title used to designate a descendant of the prophet Mohammed, but used also used as the title of a governor of a province in the Turkish Empire.
[14] "at war with the empire"
 There was an Afghani-Persian war in 1837. In it, the British supported the Afghani side, while the Russians sided with Persia. The Afghan emir was Dost Mohammad.
 Even if he was in his teens at the time of the war, Erik would be a man close to sixty or more in 1881, the year we have designated as the real time of the action of the novel.
[15] "the church in Red Square"
 Red Square has been called that from the early eighteenth century to the present day. The Russian word for "red," *krasnaya,* also means "beautiful." The church on the square is St. Basil's Cathedral (formerly the Cathedral of the Intercession). It was built between 1555 and 1560.

as all of the laborers who had worked under him. The *daroga of* Mazendaran was charged with the execution of this abominable order. Erik had done the *daroga* some favors and had amused him. He saved Erik's life by providing him the means to escape. But he nearly paid with his own head for the generous gesture. Happily for the *daroga,* a corpse half-eaten by sea birds was found on the shore of the Caspian Sea and, when the *daroga*'s friends had dressed the body in Erik's clothing, it was passed off as Erik. The *daroga* was punished for this by the loss of his wealth and was exiled. However, because the *daroga* was a member of the royal family, the Persian treasury continued to give him an allowance of a few hundred francs per month, and it was after that he came to live in Paris.

As for Erik, he went on to Asia Minor, then to Constantinople, where he entered into the sultan's service.[16] I will have made sufficiently clear the sorts of service Erik could render a sovereign haunted by all sorts of fears when I say that it was Erik who built the famous trapdoors, secret rooms, and mysterious strongboxes that were found at Yildiz-Kiosk after the last Turkish revolution. It was also he whose ingenious idea it was**[17] to make automata[18] dressed like the prince and resembling him to such a degree that they were mistaken for the prince himself. Automata that made people believe that the waking commander of the faithful was in one place when he was in fact sleeping in another.

Naturally, he had to leave the sultan's service for the same reasons that he had had to flee Persia. He knew too much. Then weary of his adventurous, formidable, and monstrous life, he desired to live *like everyone else.* And he became a contractor, an ordinary contractor who builds houses with ordinary bricks. He submitted bids for work on the Opera's foundation. When he found himself in the subcellars of that vast theater, he was mastered once again by his fantastical, artistic, and magical nature. And besides,

---

** Interview with Mohammed-Ali Bey by the special representative of *Matin* on the day after the troops from Salonika entered Constantinople.

[16] "the sultan's service"

If Erik went to Constantinople immediately after the Afghan-Persian war, the Turkish sultan would have been Mahmud II, who ruled from 1808 to 1839. After that, his sons ruled. Abdulmecid I was the sultan between 1839 and 1861, and Abdulaziz from 1861 to 1876.

[17] "whose idea it was**"

This is another of Gaston Leroux's footnotes.

[18] "Automata"

There was a plethora of beautiful, mechanically animated toys being made in Europe during the late eighteenth and throughout the nineteenth century. There were peacocks that could spread their tails, mechanical pictures, ducks with all their tail feathers in place, talking dolls, peasants making shoes, bell-ringing monks, and jiggling skeletons.

See also E. T. A. Hoffman's bitter story "The Sandman," in which a young man falls in love with a "female" automaton.

was he not still ugly? He dreamed of creating a secret home for himself which unknown to the rest of the world would hide him forever from the eyes of mankind.

We know, and we can guess, what followed. It's all there in the entire length of this incredible, but nevertheless true, story.

Poor, unhappy Erik. Is he to be pitied Is he to be cursed? He wanted only to be someone, like everyone else. But he was too ugly! And he was required to hide his genius or else *play tricks with it*. Had he had ordinary features, he would have been one of the noblest members of the human race! He had a heart capacious enough to contain the whole world, but he had, finally, to content himself with a cellar. Certainly, we must pity the Phantom of the Opera!

I have prayed over his remains asking God to pity him, despite his crime. Why did God make a man that ugly?

I am sure—absolutely certain—that I prayed over his corpse the other day when it was disinterred at the same place where the phonograph records were buried. It was his skeleton. It was not by the ugliness of his head that I recognized him, because all men are ugly when they have been dead for a while, but by the gold ring he wore. No doubt Christine Daaé had come down and slipped the ring on his finger before burying him, as she had promised to do.

The skeleton was right beside the little fountain to which the Angel of Music carried the unconscious Christine Daaé in his trembling arms when he brought her into the cellars of the Opera for the first time.

And now, what shall we do with the skeleton? Are we going to fling it into a mass grave? I say: the place for the skeleton of the Phantom of the Opera is in the archives of the National Academy of Music. It is no ordinary skeleton.

Appendix A
Bibliography

~~❧✦❧~~

Appollinaire, Guillaume. *Oeuvres en Prose Completes*. Pierre Caizergues and Michel Décaudin, eds. Paris: Editions Gallimard, 1991.

———. *Poèmes*. Paris: Editions Gallimard, 1956.

———. *Selected Writings*, Roger Shattuck, ed. New York: New Directions, 1948.

Beaumont, Keith. *Alfred Jarry: A Critical and Biographical Study*. New York: St. Martin's Press, 1984.

Berthelot, M.M., et al., eds. *La Grande Encyclopédie Inventaire Raisonné des Sciences, des Lettres, et des Arts*. Paris: H. Lamirault et Cie, n.d.

Blom, Eric. *Grove's Dictionary of Music and Musicians*, 5th ed. New York: St. Martin's Press, Inc., 1954.

Boucher, François. *20,000 Years of Fashion*. New York: Harry N. Abrams, Inc., 1987.

Chujoy, Anatole and P. W. Manchester, eds. *The Dance Encyclopedia*. New York: Simon and Schuster, 1967.

Clement, Felix and Larousse, Pierre. *Dictionnaire des Opéras*. New York: Da Capo Press, 1969.

Dauzat. *Dictionnaire Etymologique des Noms de Famille et Prénoms de France*. Paris: Larousse, 1951.

Davenport, Milia. *The Book of Costume*, Volume II. New York: Crown Publishers, 1948.

Denis, Arnold. *The New Oxford Companion to Music.* London: Oxford University Press, 1984.

Derfler, Leslie. *The Third French Republic: 1870–1940.* Malabar, FL: Robert E. Krieger Publishing Co., 1982.

Dorsey, Hebe. *La Belle Epoque.* London: Thames and Hudson, 1986.

Duault, Alain. *L'Opérra du Paris.* Paris: Editions Sand, 1989.

Dumas, Alexandre. *Le Comte de Monte-Cristo.* Paris: Editions Garnier Frères, 1962.

Feval, Paul. *La Femme Blanche des Marais.* La Baule: Editions des Paludiers, 1977.

Flanner, Janet. *Paris Was Yesterday.* New York: Viking Press, 1972.

Grand Dictionnaire Encyclopédique Larousse. Paris: Larousse, 1982.

Guicheteau, Gerard and Jean-Claude Simeon. *Histoire Anecdotique de la Belle Epoque.* Paris: Le Pré aux Clercs, 1984.

The Hours of the Divine Office in English and Latin. Collegeville, MN: The Liturgical Press, 1963.

Jarry, Alfred. *Selected Works of Alfred Jarry*, ed. Roger Shattuck and Simon Watson Taylor. New York: Grove Press Inc., 1965.

———. *The Ubu Plays,* ed. Simon Watson Taylor. London: Methuen & Co., Ltd, 1968.

———. *Ubu,* ed. Noel Arnaud and Henri Bordillon. Paris: Editions Gallimard, 1978,.

Kranzberg, Melvin. *The Siege of Paris, 1870–1871.* Ithaca: Cornell University Press, 1950.

Lacassin, Francis. *Mythologie du Fantastique: Les Rivages de la Nuit.* Paris: Editions du Rocher, 1991.

———. *La Vraie Naissance de Maigret: Autopsie d'une Légende.* Paris: Editions du Rocher, 1992.

Lamy, Jean-Claude and Pierre Lépine. "Le Vrai Rouletabille: Biographie de Gaston Leroux," in *Histoires Epouvantables.* Paris: Nouvelles Editions Baudinère, 1977.

Leblanc, Maurice. *Les Dents du Tigre.* Paris: Le Livre de Poche, 1969.

Mason, Edward S. *The Paris Commune.* New York: The Macmillan Co., 1930.

Mead, Christopher Curtis. *Charles Garnier's Paris Opera.* Cambridge, MA: MIT Press, 1991.

Merlin, Olivier. *L'Opéra de Paris.* Fribourg: Hatier Editions S.A., 1975.

The Missal in Latin and English. Westminister, MD: The Newman Press, 1962.

Missale Romanum. Boston: Beziger Brothers, Inc., 1943.

Morlet, Marie-Thérèse. *Dictionnaire Etymologique des Noms de Famille.* Paris: Perrin, 1981.

Nathan, Michel, ed. *Anthologie du Roman Populaire*. Paris: Union Général d'Editions,, 1985

Patureau, Frédérique. *Le Palais Garnier dans la Société Parisienne 1875–1914*. Liège: Pierre Mardaga, 1991.

Perrot, Michelle, ed. *A History of Private Life: From the Fires of Revolution to the Great War*. Cambridge, MA: Belknap Press, 1990.

Perry, George C. *The Complete Phantom of the Opera*. New York: H. Holt, 1988.

Peské, Antoinette and Pierre Marty. *Les Terribles. Visages No. 2*. Paris: Chambriand, 1951

Prud'homme, J. G. *L'Opéra*. Paris: Librairie Delagrave, 1925.

Queffélec, Lise. *Le Roman-Feuilleton au XIXe Siècle*. Paris: Presses Universitaires de France, 1989.

Randel, Don Michael, ed. *The Harvard Dictionary of Music*. Cambridge, MA: Belknap Press, 1986.

Royer, Alphonse. *Histoire de L'Opéra*. Paris: Bachelin-Deflorenne, 1875.

Sand, Maurice. *Masques et Buffons de la Comédie Talienne*. Paris: A. Levy Fils, Bibliothèque Arsenal, 1962.

Sedgewick, Alexander. *The Third French Republic, 1870–1914*. New York: Thomas Y. Crowell, 1968.

Seigneuret, Jean Charles, ed. *Dictionary of Literary Themes and Motifs*. New York: Greenwood Press, 1988.

Shattuck, Roger. *The Banquet Years*. Salem, NH: Ayer Compaany, Publishers, Inc., 1984.

Siepe, Hans T. *Abenteuer und Geheimins: Untersuchungen zu Strukturen und Mythen des Popular Romans bei Gaston Leroux*. New York: P. Lang, 1988.

Six, Jean-François. *1886, Naissance Du XXe Siècle en France*. Paris: Editions du Seuil, 1986.

Sue, Eugène. *The Mysteries of Paris*. New York: Howard Fertig, 1987.

———. *The Wandering Jew*. New York: Modern Library, 1940.

Vareille, Jean-Claude. *Filatures: Itineraire à Travers les Cycles de Lupin et Rouletabille*. Grenoble: Presses Universitaires de Grenoble, 1980.

Wilcox, R. Turner. *Dictionary of Costume*. New York: Scribner, 1969.

Yonge, Charlotte. *Dictionary of Christian Names*. 1884. Reprint, Detroit: Gale Research Co., 1966.

Periodicals

Bizarre. Revue Périodique, No. 1, 1953

Europe: Revue Litteraire Mensuelle, June/July 1981.

Margat, Claire. "Le Lecteur et son Double: à propos du Roi Mystère de Gaston Leroux," *Revue d'Esthetique,* Vol. 16, 1989, pp. 91–96.

Olivier-Martin, Yves. "Le Trio Fatidique: Fantomas, Lupin, Rouletabille," *Le Français Dans le Monde,* August/September 1984, pp. 15–18.

Zizek, Slavoj. "Grimaces of the Real: or When the Phallus Appears," *October,* Vol. 58, 1991, pp. 45–68.

A Checklist of English Versions of Gaston Leroux's Fiction

The Amazing Adventures of Carolus Herbert. Trans. Hannaford Bennett. London: Mills & Boone, 1922.

Balaoo. Trans. Teixera de Mattos. London: Hurst & Blackett Ltd., 1913

Bride of the Sun. London: McBride Nast and Co., 1915.

The Burgled Heart. Trans. Hannaford Bennett. London: J. Long, 1925.

Cheri Bibi and Cecily. Trans. Hannaford Bennett. London: T. W. Laurie, 1923.

The Dancing Girl. London: J. Long, 1925.

The Dark Road, Further Adventures of Cheri Bibi. New York: Macaulay & Co., 1924.

The Double Life. New York: J. E. Kearney, 1909.

The Floating Prison. Trans. Hannaford Bennett. London: Daily Express Fiction Library, n.d.

Gaston Leroux's Crime Omnibus Book. (Includes: *The Floating Prison, Cheri Bibi and Cecily, The Queen of Crime*). London: T. W. Laurie, 1930.

The Haunted Chair. New York: E. P. Dutton & Co., 1924, 1931.

The Kiss That Killed. New York: Macaulay & Co., 1930.

Lady Helena. New York: E. P. Dutton, 1931.

The Machine to Kill. New York: Macaulay & Co., 1935.

Man of a Hundred Faces. New York: Macaulay & Co., 1930.

The Man With the Black Feather. Trans. Edgar Jepson. Boston: Small, Maynard and Co., 1912.

The Masked Man. Trans. Hannaford Bennett. New York: Macaulay & Co., 1929.

Midnight Lady. Trans. Hannaford Bennett. London: J. Long, 1930.

The Missing Men: The Return of Cheri Bibi. New York: Caldwell, 1923.

The New Idol. Trans. Hannaford Bennett. London: J. Long, 1928.

The New Terror. New York: Macaulay & Co., 1926.

Nomads of the Night: Latest Adventures of Cheri Bibi. New York: Macaulay & Co., 1925.

The Octopus of Paris. New York: Macaulay & Co., 1927.

The Perfume of the Lady in Black. London: Everleigh Nash, 1911. (Also, New York: Brentano's, 1909.)

The Phantom Clue. New York: Macaulay & Co., 1926.

The Phantom of the Opera. Trans. Teixera de Mattos, 1911. (Now in Signet paperback).

The Phantom of the Opera. Indianapolis: Bobbs-Merrill, 1911.

The Phantom of the Opera. New York: Grosset and Dunlap, 1912.

The Phantom of the Opera. Trans. Bair, 1987.

The Phantom of the Opera. Trans. Leonard Wolf. New York: Penguin/Plume, 1997.

The Secret of the Night: Further Adventures of Rouletabille. New York: Macaulay & Co., 1914.

The Slave Bangle. Trans. Hannaford Bennet. London: J. Long Ltd., 1925. (The American version of this novel is *The Phantom Clue.*)

The Sleuth Hound. Trans. Hannaford Bennett. London: J. Long, Ltd. 1926.

The Son of Three Fathers. (French title: *Hardigras*). Trans. Hannaford Bennett. London: J. Long Ltd., 1927. (Also, New York: Macaulay & Co., 1928.)

Wolves of the Sea. London: W. R. Caldwell, 1923. (Also, New York: Macaulay & Co., 1923.)

Works by Gaston Leroux

1887. *Le Petit Marchand de Pommes de Terres Frites,* in *La République Francaise.*

1902. *La Double Vie de Théophraste Longuet,* under the title *Le Chercheur de Trésors, Roman Concours,* in *Le Matin,* Oct. 5–Nov. 2, 1903.

La Double Vie de Théophraste Longuet. Paris: Ernest Flammirion, Sept. 1904.

1907. *Baiochki Baiou,* in *Le Matin,* Jan. 1, 1907.

Le Mystère de la Chambre Jaune (Les Aventures Extraordinaires de Joseph Rouletabille, Reporter, I), 12 installments each of 16 pages in *L'Illustration,* Sept. 7–Nov. 30, 1907.

Under the title *Les Aventures Extraordinaires de Joseph Rouletabille, Reporter.* Paris: Pierre Lafitte et Cie, Oct., 1908.

1908.   *L'Homme Qui A Vu le Diable*, in *Je Sais Tout*, No. 38, March 15, 1908.

Republished in the collection *Le Fauteuil Hanté*. Paris: Lafitte, 1911, pp. 285–360.

Le Parfum de la Dame en Noir (Les Aventures Extraordinaires de Joseph Rouletabille, Reporter, II), in *L'Illustration*, Sept. 26, 1908–Jan. 2, 1909.

Also as 15 weekly installments in *Soleil du Dimanche Illustré*, Nos. 24–30, 1908–1909.

Le Roi Mystère, in *Le Matin*, Oct. 24, 1908–Feb. 9, 1909.

Republished in *Le Livre Populaire*, No. 58. Paris: Athème Fayard et Cie, Feb., 1910.

1909.   *Le Fauteuil Hanté*, 6 installments in *Je Sais Tout*, Nos. 58–63, Nov., 1909–April, 1910.

Republished with *L'Homme Qui A Vu le Diable*. Paris: Pierre Lafitte et Cie, May, 1911.

1910.   *Le Fantôme de L'Opéra*, daily installments in *Le Gaulois*. Collected and republished. Paris: Pierre Lafitte et Cie, June, 1910.

Collected and republished in 2 volumes with illustrations from the Universal Film (*I. Erik, II. Le Mystère des Trappes*). Paris: Société d'Editions et de Publications (Tallandier), Jan.–Feb., 1926.

Un Homme Dans La Nuit, 101 daily installments in *Le Radical* (Marseille), March 20–June 29, 1910.

Collected and republished in *Le Livre Populaire*, No. 75. Paris: Arthéme Fayard et Cie, July, 1911.

La Reine du Sabbat, 161 daily installments in *Le Matin*, August 18, 1910–Jan. 31, 1911.

Collected and republished in *Le Livre Populaire*, No. 96. Paris: Arthēe Fayard et Cie, April, 1913.

1911.   *Balaoo*, 71 daily installments in *Le Matin*, Oct. 9–Dec. 18, 1911.
Collected and republished. Paris: Editions et Publications de Jules Tallandier, 1912.

1912.   *La Hache D'Or* in *Touche à Tout*, No. 2, Feb. 1912.
Republished in the collection *Coeur Cambriolé*. Paris: Lafitte, 1922.
Republished in the anthology *Les Maîtres de la Peur*, André de Lorde and Albert Dubeux, eds. Paris: Delagrave, 1927.

L'Epouse du Soleil, 65 installments in *Je Sais Tout*, Nos. 86–91,

March-Aug., 1912.

Collected and republished. Paris: Pierre Lafitte et Cie.

1913.   *Rouletabille Chez le Tsar (Les Aventures Extraordinaires de Joseph Roule-tabille Reporter, III),* in installments in *L'Illustration.*

Collected and republished. Paris: Pierre Lafitte et Cie, 1913.

Premières Aventures de Chéri-Bibi, under the title *Chéri-Bibi,* 120 daily installments in *Le Matin,* April 7–Aug. 4, 1913.

Chéri-Bibi, in *Le Livre Populaire.* Paris: Arthème Fayard et Cie, July, 1914.

Republished in 2 volumes as *Premières Aventures de Chéri-Bibi* (Volume I: *Les Cages Flottantes;* Volume II: *Chéri-Bibi et Cécily*). Paris: Editions Pierre Lafitte, 1921.

1914.   *Rouletabille à la Guerre (Les Aventures Extraordinaires de Joseph Rouletabi-lle, Reporter, IV and V),* 135 daily installments in *Le Matin,* March 28–August 2 and Oct. 18–24, 1914.

Collected and republished in 2 volumes: Vol. I: *Le Chateau Noir;* Vol. II: *Les Etranges Noces de Rouletabille.* Paris: Edition Pierre Lafitte, Sept. and Oct., 1916.

1916.   *Confitou,* 120 daily installments in *Le Matin,* Jan. 16–Feb. 15, 1916. Collected and republished. Paris: Editions Pierre Lafitte, May, 1917.

La Colonne Infernale, 133 daily installments in *Le Matin,* April 29–Sept. 8, 1916.

Collected and republished in 2 volumes., Paris: Arthème Fayard et Cie, April, May, 1917.

Republished in the collection *Les Maîtres du Roman Populaire,* Nos. 65 and 66.

L'Homme Qui Revient de Loin, under the title *Le Monsieur Qui Revient de Loin* in *Je Sais Tout,* Nos. 125–132, June, 1916–Jan., 1917.

Collected and reprinted. Paris: Editions Pierre Lafitte, Dec., 1917.

Augmented edition in *Dimanche Illustré,* Nos. 66 and 67, June 1 and June 8, 1924.

Third edition (shortest) in *Fiction,* No. 89, April 1961

1917.   *Rouletabille Chez Krupp (Les Aventures Extraordinaires de Joseph Rouletab-ille, Reporter, VI),* 7 installments in *Je Sais Tout,* Nos. 142–148, Sept., 1917–March, 1918.

Collected and republished. Paris: Editions Pierre Lafitte, June, 1920.

Le Captaine Hyx, 63 installments under the title *Le Sous-Marin "Le*

Vengeur," first book: *Les Anges des Eaux* in *Le Matin*, Sept.,
1917–March, 1918.
Collected and republished as *Le Captaine Hyx. Aventures Effroyables
de M. Herbert de Renich, II.* Paris: Editions Pierre Lafitte, June 1920.
La Bataille Invisible, 71 installments under the title *Le Sous-Marin
"Le Vengeur,"* second book: *La Bataille Invisible* in *Le Matin,* Nov.
19, 1917–Feb. 12, 1918.
Collected and republished as *Aventures Effroyables de M. Herbert de
Renich, II.* Paris: Editions Pierre Lafitte, Dec., 1920.

1919.   *Nouvelles Aventures de Chéri-Bibi,* under the title *La Nouvelle Aurore,*
110 daily installments in *Le Matin,* April 18–Aug. 7, 1919.
La Nouvelle Aurore, 16 weekly editions, Collection "Les Romans
Cinéma." Paris: La Renaissance du Livre Editeur, Oct. 12,
1919–Jan. 1920.
Collected and republished as *La Nouvelle Aurore,* 1920.
Collected and republished in 2 volumes as *Nouvelles Aventures de
Chéri-Bibi,* (Volume I: *Palas et Chéri-Bibi;* Volume II: *Fatalitas*). Paris:
Editions Pierre Lafitte, 1921.

Les Assassins Fantômes (incorporates four works), ed. Francis Lacassin.
Paris: Editions Robert Laffont, S.A., 1993.
Les Aventures Extraordinaires de Joseph Rouletabille, Reporter (volume
one incorporates five works; volume two incorporates six works),
ed. Francis Lacassin. Paris: Editions Robert Laffont, S.A., 1988.
Aventures Incroyables (incorporates nine works), ed. Francis Lacassin.
Paris: Editions Robert Lafont, S.A., 1992.
Chéri-Bibi (incorporates six volumes), ed. Francis Lacassin. Paris:
Editions Robert Laffont, 1990.
Le Fauteuil Hanté. Paris: Le Livre de Poche, 1965.
Le Mystère de la Chambre Jaune (preface by Jean Cocteau). Paris: Le
Livre de Poche, 1960.
Le Fantôme de L'Opéra. Paris: Le Livre de Poche, 1959.
Pouloulou. Paris: Michel Lafon Editions, 1990.
Histoires Epouvantables, eds. Jean-Claude Lamy and Pierre Lepine.
Paris: Nouvelles Editions Baudinère, 1977.

Appendix B
Performances on Stage and Screen
⟫⟪

Feature Films:

1925
The Phantom of the Opera
Rupert Julian, *Director*
Universal
Lon Chaney, *Phantom*

1943
Phantom of the Opera
Arthur Lubin, *Director*
Universal
Claude Rains, *Phantom*

1962
The Phantom of the Opera
Terence Fisher, *Director*
Hammer Films—released by Universal
Herbert Lom, *Phantom*

1974
Phantom of the Paradise
Brian De Palma, *Director*
Pressman-Williams Enterprises
William Finley, *Phantom*

1989
Phantom of the Opera
Dwight H. Little, *Director*
21st Century Film Corp.
Robert Englund, *Phantom*

Television Films:
1974
The Phantom of Hollywood
Gene Levitt, *Director*
MGM-TV
Jack Cassidy, *Phantom*

1983
Phantom of the Opera
Robert Markowitz, *Director*
CBS
Maximilian Schell, *Phantom*

1990
The Phantom of the Opera
Tony Richardson, *Director*
NBC
Charles Dance, *Phantom*

In addition, there are two parodies both titled *El Fantasma de la Operata,* the first from Argentina (1955), the second from Mexico (1960, director, Fernando Cortés). Information about the credits was not available. A film of Andrew Lloyd Webber's musical, starring Michael Crawford, was left incomplete in 1990; the director of the existing footage was Joel Schumacher.

Ben Carré's set sketch for *The Phantom of the Opera* (1925)

THEATRICAL PRODUCTIONS

1975
The Phantom of the Opera
Wimbleton Theatre; London, England
David Giles, *Director*
Actors' Company, *Producer*
Edward Petherbridge, *Phantom*

1984
The Phantom of the Opera
Theatre Royal; Stratford, England
Ken Hill, *Director*
TyneWear Company and Stratford East, *Producers*
Ken Hill, *Music and Lyrics;* Additional Music by Verdi, Gounod, Offenbach, Mozart, Weber, and Donizetti
Peter Straker, *Phantom*

1986

The Phantom of the Opera

Her Majesty's Theatre; London, England (Broadway Premiere 1988)

Harold Prince, *Director*

Cameron Mackintosh and the Really Useful Theatrical Company, Ltd., *Producers*

Andrew Lloyd Webber, *Music;* Charles Hart, *Lyrics*

Michael Crawford, *Phantom*

The Phantom of the Opera

Market Theater; Albany, NY

Peter H. Clough, *Director*

Capital Repertory Company, *Producer*

David Bishop, *Music;* Kathleen Masterson, *Lyrics*

Al de Cristo, *Phantom*

1989

The Phantom of the Opera

Carousel Dinner Theatre; Akron, OH

Joseph Patton, *Director*

Prescott F. Griffith and John Kenley, *Producers*

David Gooding, *Music and Lyrics*

David Cleveland, *Phantom*

1990

Phantom of the Opera

Hirschfeld Theatre; Miami Beach, FL

Darwiun Knight, *Director*

Karen Poindexter, *Producer*

Lawrence Rosen and Paul Schierhorn, *Music and Lyrics*

David Staller, *Phantom*

1991

Phantom of the Opera

Theatre Under the Stars; Houston, TX

Charles Abbott, *Director*

Steve FRiedman, *Producer*

Maury Yeston, *Music and Lyrics*

Richard White, *Phantom*

Phantom
Drury Lane Oakbrook Terrace; Chicago, IL
David H. Bell, *Director*
Tony De Santis, *Producer*
Tom Sivak after Tchaikovsky, *Music;* David H. Bell and Cheri Coons, *Lyrics*
Larry Adams, *Phantom*

BALLETS

1978
The Phantom of the Opera
New York, NY
By Joyce Trisler Danscompany
Choreography by James Waring

1980
The Phantom of the Opera
London, England
By Marie Françoise Christout and John Percival
Choreography by Roland Petit

Bibliographic Information for Appendix B

British Film Institute. *Film Index International* on CD-ROM, 1994.

Cook, Samantan, ed. *International Dictionary of Films and Filmmakers*. 5 vols. New York: St. James Press, 1994.

Glut, Don. *Classic Movie Monsters*. London: Scarecrow Press, Inc., 1978.

New York Public Library for the Performing Arts/Billy Rose Theatre Collection, Clippings File.

Newman, Kim. "The Phantom and His 1,000 Faces." *British Film Institute Monthly Film Bulletin*, vol. 57, #677, p. 180.

Willis, Donald C. *Horror and Science Fiction Films II*. London: Scarecrow Press, Inc., 1982.

ABOUT LEONARD WOLF

Leonard Wolf's works on terror literature and film include *A Dream of Dracula* (1972), *The Annotated Dracula* (1974), *The Annotated Frankenstein* (1976), *Monsters* (for children, 1974), *Wolf's Complete Book of Terror* (1979), and *Horror: A Connoisseur's Guide to Literature and Film* (1989). His most recent books in the genre are *The Essential Dracula*, *The Essential Frankenstein* (both Plume, 1993), and *The Essential Dr. Jekyll & Mr. Hyde* (Plume, 1995). Wolf served as historical and critical consultant to Francis Ford Coppola's film *Bram Stoker's Dracula* and Kenneth Branagh's movie *Mary Shelley's Frankenstein*.

Wolf has spent most of his adult life as a writer of poetry, fiction, social history and biography, and as a professor of English, teaching Chaucer and Creative Writing. His poetry and fiction have appeared in *The Kenyon Review*, *The Atlantic*, *Harper's*, *The New Yorker*, *The Yale Review* and other magazines. He has been an O. Henry Fiction Award winner and, for his work in the horror genre, has twice received the Ann Radcliffe Award for Literature.

He is the author of a wide range of books. The *New York Times* said of his *Voices of the Love Generation* (1968), a social history of the hippy movement, that it "humanizes the subject. His observations . . . constitute some of the clearest and most level-headed commentary currently available." His book *The Passion of Israel* (1970) is a graphic account of a euphoric and tragic year in Israel's history. His *Bluebeard: The Life and Crimes of Gilles de Rais* (1980), a biography of perhaps the worst serial killer in history, has been called "the most important contribution to the problem of evil since Hannah Arendt's *Eichmann in Jerusalem*." *The False Messiah* (1984), a historical novel about Shabbatai Tsvi, a messianic figure of the seventeenth century whose brief career shook and nearly shattered the Jewish communities in Europe and the Turkish Empire in the middle of the seventeenth century, was praised by the *New York Times* for its "graphic recreation of Shabbatai's world."

Wolf is, according to Irving Howe, the finest translator of Yiddish literature in America. He has published translations from the work of most of this century's greatest Yiddish poets. The publishers of Isaac Bashevis Singer have chosen Leonard Wolf to write the Nobel Prize-winning author's biography.

The National Foundation for Jewish Culture commissioned Wolf's verse play, *Queen Esther*. Two scary plays for children, *Dracula's School for Vampires* and *Frankenstein the Thirteenth*, were commissioned by The San Francisco Children's Theatre (1986 and 1987) and were performed in San Francisco, New York, and Providence. Frank Langella has called *Dracula's School for Vampires* "marvelous entertainment for children and grown-ups alike."

Leonard Wolf's most recent novel is *The Glass Mountain* (1993).